MIDSUMMER MURDER

Books by Shelley Freydont

BACKSTAGE MURDER

HIGH SEAS MURDER

MIDSUMMER MURDER

Published by Kensington Publishing Corporation

A Lindy Haggerty Mystery

MIDSUMMER MURDER

SHELLEY FREYDONT

KENSINGTON BOOKS

http://www.kensingtonbooks.com

KENSINGTON BOOKS are published by

Kensington Publishing Corp.
850 Third Avenue
New York, NY 10022

All Kensington titles, imprints and distributed lines are available at special quantity discounts for bulk purchases for sales promotion, premiums, fund-raising, educational or institutional use.

Special book excerpts or customized printings can also be created to fit specific needs. For details, write or phone the office of the Kensington Special Sales Manager: Kensington Publishing Corp., 850 Third Avenue, New York, NY 10022, Attn. Special Sales Department. Phone: 1-800-221-2647.

Library of Congress Card Catalogue Number: 00-111183
ISBN: 1-57566-674-X

First Printing: August, 2001
10 9 8 7 6 5 4 3 2 1

Chapter
One

G ears screeched as the tour bus rounded another hairpin curve. The driver swore under his breath. Lindy Graham-Haggerty abandoned her paperback and grabbed the arms of her seat. She was glad she was sitting in the front of the bus; a communal groan erupted from the seats behind her as the members of the Jeremy Ash Dance Company lurched to the left in perfect unison.

"But I don't want to suffer for my art," whined a voice from the back. Another wild turn, this time in the opposite direction. Lindy's book slid to the floor and across the aisle. Next to her, Arabida McFee, the company business manager, groaned.

The bus driver mumbled to himself. He was looking a little green.

"I don't remember the road being this wild," said Jeremy from across the aisle. "But it's been a few years."

The company was on its way to the Easton Arts Retreat, a prestigious colony for visual artists and writers, and a summer camp for the most promising young dancers in the country. This year was the fiftieth anniversary of the retreat, and the Ash company was opening the season. Other former students who now directed their own companies would be participating in the celebrations throughout the summer.

At age fourteen, Jeremy had been the youngest dancer to ever receive a coveted Easton Scholarship. He became a favorite student, spending several summers at the camp and later forming a close friendship with the camp's owner and director, Marguerite Easton. Now at fortysomething, he had made it clear that it was payback time, and the company had been rehearsed to perfection.

Jeremy leaned forward in his seat, his anticipation palpable across the aisle as he scanned the mountains before him.

"Hang on, guys. It won't be long now. We should see the house any minute."

On cue, the house appeared in the distance, framed by lush greenery and stone cliffs.

"There." Jeremy pointed, but the brief image of stone and red slate roof disappeared as the bus took another stomach-churning turn.

Lindy glanced at Biddy, whose face was white beneath her cinnamon-colored curls. Her green eyes widened as the bus hit a pothole, and she rebounded into Lindy.

The bus swerved again and empty air loomed before them. The tires crunched on loose dirt as the bus slid onto the shoulder of the road and perched momentarily at the edge of the mountain before regaining the pavement.

"*Dios mio,*" the bus driver muttered and crossed himself.

Beyond them stretched an immense chasm. A thatch of heavily foliaged trees filled the crevice below. It had been a rainy June in New York State and the undergrowth was as thick and wild as any tropical jungle. A ribbon of blue appeared sporadically through the greenery and ended in a mirror-smooth lake that reflected the cliffs of gray granite surrounding it.

The driver maneuvered the bus back onto the pavement and continued more slowly upward through the mountains.

"There," said Jeremy. All heads turned to peer out the bus windows; the dancers farthest from the windows stood in the aisle to get a better view.

On the other side of the chasm, atop a granite bluff, stood the Easton house. But to call the edifice looming in the distance a house was a gross understatement, thought Lindy. She wasn't sure that mansion would do it justice. A castle was more like it, and a monstrous one at that. Several architectural styles fought for attention, their juxtaposition creating the appearance of a living, roiling entity.

"Wow," said Biddy. Her hand reached to push curls from her eyes.

"Jeremy, it's magnificent," said Lindy. And the daylight softened its foreboding appearance, she thought, but at night with a full moon—she shuddered.

Jeremy turned from the window and flashed her a wide grin. "Wait until you see it up close. It's a wonderful place and Marguerite is the best."

Marguerite Easton, philanthropist and society dame *extraordinaire*, was revered throughout the art world. Beloved by artists and critics alike, she had safely steered the retreat, her pet project, through the vicissitudes of the nineties. While other arts organizations floundered, the Easton Arts Retreat flourished. She didn't need to beg money from the dwindling number of charitable arts foundations. She was her own foundation, and the colony ran from the interest of well-placed investments without ever having to dip into the principal. The retreat was the paragon of intelligent arts management.

And even though it seemed to spring up spontaneously in the most inaccessible recesses of New York State, the glitterati flocked to the summer performances, driving the two and a half hours from New York City and staying overnight in the mansion's annex. Dance schools trampled over each other to get their students into the few choice spots in the summer dance program.

Lindy had never met Marguerite Easton and she felt a flutter of butterflies in anticipation. She had been out of the business for twelve years when Biddy had asked her to return to work only a year ago. She still felt like she had to prove herself again and again . . . and again. She knew it was ridiculous. Her reputation had been sound when she had retired from dancing, and she had built on it since coming back to work as Jeremy's rehearsal director. The fact that the company had been involved in more than one murder since her return was certainly not her fault.

"Do-do-do-do-do-do-do-do." Someone was singing the theme to *The Twilight Zone*. Jeremy and Lindy both turned to look, bumping heads as they leaned into the aisle.

A muscular male dancer staggered toward them. Rebo, no last name, just Rebo. His brown eyes bulged. The whites shone menacingly against his coffee-brown complexion.

"Lindy, I'm home (redrum, redrum)," he intoned. Lindy shook her head. Add Jack Nicholson to his impressions of Vanna White, Bette Midler, and Her Majesty, the Queen.

"What?" Jeremy looked a little confused and possibly annoyed. Marguerite was his mentor. Just hearing him speak of her, Lindy knew he would brook no jokes at the lady's expense.

The bus lurched again and Rebo disappeared. Lindy peered over the back of her seat. Rebo lay sprawled across Juan Esquidera. Juan's arms had wrapped around him to break his fall and lay there affectionately.

Rebo leaned back and rested his head in Mieko Jones's lap, leering at her in an over-the-top performance of dementia.

Mieko's dark eyes closed beneath black-fringed lids. She leaned forward until strands of straight black hair fell onto Rebo's face. He sputtered. She straightened up, her face as enigmatic as ever.

Then she pushed his head up and heaved him back to Juan. "Take him, he's yours, thank God."

Juan laughed and pecked Rebo on the cheek.

"Could you guys try to act with a little decorum?" asked Lindy shooting a quick glance at Jeremy.

Rebo struggled up and scratched at the red bandanna he always wore around his head. Then he snatched it off and crushed it to his chest. "I'll just look for my top hat and tails." He hoisted himself off Juan's lap. "Hey, Rose," he called and wobbled to the back of the bus in search of the costume mistress.

"Jeremy seems a little nervous," said Biddy as Lindy resumed her seat. Lindy looked across the aisle. Jeremy was staring out the window. She contemplated the back of his head. Silky blond hair waved gently down his neck and disappeared beneath his shirt collar. She touched her own hair, short, brown, and coarse to the touch. She spent a lot of time envying other people's hair. She never allowed hers to grow longer than two inches because it grew straight out in every direction.

As if feeling her gaze, Jeremy turned toward her, a slight question on his face. Blue eyes met blue eyes, his sparkling with excitement—and just a little apprehension? Tough Chicago street kid makes good, she thought; it must be pretty daunting to go back to your beginnings. She smiled at him. His mouth turned up in a quick quirk of the lips, and he turned back to the window.

The bus lurched to a stop; Lindy's stomach catapulted forward, then banged back into place. Ahead of them, a rusty Jeep hugged the outer edge of the road. Four men stared out from the windscreen with expressions of surprise. Then the driver began to inch past the bus. The bus driver pulled closer to the inside of the road. It was then that Lindy noticed the steel mesh that encased the wall of granite that rose above them. And the sign that read FALLING ROCKS.

Great, she thought. What a hell of a place to send your children to summer camp, though these campers were really young adults, ages sixteen to early twenties. She thought of her own children: Cliff at an East Coast college, and Annie, who had been in Switzerland since her junior year in high school. How many times had they gone off to camp where the dangers of the wilderness had threatened them and Lindy and Glen, her husband of twenty years, had never given it a thought.

But they had survived their camp experience. Cliff was taking summer courses at the university where he would be a junior the following September. Annie was on a European tour with the Swiss Conservatory Orchestra, where she had just graduated from high school and would continue as a university student. Actually, the snares of everyday life were more frightening than any summer camp experience.

The bus continued on its way across the mountain without further incident. Twenty minutes later, it turned off the main road and drove between two stone columns. Spanning the columns was a wrought-iron arch with the name, EASTON ARTS RETREAT, formed in filigree letters across it.

The private drive to the retreat was in much better repair than the road they had just left, and the bus purred along the smooth asphalt. *Shows you what a little care and a lot of money can do,* thought Lindy as she settled back in her seat to enjoy her surroundings.

Stately oaks and maples sheltered the wide drive. Boulders sat among the trees to each side. Wilderness, but somehow refined as if it had been designed by a very competent horticulturist to look like wilderness. The canopy of trees blocked out the sun; only intermittent splotches of sunlight reflected from the ground like glimpses of fool's gold. The bus moved deeper into the woods, and even these brief respites gave way to an unrelieved half-light, shaded and mysterious. Pockets of mist hung above the forest floor, unmoving.

The back of the bus had become quiet as the woods wove their magic. Lindy half expected pixies to begin popping out from behind the trees.

Then without warning, the bus was bathed in brilliant sunshine. Ahead of them, a wide circular driveway skirted the front of the largest, most formidable building Lindy had seen since her tour of English castles. Awestruck, it took her a minute to realize what the blinking red lights were.

Jeremy bolted across the aisle and the door swooshed open. He bounded down the steps and across the pavement to where a group of people crowded together on the stone stairs that led to the porch.

Lindy jolted out of her seat. "Everyone stay put." She turned to the driver. "Move the bus off to the side and keep everybody in place." She hurried down the steps, Biddy at her heels.

"God, I hope nothing has happened to Ms. Easton. Jeremy will be devastated," said Biddy. She stopped abruptly. "Look."

Two uniformed men wheeled a stretcher out of the woods and across the pavement toward an ambulance. Lindy strained to see the face, praying that it was not Marguerite Easton. A long, black bag lay lengthwise on the stretcher. "Oh no," she said. Her throat tightened without warning. Whoever it was, whatever had happened, there was nothing to do now but mourn.

The men hoisted the stretcher into the back of the ambulance, then climbed in behind it. The engine roared up and the vehicle began its sad journey across the mountain.

Jeremy was standing at the top of the steps, his arm around a tall, elegant woman. She stood with an imposing dignity, her symmetrical features composed and unperturbed. Perfectly white hair was pulled back from her face in a low chignon. With startling, pewter eyes, she watched the ambulance disappear into the trees beyond the house.

"There's been an accident," said Jeremy as Lindy and Biddy reached the steps. "One of the students. He fell down a ravine." Marguerite Easton flinched, and Lindy noticed that behind her serene countenance was a depth of grief that threatened to consume her.

"What can we do?" asked Biddy.

"Oh." Marguerite Easton shifted her gaze to the tour bus that was parked across the expanse of drive. She looked vaguely around until her eyes rested on a group of people that huddled in silence on the pavement. "Lenny," she called. Her voice flowed toward the group, rich and melodious. A young man looked up, his face stricken.

"Please show the driver to the Walt Whitman wing." The man nodded and began to walk toward the bus.

Marguerite's gaze moved from him to Lindy and Biddy. "I'm so terribly sorry."

Lindy shook her head. This was not the introduction she had anticipated.

"This is Lindy Graham and Biddy McFee, Marguerite," said Jeremy.

"Yes, of course." Marguerite smiled at them, good breeding taking over momentarily. "It's so very good to meet you at last. Jeremy is—"

"Ms. Easton." A burly man wearing a sheriff's uniform stepped from behind Lindy. He hitched up his belt against his stomach and readjusted his holster. Then he lifted the visor of his cap toward the directress.

"Well now," he began. He stopped and tilted his head from one side to the other; his spine made cracking noses. "They're taking the body over to County General. The parents will have to be notified."

"Yes, of course, I'll get their phone number for you, and—and—" Marguerite faltered, then continued. "Naturally, I will be phoning them, myself."

"Naturally," he replied. There was something in his tone of voice that almost suggested satisfaction. Lindy took a reflexive step backward.

Marguerite's hand lifted into the air. Jeremy enclosed it in his own. "Come inside." He led her gently toward the door. The sheriff cleared his throat, nodded brusquely toward Lindy and Biddy, then followed Jeremy and Marguerite into the house.

"Ugh." Biddy shivered.

"Ditto," said Lindy.

Lindy and Biddy settled the company in their rooms in the annex and were led by Lenny to the main house where Marguerite's private quarters were located and where they and Jeremy would be staying.

"What do we do now?" asked Biddy. She sat down in a wing-backed chair and looked around at the Victorian furnishings. Heavy green drapes hung from brass rails above the windows. Lace panels mottled the late afternoon light, their design casting a pattern of shadows on the plush carpet.

Lindy perched on the edge of a bed, tracing the pattern of the matelassé counterpane that lay across it. There was a slight chill in the room as if winter had been trapped inside. She shrugged. "Turn up the heat."

She crossed over to the far wall, richly covered in a gold brocade wallpaper. "Turn down the air conditioning," she amended. She adjusted the modern thermostat, then moved to the window and sat on the sill, letting the sun warm her shoulders.

"I wonder if they'll go on with the anniversary celebration. It's probably too late to cancel."

Biddy brought her hands to her hair. "What a hideous thing to happen. And what timing." She ran her fingers through her curls. "Please, please let this be an accident."

"What?"

"I know, that was a selfish thing to say. Imagine that poor family. You send your kid to camp and he—he never comes back."

"Don't," said Lindy. "It's a parent's worst nightmare. If you thought about what could happen, you'd never let your children out of your sight." She thought about Cliff and Annie, just starting out in their adult lives; life was so tenuous. She pushed the thought from her mind. "I suppose we should find Jeremy and see what he wants us to do. The reception for the company is only two hours away."

There was a knock on the door and both women jumped. Biddy propelled herself out of the chair and reached for the door knob.

A girl, wearing a calico dress and white apron, carried a tray into the room. "The kitchen sent this up. Ms. Easton thought you might be hungry." She placed the tray on the dresser and arranged plates of fruit and cheese on a Queen Anne table near the window. "Ms. Marguerite . . . Ms. Easton . . ." The girl bit her lower lip and shifted her weight. "She says, dinner will be delayed tonight 'cause of what happened." She shifted to her other foot. "The others have been sent to the student dining hall. It's over there." She pointed toward a fox hunting print on the wall. Lindy guessed she meant outside in that direction. The girl shifted back to the other foot as if it were a mnemonic way of remembering all the points of the message. Shift right, first point, shift left, second point.

"But Ms. Easton wants you—wishes that you—anyway, you're supposed to go to the drawing room at seven-thirty. That's where they're having drinks." She shifted again. Lindy waited for the next point. The girl grabbed the empty tray, walked toward the door, turned and shifted. "If there's anything else you would like, please dial four. That's the kitchen." She opened the door and closed it behind her.

The door opened again and she stuck her head in. "Oh, almost forgot—reception's still on." She shut the door.

Feeling ill at ease, Lindy and Biddy dressed for dinner and headed downstairs in search of the drawing room.

"It does look like that hotel from *The Shining*," whispered Biddy slowing down as she reached the bottom of the stairs.

Lindy's hand ran along the chestnut banister and she looked at the foyer below her. Carved wooden panels framed squares of fabric wall coverings. Brass sconces cast fans of light upward against the walls. Above them, a chandelier created a distant glow.

"This way, please." A tall, attenuated butler approached them and made a slight bow. His face was thin and long, like the rest of him. Sparse gray hair was slicked back from his forehead. Exchanging looks, Lindy and Biddy followed him across the hall and entered a room through a heavy wooden door that opened easily at his touch.

Jeremy and Marguerite Easton stood at the window, drinks in hand, facing each other. Jeremy was dressed in a dinner jacket and looked every bit the man of the manor.

Marguerite came toward them, a sea-green gown of chiffon floating out behind her as she crossed to where they stood just inside the door. Earrings of light green stones dangled from her earlobes. It was the only jewelry she wore. She held out an unadorned hand to Lindy and then to Biddy.

She led them into the room, and the butler appeared with a tray of drinks. Lindy took a glass of white wine and smiled at him. Were you supposed to thank servants or ignore them? She couldn't remember. She hoped the smile would suffice.

"I've been so looking forward to meeting you," said Marguerite. "With this tragic accident, I wasn't able to give you the welcome I had hoped." Marguerite shook her head. Her eyes misted over. Jeremy came up beside her, and she smiled up at him. She was a tall woman, straight-backed, and looking much younger than her seventy-two years, in spite of the lines of fatigue around those remarkable eyes. Her complexion was creamy and pink; even the inevitable wrinkles looked buoyant and alive.

They were a beautiful couple, thought Lindy as she sipped the excellent wine. Not like mother and son. No. She imagined Jeremy older; a little softer around the middle, but still strong; a maturing of the face; perhaps, a thinning of the hair. Marguerite, younger, looking at him with eyes that danced with pleasure, not the supreme sadness that filled them now. The picture of unconditional love.

Lindy always found herself contemplating Jeremy in the role of lover. She couldn't help herself; he was such an intriguing subject. No one was absolutely sure of his sexual orientation, not even Jeremy, himself. As far as she knew, he had not had any lover, male or female, since she had known him.

Marguerite's voice broke into her thoughts and she mentally kicked herself for her moment of unbridled imagination.

"Such promise. You don't find that kind of natural talent and vivacity in one person. Not very often," she said. "He reminded me a little of you at that age, Jeremy. Seventeen, blond and blue-eyed, and beautiful in a rugged way." Marguerite smiled, a whimsical smile, and then her countenance seemed to fragment. "Oh, the poor dear boy."

The butler returned that moment with a tray of fresh drinks, which everyone took, fumbling around in embarrassed silence as Marguerite fought for composure.

"That will be all, Sandiman," she said finally.

"Madame." The butler bowed. Lindy almost missed his barely perceptible glance of concern. She watched him turn and leave the room, feeling an immediate liking for the man and his discreet loyalty.

"You know," said Marguerite, rousing herself, "Jeremy was a favorite here; he still is."

"Marguerite." Jeremy looked immensely pleased, then dropped his gaze. His affection for the woman was complete. Marguerite, mused Lindy, was the only friend of Jeremy's that she had ever heard him address by their full name. Normally it would be Margie or Maggie. The use of her full name was a mark of his admiration.

"You were so serious, remember?" She returned her attention to Lindy and Biddy. "The first year Jeremy was here, he was a skinny fourteen-year-old. But he walked away with the scholarship. Three hundred boys auditioned, as I recall. Most of them older and better trained than Jeremy. But he shot across the floor like a young colt with such power and sheer exuberance that it knocked the judges on their *derrieres*. They hardly looked at another dancer after that."

Marguerite laughed, her grief momentarily held in abeyance by her memories. "And the scholarship girl that year. What was her name? Something unusual. I remember there were funny little jokes about the two of you."

"Quasimodo and Esmerelda."

"Oh yes, Esmerelda, as dark as you were fair. And just the same height, but more muscular." Marguerite's gaze seemed far away. Her eyes danced. "You hauled her around the floor, lifted her over your head, with those skinny legs quaking beneath. How we laughed. But you wouldn't let Robert make the lifts easier. You were so determined to please."

"I looked ridiculous, I'm sure," Jeremy said, obviously embarrassed.

Lindy struggled not to laugh at the imagine of Jeremy hoisting the gargantuan Esmerelda around the stage. Biddy was grinning unashamedly.

"Not ridiculous, no. And when you came back the following summer, you had filled out quite nicely."

Jeremy blushed. "I'll never be able to face my coworkers again." He shot a brief look toward Biddy.

Biddy bit back her grin, then burst out laughing.

Marguerite touched her palm to Jeremy's cheek. "A blush makes a man so handsome, don't you think? You've made us so proud." Her expression sobered. "Poor, poor Larry."

Lindy started. Larry? Then she realized that Marguerite was speaking of the boy who had just died.

"He was talented. Almost as talented as you. But he was lazy. And arrogant. He spent as much energy getting into trouble as he did dancing. But I thought we could tame that energy, focus it, and redirect it. Now, we'll never know." Marguerite sighed. "I guess he wasn't really like you at all."

The door to the drawing room opened and two men, dressed in slacks and polo shirts, came into the room, one leading, the other following slightly behind, leaning on a cane. They both appeared to be in their sixties. Lindy's attention was caught by the second man. He looked vaguely familiar, but she couldn't place him.

"Sorry we're late," said the first man, hurrying forward.

"Ellis, my dear," said Marguerite. "Look who's arrived. Jeremy, you remember my brother Ellis, don't you?"

Jeremy's drink spilled out of his glass as he turned toward the new arrivals. Drops of the dark liquid splashed on the sleeve of his jacket. His "handsome" blush fled from his face, leaving two dark patches on his suddenly pallid complexion.

"Ellis, how very nice to see you again."

Ellis strode forward, arms held out in greeting. Jeremy shifted his drink to his left hand, and stuck out his right. Ellis pulled up short, and with a quirk of his head, held out his hand and firmly shook Jeremy's. "It must be fifteen years since I saw you last. You're looking quite fine."

"Thank you. I hope you're well?"

"Yes, yes, I am." Ellis Easton looked at him with a quizzical dip of the eyebrows. "You seem surprised to see me. Didn't Marguerite tell you—" He looked at Marguerite. "Why so glum, sister? And where are Robert and Chi-Chi? Shouldn't you be heading down to the pavilion for the reception?"

"There's been an accident," said Marguerite. "I asked Sheriff Grappel to look for you in town. Didn't you see him?"

"We were out in the countryside most of the day, weren't we, Stu?"

His companion nodded.

"Anyway, that Grappel is an ass, pardon me, ladies." He nodded quickly in Biddy and Lindy's direction. "He could have found us if the man had half a brain. What on earth has happened?"

"Larry Cleveland."

"That little guttersnipe. What has he done, now? I swear we should send him home, scholarship or no."

"He's dead." Marguerite slumped. Jeremy caught her by the arm and helped her to the couch. He sat down beside her and took both of her hands in his.

"My God." Ellis took a step forward, then sank down into a wing chair next to the couch. His companion came to stand by the chair. "What happened?"

"Evidently, he sneaked out of the dorm sometime after bed check last night. His bed was empty this morning. The counselors thought he had hitchhiked into town and stayed out all night. But when he wasn't in class this morning, I insisted that we call Sheriff Grappel. Larry knew he would be sent home for something like this."

Ellis nodded his head. "And did he go to town?"

Marguerite pulled a handkerchief from the sleeve of her gown and placed it to her lips. Jeremy put his arm around her. "No. They searched the woods and found him at the bottom of the ravine near the archaeology site. He had fallen down the side. He must have lain there all night. Helpless, with everyone oblivious." Marguerite choked back a sob. Jeremy's arm tightened around her.

"Damn the kid. He knew that area was off limits. The ground is unstable. What on earth was he doing out there?"

"From the sound of this kid, just telling him something was off limits would be tempting enough to make him go there." Ellis's friend spoke for the first time. His voice was calm and rational like a lawyer explaining the contents of a contract.

Lindy looked at him again and wondered if they had met at a fund-raiser or benefit. He was tall, and quite handsome with thinning silver hair, a broad forehead, and quite athletic-looking except for the cane he leaned on.

"I suppose you're right, Stu," said Ellis, "but the rules are explicit. One infraction like that, and a student will be sent home, no appeal. I can't imagine that even Larry would have risked going back to a sweltering summer in Brooklyn, when he could be here. He was a brazen, smart-mouthed specimen, but he wasn't stupid." "I tried to call his parents, but there was no answer," said Marguerite. "I didn't feel I could leave a message without alarming them. Alarm," she repeated. "Nothing when compared to what they will soon be feeling. Where are Chi-Chi and Robert?"

"I hope you won't think me callous," said Stu, "if I ask if you have contacted your lawyers?"

Marguerite looked nonplused. "I . . . no. Of course, I should have thought of that." Her hand touched her throat. "I'm not thinking clearly. Nothing like this has ever happened in the history of the retreat. We've had accidents, certainly, but never a fatal one. Never. Not in fifty years."

Ellis stood up. "Not to worry, I'll take care of it right now."

"I'll join you, if I may," said Stu. Nodding to Lindy and Biddy, the two men left the room.

With their departure, the others dropped into another painful silence, drinks in hand but not being drunk, everyone staring somewhere in front of them, grappling with their own thoughts.

A bustle in the doorway made them all turn around.

"Chi-Chi, Robert." Marguerite rose and held out both hands. The woman who had just entered walked briskly across the floor and embraced Marguerite, her arms squeezing tightly around the older woman's waist, her head resting on her breast. "Robert needed me."

Marguerite looked over Chi-Chi's head, then extended one hand which Robert rushed to take in his.

"Jeremy." Chi-Chi left Marguerite's arms and threw herself into Jeremy's. "What a terrible homecoming."

"Hi, Chi-Chi, Robbie." Jeremy hugged Robert in turn.

"Chi-Chi and Robert Stokes." Jeremy introduced Biddy and Lindy. Robert leaned over to shake their hands, not moving away from Jeremy. Chi-Chi smiled at them with full cherry lips, whose shape, thought Lindy, would look more comfortable in a grin, but were now tight with distress.

The couple stood the same height, about five-feet-eight, Chi-Chi as substantial as Robert was frail. They were surrounded by an aura of energy. Robert appeared nervous; his hands quivered visibly as if he had more energy than his slight body could contain. His frenetic nearly black eyes darted at them like two captured animals.

His wife, as if confirming that opposites attract, was solidly built. Brilliant blue eyes broadcast from above a patch of freckles that covered her nose and cheeks, eyes that invited confidence and promised sympathy. A mass of auburn hair swirled around her face and came to rest on softly molded shoulders.

She took a glass from Sandiman, who had appeared at her side, and handed it to her husband. He and Jeremy were deep in conversation, and she had to call his name to get his attention. She took another for herself and joined Marguerite who had sunk back onto the couch.

"Please," said Marguerite gesturing to Lindy and Biddy to sit down. "I'm being a terrible hostess. I didn't even introduce you to Ellis and Stuart, Stuart Hollowell, an old family friend," she said as if making the introduction at that moment. "When I was a girl, one never lost one's manners even in the face of tragedy. I'm afraid that with all the wonderful freedoms we enjoy these days, our sense of decorum has fallen into disuse."

Lindy shook her head and mumbled something noncommittal. She felt terribly out of place. She glanced at Biddy who sat uncomfortably on the edge of her chair. Maybe they should excuse themselves and let these old friends share their grief in private.

Jeremy sat down next to Marguerite. Marguerite patted Chi-Chi's knee. Robert crossed the room and stared out the floor length window.

"I just don't understand," he said into the darkness. "How could something like this happen? He was in the dorm last night. I checked. He was there." He turned quickly from the window and stared intently at Marguerite. "There are a few of the boys, you know the ones, that I always look in on once the counselors have finished their bed check. But he was there, in his bed. I saw him."

Chi-Chi lifted her chin. Her lips quivered momentarily before she controlled them enough to smile at her husband. Marguerite patted her knee again and Chi-Chi rose to join him at the window. "You are not responsible, Robert. Is he, Marguerite?"

"Of course not. Robert, don't be so hard on yourself. Perhaps, we should have sent him home." She sighed. "There's just not the discipline there used to be. Oh, there were always a few troublemakers, a few derring-dos. But now, it seems that most of the students are more intent on having a good time than perfecting their craft. Not like it used to be." She placed her empty glass on the table behind the sofa. "But I sound terribly old-fashioned. We shan't look back. We must have dinner and then we must decide what to do about the anniversary celebration."

The others looked at her expectantly, but she leaned back against the cushions and closed her eyes.

It was an onerous responsibility, thought Lindy, and though Marguerite might consider the others' opinions, the final decision rested entirely in her hands. It would be financially and politically disastrous to cancel a season as anticipated as this one. But it would also take incredible finesse to proceed without appearing callous. Lindy was glad she didn't have to make that decision.

A few minutes later, Sandiman announced dinner. Jeremy took Marguerite's arm and the others followed them into the hall.

Ellis and Stuart were just coming down the stairs, dressed in evening clothes and looking preoccupied. Marguerite didn't ask what the lawyers had advised, merely introduced them to Lindy and Biddy, then returned her attention to Jeremy. It was obvious that this business, even something as shattering as death, would not be allowed to infringe on the dinner hour. With a small bow, Ellis took Lindy's elbow and escorted her into the dining room.

Chapter Two

The dining table could have accommodated twice as many diners as there were. Only eight of them sat around the periphery of polished mahogany, Jeremy and Robert to either side of Marguerite at the head of the table, Biddy and Stuart next to Ellis at the other end. Lindy smiled at Chi-Chi across from her as Sandiman oversaw the serving of the soup.

Marguerite lifted her spoon, cueing the others to begin. They ate in silence, except for sporadic comments on the excellence of the first course.

Lindy didn't have much of an appetite. She groped around for possible dinner topics while playing at the corners of the damask napkin that lay across her lap.

After a few minutes, Marguerite mentioned the amount of rain they had had over the past few weeks. Stuart agreed that it would help to fill the reservoirs after a dry winter. Biddy commented on the lushness of the trees. Ellis felt sure that they would have excellent weather for the performance that weekend.

The mention of the word "performance" brought another silence. Although the Ash company would not be performing until the following weekend, the students were making a showcase presentation on Saturday night. It would be necessary to prepare the understudy for Larry's parts. Everyone was thinking that, though no one mentioned it aloud. They were all geared toward thinking that the show must go on.

Jeremy's voice broke into the hush that had fallen around the table. "Do you know that Robbie and I came here for the first time the same summer? Of course Robbie was already the artistic director then. You whipped me into shape, didn't you?"

"You were easy enough material." Robert suddenly looked years younger. A stalk of fine dark hair had fallen over his forehead; he pushed it back. "That was Chi-Chi's first year, too."

Chi-Chi looked up but continued to eat her soup. Lindy tried to imagine her twenty or thirty pounds lighter and years younger, dressed in tights and leotards instead of the somewhat frilly cocktail dress she wore now. "I'm the real success story here." She took a moment to beam her smile at Lindy and then to her husband.

Lindy waited expectantly for the explanation, but Chi-Chi turned to Stuart. "And what were you gentlemen up to today, anything exciting?"

"Well, let's see," said Stuart. "We frightened away several menacing squirrels and woodchucks. Wrestled a particularly defiant tree limb that had fallen across the road. And had lunch at Bob's Diner out on the highway. I believe the latter was the most adventurous exploit of the day. Wouldn't you agree, Ellis?"

"What will these ladies think of us, Stu?"

"I hope you didn't let Ellis eat those horrible home fries with gravy. They're so unhealthy." Marguerite gazed down the table at her brother.

Ellis squirmed in his chair.

Stuart laughed heartily. "Only a few. We tough guys have to watch our cholesterol these days. Ah, but life is to be conquered, right Ellis?" He lifted his eyebrows and waggled them. "That's how we stay young and vital."

He patted the cane that was hooked over the back of his chair and turned toward Lindy. "I hope you don't think I carry this accoutrement just to beat off rabid squirrels. Hip surgery. The wonders of modern medicine." He gestured around the table to include the others. "I'm considering buying more stock in the plastics industry.

I could have hobbled around in pain for the rest of my years, but in a few weeks, I'll be hiking and golfing with the best of them. Might even take up skiing."

From the corner of her eye, Lindy saw Ellis dart an uncomfortable look down the table.

Stuart turned his arch grin on Marguerite. "Or perhaps tennis. I haven't had time to play in years."

"You're incorrigible, Stuart Hollowell. Just don't overdo."

The soup was followed by a flaky cold salmon, served on a bed of crisp green asparagus and accented by a floret of broiled tomato. Conversation finally reached a comfortable rhythm, half of the diners roused by their performing abilities to enter into the role of country weekend guests, the others so immaculately well-bred that they glided around the subject of the dead boy with coordinated grace.

Only Robert Stokes brooded over his untouched plate of food, and looked relieved when it was whisked away by the servant, only to frown again as it was replaced by the next course.

Lindy pushed aside thoughts of the accident as she became conscious of the number of calories she was packing away. She began estimating how much more she could eat without sending her relentless diet into overdrive.

Biddy was happily tucking into a slice of prime rib. There were not too many things that could disrupt Biddy's appetite or consummate professionalism. Beneath an exterior of rampant optimism and bubbling enthusiasm was a determination to make things work, no matter what the obstacles. She had succeeded in the dance business by keeping these qualities in balance, drawing sometimes on her enthusiasm to inspire those around her, and sometimes on her internal strength to bully the rest of them to rise to their best.

Lindy continued to eat, just enough to be polite, though every dish was cooked to perfection. She listened to stories of Ellis and Stuart's travels to Europe and the Far East, to Marguerite's reminiscences of how her mother had begun the retreat that had become her passion. How Marguerite had taken over and continued in her mother's footsteps.

Lindy found herself contemplating the woman, letting her words fade to a buzz as the magnetism of her person took over. Her hands played delicately in the air as she spoke. Though she wore no rings, Lindy thought that she must have been married at one time, but couldn't remember to whom or for how long. For years, her name had graced the society and arts pages of the *Times*, only as Marguerite Easton. It would have been unusual for a woman to keep her maiden name in the years that Marguerite had been of a marriageable age.

Good Lord, thought Lindy, *I'm even beginning to think like a character in a country weekend novel.* Marriageable age, indeed. Maybe Marguerite had indulged in free love and wild bohemian carousing back in the forties.

A rush of embarrassment turned her uncomfortably warm. Would she never learn to control this tendency to wild imagination? It must be because she was so focused on details in her job as rehearsal director. Like a child who went wild when let out of an arduous day in school, her mind roamed the byways of speculation whenever she had a moment of relaxation. But imagination was good for the stage, wasn't it? She'd just be a little more disciplined about her choice of subject matter from now on.

She smiled at Marguerite as she consciously erased any lurid thoughts from her mind. Marguerite caught her eye and smiled back; a smile that said any friend of Jeremy's is part of the family. It made Lindy even more chagrined at her wayward thoughts. She looked away and stabbed at a strawberry torte that had been placed before her while she was off on her mental ramblings.

"I'm absolutely stuffed," said Ellis, pushing his dessert plate away. "Let's have coffee in the library, my dear. I feel a hundred miles away from you and Jeremy. We haven't seen each other in years, and I've had to yell just to get his attention."

"An excellent idea." Marguerite rose in a fluid movement. Jeremy and Robert were immediately at her side like well-rehearsed courtiers.

The others bustled about, placing napkins on the table, scooting

back chairs, finishing up tidbits of conversation, and followed them
out of the dining room.

The library was wainscoted in dark chestnut paneling. A paisley-
and-striped wallpaper in tones of gold, burgundy, and green rose
above it to the ceiling. Bookshelves covered two walls and a knee-
hole desk stood in front of a pair of French doors, partially covered
by drapery that pooled onto the floor. A collection of leather couches
and chairs was arranged around an unlit fireplace; to its left was a
bow window with a cushioned window seat.

Lindy took her coffee from Sandiman and sat on the window
seat. She was soon joined by Stuart. He placed his cup on the window sill, lowered himself onto the cushion, and placed his cane
along side his thigh. "A nuisance, this." He indicated the cane and
reached for his cup.

Lindy smiled. "It doesn't seem to hamper your activities, and
from the look of things, you'll be throwing it away before long."

"I certainly plan to, but let's not talk about the infirmities of the
not-quite-young. I'm so glad that you were able to be here. The
preparations for the festival have been enormous. I'm always
amazed at the amount of scheduling these things require."

Lindy nodded.

"Having Jeremy here means so much to Marguerite and Ellis."

"He wouldn't have missed it." She looked across the room to
where Ellis and Jeremy stood in front of the bookcase, coffees in
hand. Ellis faced the room; Jeremy stood with his back turned so
that only his profile was visible as he listened to Ellis. Marguerite
floated toward them, said something to Ellis, then took Jeremy's
arm.

The three of them moved toward the side table and put down
their cups. Marguerite turned to the others.

"It's getting late," she said. "I'd like to go down to the pavilion
and look in on the party, if any of you would care to join me."

Robert, Chi-Chi, and Stuart rose at once, Biddy and Lindy only a
beat behind. Depositing cups and saucers, they followed Marguerite

out of the room and to the front door where Sandiman stood ready to see them out.

They walked across the expansive driveway and toward a path through the trees. To their right, the glass-enclosed lobby of the theater was lit by a band of lamps. The wooden building loomed large behind it, the rectangular roof of the stage rising above the trees and melding with the darkness of the sky. Farther along and to the left, Lindy could discern the dim outlines of other buildings.

Marguerite and Jeremy led the way, followed by Robert and Chi-Chi, then Biddy on Ellis's arm. Lindy found herself once again in the company of Stuart.

"Those buildings are the studios. There are two smaller ones off in the trees. And to your left is the dining hall." Lindy's gaze followed the direction of his uplifted hand; she smiled at him as his arm enclosed hers.

"The path changes to gravel soon. Be careful of your shoes."

The couples in front of them slowed down as the women picked their way over the stones of the path. It was slow going, and Lindy realized that it was more than politeness that had caused the men to offer their services as escorts. Their flat shoes were more able to withstand the shifting pebbles beneath their feet.

"I've suggested they pave all the paths," said Stuart. "I can't imagine why they don't have more twisted ankles than they do. But Marguerite insists on keeping everything as it has always been."

His arm tightened on hers as Lindy's heel slipped between the stones.

"Fortunately most of the students don't wear four-inch heels." He chuckled.

"I'll remember that when I dress tomorrow."

A glow of light broke through the trees. They continued toward it, the woods behind them becoming darker as their eyes focused on the light ahead. Once Lindy gasped when an otherworldly face peered at her from the side of the path where a beam of light highlighted its features.

"Statuary," Stuart informed her. "You'll meet some of the great figures of history out there in the woods, not to mention a few from mythology and some unrecognizable abstract forms of some of the resident artists. I think that one's Will Shakespeare."

The light grew stronger and the sound of dance music hummed in the air. An open pavilion stood before them; hazy yellow light emanated outward from under the roof like a giant lantern. The music was upbeat and loud, but only a few couples were dancing. Most of the students were standing in groups, talking. Rebo, Juan, and Paul were holding court to several young dancers who lounged against one of the picnic tables that were placed along the perimeter of the concrete floor.

When Jeremy helped Marguerite onto the floor, the group nearest her stood up, sending a ripple across the room. Moments later, everyone was standing, their attention focused on the newcomers. It was the first time Lindy could remember a group of young people responding so politely of their own volition.

The music faded out, and Marguerite and Jeremy led the others to the front of the pavilion. The crowd parted as they passed, gazing intently at the woman who led the way. It was like a royal cortege, thought Lindy. She wouldn't have been surprised to see the students curtsey and bow. Beneath the pavilion's roof was a silence so complete that she could hear the rustling of nocturnal creatures somewhere out in the darkness.

Marguerite stepped onto the wooden platform that held the music equipment. She surveyed the room for a moment.

"Good evening, I hope you are all getting to know our guest company members." Her voice enveloped them and gathered them to her.

Lindy could see the familiar heads of the Jeremy Ash dancers throughout the room. Beyond the call of duty, they had intermingled with the young students. Some companies held themselves aloof, approached each event in the jaded, don't-bother-me attitude that performers sometimes assumed. She felt a familiar warmth of pride as she contemplated how unique a group it was.

Marguerite called the company forward. Dancers made their way across the floor and joined Biddy and Lindy along the front. Marguerite introduced each one by name.

"Impressive," whispered Biddy under her breath. "How does she know who's who?"

Lindy nodded minutely. "Amazing."

"And this is the director of the company, Jeremy Ash, one of our most esteemed graduates." Applause broke out among the students and spread out into the night.

It was a rarefied atmosphere. Marguerite commanded an awe and respect rarely found in any group of people, much less the young who had been raised in a world of self-gratification and offhanded manners.

As the applause tapered off, she continued in a more subdued voice.

"I am sure you are all aware of the accident that took Larry Cleveland's life." Heads lowered, eyes searched hers as if seeking reassurance. A few students had climbed onto tables and benches in order to see over the heads of those in front, their concentration drawing them physically toward the directress.

"I am so terribly sorry," Marguerite continued. "Such a tragedy in our midst." Lindy saw a few heads turn toward each other, looks exchanged, a comment here and there.

"And even though I know we all feel like curling up under the covers and wishing him back to life, we cannot. We can only go forward, work hard, and try to be the best we can be. To dedicate our lives to carrying on." A few dancers brushed tears away. Arms quietly embraced them. A muffled sob here and there. And again, looks that under other circumstances would have seemed surreptitious.

"I think it would be appropriate to dedicate our performance this weekend to Larry's memory. I know it is a small thing, but it will be our best tribute." Someone coughed. Lindy was getting the idea that not everybody in the camp was mourning Larry Cleveland, and it was only their respect for Marguerite that held them in an elegiac state of mind.

"And now please continue with your party, but remember, the

rules we have are for your protection. Please, please regard them. We don't want anything to happen to any of you." She stepped off the platform, and people began to disperse. She stopped at a group that still lingered nearby. Two girls looked up, their faces brightening. Marguerite touched them lightly on their backs and then moved toward another group.

Biddy and Lindy made their way back to where they had entered and looked over the crowd. Peter Dowd, the company's stage manager, and Mieko stood at the edge of a group of students. In their midst, Rose Laughton moved her hands animatedly in the air, recounting some story that produced quiet laughter from the young dancers around her.

Rose was the company's wardrobe mistress. She was large, loud, and intimidating; not beautiful, but striking in a Valkyrie way. She struck horror into anyone who abused their costumes and had a sense of humor that often left her peers open-mouthed.

Peter, tall and dark with black hair and forbidding brown eyes, stood uncomfortably on the fringe of the group. A whiz at all things technical, he was taciturn in the social sphere. When he had announced his New Year's resolution of becoming more sociable, his statement was met with howls of laughter. If his idea of sociability meant hovering awkwardly at the edges of conversation, he was making a great start.

Lindy smiled. How someone that handsome could be so socially inept was ridiculous.

She turned from the group and her eye caught those of a boy standing in the shadows at the edge of the pavilion. His face was streaked with tears. She instinctively moved toward him. He disappeared into the darkness.

"We're going back to the house." Jeremy was standing beside her, eyebrows knit together. This was not the homecoming he had expected.

Lindy touched his arm. "We just got here." She fell silent when she realized that Robert was with him. He looked utterly exhausted. Thin lines framed his mouth. He rubbed one eye methodically with the back of his hand.

"We'll go with you," said Biddy. "We need to go over the schedule for tomorrow."

"I'll take care of it."

"Oh." Biddy looked taken aback, but she said nothing more.

"Shall we find Chi-Chi and tell her?" asked Lindy.

Robert darted his eyes in her direction. "Yes, would you?"

She nodded and led Biddy off to look for Chi-Chi's bright dress among the crowd.

Chi-Chi nodded when they told her Robert and Jeremy had left, then hurried toward the path. Lindy and Biddy followed.

"Maybe we should leave them alone," said Biddy. "Jeremy seemed to want to get away from us."

"I think he's just worried about Robert. He seems to be taking this rather too hard."

They followed the others up the path toward the house. Chi-Chi had already caught up to Jeremy and Robert. They stood together briefly, then Chi-Chi took Robert's arm. Jeremy took the other, and Lindy and Biddy were left to make their own way over the graveled walk.

From the edge of the woods, they watched the three go into the house, Chi-Chi supporting her husband as if he were an invalid. The door closed behind them.

"He sure seems dependent on his wife," said Lindy.

"Maybe we should just sit here for a minute and then go to bed," said Biddy indicating one of the benches that were spaced strategically along the path.

"We should at least say good night to Marguerite and Ellis before we do."

"We can wait for them here." Biddy sat down and contemplated a winged statue of Mercury that stood on the other side of the path.

Lindy joined her. "Don't be upset with Jeremy. You know he always gets totally involved with whatever is going on. He didn't mean to be rude."

"Of course not," agreed Biddy. "But he needs to be with his friends. We're outsiders, and it wouldn't be right to force ourselves into that friendship. Besides, it's none of our business."

"Oh, there you are." It was Stuart. "Ellis and Marguerite are right behind me. Shall we go up to the house for a nightcap?"

Brother and sister appeared at that moment, Marguerite leaning heavily on Ellis's arm. She looked tired to the bone.

"Of course," said Lindy. She saw Biddy shoot her a quick look. "Robert and Chi-Chi and Jeremy are already there. I think they wanted to talk," Lindy added.

"Then let's join them, by all means," said Stuart. With a brief look toward Biddy, Lindy stood and linked her arm around Marguerite's free one. Marguerite squeezed back and took a moment to catch her breath.

They started toward the house, Biddy and Stuart following behind.

As they entered the drawing room, Sandiman was just handing drinks to Chi-Chi and Robert who were sitting together on the couch. Jeremy had pulled up a side chair and was leaning toward them, his elbows resting on his knees. His face registered a flash of something that might have been annoyance as the others entered the room, then quickly changed to concern when he saw Marguerite.

He rose and took her from Ellis and Lindy and led her to the chair he had just vacated. "I'll get you a cognac."

Marguerite smiled at him. "Thank you, dear. I think you can go to bed now, Sandiman. We'll help ourselves."

Sandiman nodded slightly. "Good night, madame." He nodded again to the others and quit the room.

"Robert, you look ghastly," said Marguerite. "You are taking too much of this on yourself. Chi-Chi, please take him to bed."

Robert shook his head. "I've been thinking about something that happened yesterday. If only I had paid more attention . . ." He took a deep breath, which caught in his throat. Chi-Chi covered his hand in hers.

He smiled a wan smile at her. "No, it's just that—well—the thing is—Larry asked to speak to me yesterday. He seemed, I don't know, worried. It was unusual for him to seek me out, but I thought he had probably just pulled some stunt that he was sure would get him into trouble and he was trying to deflect the outcome. I put him off until after men's class today." He took a sip of brandy then held the glass cupped in both hands between his knees. "Only by today he was dead. I thought I would just let him sweat a little. He was always so sure of himself. I figured that giving him time to stew over it would at least make him think twice about doing it again. Whatever it was." Robert lowered his head and stared into the brandy snifter. "I didn't realize he was so disturbed. I should have talked to him then and there. What have I done?"

Marguerite was out of her chair and sitting next to Robert before the others had time to react. "Stop it this instant, Robert Stokes. It was probably just what you thought it was, and talking to him wouldn't have changed a thing."

Robert looked at her bleakly. "But what if—"

"He had an accident, plain and simple."

"But what if it wasn't an accident? If he was really troubled and I turned him away. He might have been desperate." Robert's voice broke off. His head jerked from one face to the other.

"Are you suggesting that the boy might have killed himself?" asked Stuart.

"Nonsense," said Marguerite. "Larry Cleveland was not a boy to commit suicide. He took one too many chances, and his luck ran out. There it is." She looked around the room. "I will not have Robert taking the blame on himself. I'm sorry the boy is dead, but no amount of second guessing will bring him back."

"Did you tell this to the police?" asked Stuart.

"No, I—I didn't think about it until after they had left. I'm still not sure it has anything to do with what happened."

"Perhaps you should."

"I hardly see how that would help." Ellis walked back from the window where he had been standing. He looked at Stuart. "Well, if he must, he must, but I still don't see how it will help."

"I'll tell them first thing in the morning, I'm sure they'll be back," Robert said bitterly. "Though I'm not looking forward to talking with Byron."

Chi-Chi patted his hand. "I think we'll go home now." She took his glass and set it on the table. Robert obediently stood up.

"I'll walk you out, and then I'll take myself off to bed." Marguerite walked beside the couple as they left the room. "Good night," she said and closed the door behind them.

Stuart moved to the couch and motioned Ellis to join him. "I don't envy Robert facing Grappel in the morning," he said. "But really, it can't be helped. In view of the possible ramifications, we must do all we can to assist the police in their investigation."

"Investigation?" asked Biddy.

"Just normal procedure. Nothing to worry about."

Ellis's mouth pulled into a grim line. "Be assured that nasty son of a bitch, uh, pardon, ladies, will make things as uncomfortable as possible. Miserable bastard."

Lindy wasn't sure whether Ellis had been referring to Robert or Sheriff Grappel with his last statement.

"The sheriff doesn't seem too popular," she ventured.

Stuart lifted his glass to her. "I think we can all drink to that, my dear. You would be hard put to find a meaner piece of work than Byron Grappel. Backwoods inbreeding or something of the sort."

Ellis choked on his drink. "Stuart."

"Well, it's true."

"He's always been a hothead," said Jeremy. He had been so quiet that Lindy had almost forgotten he was in the room.

"Surely, he wasn't sheriff here when you were a student," she said. "He doesn't look that much older than the rest of us."

"No." Jeremy spoke slowly as if his thoughts were miles away.

Ellis took up the explanation. "I think he had just started as a patrolman, the first year you were here." He raised his eyebrows and leaned forward. "He was engaged to Chi-Chi."

"Chi-Chi?" Biddy and Lindy said simultaneously.

"And therein lies the rub. He and Chi-Chi had been childhood sweethearts. Everyone in town expected them to marry as soon as Byron had saved enough money."

"You mean she's a local girl?" asked Biddy.

"Oh yes. She was here working as a maid that summer. She fell head over heels in love with Robert, didn't she, Jeremy."

"What? Oh, yes," Jeremy agreed and returned to the contemplation of his brandy.

"They were married at the end of the summer, the last day of camp. Best thing that ever happened to Robert . . . and to Chi-Chi," Ellis said as an afterthought. Then he chuckled. "You would have enjoyed that, Stu. Byron showed up the night before the wedding with a shotgun. Chi-Chi walked right up to him, stuck her nose in his face, and kicked him in the shin so hard that he dropped the gun. While he was hopping around on one foot, rubbing his leg and cursing like almighty thunder, Chi-Chi takes the gun, walks over to the lake, and chucks it right in. God, the girl had an arm." He laughed again, pulled out a handkerchief and wiped his eyes. He leaned back against the couch, still chuckling. "You know, Jeremy, I haven't thought about that wedding in years."

"A formidable lady," said Stu.

"Yes, she was," agreed Ellis. "Gave a whole new meaning to the expression 'shotgun wedding'." His eyes danced with amusement, then came to rest on Jeremy's. "That was quite a summer, wasn't it?"

He was answered by a rumble of thunder, so close that they all jumped. "And on that note," said Ellis, "I think I'll say good night."

Chapter
Three

Rain descended on the mountain during the night. Lindy was startled from sleep several times by claps of thunder and the sky flashing bright through the window. By morning the storm had changed into a steady downpour that lashed at the window-panes and thumped heavily on the sills. The sky was gray and depressing.

Biddy groaned from the other bed. "Ugh, rain, and I didn't bring an umbrella."

"I'm sure they will have plenty downstairs." Lindy went into the bathroom and turned on the shower, letting it run until clouds of steam thickened the air.

When she emerged from the bathroom, Biddy was sitting at the window, arms wrapped about her and wearing a thick Spoleto Festival sweatshirt over her nightgown.

"Nice look," said Lindy. She shivered as she grabbed clothes from the bureau. "Pretty damn cold for July, if you ask me."

"And nasty running from building to building in the rain just to work. Give me the city any old day."

"Sissy. We'll have you hiking and rowing and swimming in the lake before you know it."

"Hiking maybe, as long as there's a path, but swim in a place where icky things live and brush up against your legs and bite your toes? Yuck! If we get two seconds off, I'll curl up with a book and look out the window at the view."

"Very literary, but even Eliza Bennet schlepped through pastures and climbed over stiles in the rain to visit Mr. Darcy."

"Yeah, but Austen didn't put in any snakes or mosquitoes or wild dogs. I'll just be the perfect weekend guest and get the vapors anytime someone suggests mountain climbing." Biddy walked into the bathroom. The sound of running water drowned out her next words.

"Well, suit yourself, I intend to explore every nook and cranny," Lindy said above the noise.

A few minutes later, Biddy came back into the room scrubbing her hair with a fluffy pink towel. "I suppose it's useless to dry my hair. It'll just get wet again."

"Yep, hurry up. I want to go make sure everything is running according to schedule. I'm sure Jeremy has taken care of it, but he did seem distracted last night."

"I'll say." Biddy's face clouded momentarily. "It sure would be a lot easier on all of us if he didn't try to carry the weight of the world all by himself. Between him and Robert there's enough responsibility-taking to spread over an entire camp of pampered, undisciplined dancers."

"Next, you'll be giving a speech about the old days, when we had to walk through the snow to class, and only had one pair of black tights, that we had to wash out in the sink every night. Get dressed."

"Well, I think Marguerite is right. There just isn't the discipline there used to be."

"You don't think our dancers are disciplined?"

"They're the exception. And that's because of Jeremy. And even they like to party too much."

"Some people . . ."—Lindy arched an eyebrow at her friend— "have a short memory."

Biddy made a face and pulled on khaki slacks, then reached for her sweatshirt. "I wonder how Robert is this morning. I felt sorry for the guy. He was so upset."

"It's a good thing Chi-Chi is so nurturing," said Lindy. "I wonder if they'll let her sit in on Robert's interview with the sheriff."

"If I were the sheriff, I'd lock the door. I wonder what's for breakfast?"

Biddy grabbed her dance bag, and Lindy followed her down the stairs. The spicy smells of coffee, eggs, and breakfast meats greeted them as they entered the dining room. With a contented sigh, Biddy headed for the row of chafing dishes on the side board. "I could get used to living like this." She reached for a plate.

"Yeah, *you* could. You never gain weight. I'd be too wide to get through the door after about two weeks."

Biddy only nodded. She was already tucking into a pile of scrambled eggs.

Lindy watched Biddy eat while she sipped at black coffee and separated wedges of an orange. It was not great for her stomach, but her thighs would be thankful. After what seemed like an age of watching Biddy pack away eggs, toast and jam, and bacon, Lindy stood up.

"If you're feeling revived enough for a walk, I think we should go check on the classes. Rebo is teaching modern technique to the students, if Jeremy didn't change his mind."

Biddy put her napkin on the table and pushed back her chair. "I'm feeling much better, thank you," she said. "Let's see if Jeremy has started company class. I don't know why he didn't let you teach it like you normally do."

"Because this is his show," said Lindy. "He wants to give it everything."

"Yeah, well, after meeting Marguerite, I see where he gets his energy."

Stuart was standing on the front porch, unfurling a giant umbrella. "Big enough for three," he said. They gratefully squeezed themselves under its protection and let Stuart lead them down the steps.

"And where are you ladies headed this morning? This rain

shouldn't keep up for much longer. It's supposed to clear up by this afternoon."

The sound of engines caught their attention. Two police cars turned into the drive and came to a stop in front of the steps, virtually blocking their passage.

"Insufferable bugger," muttered Stuart. "Good morning, Sheriff," he said in a louder voice and directed a polite smile at the man getting out of the passenger side of the first car.

Sheriff Grappel nodded. "Is Ms. Marguerite inside?"

"I believe so. Sandiman will announce you. Now, if you'll excuse us." Stuart tipped his head slightly toward the sheriff and scuttled Lindy and Biddy across the drive, one hand holding the umbrella, the other maneuvering his cane between their feet.

At the theater, Biddy left them to look in on company class.

"I'll check on Rebo, but first: Stuart, is there an infirmary and doctor on the grounds?"

Stuart raised his eyebrows. "Of course, are you in need of one?"

"No," said Lindy. "But I thought the kids could use some grief counseling. There was one boy I saw last night that seemed particularly upset. Do you think it would be impolitic to suggest it?"

"Not at all. I expect Dr. Addison has already set something up. She's a superb physician. An old friend of Marguerite's. It's this way."

They walked down the path they had followed the night before, past the student dining hall, then Stuart veered off to the left. The trees sheltered them from the worst of the rain, but drops fell from the leaves and made thudding noises as they hit the surface of the umbrella.

After a few minutes, they stopped in front of a brown, wood-shingled cabin. A sign of whitewashed wood hung to the left of a screen door. INFIRMARY was carved into its surface and painted black.

Stuart stepped onto the porch, collapsed the umbrella, and shook it vigorously. The screen door rattled beneath his knock.

A husky voice answered from inside. "Come in."

"I'll wait for you out here and escort you back. Wouldn't want you to get lost on your first day."

Lindy considered telling him that she thought she could manage the cultivated wilderness of the camp on her own, especially since each path was marked with a sign bearing names like Hemlock Lane, Elm Hollow, Two Rocks Way. But it would be an affront to his Old World manners, so she just said, "Thank you" and went inside.

The difference between the rough exterior of the outside of the cabin and the high-tech interior stopped her just inside the door. Behind a metal desk sat a diminutive woman, dressed in a tailored pantsuit that would have been more appropriate for holding office hours on the upper East side of Manhattan.

She looked up at Lindy and tilted her head. The motion sent her sleek black page boy swaying to the side. Black horn-rimmed glasses added to the general severity of her appearance, the thickness of the lenses distorting and amplifying the size of her eyes.

"Dr. Addison?"

"Yes," she said in a voice much too throaty for the thin, business-like woman who stood, took off her glasses, and held out her hand to be shaken.

"Lindy Graham," said Lindy holding out her own hand, which was taken in a firm grasp. "I'm the rehearsal director for the Jeremy Ash Dance Company."

"A pleasure. Please be seated. How can I help you?" She motioned to a chair at the side of the desk and resumed her seat.

"I was just wondering . . ." Lindy felt momentarily at a loss for words. She couldn't imagine this woman unwinding enough to invite dialogue with young men and women over their feelings about the death of a friend. "I noticed that some of the students seemed particularly upset about the accident, especially one boy—"

"Connie, most likely."

"Pardon me?"

"Connie. Connover Phillips. He's taking this harder than the others. He was infatuated with Larry, though I can't imagine why. Larry never gave him the time of day. But that's neither here nor there, is it?"

Lindy shook her head. She was beginning to feel that she had misjudged Dr. Addison. "Everyone has been quite preoccupied with the, um . . ." She deflected the air with her hand. "I wasn't sure if anyone had thought to—"

"Consider grief counseling?" Dr. Addison smiled. "We're on top of things here, in spite of the rather rustic ambiance. We have to be. With the nearest hospital a good half hour and a harrowing drive across the mountain, we try to be prepared for any emergency."

"I didn't mean to—"

"Don't worry about butting in. You have to if you want to fit in here. Anyone who works for Marguerite is expected to plunge head-long into the fray. I expect you'll find yourself more involved in things than you can imagine. I hope you'll enjoy it; it's quite exhilarating."

"I'm sure I will." Lindy rose to leave.

"Would you like a tour? I think you'll be impressed."

"Yes, thank you." Lindy was taken off guard by the sudden invitation. She followed the doctor into another room. The walls were painted in white enamel and glistened in the fluorescent lighting. A metal examination table stood on the left and to the right, two hospital beds were neatly made in crisp white sheets and blankets. The room was crammed with gleaming metal, state-of-the-art equipment.

"Rather impressive for a summer camp, wouldn't you say?"

Lindy could only nod. It was an amazing array of medical technology.

Dr. Addison pointed out one machine after another, her sleek hand gliding across each instrument as she spoke. At the far end of the room were two doors: one marked, X-RAY, the other, LAB. The building was much longer than its humble facade had suggested.

"Just about anything you would need for a physical emergency, but we are also equipped to deal with emotional and psychological problems, in a triage sort of way. We, of course, rely on outside expertise when necessary, but quite frankly, Lindy—may I call you Lindy?"

Lindy nodded.

"My name is Adele—our equipment is probably more advanced than any they have at County General. Of course, I'm only a Manhattan cardiologist, but I've taken quite a few courses in other fields. One must be prepared."

She sighed suddenly. "I've worked here for ten summers. I find shin splints and poison ivy a welcome relief from triple bypasses. But I confess, I wasn't prepared for this."

She led Lindy back to the door and flipped off the lights. The room behind them was plunged into darkness, except for a series of emergency lights that blinked on.

"You're probably wondering what would bring a cardiologist to summer camp every year."

"Actually, I was," agreed Lindy.

"Marguerite, of course. She's the reason we all keep coming back. We've known each other for years. We were at Hall's together, back in the Dark Ages. She was in the senior division, I a mere second grader. She spent many a night singing a homesick seven-year-old to sleep."

Lindy looked at her, astonished. It was hard to imagine this sleek professional as a child, much less a lonely child in need of comfort.

They reached the entrance door. "Thanks, Adele. I'm quite overwhelmed."

Adele smiled. "Welcome aboard, Lindy."

The rain had let up while she was inside the infirmary. She found Stuart on the gravel clearing, chucking stones with his cane.

"Working on my golf swing," he said a little sheepishly. "I can't stand being idle. Something I learned from my father. Never let an opportunity for action go by, accept every challenge, and you'll stay young until the final hour." He offered Lindy his arm. "Shall I show you where class is being held?"

They retraced their steps along Two Rocks Way. Piano music drifted toward them through the trees.

"Thank you, Stuart. I think I can find my way from here."

"My friends call me Stu." He smiled, his blue eyes crinkling. His father had the right idea, mused Lindy as she walked toward the studio. Stu looked very boyish in spite of the fine lines in his face and the slightly flaccid skin around his jaw line.

The Loie Fuller studio was shingled like the infirmary. Inside, a small foyer was crammed with piles of dance bags and water bottles; rain gear hung on pegs along the back wall, and leaning on the half wall that looked into the dance space was Jeremy, watching the class with total concentration.

Lindy walked up beside him. "Who's teaching company class?" she whispered.

"Mieko." He didn't take his eyes off the room. Rebo walked among bodies that were stretched out on the floor, performing a series of contractions.

"And lift, contract, stretch the arms, and release." He leaned over to reposition the arms of one of the students. "And lift, contract . . ." He made his way around the room, adjusting the position of one dancer, kneeling and suggesting something to another. After a few more bars of music, he stood up and stopped the pianist, who was sitting behind a baby grand Baldwin in one corner of the studio.

"Listen, everybody. You don't grab at the abdominals for a contraction. You must lengthen and scoop—and keep the tension out of your shoulders." He looked around at the dancers, some still lying down with only their heads turned toward him, some propped up on one elbow, some in a sitting position.

"It should feel like this." He chose a boy near to him. "Lie back." The boy flashed him a grin. Rebo grabbed both his hands and placed one foot lightly on his navel. "When you lift up, the stomach should scoop out." He pulled the boy up by his arms keeping his foot in the hollow of the boy's stomach. "The knees bend because of the tilt of the pelvis. The spine curves; the shoulder girdle remains flat." He transferred his foot to the boy's chest. "Keep the chest flat across."

The boy straightened his shoulders; his abdominals grabbed and his ribs expanded. Rebo transferred his foot back to the boy's gut. "Without letting the abs pop up." The boy scooped out his stomach until his waist was pressed against the floor and his shoulders were parallel to the ceiling.

"Voilà," said Rebo. "The method is a little S-and-M, but it works."

There was a burst of appreciative laughter. He grinned. "Now try it without me."

The boy curved his spine. His knees released upward. His chest rose straight to the ceiling.

"And release."

The boy returned to a lying position on the floor.

"Now, everybody. Once again."

The music began. "And lift, contract, and stretch the arms . . ."

"Things look good here," said Lindy. "Why didn't you let me know you weren't teaching company class? I would have taught."

"I know," said Jeremy, still watching the class. "I was going to do it, but then I decided to take a look around instead."

Read that as too agitated to stay in one place, thought Lindy. Jeremy always pulsed with energy when he was upset. She could feel it now.

"It will be good experience for Mieko," he continued. He didn't look at her when he spoke. His attention was focused on the activity in the studio.

"Thought I'd find you here." Jeremy jerked around at the voice. Sheriff Grappel stood with his thumbs hooked in his belt loops. His shoulders and arms were brawny to an extreme, but his pants were belted low, and the buttons of his shirt stretched against the button holes.

When muscle men turn to fat, thought Lindy with an internal shudder. *Ugh.*

"You were looking for me . . . Sheriff?" Only the slightest pause before the title betrayed Jeremy's contempt. There was not a hint of it in his voice, but the sheriff's jaw tightened.

Lindy tried to imagine what Chi-Chi could ever have seen in this man. Or maybe, it had never been something she thought about; it was just expected that she would marry him, and so she would have if Robert hadn't come along.

Ugh, she thought again and turned back to watch the class. The students were now lined up in the far corner, ready to begin moving across the floor. Rebo was demonstrating the steps, but most eyes were focused not on him but toward the entrance where Byron Grappel stood contemplating Rebo.

Grappel shook his head slowly, his mouth tight with disgust. Jeremy turned back to the room following his gaze. Lindy was afraid to look at him. The emotion between the two men thickened the air.

"Initial postmortem report's in," said Grappel over their shoulders. His voice was low and hardly above a whisper.

Jeremy twitched slightly but didn't turn around.

"He didn't die immediately." There was a pause. The coffee and orange slices began to burn Lindy's stomach.

"Looks like he tried to crawl back up the side of the cliff."

Another pause, while Lindy listened to the sound of his breathing.

The sheriff snorted. "Don't know why he bothered. He musta taken a flying leap to get to the bottom in the first place. Too many ledges and things to break his fall, if he had just slipped down."

She felt Jeremy sway.

"Pretty nasty way to die." The sheriff unsnapped his holster and resnapped it. " 'Course, he might have had help."

Jeremy swung around. "Why don't you say it all at once, Byron?"

Dancers moved across the floor, diagonally from corner to corner. Lindy forced herself to watch their movements. Triplet, step and spiral, step to the side, run, run, *jeté*. She willed herself not to turn around. There was silence behind her. A standoff between Jeremy and the sheriff.

Rebo seemed to sense that he was losing the class's attention. His voice rose, booming over the music. "Push from the back leg, when you *jeté*. Come on."

He followed each dancer across the floor, correcting, cajoling. "Move. That's really nellie, you can cover more space than that."

Lindy heard Grappel snort again. "He had sex before he died."

This time Lindy did turn around. She stared at the man, thinking how satisfying it would be to smack the nasty expression off his face.

"That kind of sex." Grappel nodded toward Rebo who had just

lifted a boy under the shoulder propelling him another foot in the air.

"That's better," yelled Rebo. "Now do it yourself." The boy jumped higher on the next attempt.

"Too bad Larry Cleveland didn't stick to doing it himself," said the sheriff with a shrug.

"For Christ sakes, Byron, the boy was seventeen."

"Not a consenting adult."

"What's that supposed to mean?"

"It means that I'm going to be taking a good look at his death. Maybe it wasn't an accident after all." His lips moved like he was chewing something unpleasant. "A boy that age in a place like this. It isn't natural." Byron lifted one eyebrow, looked again across the room and turned his back on them.

"And you were buggering farm animals when you were twelve." Jeremy said the words under his breath, but Lindy saw the minute hesitation in Grappel's step before he continued toward the door.

What a stupid thing for Jeremy to have said. Lindy waited until the door slammed behind the sheriff, then turned to him. She started to speak, then saw the look that flared from his eyes as he stared at the closed door. It was a look she had only seen once, and it had not boded well for the person at which it was aimed.

"Do they raise a lot of sheep in New York State?" she asked.

They waited for Rebo to finish class. The students bowed first to Rebo and then to the pianist, then burst into noisy applause. Rebo made an exaggerated kowtow, circling his arm in front of him until it slapped the ground. He was surrounded by a group of young dancers.

"That was great! Thanks. Are you teaching again?"

"Tomorrow at eleven," said Rebo. "And make sure you get to ballet class with Andrea Martin. She's a fantastic teacher."

"Ballet's so old-fashioned," countered one of the girls.

Rebo slung his arm around the girl. "Ballet is the foundation of all theater dance, Miss Thing."

Too bad the sheriff hadn't seen that, thought Lindy. Maybe he wouldn't be so quick to judge if he knew that dancers treated everyone with affection.

The group split up in the foyer. The dancers grabbed dance bags, threw raincoats and ponchos over their arms, and began drifting toward the door.

Rebo waved goodbye as he walked over to Lindy and Jeremy.

"Nice class," said Jeremy.

"Considering that I was playing opposite the Vampire Lestat of New York. Talk about being upstaged." Rebo bared his teeth and hissed. "What did the ghoul want?"

"To let us know that Larry Cleveland, the dead boy, was sexually active." Jeremy's voice was dry as sand.

Rebo shrugged. "Him and the rest of the world. What's the big deal?"

"I believe that Jeremy is saying that Grappel would like to make things uncomfortable for everyone," said Lindy.

"For someone who's got his head stuck where the sun don't shine, he's got a lot of nerve. I hate guys like that."

"We all do," she agreed. "But maybe we should keep a low profile until this is over."

Rebo looked abashed for a moment. "Thank you, mama, but I wouldn't mind a little grapple with Grappel. No thick-necked homophobe is driving me back into the closet. Where are you guys off to?"

"Scheduling meeting with Robbie at the dining hall," said Jeremy.

"Well, I'm off to the what's-it . . ." He pulled a piece of blue paper from the pocket of his dance bag. "Deni-Shawn Studio. Eric and Juan are teaching composition. I'll just kibitz."

"What's that?" asked Lindy, pointing to the paper.

"A program insert from last season. Robert wrote out a schedule for me. All the notices are handwritten, even though there's a computer in the office." Rebo touched his fingertips together. "In keeping with the rustic ambiance. So quaint," he said in a breathy falsetto. "I'll just take my two Grecian urns and run along Hemlock

Lane to visit with Ted and Ruth." He skipped out the door and down the path.

Jeremy groaned. "Low profile, right."

Robert, Rose, and Biddy were sitting at a picnic table in the dining hall when Jeremy and Lindy entered. Beige coffee mugs and a scattering of papers covered the planks of the table.

Biddy was wearing a pair of reading glasses that she had begun using in the last several months. No one had ever acknowledged the addition. In a profession that depended on youth and good looks, nobody liked to mention the inevitable march into middle age. It wouldn't be long before Lindy joined her. She was already having to hold books and menus at arm's length to get the words in focus.

"There you are," said Biddy, snatching the glasses from her face.

Jeremy smiled. It was the first time he had smiled that morning, but Biddy had that effect on just about everyone. She always knew how to make people comfortable. Her glasses were just another prop in her repertory of techniques.

"What are you two smiling at?"

Lindy straightened her mouth. "Where's Peter?"

"Still at the theater," said Rose, reaching for a pencil that was stuck through braids that wrapped around her head. She began scribbling on a legal pad in front of her. "He's adapting the lighting plot for the student prod to coincide with ours." She finished writing and stuck the pencil back into her hair. "And I think he wanted to stick around for a few minutes to give Mieko some moral support. It's the first time she's taught." She raised one eyebrow at Jeremy.

Finding him unresponsive, she continued. "You know, I bet if Peter had started going out with Mieko last year instead of Andrea, they would still be together."

"Rose, why are you dressed like Heidi this morning?" asked Jeremy.

"In keeping with the situation, boss. You like it?" Rose turned her head side to side, displaying heavy braids that wrapped her head like strawberry-blond sausages.

Jeremy just shook his head.

There was no one in the world more un-Heidi-like than Rose Laughton. At nearly six feet, arms and legs built up from years of aikido training, and a mouth that could burn the ears off a sailor, Rose would never be mistaken for a cute little girl sitting at the feet of her grandfather. Rose usually had people groveling at her feet, even if she had to wrestle them to the ground to get them there. But she was the best costume mistress in the business and Jeremy had jumped at the chance of hiring her last year.

Jeremy swung one leg over the bench and straddled it. "So, where are we?"

"I think things are in pretty good shape, considering," said Robert. "Biddy's got everything organized. She's a whiz, Jeremy." Robert reached for his cup.

Coffee was the last thing the man needed, thought Lindy. His thin fingers trembled as he took the cup and brought it to his lips. His face was a shade of off-white. Lindy wondered if he was always this nervous or was it because one of his charges had had a fatal accident. She felt sorry for him. It was a feeling she hated. Especially when the person was so likable.

Peter strode through the door carrying a black portfolio. "Sorry. Lots of stuff to do." He sat down and opened the portfolio. Lindy peered over his shoulder at a series of scribbles and geometric shapes that filled the page.

"There's coffee in the urn on the counter," said Robert. "Stays on all day and can get pretty intense by late afternoon, but it's still pretty fresh now."

"Thanks, but I've already had my quota for the day. So, where are we?"

Lindy smiled as she recognized Peter's echo of Jeremy's question. For two men who had begun their working relationship as dire enemies they had covered a lot of ground toward becoming friends.

"We expect a full house of parents, friends, and critics for this weekend. Box office is more than good for next week," said Biddy. "Robert has the programs finished; we'll just have to insert the name of Larry Cleveland's understudy." She held up a slick pamphlet with a picture of the entrance to the retreat on the front. "He did a great job, don't you think?"

"Chi-Chi did," said Robert.

"Chi-Chi," corrected Biddy. "You'd be amazed at how much work she gets done. She's in charge of the restaurant and annex. And helps Robert with programming, *and* takes care of the students, *and* runs the student dining hall. She's indefatigable."

Robert smiled. It animated his pale face and straightened his shoulders.

Biddy turned toward the costume mistress. "Rose?"

"All the costumes are out of the trunks and waiting to be fitted." She consulted her notes on the legal pad. "There's a fitting tomorrow morning. I'm guessing at a few minor alterations. Then I have a costume crew coming in the afternoon to help with the sewing and steaming."

Rose leaned forward on her elbows. The others readied themselves for one of her expostulations. "It's great. All the students that aren't performing until the next student production are working as crew for this one, then they exchange jobs for the next show. The camp trains them not only to dance and choreograph, but gives them experience in wardrobe, lighting, publicity, and stagecraft." She banged her hand on the table. Robert jumped. "That gives them so many more options. Those that don't make it as dancers still have the opportunity of staying in the field. We should all have such foresight."

Jeremy cleared his throat.

"It was Marguerite's idea," said Robert. "She took me on as director after I—after I snapped my Achilles tendon."

Rose looked momentarily nonplused. Then in her typical way, she recovered. She slapped him on the back. Robert pitched forward. "And look what you've built. You must be so proud."

"Yes," he said. "I am."

Whether he was happy with his situation or not, he certainly wasn't going to contradict her. Her hand was still resting on his shoulder. She could knock him off the bench with a flick of her wrist.

Peter wrestled with a smile, then found his composure. It was too bad, thought Lindy. His smile brought his already handsome, if terse, features into the realm of Romance Hero. Maybe that was why he showed it so infrequently.

"The student crew will be watching rehearsal this afternoon," he said. "Just to get their bearings. We've already done some hanging and focusing. If it's okay with you, Jeremy, I'll take some time during the tech tomorrow to let them experiment with some things."

"Sounds good," said Jeremy. "Anything else?" He looked around the table.

"I feel like I'm on vacation," said Lindy. "Shall I take the rehearsal this afternoon?"

Jeremy shook his head. "I'll do it."

"Company class tomorrow morning?"

"No." Jeremy looked at her, his brows drawing together slightly. "I need you just to keep an overview—of things—mainly."

It wasn't like Jeremy to be so inarticulate. She immediately felt insecure. Was he trying to tell her something? Did he not like the way she was working? God, she wasn't about to get fired, was she? She glanced at the others around the table. They seemed oblivious. She was just being paranoid. But with understudies waiting in the wings for your entire career, insecurity became an occupational hazard. She shook it off.

"Okay."

The door opened and Ellis stepped inside. "Sorry to interrupt, Jeremy, but Grappel has been upsetting Marguerite. When you're finished here could you come up to the house?"

Jeremy started to rise. "I'll come now."

"That isn't necessary. Please, continue with your meeting." He nodded to the others and left.

"It's going to be very unsettling having Byron around," said Robert. "He hates everything about the camp, especially me." He tapped his pencil on the table. Between the trembling of his fingers and the intensity of the tapping, the pencil threatened to snap in half.

"Jeremy," he said.

"What?" It was obvious to Lindy that Jeremy was not paying attention.

"Maybe, you should go up to the house. I think we're finished here."

"Yes." Jeremy left them without a word of "goodbye" or "see you later."

Biddy widened her eyes at Lindy. Lindy shrugged back.

Chapter
Four

Lindy sat next to Robert in the Loie Fuller studio, notebook resting on her lap, pen in hand. Finding herself at loose ends, she had offered to take notes during the student rehearsal.

The day had turned hot and humid after the rain. Inside the studio the air was muggy, though a slight breeze occasionally wafted through the open windows. Unlike the house and theater, the studios were not air conditioned. Cold air was bad for dancers' muscles.

Bach's Partita and Fugue filled the air. A *corps de ballet* of eight girls were posed in two diagonal lines that met in the center upstage. In front of them a *pas de deux* was being performed by a boy and girl. A man and woman, really; they were both in their early twenties.

The boy was dressed in gray tights and a white tee shirt, tied tight at the waist. Conservatory trained, thought Lindy. The girl wore bright red nylon gym shorts, bare legs and pointe shoes covered with pink ankle warmers. Her long legs ended in boatlike feet that arched so much they threatened to break the shank of her shoe.

"Pull out of your feet, Ginny." The correction came out in a thick accent. Katarina Flick, the oldest of the teachers at the camp, beat the floor with a stick. "Ach, why don't you lift up?" She raised the stick in the air. Madame Flick was dressed entirely in black and had seen thinner years. And though she couldn't be over five feet tall, she commanded the room like a general on horseback.

Ginny prepared for a pirouette in front of her partner. She pushed into *passé* position and began the turn; the boy's hands encircled her waist to support her. She was leaning to the right. Lindy shifted in her seat in the opposite direction as if the motion could bring the girl back on balance. The boy had to pull her back into position.

The stick banged several times on the floor. "Stop, stop." Madame Flick ambled forward onto the dance floor. Ginny collapsed forward on straight legs, pressing her hands to the floor.

"Sorry," she said. "It's just that it's so hot and humid. I can't find my energy."

"Ach, and dressed like that." Flick pointed her stick at the red shorts. "You should complain? Come. We are aaall waiting." She turned her back on the girl and looked over her shoulder. "I knooow you can do it." The music started; Ginny took her preparation and completed a perfect triple pirouette. Her partner stopped her in *passé* and her leg *developé*d to the side until her foot pointed to the ceiling. Then she rotated to an arabesque. The boy dipped her forward into *penché*. The *corps* began to *bourrée* across the floor.

Flick rested both hands on her stick, weight balanced between her two feet. "Sooo talented," she said with an exasperated sigh.

The piece ended a few minutes later and the dancers flocked around Madame Flick. She disappeared from view. Only the sound of her corrections could be heard echoing from the crowd that surrounded her.

The dancers for the next piece took their places, forming a circle in the middle of the floor. They were barefoot and wore various styles of gym clothes. They were already sweating from warming up on the sides of the room.

Lindy felt the sweat trickle down her neck. She ran her hand under her chin.

"It's the rain," said Robert. "One minute it's chilly and they're all wearing sweats, and then the sun comes out and off come the clothes."

Robert popped a tape into the music system that sat on a trolley next to him. *"There is a Time.* I reconstructed it a few years ago and it was so successful, I decided to bring it back this year."

Lindy nodded. "It's one of the great classics." José Limon, the choreographer, was the protégé of Doris Humphrey and the Rise and Fall school of modern dance. Not only an accomplished dancer, master choreographer, and superb painter, José had been the consummate gentleman. And though he had been dead for twenty years, he had been an inspiration to several generations of dancers, including Lindy's. She knew that these young dancers probably only knew of him from dance history courses. Perhaps, a few had never even heard his name.

"They should have a chance to experience where their craft has come from."

"And you can't do better than *Time.* It's my favorite."

The Della Joio music began. The dancers rose on demi pointe. Lindy's feelings rose with them, and her eyes misted over. It happened every time she saw this piece, whether in the theater or on the crackling and slipping old 35-millimeter films that were housed at the Library of Performing Arts.

Robert glanced at her and broke into a smile, a lovely smile that washed away all the tension and nervousness from his face. "I get the same reaction. Every time." He stood up and moved closer to the dancers. Soon he was moving among the group as they went through their steps and formations, correcting, counting out sloppy passages, moving them bodily to the correct positions.

In rehearsal, Robert Stokes blossomed. His energy was directed and persuasive. He even seemed to grow larger in Lindy's eyes. She wrote everything he said, every physical correction he made, as quickly as she could, using her own adapted shorthand, writing with one hand, and flipping pages with the other. By the end of the first section she was sweating as much as the dancers.

As the notes of the next section began, Robert walked past her, eyes on the dancer who had taken his place upstage right. "Larry's understudy," he said under his breath and continued to walk in an arch around the front of the studio.

The boy began the series of steps, mechanically, each one executed separately without the flow that should drive them across the floor.

Lindy glanced at Robert. He stood watching the dancer, head tilted to one side. His shoulder pulsed forward with the music, a nonverbal prodding movement, that said "more, more."

The boy faltered on the next phrase and shot an apologetic look toward Robert.

"We'll fix it later," said Robert, just loud enough to be heard over the music. Just loud enough to be heard by the boy and not the other dancers who were waiting at the edges of the studio for their next entrance.

Lindy wrenched her eyes from the soloist and took a quick look around. Every eye was trained on the dancer on the floor, the energy intense and expectant. Lindy felt her own nervousness increase. It was a typical kinesthetic reaction to watching a less-than-prepared dancer. If you didn't command the stage, the whole audience became uncomfortable.

He continued to struggle through the phrases of movement. It was obvious that he wasn't sure of the music, much less the steps. With each mistake be became less sure, more nervous, and consequently made more mistakes.

"Come on, come on," Robert said though he was only talking to himself.

Finally, he waved his hand in the air without taking his eyes off the dancer. The music stopped, and Lindy looked up to see one of the other teachers remove his hand from the tape player, then shake his head.

The room dropped into total silence. The boy halted midphrase and stood looking at the ground, biting one side of his lip, as he waited for Robert to approach him.

"Dylan, do you know the steps?" His voice was quiet and soft like a massage.

"I thought I did." Dylan's voice quavered. He rubbed his arm across his eyes. He was sweating profusely. Rings of moisture soaked his tee shirt beneath his armpits and spread in a diamond shape across his chest.

"Try it again. Just clear your mind of everything but movement and music." Robert held up his hand. The teacher recued the tape. Dylan listened for a second, found his cue, and began again. He had everyone's full attention. No one marked steps in the corner. No one reached for a water bottle or a towel. There were not the usual whispered conversations on the side lines. Every dancer in the room was focused on Dylan. Lindy was sure he could feel their attention, and it only made it more difficult to carry on. This was not the opportunity that understudies dreamed of. No dancer wanted a part because of someone else's injury, and especially not because of a death.

Her heart went out to this boy, who not only struggled with the steps of the dance, but also with the ghost of Larry Cleveland.

Again Robert motioned to stop the tape. The dancers who were watching lowered their eyes, or turned and began stretching on the bar, or leaned over to adjust a leg warmer. It was a situation they all dreaded—not to be up to the part when you at last got the chance.

"It's okay." Robert patted the boy's shoulder. "You just need extra rehearsal. We'll do it afterwards." His voice rose. "Let's cut to the next section."

The boy walked slowly to the side of the room.

Robert came to stand by Lindy. "I shouldn't have pushed him out like that with no preparation. But he knew it perfectly last week."

Lindy nodded sympathetically.

"I can't." The words were painfully muffled. Robert turned slowly toward the voice. Lindy's head jerked toward the dance floor.

Dylan was standing two thirds of the way across the floor, hands clenched by his sides. He shook his head several times. "I can't do it."

"Of course you can." Robert walked toward him. "You just need more rehearsal." It was the voice someone used when trying to coax a kitten out of tree. "I should have given you a rehearsal before we began today. But it's fine. There's plenty of time. We'll rehearse this afternoon."

"I can't. I'll never be able to do it as well as Larry."

Robert reached him and clasped his shoulder. "You're under a lot of pressure, anyone would be. You can do it."

"No—he—can't." A shrill cry came from the back of the room. It was a slight boy with dark hair that curled over his forehead. His shoulders were hunched over, his arms clutched across his stomach. "He can't do it as well as Larry."

He convulsed forward and vomited on the floor, liquid spattering as it hit the wooden surface. Dancers jumped back. With a groan, the boy ran toward the door.

Lindy recognized him as the boy that she had seen at the pavilion. The one they called Connie. She jumped automatically to her feet and then sat down again. She wasn't the director here, but everyone else was frozen on the spot like the final tableau of a period piece.

Then Robert turned slowly around and looked at her.

"Go after him," she mouthed. He turned and ran. Talking erupted around the room. Someone was sent for a mop. Madame Flick's voice rose in a rumble.

"Take a five minute break—outside. Get yourselves back into your concentration. This is a woorking break."

Lindy followed the others outside. She walked to the edge of the clearing and searched each path trying to catch a glimpse of Connie and Robert. Should she call for Dr. Addison? It was probably just emotion that had expelled Connie's lunch onto the floor.

She peered beyond the trees, but the two did not return to the studio. After a few minutes, she followed the students back inside. The teachers were grouped around the tape recorder, holding a conference. There was nothing she could do here. She gathered up her things and headed for the theater.

"Where have you been?" Mieko intercepted Lindy just as she stepped backstage.

"At the student rehearsal. Jeremy said he wanted to take rehearsal this afternoon."

"We're the ones having to take it." Paul Duke stuck his head out from the wings and rolled his eyes.

"Paul, you're late for your entrance." The voice was Jeremy's. Thunderous, directed from somewhere out in the house, but exploding onto the stage. Paul disappeared back into the wing.

Lindy looked at Mieko for an explanation. Jeremy never yelled at his dancers; his speaking voice was authority enough.

"He's been like this all afternoon. Andrea has already cried twice. Rebo's grumbling, and half the company are tripping over their open mouths just getting onto the stage."

"Yikes."

"He even snapped at Peter." Even though Mieko's face and voice didn't betray her agitation (Rebo often call her the Ice Queen in reference to her combination of *sang-froie* and Asian inscrutability), Lindy had learned by now to read her body language: the way she pulled her elbows close to her side; just the hint of narrowing of her almond-shaped eyes; the studied calm as if she had withdrawn her energy inward. "I'm surprised Peter didn't drop him on the spot."

"I'm on my way out front," said Lindy. Something was up. Jeremy never lost his temper. In his own way he was as controlled as Mieko, but whereas Mieko seemed comfortable with this undemonstrativeness, Jeremy was not. Lindy often thought that it was this quality that made him such a good choreographer, that sublimation and redirection of energy.

Only it wasn't sublimated now, and it was directed at Paul who continued to dance while glaring out into the house.

Jeremy was standing in the center aisle, hands on his hips. Peter sat behind a plywood board that had been placed across the seats in front of him and which held a laptop computer and a book of lighting cues. His eyes were riveted to the stage as he talked into a headset to the lighting man in the booth at the back of the house. Next to him sat Biddy, scrunched down in her seat, feet resting on the edge of the cushion, hands clasping her knees. If she got any smaller, you wouldn't be able to see her over the tops of the seats. Maybe that was what she intended.

Lindy walked up the side aisle, then scooted between two rows of seats until she was behind Jeremy and at the end of the row where Peter and Biddy were sitting. Biddy dropped her feet to the floor and straightened up. She jerked her chin for Lindy to join them. Jeremy walked down the aisle to the edge of the stage.

There was no orchestra pit. The house came right up to the apron. Jeremy placed both hands flat on the stage, but instead of jumping up onto the stage, he stood there looking at his dancers who continued to plow through their steps, faces carved in frowns of concentration. They were not happy campers, thought Lindy.

He turned suddenly and strode back up the aisle toward the three of them. They simultaneously braced themselves, one-two-three, like soccer players ready to block a kick.

"I'm sorry," said Jeremy pushing his fingers through his hair. Not the first time he had done that today, thought Lindy. "Can we take it back to the adagio, Peter?" Peter spoke into the headset; the tape stopped. The dancers looked out into the dark house.

"Let's go from Paul's entrance again," said Jeremy, his voice weary. "Try to settle down."

The dancers took their places for the earlier cue.

Jeremy ran his fingers through his hair again.

"Why don't you let Lindy take over for a while?" asked Biddy.

"I don't—just stay out of this." He turned and took two steps down the aisle, a movement that effectively cut him off from the others.

It was too dark in the house to see Biddy's features. But Lindy knew Biddy's reactions as well as she knew her own. Her face would be suffused with red, and her lips would be pursed to keep them from quivering. They had been friends for twenty years, worked, played, laughed and cried together. Lindy felt an empathetic burn in her gut. Peter merely glanced Biddy's way and then returned his attention to the stage.

After what seemed an interminable length of time, Jeremy called a halt to the rehearsal. He walked once again to the edge of the stage and stopped. "It's me, not you." It was not much of an apology, but it was enough.

"It's okay, boss. We weren't at our best either," said Rebo.

"Just gotta get our focus back," said another dancer.

"Sorry, Jeremy," said another.

"Go have some fun," said Jeremy. "We'll start fresh tomorrow." The group started to clear the stage. "Andy?"

Andrea Martin walked slowly downstage. This time Jeremy did pull himself onto the stage and sat with his legs dangling over the edge. Andrea sat down next to him, her legs crossed in front of her. There was a brief conversation. Andrea gave him a tentative smile and stood up.

Jeremy watched her walk toward the wings, then pushed himself off the stage.

"I think I'll just get my swimsuit," said Biddy. "Those icky things in the lake would be better company." She scrambled over Lindy's legs and was up the aisle before Jeremy reached them. He glanced up the aisle after Biddy, then turned to Lindy and Peter. The corners of his mouth tightened.

Peter snapped the laptop closed. "I think it's about time for a beer. Chi-Chi said we were welcome to use the bar, even though it won't open officially until Thursday night."

He grabbed the computer and inched his way past Lindy. She watched the two men pass silently up the aisle. Marguerite and Peter were the only two people that Jeremy didn't have a nickname for. His formality toward Marguerite was a show of deep respect. He respected Peter, too, but it was their tenuous relationship that prevented Jeremy from breaking down and calling him Pete or Petey or some other silly name of affection. He didn't know how Peter would react, and he wasn't willing to take the chance.

Lindy sighed as she once again gathered up her belongings, feeling more useless than ever. The performing arts was an intensely emotional world. It had to be, but it was also claustrophobic. So much of their time was spent on tour, where you couldn't get away from the situation or the participants. When people needed to vent, they usually took it out on each other. Like rioters in the ghetto, they only hurt themselves. "We always hurt the one we love," she sang to the empty seats as she left the theater.

Chapter
Five

Sandiman opened the door as Lindy reached the top of the stone steps. Slightly taken aback by this bit of seeming omniscience, she walked across the porch and managed, "Good afternoon."

He bowed slightly, and she stepped inside. He was dressed in full sartorial splendor: black trousers, gray coat, an impeccably starched shirt front with a black tie riveted in place by a diamond stickpin.

"Madame and Ms. McFee are in the morning room if you would care to join them for tea."

"Thank you, Sandiman." Actually what she had in mind was something a little stronger than tea, but she followed him down the corridor, past the drawing room and library to a door behind the wide staircase.

She was aware of Marguerite and Biddy turning toward her, but for a moment she was too dazzled by the room to acknowledge them.

An assortment of tables and pedestals was topped by potted ferns, aspidistras, browallia, geraniums, and other plants whose flowers created a palette of yellow, orange, blue, and violet. Shades and textures of green shot upward dramatically or flowed luxuriantly across the tables. The variegated leaves of trailing ivy spilled off the edges and spread across the carpet.

In the middle of the room stood a tea table and several small but comfortable-looking chairs. Dumb canes and ficas stood beside them like dutiful servants. A silver tea service had been placed on the table next to a tiered plate of dainty sandwiches and pastries.

"You like it," said Marguerite. It was a statement of sheer delight. "We don't have the leisure or the extra room for a conservatory, so I've combined functions into one room. In the mornings, when the sun is rising—" A graceful hand floated toward a bank of windows in a balletic pantomime. "It is a wonderful place for writing letters, reading, or just thinking."

Her hand moved in a smooth arc from window to tea tray. "Milk or lemon?"

"Lemon, thank you."

Biddy turned from the window. "Come look at the view. It's incredible."

An expanse of plate glass framed a mauve sky interrupted by bold white clouds that scudded into view and then passed away. In the distance, the tips of a mountain range, gray-green in the waning daylight, disappeared into the clouds. A flare of sunlight broke through an unseen hole in the sky. Nature's spotlight, radiating downward and transforming the muted shadows to emerald green. And before the mountains, miles of wilderness, crushed and up-ended from the glacial thaw thousands of years ago. And though its roughness was tempered by trees and shrubs, one could almost feel the vestiges of violence that had once thrust the earth in on itself, compacting and spewing up rock in some places and rending it into vast chasms in others. Thousands of years of time had made this country and it was overwhelming.

Lindy scanned the vista, then came to focus on the land closer to the house. There were three terraces carved from the granite substratum. The lowest housed a multiple-car garage and storage sheds. Above it, four tennis courts, stood back to back, perfectly paved, and devoid of players.

Directly below the window was a parking lot. A laundry truck was parked off to the right. Two men carried bundles of white linen beneath a roof and into an unseen door. Seconds later, they returned, jumped into the van, and drove away. One lone car remained in the lot, facing the view like a tourist stopped at a scenic turnoff: a white car, with the words, COUNTY SHERIFF, written in black on its door.

"Yes, he's still here," said Marguerite as she turned from the window. She walked deliberately to a chair, then sat down suddenly. Her teacup rattled in its saucer. She smiled apologetically. "I'm beginning to despise that man."

"He was here, talking to Marguerite when I left rehearsal," said Biddy.

"Absolutely galling," added Marguerite. "I actually believe he is enjoying this, the despicable creature." She placed her saucer on the table next to the chair and flicked a piece of imaginary lint from the Battenberg tablecloth.

"It wasn't pleasant," said Biddy under her breath.

Marguerite leaned back against the chair and closed her eyes. "He was making all sorts of innuendoes." She opened one eye and shifted it toward the two women. "Sexual ones." The eye closed. "We try to keep a careful watch over the students. Not all of them are adults. But it becomes more difficult each year. All this political correctness. Threats of lawsuits if you so much as breathe heavily in their direction." Marguerite laughed abruptly and sat up.

"See what I mean? 'Breathing heavy' has automatic sexual connotations, even though what I meant was entirely different. Sometimes I think I'm not fit for this world. We should be mourning the loss of a young man whose life was cut off in his prime. Instead the sheriff is trying to muck up any dirt he can just to make the Easton family uncomfortable." She brought two elegant fingers to her brow. "Insidious."

Lindy left Biddy at the window and sat down next to Marguerite. Perhaps she could be of some use here. She certainly had struck out with everyone else today.

"And Larry's parents are on their way. Only to be bombarded with horrible speculations about the life of their son." Marguerite flicked at the tablecloth again. Her nails were neatly manicured but unpolished. "I think I could murder the man, I really do."

Lindy smiled at her, a humorous smile. She didn't for a minute think Marguerite would ever have to resort to such extreme measures, not with her money and family name.

"I expect there are more efficient ways to deal with Sheriff Grappel," she suggested.

"Of course I would never do such a thing," Marguerite said seriously, "but it's a satisfying fantasy." Her shoulders twitched. "Do you know, my dear, he actually had the effrontery to suggest that I had more than an artistic interest in the boys. Quite ridiculous in view of the medical report."

So that was what set this off, thought Lindy. Grappel had told Marguerite about the postmortem examination. Surely that was crossing over the bounds of police procedure. She remembered the tight-lipped Bill Brandecker who had been involved in her two experiences with murder. He and his policemen friends refused to give out the smallest bit of information.

"Yes," replied Lindy distractedly. Her thoughts had receded from the immediate problem to the former deaths she had encountered, and the thought of Bill Brandecker, who always sent her mind into overdrive.

"When I pointed this out to him, the man said perhaps that was exactly what caused Larry to kill himself. Suicide! What a deplorable imagination. He even suggested that I was jealous of the way the boys carried on."

Lindy was taken aback. She couldn't imagine anyone having the nerve to say something like that to Marguerite Easton.

"I called him a crazy rural throwback." Marguerite smiled ruefully. "I don't know what came over me." She looked at Lindy for a moment. "He's taking pleasure in our misfortune. I should have handled him with more finesse."

"I doubt if he would have recognized finesse if you pronounced it in one syllable," said Lindy.

"Anyway," said Biddy looking out the window, "Chi-Chi has taken up where you left off." She motioned them over. Without a word, they hurried to the window.

Byron Grappel was attempting to get into the driver's side of the police car. Chi-Chi had taken hold of his sleeve. He turned toward her, his free hand still on the open door. She was doing all the talking, or possibly yelling, the way her body was thrust forward. Grappel just stood there looking sullen.

"Go for it, Chi-Chi," whispered Biddy.

Chi-Chi stuck a fist toward the sheriff's face. Lindy heard the intake of Marguerite's breath behind her. The sheriff grabbed Chi-Chi's wrist and flung it aside, jumped into the car and slammed the door.

Before Chi-Chi could move, the car jolted into reverse, jerked to a stop, then lurched forward, tires squealing as it disappeared around the side of the house. Chi-Chi watched it leave, then turned and walked back across the parking lot until their view of her was blocked by the roof that covered the delivery entrance.

"Why must men always do that with their cars when they're angry?" asked Marguerite. "It's so unimaginative."

Marguerite left them a few minutes later in order to rest before dinner. Biddy dropped into the chair across from Lindy. "I'd like to wash that goon right out of my hair," she sang.

"He's a mean one, Sheriff Grinch," countered Lindy.

"A man like that would kill his brother," agreed Biddy.

It was a game they often played, adapting old songs to fit the situation. It had begun years ago out of boredom during the long travel and tech days on tour. In their younger years, they could sing entire conversations without missing a beat. They had picked it up again years later when Lindy had returned to work. Sometimes, it was more soothing than actually tackling a subject directly.

"And while we're at it," said Biddy, "how do we solve a problem like—" She stopped singing. "Jeremy."

"Try to ignore him?"

Biddy expelled air through her lips, a cross between a raspberry and a motor boat. "A little difficult to ignore; he *is* our boss."

"Yeah, I know. But I do think that if we just give him some space, he'll pull himself together."

"Any more space and we'd be in Siberia."

"At least there wouldn't be mosquitoes and this hideous humidity in Siberia."

"Stuart says the weather will clear up and get cooler," said Biddy.

"Yeah, he told me, too."

"But to get back to Jeremy . . ."

"I really think things will work themselves out," said Lindy. "You know how he overreacts to things. This is so important to him. He must be feeling horrible for what Marguerite and Ellis and Chi-Chi and Robert are going through. I bet if we could deep-six Sheriff Grappel, things would get back to normal pretty quickly in spite of this tragedy."

"You're right. I just hate to see him angst so much. He always takes responsibility for everyone's problems. It makes him soooo . . ." Biddy's eyes searched the air around her, a habit of hers when she was at a loss for words.

"Repressed?" Lindy finished for her.

"Jeremy isn't repressed," said Biddy indignantly. "Just self-contained."

"Do you know something I don't?" Lindy raised both eyebrows.

"Would you stop that? I don't know why you insist on playing matchmaker. It isn't going to happen. Jeremy and I have a perfectly good platonic relationship, at least until this week, and that's fine with me."

"If you say so."

"I do, and anyway, how did we get onto the subject of Jeremy's love life?"

Lindy shrugged. "I don't know. He's such good material."

"I did learn a little dirt, however."

"About Jeremy?"

"Yeah. Not about his sex life, but Stuart told me that during Jeremy's 'dark years'—" Biddy paused a moment to give Lindy time to come up to speed. Jeremy's dark years: several years when he had disappeared and fallen into a life of drugs and alcohol brought on by guilt and self-loathing. She nodded to let Biddy know that she was with her.

"That during those years, Marguerite supported him financially.

Stood by him, even though he refused to see her or have any contact with her. Evidently, she had complete faith in his being able to bounce back. And she was right."

"Wow. Though it doesn't surprise me. It sounds just like something Marguerite would do. But how did Stuart know about it?"

"Stuart seems to know just about everything that goes on in the Easton family. And he's not averse to a little gossip."

"Hmmm."

"In case you haven't noticed, I think he is Ellis's friend." Biddy gave her a knowing look. "You know—his 'particular' friend."

"Particular friend? God, Biddy, have you been reading Victorian novels again?"

Biddy laughed. "No, it's just the artistic ambiance, but I do have a great Regency romance that you can borrow when I'm finished. 'Erect shafts' and 'throbbing manhoods' every seventy-five pages like clockwork . . . or if you delete the 'L' . . . "

Lindy shook her head. "Do you know what I love best about touring with you?"

"Please, spare me. Hey, speaking of particular friends, is Glen coming this weekend, or is he going to cancel again?"

"So far so good." A year and a half ago, Glen had been promoted to overseas consultant for the telecommunications firm he worked for. It required a lot of traveling, and he had ended up canceling more of their plans together than he had been able to make. "He has a charity golf tournament at the Clarendon Club on Friday. I'm sure he won't miss that. Then he'll come over for the rest of the weekend. You'll lose your roommate for a couple of nights. Maybe, I *should* borrow that book. So I can 'bone up' on the 'erect shafts' parts."

Biddy burst into laughter. "Oh criminy," she said, looking at her watch. "I didn't realize it was so late. We'll have to hurry to get dressed in time for drinks."

"Drinks? Now there's an Old World affectation. What happened to 'cocktails' or 'happy hour'?"

Biddy was already heading for the door. "Well, at least you can beg off for a couple of nights and have a romantic dinner for two in the restaurant."

"Yeah, with half the company looking on."

"Did you tell him about what happened, yet?"

"You mean Larry Cleveland? Good God, no. He'd be furious if he thinks I'm involved in another death, accident or no. On second thought, maybe he'll have a satellite disaster, and he'll have to go to—someplace really far away."

Biddy opened the door and waited for her. "I think he's just jealous that you get all the excitement."

"Glen? He doesn't have a jealous bone in his body." Lindy scrunched up her face. "How many plays on the word 'bone' do you think there are?" She tap-danced through the door.

Biddy joined in behind and they shuffled and ball changed their way to the bottom of the stairs.

"God, what if Sandiman saw us?" Lindy widened her eyes and looked around.

"He'd say," said Biddy, "'Thank you, madam, for making me laugh.'" She gave Lindy a quick hug and ran up the stairs.

They arrived at the door of the drawing room only five minutes late. In any other palatial home it would be called the living room. But the Eastons lived an artistic, almost literary existence: from the studios named for famous dancers to the volumes of Shakespeare on the library shelves; from the Walt Whitman and Emily Dickinson wings of the annex to the statuary displayed among the trees.

Lindy looked heavenward and opened the door. Ellis stood by the fireplace, drink in hand. Sandiman hovered nearby, tray of glasses at the ready.

"Ah, there you are," said Ellis, coming forward to greet them. "I'm afraid it's only us this evening. The Clevelands have arrived, and Jeremy and Marguerite are with them. Chi-Chi and Robert have begged off, and Stuart is up to his eyeballs in business calls. I don't know why he can't just let Stu Junior sink or swim on his own. Given half a chance, the boy might learn something about running a business."

Stuart joined them as they entered the dining room, apologizing for being late. There were only four places set. Fortunately, they were all at the foot of the table instead of being spread evenly across the great distance of mahogany.

It was curious to Lindy that Ellis had not graduated to the head of the table tonight in Marguerite's absence. It was even more curious that Marguerite sat at the head when a male Easton was present.

Yours is not to judge, she thought, then wondered if she would be speaking in iambic pentameter by the end of their two-week stay.

Stuart and Ellis were more relaxed and spontaneous than she had seen them before. They talked easily about any subject that happened to come up. Ellis was knowledgeable in all areas of art and travel, and Stu added a refreshing slant on business and finance.

It was obvious that the two men enjoyed each other's company and appreciated the chance to show off to an appreciative female audience. By the time the main course was served, they had moved on from the museums of Europe to wild tales of African safaris and cruises up the Nile.

Ellis recalled Stu's scheme for tours into Machu Picchu. "Sort of a Club Med Among the Natives. A lunatic idea."

Stu laughed. "Not at all. It was a challenge."

"What happened?" asked Biddy.

Stu's laughter subsided to a chuckle. "While I was busy wheeling and dealing with the authorities, Ellis goes and gets lost in the Andes." He leaned forward and lowered his voice to a conspiratorial level. "When we finally found him—days later, I might add . . . " He cast an amused look at Ellis. "He had been adopted by a tribe of local Indians; waited on hand and foot by a score of topless, nut-brown maidens."

Ellis blushed.

Stu laughed louder. "The man who would be king. I wish you could have seen it."

They lingered over coffee and brandy without leaving the table. Lindy was having such an enjoyable time, that she forgot about the sad duty that was being performed elsewhere in the house.

When their coffee was finished and they were standing in the hall, Ellis excused himself. "Thank you for putting up with the memories of a couple of old men. If you'll excuse me, I'll just check on how things are faring in the library." With a nod, he left them.

"Speak for yourself, old boy," said Stu flipping his cane toward his friend. "I'm ready for twenty more years of the same. But in the meantime, I'm off for a postprandial stroll among the trees. Would you ladies care to join me?"

Biddy and Lindy thanked him, but declined, saying they had to get up early the next day. That was true, but Lindy had no intention of strolling darkened paths where a boy had just fallen to his death. She had to bite her tongue in an effort not to warn Stuart to be careful and thus bring up the subject they had managed to avoid all evening.

Chapter
Six

Rolls of thunder reverberated through the night air. Flashes of lightning lit the window, followed by cracks that sounded like a bull whip. A piercing ring jolted Lindy from sleep. Bleary-eyed, she reached out from the covers and turned off the alarm clock. Beyond the window, the sky was a clear blue, washed of imperfections from the continuous falling of rain during the night.

"Is he gone?" croaked Biddy.

"Who?"

"The guy with the black cape and fangs." Biddy sat up, blinking. "I swear that was the most Bela Lugosi night I ever didn't sleep through."

There were dark circles under Biddy's eyes. Her hair was even wilder than usual, her cinnamon curls splayed out from her face like an electric shock.

"I think you should get a couple more hours of sleep," said Lindy throwing back the heavy comforter and dropping her feet to the floor.

"Hmmm," said Biddy and the blanket went back over her head.

Lindy hurried to the bathroom, shivering. Her feet flinched away from the cold tiles as she walked quickly across to the bathtub and turned on the tap.

A few minutes later, she forced herself from the hot shower, donned walking shorts and a sweatshirt, hurriedly gulped down a cup of coffee, and made her way to the theater. It was 9:05.

The theater was fifty years old and had been converted from an existing building. Like the main house, it was built at the edge of the clearing with a downward slope at the back, which created an extra floor for wardrobe, scene shop, and dressing rooms below the stage level. She followed the loading drive around the back to the stage door. The driveway was enclosed on one side by the concrete of the theater foundation and on the other by a steel handrail painted green. A mesh elevator for loading equipment and scenery was housed in a wooden silo that jutted out from the far end of the building.

She entered the stage door, passed several dressing rooms that were now empty, and followed the sound of Rose's voice down the hall to the wardrobe room.

The room was a narrow rectangle. Racks of costumes surrounded the walls. Below them, black theater trunks had been pushed up against the wall to clear as much space as possible. An ironing board and steamer claimed one end of the room along with a table covered with sewing boxes, scissors and portable sewing machine.

In the center of the tightly packed space, Rose was stalking around a girl dressed in one of the Ash company costumes. Beneath it, she was wearing tights and a leotard. A pair of Birkenstock sandals completed the ensemble. Rose talked nonstop as she circled the figure, gesturing with her hands. She pulled at the bodice, added a straight pin to a seam, and began adjusting the waist.

Four girls followed behind her like a brood of baby chicks. They were already dressed for ballet class, which by Lindy's calculations had started five minutes ago. But Rose held her audience captive. They hung onto every word while they stood on tiptoe to see over her shoulder or bent to the side to see around her. They moved in a circle with her as she explained how to baste the seams before sewing them on the machine, how to fold back the elastic straps without cutting them, so they could be let out again for the next person who would need to wear the costume.

"Okay, that does it," said Rose as she unzipped the dress. "If you all hurry, you can get to ballet before the end of *tendus*. Tell Andrea that I'm sorry we ran over."

The girls grabbed their dance bags and made for the door.

"Be back at twelve, and we'll start with the alterations," she yelled as the girls hurried away. "Bring your lunch."

"Holy Moly." She sank onto a closed trunk and unclipped a barrette from the top of her head. Two long plaits fell down on either side of her ears, ending just at her bustline. "That took forever. They had a million questions. I don't think one of them had ever seen a needle and thread before, except maybe in a museum." She sighed a martyr's sigh.

"Better you than me," said Lindy.

"Ask not for whom the bells . . ." She finished the quote by tilting her head side to side. The ends of the braids swung back and forth in an arc across her shirt front. "They toll . . ." the braids swung again, " for me. What do you need?"

"Nothing. Just wondering . . . how things are going."

"Well, you saw for yourself. Slow but energetic. I don't know how much they learned about costuming, but I got an earful of camp gossip." Rose stretched her mouth into an Emmett Kelly frown. "Whose calves are too big, who should never wear a unitard, who's a binge eater, who sneaks off into the woods to 'do it.' Their words not mine. God, were we ever that young?"

Never, they agreed.

"I also got the lowdown on Larry Cleveland and the kid that threw up in rehearsal yesterday. It's the morsel of the week."

Lindy swallowed. This was not a good topic on a stomach whose only contents were coffee.

"I guess this Larry kid was a piece of work. Gorgeous on the outside but a conniving little bastard on the inside. It seems he used them in more ways than one. He passed around a lot of favors, but they had to pay."

"How so?"

"Money, gifts, stuff like that. He even made one girl do his laundry. His death has the camp split down the middle. Those who loved him, and those who would be glad he's dead if they were old enough to realize it."

"A pretty elaborate setup for someone only seventeen."

"Yeah, well everything else happens sooner these days, why not that? I got the distinct impression that he liked girls as well as boys, to tell by the blushes that the mention of the autopsy report brought on. My guess is there will be a lot of ballerinas running for AIDS tests as soon as they leave camp."

"How did you get them to tell you all of this?" asked Lindy. "My kids clam up whenever I try to bring up the subject of sex. They think anyone over forty doesn't have a clue."

Rose shrugged. "Give 'em twenty years." She heaved herself off the trunk. "Costume fittings are like a crowded bar with me as the bartender. I don't think they even realized what they were saying."

Jeremy was giving company class on stage. He looked a little haggard, but he seemed more like himself.

Lindy left the theater and checked in on Andrea's ballet class. Things were fine there, too.

Well, she thought, *there's nothing for me to do but . . . enjoy my surroundings.* A hike would be perfect exercise before an afternoon in a dark theater with the students. Though, between Robert and Jeremy and the rest of the teachers, she probably wouldn't be needed there, either.

Behind the theater, she climbed down a set of stairs that had been carved out of the rock. The day was cool. The leaves of the trees were still wet and dripping from the night's deluge. The smell of wet earth and moldy leaves invigorated her. Her sneakers made crunching noises in the gravel as she broke into a jog.

The path ran downward in an easy slope, then veered off to the right. She picked up her pace as the path left the trees and followed the edge of the mountain. A guardrail prevented inattentive hikers from pitching down to the path that snaked its way below her.

She pulled her sweatshirt over her head and tied it around her waist without breaking her stride. Several yards later she slowed to a walk. A man was standing at the curve of the path where the shape of the land made a natural lookout point. His hands rested lightly on the guardrail and he gazed out at a vista that rivaled the view from Marguerite's sitting room. He turned as he heard her approach.

"Good morning, Lindy. Lovely day for a hike."

"Morning, Ellis." She sat down on a wooden bench that was supported by two boulders. She grabbed her foot with both hands and stretched her calf, then repeated the action with the other foot. "I expect it's easier going down than it will be coming back up."

"Indeed. Though this is as far as I usually go. One of the best views you can find." He took an invigorating breath. "I told Marguerite the weather would be good for the weekend." He smiled as if he had been instrumental in bringing it about.

They sat and stood in silence for a few minutes admiring the view.

"Easton country," he said with a sigh.

"You own all of this?" The landscape stretched for miles—and miles.

"Most of it, except for the town, and where we leave off the park service takes over."

"It's so big."

Ellis smiled. "You can see all the way to the Hudson River from the point right beyond this rail."

Lindy stood up and leaned over the rail, trying to catch a glimpse.

"But don't be tempted. We've had to close off the lookout. One too many mud slides." He shifted uncomfortably. "They say that's where the Cleveland boy lost his footing."

Lindy backed away. "What are those towers?" She pointed emphatically at one of the brown obelisks that rose above the trees, while she tried not to think about where they were standing. "There and there and over there?" Her hand moved to indicate each one.

"Ranger stations. During the dry season—we do have one, you know—later in the summer—there is a real danger of forest fires. And when the weather is like this, they keep an eye out for rock and mud slides. There's a sublayer of granite over much of the land. The camp is built on one. But the top layers of dirt and rock can be highly unstable."

"There was mesh over the rocks on the road."

Ellis nodded. "We still get an occasional boulder falling onto the road. Only last season, one barely missed a family on its way to the camp. No one was hurt, thank God. It doesn't happen often. Usually we just get a lot of mud across some of the paths. The park service is good about clearing the main road. There are a lot of tourist attractions near here—near as the crow flies, anyway."

"None of your land is developed?"

"Heavens no. Not that I have anything against tasteful development, ski slopes and golf courses, and the like, as long as they don't get too close. But the land has been in our family for generations. Several hundred acres are held in trust for the camp. Marguerite would never let the homestead be 'corrupted,' as she calls it." Ellis lifted his shoulders in an amused shrug.

"A daunting job."

"Oh, she doesn't have the sole voice. I get to put in my two cents worth on occasion. There is a board of trustees, mostly family members." He smiled, a wistful tilt to his head. "Unfortunately, there are not that many of us left. Only two out of the original six children. Two dead in World War II. One in childhood. Samuel of a heart ailment. Lord, how I miss him. He did leave a daughter, but she lives in London and is not much interested in the family business.

"It doesn't really matter. The trust practically runs itself. Our mother was very farsighted. When she saw her first performance of Ted Shawn and Ruth St. Denis, she fell in love with dance. She modeled this camp along the same philosophy as the one run by Shawn. Of course as an early suffragette, she included girls." His eyes twinkled.

"Our resident writers and visual artists have their living quarters and studios over that ridge, closer to the county road. They keep pretty much to themselves, communing with nature, and all that."

Lindy followed the direction of his finger but could see nothing but trees.

"And we have our own resident archaeologists. I think Van Zandt has been here as long as some of the fossils he's looking for. They haven't found anything but a bunch of oyster shells, but they keep plugging away year after year."

"I don't suppose they would be too enthused about any development of the area, either."

"Just mention developers and Van Zandt goes berserk. His crew have had more than a few run-ins with the locals over it."

"The locals? They're in favor of development?"

"Mainly they're afraid that if the archaeologists *do* find something, the Indians will claim the land and put up a casino. This is a depressed area. Has been for years. First the sawmills shut down. Then all the young people started moving away. When the highway came through, they hoped it would boost the local economy, but nothing materialized. All the money-making ventures seemed to spring up all around here but just out of reach. The locals figure if anyone is going to make money off the land, it had better be them."

"I can't believe that anyone who lives in such a beautiful place would be willing to sacrifice it for a few extra tourist dollars."

"I think most people would sacrifice just about anything to make life better for themselves or their children. Fortunately, I've never had to make a choice like that, and I'm not eager to judge those who do."

Lindy regarded him thoughtfully. Until now, Ellis had seemed shallow and ineffectual, though he was entertaining. But this small window into his thoughts, and the unexpected compassion she had found there made her readjust her opinion of him. It also made her angry to think that one man was intent on bringing his family to grief.

"Is that why Sheriff Grappel is so antagonistic?" she asked.

Ellis expelled an explosion of air. "Byron Grappel is an ass—in the *Equus* sense, mind you."

Lindy didn't know if he meant the genus or the play by Peter Schaffer.

"*Equus asinus*," Ellis clarified. "But to answer your question. There are a few movers and shakers in town who have their eyes on the property. Some parcels could be sold off within the terms of the trust, and they would love to put up ski resorts, shopping outlets, and a theme park. And the sheriff, being a paid county employee, wouldn't mind feathering his own nest. But the reason for his 'antagonism', as you understate it, doesn't have to do with the land." Ellis brushed his hands together. "How did we get onto such a sordid topic? I shouldn't have distracted you."

"I'm glad you did, I enjoyed talking with you." Lindy rose from the bench and rubbed the front of her thighs. "But I'd better get going. I'm already getting stiff from sitting too long."

Ellis nodded. "Another twenty minutes down the path, there's a bridge where you can dip your toes into the stream."

"Sounds heavenly." She continued her jog down the path while Ellis walked slowly back toward the theater.

She passed under a canopy of trees and swatted at a few mosquitoes that buzzed around her face in the damp air. The path wound slowly downward—through thick forest, then past a meadow filled with blue bachelor buttons and into the woods again.

After half an hour she slowed her pace, sweat dripping into her eyes. She'd be sore tomorrow. She had no idea where she was; she hadn't come to the bridge. Perhaps, she had gotten off the main path, there were no signs here. She had left the graveled path some minutes ago, and only hardened earth, deeply rutted with erosion, met her feet.

Once again she found herself on a ledge of rock, and below her was a rushing, stream swollen from the recent rain. To the right were the bridge and the path that wound back into the woods. She had taken a detour and it would take her forever to retrace her steps and then continue to the water. Her feet burned inside her sneakers; the water beckoned. She looked over the side. Rough, but enough places for hand and footholds. A shortcut. She had been running for an hour, and would have to hurry to get to the water if she didn't want be late for rehearsal. She wondered for a moment if Jeremy would notice if she were.

To hell with him, she decided. Taking hold of a sapling she stepped downward. Loose rocks, dislodged by her shoe, clattered down the slope before her. Testing the solidity of the ground, she took another step. She skidded, but her grip on the sapling helped her to recover her balance. Carefully, she continued downward, searching for secure stepping places among the roots and stones that littered the way, trading the sapling for a bush and then an over-hanging limb. Halfway down the side, she skidded on wet leaves. The mass of vegetation slid downward, taking her with it. She leaned forward, bending her knees to keep her balance. Her arms stretched to her sides as she navigated past the blurring scenery. Mountain surfing, she thought wryly. This was a little more excite-ment than she had planned on. Her adrenaline was pumping and was she wrecking the ecology. Guilt, mixed with panic and excite-ment accompanied her to the bottom.

She had barely reached the base of the cliff, still standing, but heart beating wildly, when a figure rushed at her from behind a tree. It took a heart-stopping second to realize that its hind legs were cov-ered by jeans, and the arms that were waving furiously were flesh, not fur. Not a bear, but a suntanned young man wearing a Grateful Dead tee shirt.

He rushed up to her and skidded to a stop.

"Are you okay?" he asked breathlessly. "I saw you hauling down that cliff, and I thought you were a goner for sure."

"I was just taking a shortcut to the stream. I hope I didn't destroy any flora or fauna on my way."

His eyes widened. They were a light hazel. "Don't worry. Stuff is always falling down these cliffs." His eyes narrowed. "Are you sure you're all right?"

He seemed to be in worse shape than she was. His sun-bleached hair was pulled back in a ponytail, leaving two high cheek bones ex-posed to view. One was covered by a considerable-sized bruise that had faded to an ugly greenish yellow.

"Looks like you know whereof you speak," said Lindy pointing to the bruise.

"Huh? Oh, you mean this." He touched his cheek. "Nah, I got that at the local bar." His expression changed from concern to em-barrassment. "I'm twenty-one."

"Ah, that makes all the difference."

"It wasn't my fault. Hey, you're bleeding."

Lindy twisted her arm around and looked at her stinging elbow. "I think I sideswiped a couple of trees on my way down." She laughed, suddenly feeling weak in the knees.

"Maybe you'd better sit down."

"I think that would be a good idea."

He enclosed her upper arm with strong fingers and led her to a log that lay near the edge of the stream. Pushing her onto it, he began to examine her elbow. "Not too bad, but I can give you a Band-Aid if you come down to camp."

"You're an archaeologist?" asked Lindy.

"How could you tell?"

Lindy lifted her chin toward a scene of activity farther along the water where the stream had washed out a wide area before twisting in the opposite direction. Several tents were pitched near the streambed. A battered Jeep that had probably been red in a former lifetime was parked on a ledge behind them. Along the stream, several figures squatted in ankle-deep water within an area marked with stakes and string.

He followed her gaze. "Oh, yeah." He shrugged. "Actually I'm not an archaeologist yet. But I will be. I have another year of undergrad work. There are a bunch of us doing our independent study with the old man this summer."

"The old man?"

"Dr. Van Zandt, I mean," he mumbled. His mother couldn't have provoked a more embarrassed response.

"Actually, he won't be too pleased to see you here. It's off limits to anybody but staff, and I'm already on his shi—on his bad side."

"Oops, too late," said Lindy. Dr. Van Zandt, it could be no one else, was puffing toward them. "Unless the bears here wear canvas hats and work boots."

"Yep, that's the old man, all right," said her rescuer, sounding decidedly unhappy.

"Paarrker," Van Zandt bellowed when he was still a hundred feet from them.

"That's me," said the young man. "Donald Parker."

"Nice to meet you."

Van Zandt continued to lumber toward them, oblivious that he had left the shore and was splashing through the shallow water and soaking his trouser legs. He was short and husky and his stomach bounced as he ran. He looked just like an archaeologist, thought Lindy, at least like the ones she had seen on television.

He must have stepped in a hole in the streambed, because one side of him shifted abruptly downward, sending his glasses flying off his nose. Lindy gasped. They bounced on his chest as he recovered himself and began running even faster. Instead of plummeting into the water, the glasses continued to bounce against his chest. A thick black strap was attached to each earpiece and hung around his neck.

He plowed up a deposit of rocks, feet slipping and scudding on their slippery surfaces with a bizarre kind of grace. "Paarrker." This one started low and quiet and continued to crescendo, then died *subito* when he stopped before them, red in the face and puffing mightily.

Lindy stood up ready to make her apology, then changed her mind. After all, she *was* a guest of the Eastons.

"Who is this person?" Dr. Van Zandt scowled. Lindy could swear that one eye looked at her, while the other pinned an uncomfortable student assistant. Then she realized that one eye was slightly askew. Bad eyesight must surely be a liability for an archaeologist, she thought.

Van Zandt replaced his glasses and scrutinized her. She quickly improvised an explanation that would get her and Donald Parker off of the doctor's list.

"I'm sorry," she barked. "Didn't realize this was off limits." She yelled at him as if he were slightly deaf. She had no intention of backing down before this bad-mannered eccentric. "I'm a friend of Marguerite Easton's." She stuck out her hand. "Lindy Graham."

Open sesame. Van Zandt's features broke into a beatific smile. His color returned to normal. His teeth flashed. "A friend of Marguerite's, eh? Glad to meet you." His hand shot out.

When Lindy's teeth had stopped rattling from the handshake, she apologized again.

"Don't worry about it, but it's dangerous around here, especially with all the rain we've been having. They've already had one tragedy up at the house, they don't need another. Parker here will show you back to the path." He turned to leave, then stopped. She felt Donald tense beside her. "And you, Parker, will type this week's field notes tonight instead of going into town." They watched his broad back bound away over the rocks.

"This way," said Donald. "Sorry about not getting you a Band-Aid."

"That's all right. I'm sorry if I got you into trouble."

Donald began leading her away from the stream. "No problem. He's been unhappy with me ever since I talked to the police about the accident."

Lindy stopped. "The police questioned you about Larry Cleveland?"

"That was the kid's name?" Donald sighed. "It's a damned shame what happened to him. And the old man is worried that the town will just make the accident an excuse to try to close the camp. I mean, he cares about the kid, of course, but if the town develops this area, it will ruin the beds. I know oyster shell middens aren't as glamorous as pyramids but it's important work. They're the major source of our knowledge about prehistoric man on the eastern seaboard." He looked suddenly embarrassed. "Sorry, I guess it isn't really very interesting."

"I understand the importance of work without glory; consider me an appreciative audience."

Donald's face broke into a gratified smile. "Thanks." He started walking again.

"What did the police question you about?" asked Lindy, running to catch up and trying to lasso the conversation back into the modern era.

"Well—" He stopped suddenly and Lindy pulled up short behind him. His head lifted and he searched the surrounding cliffs.

He pointed to a tiny break in the trees above them. "That's where they found the body. You can't see the bottom from here, but it's a pretty nasty area." He shook his head. "They mainly just wanted to know if we saw or heard anything that night. Of course we didn't; we're like the Neanderthals, to bed with the sun, up with the sun." He touched his cheek. "Most nights anyway."

"I don't see why that would get you in Dr. Van Zandt's bad graces."

"Oh, that didn't. It was what I said about the Jeep."

"What Jeep? Your Jeep?"

"Nah, not that heap of junk. A big, black four-wheel-drive number. We've seen it several times during the last few weeks. The old man thinks it's spies, but I told him it could be some pervert—there are a lot of kids up at the camp." He grimaced. "I thought the cops should know."

"And?" prompted Lindy.

"So, I told 'em about it, and that sheriff made some snide remark about the kinds of people up at the house, and the old man took offense. Now I'm the one typing field notes every night."

Lindy laughed sympathetically.

"I don't mind. He thinks it's a big punishment, but I know he doesn't trust anybody else to do them, and his eyesight isn't getting any better. So it's okay." He came to a stop at the edge of a graveled path.

"How did we get back here so fast?" asked Lindy. "I was running for over an hour."

"There's a huge network of paths and subsidiary paths, some still used and some overgrown. You just have to know where you're going. See ya around." Donald turned his back to her and loped off through the woods.

Lindy passed several small cabins and another building that she thought must be the student dorm. Groups of dancers hurried down the path. Another group appeared on the porch letting the screen door slam behind them. They waved to Lindy as she passed. She waved back.

At least she hadn't missed rehearsal. A quick cleanup and she would be ready to face the afternoon. She felt exhilarated by her jog, fascinated by the people she had met, and a little apprehensive of what was to come.

She walked around the back of the annex to take the service entrance. There was a back stairway for the help, and she didn't want to track mud and leaves into the main house. She held the door for a delivery boy, grunting under a load of cardboard vegetable boxes, then followed him inside.

The sounds of activity surrounded her as she made her way down the hallway. Clanging of pots, and doors slamming, a vacuum cleaner, two vacuum cleaners, maids pushing trolleys of cleaning supplies and stacks of fresh white towels. Through the entrance of the dining room, she could see girls placing vases on white tablecloths, hear the clatter of silverware being poured into stainless steel containers.

She passed the bar where a freckled boy looked up from the glass he was polishing and smiled at her. Another boy hefted a crate filled with lemons and limes onto the counter.

The annex was as busy as any theater on opening night. And throughout the commotion, Chi-Chi's voice burst like exclamation points—directing, encouraging, making suggestions—choreography in a different sphere.

A salutary reminder, thought Lindy, of her own responsibilities. She took the stairs two at a time, splashed water on her face, grabbed her dance bag, and was at the theater in less than ten minutes.

Chapter
Seven

The theater was in a state of barely controlled chaos. Several girls sat on trunks in the wardrobe room. Piles of chiffon slid across their laps as they attacked the fabric with needles and thread as if poking pins into voodoo dolls. Rose bent over another girl at the sewing machine. One of her braids had come loose from the Heidi coil and swung in the air like the ear of a demented rabbit.

In the girls' dressing room, Andrea and Kate were helping the less experienced dancers with their makeup. Other young dancers hurried up and down the stairs, retrieving forgotten shoes or calling for a dancer needed on stage.

On stage, the *corps de ballet* walked from one formation to another, marking their spacing. Their white tunics and pink tights were tinged with a murky blue.

"Hold it," Peter commanded from where he was sitting in the house, surrounded by the student crew. He pulled the headset off the boy sitting behind the makeshift manager's board. Putting it on his head, he turned to look back at the booth, and began speaking into the mouthpiece.

The dancers continued to move through their positions. The light changed from blue to mauve; the tunics turned a dirty gray. "Are you in the correct cue?" Lindy could hear his voice rise even though he was still talking into the headset. He wasn't at his best in crowds even on a good day, and this didn't appear to be one of those.

The stage changed from mauve to amber then suddenly went black. "Freeze!" yelled Peter. There was no light in the house except for the small lamp on the board and an eerie glow from the lighting booth at the back of the house. The stage lights popped back on. Mauve again.

The dancers who had frozen midmovement, relaxed and stared out into the house. Peter pulled off the headset and walked up the aisle to the booth. He rolled his eyes as he passed Lindy.

A few seconds later the stage was washed in a soft blue that molded the white of the tunics into voluptuous folds. Peter returned down the aisle. "We're a little behind." He squeezed past the row of seats and sat next to the boy who was calling the cues. "Not your fault," he said.

Robert and Jeremy were standing down front looking toward Peter. They turned back to the stage. The piece continued in silence. It was a spacing rehearsal: marking the steps while learning stage positions, deciding which wings to use for entrances and exits. It was a necessary process in transferring a piece from the studio to the stage. Even the most professional dancers took a tech day for setting lighting cues and spacing. They were long and boring even on the most efficient days.

Lindy gritted her teeth. She hated tech days. Everybody did. And this was a tech and run, which meant after each piece was spaced they would dance it full out, in costume, with the music—a combination tech and dress rehearsal. It was only 2:30, but at this rate, they would be in the theater all night.

Her eyes scanned the house. Silhouettes of dancers appeared, stretched out in the aisles or in the audience seats. Should she tell them they weren't supposed to sit in their costumes? No, she would leave it to Rose. She would be more effective. Being yelled at by Rose was an instant education. Lindy remembered her own first summer stock experience. She hadn't known what a prop table was. She had left something—what was it, a cup?—sitting on one of the frames of scenery. In the middle of the next scene, the cup had come flying onto the stage, breaking into several pieces that scattered across the floor. "There's a prop table, goddamn it," thundered the stage manager's voice from the wing. Lindy never forgot to return her props to the table after that. Sometimes, drama held a more lasting impression than polite entreaty. She smiled; Rose would deal with it.

Feeling at loose ends, she strolled to the back of the house. In the farthest corner seat sat Biddy, legs thrown over the seat in front of her. There was no mistaking the shape of Biddy's hair even in the darkness.

"What's up?" asked Lindy walking up behind her.

"Bedlam everywhere you look."

"Think we should help out?"

"Not me. Until Jeremy's back to normal, I'm determined to keep a low profile."

"I wish they would." Lindy motioned down to four dancers sitting halfway to the stage. Rebo's arm was draped across the back of Juan's seat. His fingers played with a lock of Juan's hair. The stage lights made it a perfect dumb show. Next to Rebo was Eric, head to head with . . . Paul? Lindy looked more closely. Of course not, Paul was as straight as they came. This silhouette wasn't familiar. Oh shit, it must be a student, and if Grappel made an appearance . . . That's all they needed. She walked down the aisle and slipped into the row of seats behind them.

"Don't you guys have something to do?" she asked.

Rebo tilted his head backward over the seat until he was looking up at her. "We're doing it." His eyes widened and he made choking noises. "We're dying of boredom."

"Don't be a wuss," said Eric. "No one ever dies of boredom, they just fade . . ." He began slipping down in his seat. "Fade." The word was muffled. He dropped to the floor. The seat bottom flipped up. "Awaay."

The boy laughed. He was wearing a silk shirt and pants from the Holberg Suite, and they were wrinkled.

"What about this one?" Lindy indicated the boy with her head as she directed the question to Rebo.

"We're the last piece," volunteered the boy. "I've already warmed up twice and we probably won't even get to it today."

She was getting a headache. She went directly to Rose, who was now backstage, adjusting the drapes of the tunics as dancers made their exits.

Moments later, she heard Rose's voice reverberate through the house. In a few minutes every dancer was standing backstage, wrinkles and all.

Lindy went back out front. She passed Robert who had shifted his position to check the sight lines for stage right. She smiled even though he didn't seem to notice her. He shouted a correction. His voice had the raspy quality of someone coming down with a cold. A line of eight dancers shifted a step to the left. "Good." Robert returned to the center aisle.

She couldn't just keep wandering around the theater all day; it would drive her crazy. And Biddy was no help. "I feel just like that rat in his cage," she sang under her breath as she walked back up the aisle. It was a song that Cliff had listened to on one of his long weekends home. It played constantly on the radio and he had bought the CD. Even though Lindy knew she had heard the song at least a hundred times that weekend, the only lyrics she had been able to identify were the rat in the cage part.

She pushed open the padded swinging doors to the lobby and walked through. It was sunny. She blinked a few times until her pupils adjusted.

Beyond the glass front all was quiet. The theater's parking lot was covered with drying puddles. Across the drive, the main house looked cleansed by the night's storm. Even the annex, that ran behind a copse of trees, looked deserted, though Lindy knew there was plenty of activity inside.

She turned her back on the scene and read the words of a plaque that ran along the back wall of the lobby. 50 YEARS OF EASTON STU-

DENTS. Beneath it, rows of photographs stretched from the corner to the ticket office.

She passed along the line of pictures until she reached the beginning of the display. Two rows of healthy, plump young men and women were dressed in dreadful black knit tights or gym shorts gathered at the waist and white, cap-sleeved shirts that buttoned up the front. Below it hung two individual pictures of the scholarship students for that year. She moved along the line, stopping here and there as she recognized names of dancers who had made it, and wondering what had happened to the ones who hadn't.

About two thirds of the way down, she saw a familiar face. Jeremy at fourteen, blond hair curling over his ears, scrawny and spindle-legged, with a devilish smile on his face. In the next frame, a serious young woman, already buxom, dark hair pulled severely back in a bun. Esmerelda Lanterna. Puberty would not be kind to that figure, thought Lindy.

A few pictures later, another shot of Jeremy, looking stronger and more mature. And in the third—he must have been about sixteen when the photo was taken—tall with muscles that had filled out during the preceding year, and incredibly handsome. He was standing next to Marguerite, who looked as grand as she did today, only younger and dressed in a beaded gown. She looked up at him as he smiled at the camera.

The pictures that followed captured the changing standards for dancers. Sleeker bodies. Shorter torsos. Longer legs. Flat-chested girls and high-arched boys. And each year, getting thinner and thinner.

She stopped suddenly, her breath catching. Before her was the picture of this year's scholarship student, Lawrence Cleveland. She forced herself to look at the boy who until now had been faceless to her. Blue eyes, high cheekbones, a smile that held the slightest hint of malice, a wave of blond hair swept across his forehead. Her throat tightened. She had expected him to be darker, she didn't know why. And more muscular. But this boy was tall and lanky with a special grace that had been captured superbly by the photographer. She looked at the group shot above it, her eye going immediately to the figure of Larry, the focal point of the group, looking smug and at ease, surrounded by sixty other dancers. She ran her finger over the names printed below the photo until she came to Connover Phillips, then transferred her finger to the corresponding face. Connie, in the back row, head tilted down, eyes looking shyly out from beneath dark curls, lips pursed as if he could barely manage a smile for the camera.

She was still gazing at the picture, her hand resting on the wall next to it, when she heard the front door open behind her. She glanced over her shoulder. Ellis held the door for a policeman that Lindy didn't recognize. At least it wasn't Sheriff Grappel, but what on earth could he want?

He walked across the lobby, nodded "ma'am" and went into the house. Darting an unhappy look at Lindy, Ellis followed him. Lindy slipped through the door behind them before it had a chance to close.

The two men stood in front of her, getting their bearings in the dark. Then Ellis pointed in the direction of the stage where Jeremy and Robert stood talking. The policeman strode forward, bracing his feet against the rake of the auditorium.

Ellis came to stand beside her. "Byron wants to talk to Robert. What the hell, pardon, can that lamebrain be up to now?"

She saw Robert, backlit from the amber stage light, turn a shocked face toward the policeman, then watched as the policeman escorted him up the aisle. Jeremy stood rooted to the floor. First one dancer stopped, then another, until the whole stage was staring at the strip of sunlight left by the closing door. Then Jeremy bolted up the aisle, slowing down long enough to exclaim, "They're taking him for questioning," in a voice so filled with hurt, that Lindy felt it in the pit of her stomach.

Biddy met Lindy and Ellis at the door. "I saw what happened. Feel like we've been here before?"

They arrived at the house to see the sheriff's car parked at the front of the steps. Lindy was vaguely aware of people behind her. Then she saw Robert in the back seat of the car and forgot about everything else. Grappel got in the passenger side, slammed the door, and the car drove away. Chi-Chi came out of the annex at that moment. Dropping a dish towel, she began running after the car.

Jeremy caught her around the waist and held her tight. She struggled to free herself as if she intended to chase the car down the mountain and into town.

A movement on the steps caught Lindy's attention. "Jeremy," she cried. It was a reflex action. There were other people standing closer to Marguerite, who had slumped against a column and sank to the ground.

Jeremy propelled Chi-Chi in Lindy's direction and raced for the porch.

"I'm okay," she said. She had recovered herself faster than Lindy dreamed was possible. "I'll get Dr. Addison."

Chi-Chi took off down the path to the infirmary. Lindy turned to watch her and met instead the anxious faces of sixty young dance students.

Madame Flick's voice came from somewhere within the group. "Coome, cooome. It will be all right. Let us get some work done so we will have something goood to show Ms. Marguerite on Saturday night." The other teachers began to gather the students back toward the theater.

"It was a stampede," said Peter coming up to Lindy. "First one student, then another and they were all heading for the door like someone had yelled fire. You taking over?"

Jeremy had lifted Marguerite and carried her into the house. Dr. Addison passed them at a full run followed closely by Chi-Chi.

"Yes. Biddy, let me know the minute you hear anything."

Biddy and Lindy sat with Stuart and Ellis at the dining table. Marguerite was "resting comfortably" according to Dr. Addison after a mild "spell." She didn't elaborate, but said she would be in her office until late that night. Jeremy had driven Chi-Chi into town to the sheriff's office.

The four of them picked at their food, attended only by Sandiman, who hovered tragically at the sideboard when not serving the courses of food that went virtually untouched.

Stuart tried valiantly to keep a thread of conversation going, but by coffee, even his determination had faltered.

"Should we cancel the student show?" asked Ellis. Sandiman bobbled the brandy snifter he was placing before him. "Oh, do stop hovering, man." Ellis shooed him away with a flourish of his hand. "Get yourself a glass and sit down."

Without a word, Sandiman retrieved another glass from the sideboard, poured out the brandy, and took his place at Lindy's left.

She widened her eyes at Biddy.

"Unorthodox, you're thinking," said Ellis. "Sandiman is a family retainer in both senses of the word. He's an anchor as well as a butler. And he knows better than the rest of us what is good for Marguerite."

"Thank you, sir."

"So what do you think?" Ellis swirled his brandy snifter until the liquid threatened to spill out.

"Let's not be hasty, Ellis," said Stu. "We need to staunch any speculation, not give in to it."

"Speculation?" asked Biddy.

"The sheriff obviously is going to make more of this than there is," said Stu. "Why else would he have Robert taken away in full view of the entire camp? He could easily have questioned him here. He questioned the rest of us without taking us ignobly away to the pokey."

"He questioned you?" Lindy looked from Stu to Ellis.

"Yes. He's determined to cause trouble," said Stu. "Evidently they found some papers in Larry's locker that are 'suspicious' according to Grappel, though that is all he would say."

Ellis returned his glass to the table. It caught the edge of his saucer. The brandy splashed over the rim and rolled down the side. "It's ridiculous. I won't have Marguerite placed under any more stress. I don't know what I'd do if . . ." His voice faltered. "If something happened to her."

Stu reached across Biddy and placed a hand on his forearm. "We're not going to let anything happen to Marguerite."

Ellis looked at Sandiman. "I think we should close the camp until this whole thing is cleared up."

Sandiman returned his employer's look with a candor that surprised Lindy. She had no personal experience with servants, but she had read enough to know that they were not usually consulted on family business.

"Ellis," began Stu.

"You said only last night that we should—"

"Should be prepared to do what is necessary for the survival of the camp." He motioned to Biddy and Lindy. "By way of explanation, Cleveland's parents were quite upset as you can imagine. The father especially—"

"Like father, like son," said Ellis.

"Well, yes. He made some rather outrageous accusations and threats. The poor mother was mortified. If he does decide to sue, especially if there are any circumstances that would suggest suicide or negligence on our part, it could be extremely damaging to the image, not to mention the solubility of the trust and, consequently, to the camp."

He sounded just like a lawyer. When Lindy had asked him earlier what he did before he retired, he had answered, "Oh, a bit of this and that." She wondered now if some of the this and that had included legal work.

"All the more reason to send everyone home. I won't have Marguerite dragged through the mud because of that vindictive ass of a sheriff."

"We agreed to sit this out," said Stu firmly.

"But if it does blow up, it could ruin us; it would kill Marguerite."

"But if we win, there will be no stain or questions about the reputation of the camp or the family."

"Sandiman?" Ellis's question held a twinge of desperation.

Sandiman cleared his throat. "What would Madame want, sir?"

Ellis slumped back in his chair, defeated.

Lindy looked at Sandiman in astonishment. Sitting ramrod

straight on the edge of his chair, long bony neck swathed in starched collar and impeccably tied jabot, patrician nose slightly hooked at the tip, thin lips, sparse hair, oiled and combed straight back from a high forehead, he was the perfect stage butler. Never again would Lindy think of servants as part of the furniture. Like Rose, Sandiman heard things people didn't even realize they were saying. And like Rose, he obviously had the clout to influence others.

With one short sentence, delivered without inflection, the Eastons' butler had declared war on Sheriff Grappel and public opinion.

The sound of an arriving car sent Biddy to the window.

Chi-Chi and Jeremy entered the dining room a few minutes later. Sandiman returned to the sideboard and set two additional places at the table.

"Not for me, Sandiman," said Chi-Chi. Her round, buoyant face sagged. Gone was the bustling commandant of the annex. The Chi-Chi that stood before them was a tired, washed-out, rather dumpy middle-aged woman.

Sandiman continued to place silverware on the table. He pulled the chair out and Chi-Chi sat down.

Jeremy poured himself a brandy and went to the window. He stared out into the night.

"Sit down and eat something," said Biddy. Her voice was like a cooling balm. Lindy had heard that voice calm the most agitated hearers.

"I'll eat when I'm hungry," said Jeremy without turning around.

Lindy saw Biddy's throat tighten as she swallowed her next words.

"How is Marguerite?" asked Chi-Chi between mouthfuls. She was already beginning to look younger and more energetic.

"Nothing to worry about," said Stu when he realized Ellis wasn't going to answer. Ellis was staring over his shoulder to the unmoving figure at the window. "Adele says she just needs to rest. She'll be fine."

"If she isn't put through any more of this absurdity." Jeremy turned on them, shot Ellis an angry look, then turned away.

Ellis looked surprised and hurt and a little confused. Lindy wondered if he would be able to hold up under the strain any better than his sister.

"Byron refused to let us see him." Chi-Chi's eyes were focused on the unlit candelabra that sat in the middle of the table. It gave the effect of her talking to unseen dinner guests at the other end. "They're going to keep him in the jail until the last possible moment, and they have absolutely no right."

Sandiman filled her wine glass.

"I know he's going to hurt him, I just know it." She took a gulp of wine and choked.

Stu patted her on the back. "Now, now, he knows better than to do anything to Robert. They can only keep him for twenty-four hours without arresting him."

"Arresting?" Chi-Chi's face crumpled. "For what? What can they possibly think he has done? He wasn't derelict in his care for the students. It isn't really his job to oversee them. We have counselors, and assistant counselors, and—me."

Stu's hand rested on her back. "Whatever Grappel is up to, he's no match for us."

Jeremy returned his glass to the sideboard and walked quickly toward the door. Sandiman barely managed to get there before him.

An uncomfortable silence settled around the table. Ellis and Biddy stared at the tablecloth. Stuart continued to pat Chi-Chi mechanically on her back. Lindy tried to read a clue from Sandiman's face, but he had slipped back into his role of butler.

"You really didn't have to do this," said Chi-Chi opening the door to the cabin that she and Robert called home. "I'm perfectly all right. Jeremy is taking this harder than I am."

"We were glad to come along," said Biddy. "And don't worry about Jeremy. He always takes things too much to heart, doesn't he, Lindy?"

"Huh? Oh, yeah. Marguerite sure keeps up to date, doesn't she? Between the infirmary and this . . ." Lindy gestured to an elaborate computer console that covered an entire wall of the tiny living room. A wooden desk stood in front of the equipment leaving just enough room to move from one to the other. Its surface was scattered with papers. To one side, a mayonnaise jar held pencils and pens. More paper was stacked haphazardly at the corner of the desk. A glass with the remains of a murky orange liquid rested on top of the paper.

"This is office as well as home." Chi-Chi looked lovingly around the room. "It does take up a lot of space, doesn't it? It was Marguerite's idea. When Robert and I were married, she decided that I should learn the hotel business." She shrugged. "She wanted me to feel like I was needed. I never even finished high school; too smart for my own good." She laughed, a fragment of cheerfulness making a brief resurgence. "So she sent me to a hotel management course, and I started running the annex. It wasn't so big then. It seems like another lifetime."

Chi-Chi looked up, her eyes round and slightly expectant. "Would you like a cup of tea or something?"

Lindy would like nothing more than to go to bed. It had been an emotionally exhausting day, and her calves and thighs were feeling the strain of her morning hike.

"That would be great," said Biddy.

Chi-Chi left them, snatching the used glass off the desk as she passed by. Pretty soon the noises of tea preparation were heard from the other room.

"Thank you, Miss Nurturer," said Lindy.

"I don't think she wants to be alone. And anyway—" Biddy took a breath.

"No songs about walking alone in a storm, please. We've had enough rain as it is."

"How about: Picking yourself up, brushing yourself off—"

"And starting all over? No thanks." Lindy walked over to the desk. "Get a load of this equipment. Glen's office isn't this sophisticated."

"The entire management of the annex and retreat is done on that computer," said Chi-Chi. She carried a wicker tray of tea things and put them on a coffee table in front of a sling-back couch. Lindy and Biddy sat in two butterfly chairs that faced it.

"I can do all the ordering, keep the books, link up to the reservation desk, plus help Robert with scheduling for the camp. All from my living room." Her hands moved around the tea things. Talking about her work seemed to revive her. "We even print the programs on that laser printer. The quality is really good."

"The program we saw yesterday was printed here?"

Chi-Chi handed Lindy a cup. "I did it a couple of nights ago. The hardest part was getting Robert to write down all the information."

"I was wondering about that stack of scratch paper," said Lindy with a laugh.

"Some of us are mechanically-minded and some of us are creative. We're perfect together." Chi-Chi sighed. "I hope he's all right. I don't trust Byron." Her features squeezed together. Lindy looked away while she composed herself. "Oh, please don't let him hurt him."

"I'm sure he'll be all right," said Biddy.

"They wouldn't even let me give him his allergy pills," she said with a final sniff.

"Allergies," said Lindy trying to disentangle her mind from the image of Byron Grappel standing over Robert with a rubber hose. "That must be unpleasant in these surroundings."

"Poor darling. His eyes water and his nose and throat close up without antihistamines and his power drink."

"The glass with the orange stuff in the bottom?" asked Biddy.

Chi-Chi nodded. "I make a pitcher of it every day. Orange juice, brewer's yeast, echinacea, and a few other things. It fortifies the immune system."

Lindy grimaced.

"Robert doesn't like it, either, but it's only for a few months of the year. He's perfectly fine in the city." She bit her lip. "Marguerite doesn't know; she'd refuse to let him come."

"Mum's the word."

Chi-Chi relaxed. "A few months of sneezing is a small price to pay for all Marguerite has done for us. And she worries too much. I don't think she believes any of us have completely grown up."

They took their leave a few minutes later.

"You could sleep up at the house tonight," said Biddy. "Are you sure you'll be okay alone?"

"No. But Robert will be back tomorrow. I'll just have to make do until then."

"I hope she's right," said Lindy as they made their way back to the house.

Biddy only nodded.

Chapter
Eight

"I can't understand what is taking him so long." Ellis stood looking out the window of the dining room in exactly the same position Jeremy had occupied the night before.

"I'm sure he'll be back soon," said Lindy. She played with the cup of coffee that sat on the table before her.

"He shouldn't have insisted on going by himself. He says his hip is fine, but driving down the mountain—if he needed to use his reflexes quickly . . ."

"He probably just decided to do a little shopping while he was in town." Biddy didn't look at him, just continued to play with her plate of cooling eggs.

It was the first time Lindy had ever seen Biddy pick at her food. Her stomach, unlike Lindy's, never seemed to be affected by stress or worry.

"Maybe he stopped in at the police station to see about Robert." Lindy took a sip of coffee. It was cold. She wondered if it would be okay to exchange her cup for another with hot coffee.

"That must be it," said Ellis, suddenly sounding years younger. "I don't know what we would do without him." He walked over to the sideboard and began to fill a plate from the chafing dishes.

The door opened and they all turned to see if it was Stu. Jeremy paused long enough to cast a cursory glance over the table and poured himself a cup of coffee.

"Morning, Jeremy," said Ellis. "Stu went into town to collect the papers. He said we shouldn't wait until they were delivered this afternoon. Better to be prepared for whatever they might be saying about us."

Jeremy gave him a long look. "I'm sure he's right." He sat down several chairs away from the others.

Lindy stifled an urge to get up and kick him. He wasn't the only one distressed by the events of the last three days. He should stop acting like such a brat and start helping the others to cope.

"How is Marguerite this morning?" Biddy asked, looking at him quickly before returning her gaze to the now-cold scrambled eggs.

"She seems okay. A little tired. Adele told her to stay in bed today. But you know Marguerite."

Actually, they hardly knew Marguerite at all, but Lindy refrained from saying so.

"Ah, here he is." Ellis put his plate back on the sideboard and went out to meet Stu.

Lindy, Biddy, and Jeremy drank their coffee in silence.

Lindy wished Jeremy would just get things off his chest. He was making them all uncomfortable, Biddy especially. She was completely loyal to him and the company and Lindy knew it hurt her to be left out of things that were affecting him.

He had a way of letting things build up until the very space around him seemed to vibrate. Sometimes the mood blew over without any of them knowing what had caused it. Other times his revelations about his feelings had been shocking and unsettling. Lindy hoped this would be one of the former kind. Between the student performance, their own performance, a death, Marguerite's health, and Robert's stay at the police station, they had more than enough to deal with already.

Ellis returned to the dining room with Stu in tow. Neither of them looked happy. Stu slapped down a stack of newspapers and went to pour himself a cup of coffee. Ellis took up the paper on top.

"Fatal Accident at Easton Arts Retreat," he read aloud. "That's not so bad." He turned to the next paper without reading the article of the first.

"Oh my God." He didn't even apologize for his blasphemy, but sank into a chair that fortunately was placed right behind him. *"Student Found Dead at Academy. Police Investigate."* He tossed the paper aside and reached for the next. A hand closed over his wrist. Stu stood next to him.

"I don't think we need be too concerned about the headlines. It will all blow over in a couple of days and then will be forgotten."

"If there's an earthquake or a war," said Jeremy without looking up.

Lindy gave him a stern look, though he couldn't see her. He was staring into his coffee cup. She willed him to get the message. He lifted his eyes in her direction. At least he had the decency to look chagrined.

Biddy pushed her chair back and left the room.

Oh great.

"Blow over." Ellis extracted his wrist from Stu's hand. *"Child Plunges to his Death at EAR?"*

"I almost didn't bring that one back." Stu placed both hands on the table. "Ellis," he said levelly. "It's only the local paper. And you know how the editor feels about gaining these lands for the town's benefit. He's in cahoots with the mayor and those local real estate people."

Stu straightened up and squeezed Ellis's shoulder. "It has a circulation of less than two hundred readers. It won't affect any public opinion but theirs, and we already know where the town stands."

"Sandiman!" Ellis bellowed the name so loudly that the others jumped. Sandiman appeared magically from behind the baize door to the kitchen.

"Yes, sir."

"I don't want Marguerite to see the papers today, or tomorrow, or any day until this has blown over, do you understand?"

The idea was ludicrous. Lindy imagined the servants hiding in the scullery cutting out the headlines of all the papers that entered the camp. A scene right out of a Victorian novel. It occurred to her that Marguerite might need less protecting than her brother.

"Very good, sir." Sandiman uttered the remark with a completely straight face, but Lindy guessed that if Marguerite wanted to see the newspapers, all she had to do was ask.

"That will be all." Ellis waved his hand in the air, dismissing Sandiman, the same man who only last night had sat with them tête-à-tête over brandy.

Sandiman bowed and disappeared behind the door.

Lindy found that she had an almost uncontrollable urge to laugh. Sandiman came and went like a jack in the box. Ellis changed his role in the family as readily as he changed his clothes. Stu was beginning to act like the friendly family solicitor, and even she and Biddy were beginning to think in terms of "tête-à-tête" and "particular friends." Only Jeremy seemed resistant to the Old World influences around him.

"Can I see one of the papers?" he asked, his voice as bland as if he were asking the loan from a fellow commuter on his way to work.

Stu tossed it toward him. Their eyes met for a second before Jeremy opened the paper and began to read.

Ellis was reading the article in the local paper. He opened to the continuation and he was hidden by the double pages of newsprint. An occasional grunt came from behind the paper. Lindy tried to read the front page that Ellis held from where she was sitting.

"For crying out loud," she said and grabbed the remaining paper.

It wasn't pretty. The paper wasn't local, but even they mentioned the fact that the police were investigating the circumstances of the case. She had no doubt who the "spokesman" for the county police was.

Everyone looked up from what they were reading at the sound of another car coming to a stop at the front door. The slam of a car door, and the car drove away. A few seconds later Robert entered the dining room.

He couldn't have looked much worse if the sheriff *had* been beating him all night. His clothes were rumpled; his hair was flat on one side; a cowlick stuck up on the back of his head as if he hadn't even been allowed to comb it after his long night in the county jail. But the worst part of his appearance was his face. His eyes were red-rimmed and bloodshot. There were puffy circles under his eyes and when he spoke, his voice was thick with congestion.

"How is Bu-arguerite?"

"Oh God, Robbie." Jeremy jumped to his feet and poured the man a cup of coffee, the only breakfast item that was getting any attention at all.

Robert shook his head. "How is she?"

"She's okay. Nothing to worry about. You look like hell."

"I fell like hell. I dond dnow what they put in dose maddresses. I gotta get cleaned up and let Chi-Chi dhow I'm all right."

"Sit down," said Jeremy. He helped Robert into a chair and then headed for the kitchen.

Robert began drinking the cup of coffee that Jeremy had poured for him, but waved away Lindy's offer to fix him a plate of food.

In a few minutes, Jeremy returned, out of breath and holding a bottle of pills. He poured two into his palm and handed them to Robert.

Robert popped them into his mouth.

"What are those?" asked Ellis, alarmed. "What's wrong with you, boy?"

"I'm fide. Something in the jail, bade me stuffy, that's all."

"God knows what kind of molds and mildew are growing in that jailhouse. It's got to be a hundred years old," said Ellis, mollified. "Remember when we were in DC for the cherry blossom festival?"

"I remember you sneezed your way through the weekend," said Stu, "including the receiving line at the White House. I thought I'd bust a gut trying not to laugh; I think the First Lady did, too."

Ellis turned pink. "First and only time I was ever affected by pollen. Nasty experience."

Robert's breathing was returning to normal as the antihistamines went to work on his nasal passages. "Me, too," he said.

Lindy glanced over to Jeremy. No response.

The kitchen door swung open and Chi-Chi rushed into the room. Robert stood up and she threw herself into his arms. "Are you okay?

I was so worried." Questions continued to pour out as she touched his face, smoothed his hair, took his chin in her hands and then hugged him again. "I was so worried," she repeated.

"I'm okay. The worst part was missing you."

"I was so afraid he would hurt you."

"Don't be silly."

The others listened to this exchange of affection until they couldn't stand it any longer.

"What happened?" they chorused together.

Robert and Chi-Chi looked at the others, surprise on both their faces.

"Uh, sorry," said Robert. He placed Chi-Chi in a chair and sat down in the one next to it. Lindy could tell they were holding hands under the table.

"So they come and get me out of rehearsal. Byron is waiting and says he has some questions for me. I say fine, and he says down at the station." He took a breath. "I figure this is pretty strange, but typical of Byron, so I get in the car. But when we get to the jail, instead of questioning me, they throw me in a cell."

Chi-Chi must have squeezed his hand, because he winced and turned to her. "They didn't 'throw' me, that was just a figure of speech. After a while they lead me to the interrogation room. It was printed right on the door. It was pretty daunting. If I did have anything to confess, the sign alone would have undone me."

"They wanted you to confess?" Lindy couldn't help herself. The question just came out.

Robert frowned. "I think so. But Byron was kind of vague on what it was he wanted me to confess to. Evidently they found some notes in Larry's locker that they hinted had to do with his fall. Of course that was stupid, and I told them so. I did think that Byron was going to hit me then, but there was another guy with him, and he seemed much calmer about the whole thing."

He pushed at his cowlick. "They woke me up twice during the night to question me again—"

"Can they do that?" Chi-Chi asked Stu.

Stu shrugged. "We should have gotten you a lawyer, but it

seemed so unnecessary at the time. We thought for sure you'd be back in a couple of hours."

"I told them everything I thought would be helpful, but I guess it wasn't what Byron wanted to hear. He kept trying to make out that Larry killed himself because he had been seduced. Byron doesn't know quite what to think, but he would like the seducer to be me."

"That's preposterous," said Chi-Chi.

"Absolutely ridiculous," said Ellis.

The others added their reassurances, even Lindy, who really had no idea whether it could be true or not. Only Jeremy sat quiet at the end of the table, slowly biting his lip.

Lindy taught company class that morning. When Jeremy tried to argue, she politely told him that he was driving everyone crazy and that he should go down by the lake and do some deep-breathing exercises.

She was as shocked at herself as Jeremy appeared to be, but she managed to stare him down. It was an odd feeling. She had probably been privy to more of his feelings than most of the others, but even so, she never had spoken to him in anger before. It was so useless. He took whatever reactions people had to him and absorbed them. Lindy often thought that he would be a lot better off if he would just throw them back and be done with it.

But he never did. He seemed to have an immense capacity for carrying everything inside himself.

When he at last gave in, and Lindy had drawn a shaky breath, already regretting her words, all he said was, "I am who I am." And left her to stew in her own irritation.

At lunchtime, Lindy wandered toward the student dining hall. She didn't really want to face any of the family at lunch. In fact, she and Biddy had decided to begin having their meals in the annex dining room that would be opening for the weekend.

The sun was shining, but it was not so humid as the day before, and clusters of students were having their lunch on the lawn or at the picnic tables beneath the trees.

Lindy passed down the line of food and took a sandwich and a glass of iced tea. The sandwiches were freshly made and the tea was brewed, not instant. Chi-Chi's doing, she was sure. It was amazing how much one woman could accomplish. Chi-Chi had been totally involved with the guest quarters in the annex. Except for brief appearances like the one that morning, no one had seen her except at a distance, ordering squads of waiters and directing deliveries. She must have really trained her staff here well, because there was no falling off in the quality of food given to the campers even in her absence.

Lindy saw several of the Ash dancers sitting in a group in the sun. She walked over to them.

"Have a seat, Lindelicious," said Rebo. He was lying on the ground, his head in Juan's lap. "Nothing like dining al fresco. Watch out for the anthill."

Lindy moved away from the line of red ants. Eric scooted over to make room for her.

Mieko snatched a carton of yogurt away, just as Eric's hand hit the dirt where it had been. Lindy sat down, molded a place for her glass in the ground, and opened her sandwich.

"How was your class this morning?" she asked Rebo.

"A little dance and a whole lot of talking." Rebo pushed Juan's knee aside to see her better. "They were so logy during the warmup, I made the mistake of asking what was wrong. Did I get an earful." Rebo's eyes rolled upward and he batted his lashes. "Maybe I've missed my calling. Once they got going, they didn't stop. Pretty soon we were all sitting on the floor like some New Age therapy session."

"Feelings—" crooned Eric in a falsetto.

"Yikes. I thought Dr. Addison was talking with them," said Lindy.

"No offense, Lindelicate, but sometimes it's easier to talk to some one nearer your own age. Especially with the things they talked about. Honey, it made me feel out of the loop."

He took a bite out of a peach. Juice dripped down his chin. Juan wiped it away with his finger.

"And who appointed you slave of the day?" asked Lindy.

Juan grinned. "I make him pay."

Lindy smiled, but she suddenly felt uncomfortable. In light of the implications Sheriff Grappel was making, should she suggest they be more discreet? She pushed the thought aside. How could she even allow herself to be influenced by a man like the sheriff? She couldn't care less what he thought about them. And yet . . .

Rebo was looking at her with a faint question on his face. "So don't you want the skinny?"

"Uh, yeah," she said. "They needed to work through their grief, right?"

"Grief, schmief, there's not a whole hell of a lot of grief being felt over Larry Cleveland. Seems this kid was a real piece." Rebo sat up, crossed his legs and leaned on his elbows. "Don't get me wrong, there are a few that are upset. That started the discussion. Then it comes out that this kid had dirt on just about everybody in camp. He must have been spying on them constantly. I'm surprised he had time left over to learn any steps. Half of them had lost all their money to him, not to mention care packages, jewelry, books, just about anything they had."

"Didn't the counselors or Robert have an idea of what was going on?"

Rebo gave an exaggerated shrug. "They're into *daaaance*. I don't think they have a clue what kids are like these days. Larry was also getting it on with boocoodles of campers—girls, too." Rebo shrugged again. "Go figure."

"Some men like women." Mieko's uninflected statement stopped him for a second.

"Oh—right." He grinned at her. "I like you, but it makes Juan jealous."

Juan rolled over and rubbed his cheek against Mieko's bare arm. "I like you, too."

"Bonehead." She shoved him away.

Rebo clapped his palm to his forehead. "Lordy mercy, Lin-descriminate, I never thought that *I'd* be giving *your* safe-sex lecture." He whipped his bandanna from his head and leaned forward. "Do you see any gray hairs?"

There was no hair. Rebo shaved his head. "Only a five o'clock shadow," she said.

"Maybe I should grow it out," he said patting his skull.

"You always say that people *are* being safer about sex."

"Well, they will be now. I scared the shit out of them. Do you think I should grow it out?" He turned the top of his head to Mieko. She groaned and fell back on the ground.

"It's so hard to believe," said Lindy. "He was so young."

"You're talking like a mother, Lindecorum. He was seventeen."

"A child."

Rebo laughed. "No babe in the woods, but a babe from all accounts."

"Have they told all this to the sheriff?"

He shook his head. "They might not share the same feelings about Larry Cleveland, but the one thing they agree on is the sheriff. He won't be getting any cooperation from them."

"The man is vindictive and dangerous," said Lindy. She felt distinctly uncomfortable. "Maybe we shouldn't give him any ammunition." She narrowed her eyes at Rebo.

"Lost me, doll face."

"What I mean is . . ." What did she mean? Should they put on an act for some jerk that didn't deserve their attention? Was that playing into prejudices and fears or was it being smart?

Mieko sat up. "She means you should keep a low profile."

"Oh, right." Rebo looked confused. Then Lindy saw the comprehension dawn on him. "Oh no. I'm not crawling back into the closet because of some redneck, homophobic, two-inch needledicked hillbilly. Nuh-uh. Forget it."

"I'm not saying you should crawl anywhere." But wasn't that just what she was trying to say? "You don't know what's going on with Sheriff Grappel."

"We have an idea," said Eric.

"He's been trying to find out who Larry's lover was," said Rebo.

"And did anybody tell him?"

"Hell no. They're too numerous to mention."

Lindy took a breath, deliberating whether to let them in on what she knew. They had never failed her in the past. "Grappel is trying to implicate Robert. And then make this a suicide, because Larry was so ashamed of what happened. The town wants the camp for development. They're only looking for an excuse to discredit the Eastons."

"Robert?" Rebo guffawed, then looked at Juan, then Eric. "No way." They both shook their heads. "No," he said again, this time more slowly. "I don't think so. None of them mentioned him, and, believe me, they mentioned everything else."

"You don't think they would keep that from you because they thought you might tell? They could be protecting Robert." Why was she even asking this question? Robert was obviously in love with his wife. But what about all those sex offenders whose wives never knew?

"I know what you're thinking: camp counselors, Little League coaches, Boy Scout leaders, but . . ." He didn't sound convincing. Lindy could practically hear him thinking.

"Maybe he was pushed by a jealous lover." They all stared at Mieko. "It's a possibility."

"Yeah," said Rebo.

"Hell, why can't they just say he fell down the damn hill?" asked Juan. "That's probably what happened."

"It probably is," said Lindy. "But that's hard to prove. It would be easier to find someone to blame."

"Even so, that doesn't mean it was a male lover," said Mieko. "A girl could have pushed him just as easily."

"Yeah," agreed Juan, his eyes brightening. "There's a perfect example." He pointed behind them. Andrea and Paul were sitting on a bench under the trees. Paul's arm was around her waist. His hands were busy.

They waited for Juan to continue.

"I'm not saying this would happen, but just say—Andrea dumps Peter for Paul—"

"She didn't dump him," said Mieko. Her eyes were mere slits. Lindy looked down. Her elbows were pressed close to her side. Mieko wasn't liking this scenario.

"I didn't say she did, I'm just hypothesizing. Say she did or something. Anyway, Paul's standing by the edge of a cliff. Peter could be walking by and poof, over he goes. But it could just as easily be Andrea, say if Paul pissed her off or she had a change of heart, or something. She walks right up and poof. If Paul were close enough to the edge, it wouldn't really take too much strength to . . ."

"Poof," they said in unison.

Juan grinned. "Am I right or am I right?"

"You're right," said Lindy. "I'm living proof that it doesn't take a great amount of strength to push someone into oblivion. But that was a terrible example." A year ago, Andrea had been madly in love with Peter. They weren't really suited and after a few months, the affair had died a natural death. If only the same could be said for Larry Cleveland.

"Well, see what you can find out," said Lindy. She wadded up her sandwich wrapper, retrieved her empty glass, and stood up. "Oh, what about this boy—Connie?"

Rebo nodded.

"Him, too?"

Rebo nodded again. "He wasn't in class today; the others are worried about him. He's taking it pretty hard. He didn't have many friends. Extremely shy." Rebo winced. "A perfect candidate for jealousy."

That afternoon, the first call came in. A worried father who had read of Larry's death in the newspaper that morning. Was the camp safe? Why were the police investigating? Was there anything to worry about?

The call had been handled by the switchboard operator. The next one, she transferred to the house. Sandiman came with the news. Parents were panicking and the press demanded answers. At 1:30, two girls were taken away by their parents. Marguerite stood on the steps of the mansion and waved goodbye. The girls waved out the back window, the tears streaming down their faces. By two o'clock, the main gates had been locked to prevent press cars from choking the driveway.

On her way to the student rehearsal, Lindy saw Stu talking to one reporter who had managed to sneak in before the iron gates had closed. "The family will be issuing a statement," was all she heard.

Lindy sat in the dark theater, half watching the ballet students. There were two empty places in the line of the *corps de ballet*. There were no understudies to fill the spots.

"We will leave the spaaces," said Madame Flick. "Keep to your own positions." She shook her head as she walked back up the aisle.

Several minutes later, Biddy sat down in the seat next to Lindy. "Ellis has gone up to the highway to give a statement to the reporters."

"Ellis? They would have done better to send Sandiman. Why didn't Marguerite go? She's by far the best spokesperson for the camp."

"She wanted to, but Ellis put his foot down, and Stu backed him up." Biddy sighed heavily. "Stu was coaching him on what to say when I left."

Ellis was a dear, but Lindy wondered if he would be up to handling the reporters' questions. Marguerite should have gone. She would have been able to handle the press and the parents. But was she really too sick? The idea was frightening.

Could things get any worse?

Chapter
Nine

A few minutes later things got worse. They changed over from the ballet to *There is a Time*. The dancers took their places, forming the opening circle.

Madame Flick was talking to the modern teacher, Victor Slaton, who was in charge of the rehearsal, while Robert rested from his night in jail. They looked up at the stage. There was a gap in the circle. Someone was missing.

"Places," Victor yelled.

The dancers in the circle turned to look at him. They *were* in their places.

The teacher looked around the house. No latecomer was rushing to the stage.

"Who belongs there?" He pointed to the gap in the circle.

The dancers to each side of the empty position looked at each other.

"Connie Phillips."

"Well, where is he?"

Shoulders shrugged.

"Anybody seen Connie?" asked Victor. The dancers on stage shook their heads. Victor turned to the rows of seats. No one had seen him.

"Lenny, go look for him."

Lenny got up from where he was sitting in the audience.

"No, not you," said Madame Flick. "You don't have shoes on." She motioned to one of the girls on the crew. "Go loook for him, pleease."

The girl ran up the aisle and out the front door.

The music started. They danced the first section without the missing boy.

The piece ended and there was still no Connie. The girl came rushing back into the theater.

Victor and Madame Flick looked at her expectantly. She shook her head.

"I looked in the dorm, in the dining room, the studios, even down some of the trails. He's not anywhere."

"He must be somewhere," said Victor. He turned to the group of dancers waiting to rehearse their bows. "Doesn't anybody have an idea of where he is?"

"He was real upset," said one.

"He wasn't at class this morning."

"Not at breakfast, either."

Lindy walked down the aisle until she was standing next to the two teachers. She felt a tight wad of panic in her gut.

"That's all we need," Victor said. "Could he have left with the Morrisons this morning?"

"The people who were driving away with the two girls? I only saw the girls in the back seat," said Lindy.

"We'd better inform Robert and Ms. Marguerite," said Victor. "He's probably off being self-indulgent somewhere. It's the age, you know. Those hormones. Everything seems like the end of the world."

For Larry Cleveland it was the end of the world, thought Lindy.

"I'll go," she said.

A few minutes later, she returned to the theater, followed by Jeremy, Stu, and Ellis. Robert, looking marginally better than he had that morning, joined them a minute later.

"Sandiman rang the bungalow," he explained.

Madame Flick began the next rehearsal. The others went to the lobby where they could discuss what to do without being overheard by the students.

"I think we should call the police," said Ellis before anyone else had the opportunity to speak.

"Ellis," said Stu. "Let's not jump the gun. Grappel would love another excuse to harass us. Let's try looking for him ourselves, first."

"But . . ."

"If we don't find him in a few hours, we'll call the authorities."

"Is it possible that he called his parents?" asked Lindy. "He might just want to go home," she added hopefully.

"They would have to check him out," said Stu. "And he hasn't been checked out. I looked at the roster first thing when you told us he was missing." His eyes were troubled. "And we can't call the parents and ask if they took him away without notifying us. If they didn't . . ." Stu looked apologetic. "There's no reason to worry them unnecessarily."

"But where would he go?" asked Ellis, his voice rising.

They all looked at each other waiting for an idea.

"Someplace quiet to think," said Jeremy at last.

"We'll organize a search," said Robert.

"You can't send students out looking for him. They might get hurt," said Ellis.

"Then what do you suggest?" Jeremy asked the question with a pointed stare.

Ellis lowered his eyes. Then he looked at Stu.

"We'll have them search in teams," said Robert.

"Put one of our company members in charge of each team," suggested Lindy. "They can keep anyone from wandering off on their own."

"Excellent." Stu smiled at her. His voice was assured, but his eyes were restive.

"I'll round them up." She took off at a jog.

Twenty minutes later, the dancers had been divided into twelve groups and were assigned areas in which to search. Two dancers of the Ash company led each group. Rose and Peter took another. Lindy and Robert, Stu and Victor, and Jeremy and Ellis were to go with the remaining three groups.

The rest of the teachers would stay to coordinate the groups' activities. It was arranged very efficiently. With that many choreographers and rehearsal experts, it was easy. And for once, artistic temperaments didn't get in the way.

"I don't think Stu should go," said Ellis.

"Ellis, dear friend," returned Stu. "I'm not going spelunking. I'll stick close to camp." He twirled his cane like a baton. "You don't have to worry about me. But—" He pointed his cane at the young dancers congregated around the leaders. They took a step backward. "No one is to veer from the paths. Absolutely no one is to go into the restricted areas."

The archaeologists, thought Lindy. "Does Dr. Van Zandt have a cell phone?" she asked Stu. She didn't know why he was the one to ask, but he seemed to have taken over leadership of the search.

"Good thinking, Lindy." Stu called Victor over. "In the Rolodex in the library is Dr. Van Zandt's cell phone number. Call him and ask if he's seen anybody where they shouldn't be."

Victor nodded.

"On second thought, Van Zandt thinks everybody is where they shouldn't be. Just tell him that . . ." Stu drummed his fingers on the head of his cane.

It was the first time Lindy had seen him at a loss for words.

"Just ask him if any of the boys have gotten too close to his site."

Victor nodded again, waited a second to see if there would be another change in his instructions, then took off toward the house.

Stu lifted his cane in the air. "All right, troops. Move out."

By six o'clock, all the search groups had returned, hot, dirty, tired, and discouraged. None of them had found a sign of Connie Phillips.

"Now, we call the police." The side of Stu's trousers and one shoulder of his polo shirt were covered in umber dust.

"I told you you shouldn't go traipsing around the woods," said Ellis. He started brushing at Stu's pants leg.

"Just slipped on a patch of loose dirt." Patiently, Stu waited for Ellis to finish brushing him off. "We really have no choice but to call in Grappel."

"Just what you'd expect," the sheriff grumbled. "You've lost another one." He shook his head. "And you've mucked up any clues that might have given us a lead—and it's getting dark."

He looked over the group that was sitting on the front steps of the house. They hadn't wanted to go inside and dirty up the drawing room.

"You here, Stokes?" His lip turned up in a sneer. It was almost comic. Almost. "Shoulda never let you out of jail. No telling what's happened to that kid."

Robert looked totally nonplused. It was Jeremy that had to be restrained by Peter and Rose.

Grappel shot him a quick, deadpan look, and turned away.

They watched him walk toward the several police cars parked in the driveway; stood silent as he conferred with the other policemen; then waited until they had spread out toward the woods.

"I think we should leave them to it," said Stu. "Perhaps we could reconvene in the drawing room in, say, an hour?"

Biddy was waiting at the door to their room when Lindy reached the top of the stairs, tired, depressed, and growing increasingly frightened.

"No news?"

Lindy shook her head. "The police are here."

"I saw from the drawing room window."

Lindy turned on the shower.

Biddy followed her in and sat on the lid of the toilet. "I spent the afternoon with Marguerite."

Lindy stuck her head out of the shower curtain.

"I was trying to distract her. I didn't want her to find out about Connie being missing." Biddy shrugged. "I think she knew, but she played along. She reminisced about the good old days."

Lindy turned off the water and stepped out.

Biddy handed her a towel. "She loves this place so much. I don't know what she would do if she lost it."

"Do you really think she could lose such a huge enterprise, just because one person died? It doesn't seem possible. They must have insurance out the wazoo. Not to mention lawyers. You always have to sign waivers before you send your kid to camp. And most of these 'kids' are adults."

"Yeah, she seems to be well covered. They keep the underage campers in a separate dorm. They're strictly overseen. Those over eighteen live in the cabins and are allowed more freedom. But even then, the retreat brooks no infractions of the rules and they are numerous. I saw the list."

"So why is everyone so worried about losing the camp? It's a trust, for crying out loud."

"I guess that's what her lawyers are saying. They don't seem to be too worried about it. But Stu told her if they could prove extreme negligence, it would cost."

"I can't imagine that whatever the payout, it would even make a dent in the family's money."

"It isn't the money that is an issue with Marguerite. It's the loss of trust."

Lindy nodded. Years of dedication and love destroyed because of one accident. It wouldn't matter what the outside world thought or did, Marguerite would never forgive herself. She was like Jeremy in a magnified way. That over-responsibility. Having met Marguerite, she understood him better. She had been a great influence on his life; what affected her, would affect him. And if she were destroyed? Lindy shuddered.

"Someone walk over your grave?"

"Something like. Come downstairs with me."

Ellis's face was flushed. Jeremy stood facing the window. Biddy hesitated at the door of the drawing room. Lindy nudged her forward.

"Ah, there you are." Ellis came forward. His relief was obvious. "What would you ladies like to drink?"

"I'll do the honors." Stu stepped into the room behind them and walked toward the drinks table. His gait was a bit stiff and Lindy wondered if he had injured his hip that afternoon. He handed drinks to Lindy and Biddy and then poured one for himself. He looked more at home than either Jeremy or Ellis.

They were soon joined by Robert. "Chi-Chi's swamped with arriving guests, but she'll make sure they save some dinner for us."

"Nothing from Grappel?" Stu asked the question of Jeremy.

"They've called off the search until light."

Stu nodded. "Well, in the meantime, we had better decide on a line of battle." He gestured toward the couch. Biddy and Lindy sat down. Stu sat in one of the wing chairs that faced the couch and Ellis took the other. Robert pulled up another chair and sat down. Stu eyed Jeremy.

He walked slowly toward the couch like a recalcitrant child and sat next to Biddy. Lindy felt her move closer. She moved over to make more room.

"What do we do?" asked Ellis. His eyes looked expectantly to Stu.

"First we have to do something to stop the adverse publicity. Your statement was good, Ellis. Very genuine. But perhaps we should show a little more good will toward the community."

"Like what?"

"I don't know. Give them something."

"Like what?" repeated Ellis. "They already have a lease on two of the club houses at the lake. They have swimming and boating rights and a section for camping. There used to be rock climbing, but they couldn't afford to keep up the insurance." Ellis stood up. A look from Stu and he sat back down.

"I'm sure if we put our heads together, we can come up with something."

"They won't be satisfied until they can put up condos." Ellis sighed heavily. "Maybe things have come to that."

"Never." Marguerite stood in the doorway, supporting herself on the doorframe.

"Marguerite, should you be out of bed?" Ellis's alarm sounded in his voice.

"You give in too easily, Ellis. I won't lose this. Even if I have to fight them alone."

"Now, my dear, I didn't mean . . ."

"Shut up, Ellis, you've done enough harm already." Jeremy was already crossing to the door. He took her hand in his. "You are not going to face anything alone."

Lindy felt her stomach knotting. She tried to give Ellis a reassuring smile. He was staring at his hands.

"Ellis was only expressing his frustration," said Stu. "He wouldn't dream of letting them get their hands on your property."

"Don't patronize me, Stuart. It doesn't become you."

Stu looked befittingly chastised. "But you make everyone want to protect you. You bring out the *galant* in us mere mortals."

He was flirting with her. There was no other word for it. Jeremy's expression could have withered a sequoia. Stu was totally unaffected by it. "Take my chair." He disengaged Marguerite from Jeremy and sat her down. "Can I get you a drink?" but Jeremy had already started for the bar.

Lindy and Biddy exchanged glances. Biddy rolled her eyes just enough for Lindy to see. It said: Male power struggle in progress.

Lindy was about to lose her patience. One boy was dead, another missing. Robert was suspected of molesting a minor, and two ridiculous males were circling Marguerite like hyenas over their prey. "So does anybody have any ideas?" she asked.

Marguerite gave a hint of a smile. Barely a movement of the lips, but it spoke loud and clear.

"Larinda Gibson called this afternoon. She wanted to know if I was still going to open the fireworks on Sunday."

"Marguerite . . ."

She stopped Ellis with a lift of her hand. "I told her of course I would. I've opened the display for the last twenty years. This year will be no different. I will tell them exactly what is going on and what we are doing about it. I have friends in this town. Not everyone on the mountain is as eager to throw us to the dogs as you imagine."

* * *

Lindy and Biddy left a few minutes later and went to the restaurant to meet Rose and Mieko for dinner. They passed through the double doors that led to the annex and entered a wide hall. To their right, the reception area was bustling with arriving guests. On their left the hall was filled with alcoves and picture windows that looked out over the valley. Chairs and sofas were placed for contemplation and quiet conversation.

The restaurant was immense and yet set up to give the effect of intimacy. Plants hanging from pedestals and trees planted in huge ceramic urns separated groups of tables. Antique statues were placed throughout the room, and the combination of sculpture and greenery gave it the appearance of a secluded garden.

Chi-Chi greeted them at the door. She was dressed in a light yellow linen suit, her hair swept back and clasped in a cascade of soft waves. She led them to a table where Rose and Mieko were sitting with Peter.

"Hi, girls. We've brought along an escort," said Rose.

"Finally finished at the theater," said Peter. "I had to go back and fix a few things, since the rehearsal was cut short. I didn't think I should leave it until tomorrow."

"Glad you could make it," said Lindy. *And that you seem to be enjoying yourself,* she added to herself. It had been a long process, but Peter was pulling himself out of his self-inflicted exile from the rest of the world. He had gained weight during the last year, though he was still a bit too thin. There was no longer the line of anger etched permanently on his face, and the scars of teenage acne only leant a rugged appearance to his handsome face. And he seemed more relaxed, if that could be a word to describe him. He was still more comfortable with his lighting equipment than he was with people.

Andrea had been partially responsible for his reemergence into the world. But that had ended amicably on New Year's Eve, and Andrea had immediately taken up with Paul. Peter seemed perfectly at ease with the situation. But Juan's words came back to Lindy as she looked over the menu, and she wondered for a moment how Peter really felt about Andrea's affair with Paul.

Surely no sane person would be jealous enough to kill their lover. Especially not one who was known to be as promiscuous as Larry Cleveland.

She ordered Chicken Florentine. It was as far down the menu as she had read when the waiter returned. She handed back the menu. But what if the person wasn't sane? Teenagers were as close to being irrational as you could get—attempting to find their place in the adult world, while battling raging hormones, and not really wanting to give up the comforts of childhood. A shy, friendless boy might lash out if he thought his hero was betraying him. And then panic and run.

She shook herself. Grappel's insinuations were beginning to affect her objectivity. He had presented absolutely no evidence, just innuendoes and speculations. And if he could affect her in this way, what could he do to people who knew nothing of what was going on, were concerned for the safety of their children, or wanted to believe the worst?

What could lead a man to desire harm at the cost of the truth? She looked over at Peter, who was talking to Rose. A good man, a compassionate man, and yet, at one time he had almost killed a man because of his anger.

People committed murder for bizarre, sometimes insignificant, reasons. You could read it in the newspapers every morning, hear it on the news every night.

She had lost her appetite. She was pushing a piece of chicken around her plate, when Biddy's foot pressed hers.

Lindy looked up and then followed Biddy's gaze across the room. Marguerite had entered the restaurant and was stopping at tables, greeting the guests. Damage control, and a brilliantly strategic move. She seemed a little pale, but that could be from the muted candlelight.

Marguerite chatted for a few moments with Rebo, Juan, and two other company members sitting nearby, then said hello to a couple next to them. She called them by name. The Kravitzs. She probably knew everyone's name. The sign of an accomplished hostess. Know your guests. Especially if they're paying a fortune to send their children to your summer camp.

She stopped at their table. "Peter, Rose, I hope you've found everything you need in the theater?" Polite agreements. "And Jeremy tells me that you taught company class for the first time yesterday, Mieko." She smiled at Mieko. Marguerite, as far as Lindy knew, had never even seen Mieko except the first night when the company was being introduced at the pavilion.

Any other person would have been nonplused, but Mieko just looked attentive and said, "Yes."

"And you were quite a success."

Mieko blinked. She must be rattled, thought Lindy.

"Thank you," she said.

"You're interested in teaching?"

"I—I suppose I might be."

"We always need good teachers. It's so hard to find people who not only know their craft but can instill that knowledge in others. I know you're young, but keep teaching in mind for when you retire. It pays to think ahead." Marguerite tilted her head. "Or do you plan to return to chemistry?"

"Chemistry?" Lindy said the word out loud.

"It wasn't a secret was it?"

Mieko shook her head. "My father thought I should have something to fall back on."

"Very wise of him," said Marguerite. She took her leave and continued her round of the room.

"You have a degree in chemistry?" asked Lindy. "I had no idea."

"I knew," said Peter.

"I didn't," said Rose. "Why didn't you say so?"

Mieko's lips pressed together. On anybody else it would have been a shrug. "People tend to treat you the way they think you are, not as you really are. A degree in chemistry is a—liability."

Lindy saw Peter cock his head as he regarded the girl thoughtfully. *Bet you didn't know that*, thought Lindy.

"I see what you mean," said Biddy. "It's sometimes best just to let people take you at face value than try to construct you out of what your past has been."

"But your past is a large part of what you are," said Rose.

"Of course it is," said Biddy. "But a person is more than a sum of past experiences. They affect you, but they don't always make you what you are. It's how a person shapes his past and his future."

Lindy nodded her head in agreement. Biddy was a clear example of that. Biddy's one great love had died of AIDS. And whereas it certainly had curtailed her love life for a while, it hadn't made her bitter.

"Well, I don't know how we got so philosophic," said Biddy. "Being at an arts colony, I guess. Did you know that Eudora Welty actually spent a month here?"

The conversation turned to literature. Peter showed an unexpected knowledge of feminist writings. Rose confessed that her favorite reading matter was forensic thrillers, which led into a debate on whether genre fiction should be considered literature. Lindy hadn't had so much fun since her night course in the Brontës at the local community college.

The restaurant was empty by the time they left the table. They separated in the hallway, and Lindy and Biddy returned to the main house.

They were walking along the hall when a motion in one of the alcoves caught Lindy's attention. She stopped abruptly. Two figures were concealed partially in shadow. Two male figures, arms linked around each other, looking out into the night. Rebo's hand slipped down to Juan's butt. Lindy bolted forward.

Biddy grabbed her by the elbow. "What are you doing?"

"Stopping a public display that has no business being public." She stalked over to the couple.

Rebo turned around. "Hi, Lindelightful. Want to join us?" He raised his eyebrows and ran his tongue over his top lip.

"No, and I think the least you two could do would be to save this for the privacy of your own room."

Rebo's eyes widened. Juan frowned.

"Hey, what's wrong with you?" Juan asked.

"It isn't what's wrong with me—"

"Is something wrong with us?" asked Rebo, scrutinizing her with questioning eyes.

"Uh, no. But in light of recent events, I think you should keep your feelings and actions to yourselves."

Neither man replied, just looked at her incredulously. Lindy's stomach began to burn.

"There's nothing wrong with what we're doing. It's not like I threw Juan on the floor while the world watched on." Rebo's rich voice was suddenly cold. "Don't expect me to change my beliefs to fit this week's fashion," he said.

"You're *not* Lillian Hellman, but this could easily turn into a witch hunt. Think what you are doing."

"I'm looking at the stars with the man I love."

Lindy was taken aback by this straightforward declaration. She hadn't thought of Rebo and Juan as being in love. Just two people thrown together and making the most of it. Rebo's use of the word "love" startled her.

Juan attempted to move away from Rebo. Rebo tightened his arm around him. "Do you have a problem with that, Lindy?"

She swallowed. "You know I don't—ordinarily—but—" She felt her face grow hot. "It's just that Grappel . . ." She stopped. Tried again. "I just don't want to give him any more ammunition."

"Is that what it really is? Or is it that you don't mind knowing about us, as long as you don't have to see it?"

"Rebo . . ." Juan whispered.

"No, Juan. I'm sick and tired of always having to fight everybody just to be able to be myself. It's okay if Paul mauls Andrea in front of the entire camp, but Juan and I are not even allowed to act natural." He turned on Lindy, his voice vibrating with anger and disappointment. "It's okay for a bunch of football players to prance around in the end zone and pat each other on the butt." His voice dropped an octave. " 'Cause it's a man's sport." He cocked his head at her and said in his normal voice, "Ever wonder what goes on in those locker rooms?"

"I don't care what goes on in their locker rooms. They're not my problem."

"I'm not your problem." He paused. Took a deep breath. "You're just like all the rest of them."

She shook her head. "You know that I'm not." She looked at Juan. His eyes moved away.

"You're just as hypocritical as the rest. People like you make me sick. You're even worse than the guys that dress up in sheets and burn crosses. At least they're honest." He grabbed Juan by the hand and dragged him away.

Lindy stood alone in the alcove, heart beating against her sternum, searing heat shooting through her stomach, her throat constricted. She wanted to call him back, apologize, but she only stood there while the tears formed slowly in her eyes. Was she a hypocrite? She hadn't thought so. But she had never been confronted with . . . what? She'd never felt uncomfortable about displays of affection before, not until they had come here. It was because of what had happened. Didn't Rebo understand that?

No, he saw her as a traitor. A liar. A hypocrite. And maybe that's just what she was. How could she let one incident, one vengeful man that she didn't even like, make her turn against her friends?

She should go after him. Try to explain. But her sense of shame kept her riveted to the spot.

God, she had botched that. She meant to protect them, but she had only alienated one of her best friends. But dammit, he knew she was his friend. If he hadn't been so uptight, he would have realized what she was trying to do. It was just as much his fault as it was hers. To hell with him.

Her righteous indignation lasted her through the walk back to the main house.

Self-recrimination joined her as she went upstairs to bed.

Chapter Ten

The police returned early the next morning. Lindy was awakened by the sounds of cars in the parking lot below their room. She and Biddy watched from the window as the men received their orders from Sheriff Grappel and dispersed. One of them was accompanied by a dog. It seemed ludicrous, one dog, ten men, and thousands of acres of treacherous wilderness. Where were the helicopters? The teams of search specialists?

At breakfast, they learned that Grappel had set up a command post in the Loie Fuller studio. They would make uncomfortable housemates, thought Lindy. Fuller, an early twentieth-century iconoclast and pioneer in the use of lighting for the stage; Grappel as stuck in his ways and resistant to change as anyone could be. Or was he? Did he plan on letting things get out of hand here, so he could clean up on the proceeds from the town take-over? He was fighting a losing battle if that was the case. The town would never get this land, and in the meantime, young people were being sacrificed to someone's greed.

Unless Grappel was right about Robert, and Lindy was letting her own prejudices influence her thinking. It was no good. She had to be objective. Someone needed to look at the situation without all this emotional involvement. Even Biddy, who would normally have a list of suspects by now, seemed unable to act. She was more upset about the way Jeremy was treating her than she admitted. Lindy glanced across the table. She had never seen Biddy disengage herself from a situation before. She must be regrouping, gathering her strength. But for what?

Surely, Larry Cleveland's death was an accident. The sheriff had no evidence that she knew of that said otherwise. If any other official had been in charge of the investigation, it would have been cleared up by now.

That's what they needed, Lindy decided, as she and Biddy left the house for morning class. An unbiased investigator. But could a person just call another police station and say things were being mishandled and could they please send in somebody else? She didn't think so, but she knew who to ask.

As soon as she thought about Bill Brandecker, she became calmer. He would know just what to do. Of course, he would yell at her first. It had become almost a ritual with them—like being read your rights. Twice Bill had helped them when the company had become involved in murder. After the second case, Lindy and Bill had become friends, meeting once or twice a month for lunch when Bill's teaching schedule at John Jay College of Criminal Justice and her schedule as rehearsal director had permitted.

It was an uneasy alliance. Bill was amiable—usually—confident, refined, and wonderfully clear thinking, but he had a quick fuse, and Lindy had been the brunt of his exasperation more times than she cared to remember.

Should she call Bill and ask for his help? It was summer. He wasn't teaching. And as far as she knew, he was sweating July out in the city.

"Hey, isn't that Glen's car?" asked Biddy.

A silver BMW pulled into the driveway.

"Looks like it, but he isn't supposed to be here until tomorrow." Lindy squinted against the sun. "Nope, there are two people in the front seat."

She and Biddy continued across the driveway and the car came to a stop. The passenger door swung open.

"Hey, Mom! Wait up. It's me."

Lindy whirled around as she recognized Annie's voice. Annie? Here?

Her daughter ran across the drive, legs lean beneath her shorts, thin arms pumping as she ran. She threw herself at Lindy and hugged her. "Surprise!"

Lindy glanced over her head at Glen who was getting out of the car, then back to Annie. "Are you okay? Why aren't you in Europe? Is anything wrong?"

"Nothing, except the last three weeks of our tour got canceled. So instead of moping around in Geneva for the summer, I called Daddy and hopped on the first flight to New Jersey." Annie pulled away and looked at her. "Glad to see me?"

"You bet." Lindy gave her a squeeze.

"I didn't expect you until tomorrow," she said to Glen.

"Figured I'd drop her off and get over to the tournament." He leaned forward and gave her a peck on the cheek. "I'll try to get back tomorrow in time for the performance."

Lindy held Annie at arm's length. "I think you've grown."

Annie pulled her shoulders back and stuck out her chest. She wasn't wearing a bra. "Hope springs eternal," she said.

Lindy gave her a mother's once-over. She looked healthy and happy. She had inherited her mother's lean body, but her hair and eyes were dark brown like Glen's.

Lindy hugged her again.

"Hi, Biddy, have any murders for me to help investigate?"

Biddy winced. "Great to see you, too, Annie."

Just then two uniformed policemen emerged from the dining hall behind her.

Glen's groan made Lindy turn around.

"What's going on?" he demanded. "Annie, get back in the car."

Annie rolled her eyes at Biddy and Lindy, a habit that was reminiscent of her mother. "Yeah, what's going on? Oh boy."

Ignoring Annie's enthusiasm, Lindy turned to Glen. "One of the boys is missing. He was . . . uh . . . homesick, and he probably just hitchhiked home, but you can't be too careful."

"Lindy . . ." Glen's eyebrows drew together. He had no patience with his wife's "indulging in disaster," as he called it. If his mouth tightened, she knew she was in trouble. She watched his lips. Nothing yet.

"Oh," she said. "And there was this accident. Another boy fell down a cliff."

Glen's mouth tightened.

"It happened before we got here," she said quickly.

"Annie, get in the car. You can come with me to the golf tournament."

"Daaddy," Annie whined. Her eyes opened wide. It was Lindy's turn to roll her eyes. Glen was a sucker for his daughter, and she had learned to manipulate him while still a toddler. "Golf is sooo boring. And they all wear such ugmo clothes."

"There's really no danger," said Biddy. "One of the boys broke the rules and went to a place that was off limits. The land is clearly marked. There's no danger—"

"For anyone who follows the rules—Annie."

Annie gave Glen an angelic look then turned a wicked smile on Lindy and Biddy.

"I'll check you in," said Glen with a resigned sigh.

"Oh, I thought I'd just bunk down with Kate and Mieko." She turned to Lindy. "Are they still rooming together? Do you think they would mind?"

"Yes, they are and I'm sure they would love to have you." Annie had only been home for a few visits since Lindy had gone back to work. But she knew everybody in the company and had adopted them with the same enthusiasm she showed toward every new encounter. At twenty-two, Kate was only four years older than Annie, and there had been an instant rapport between the two girls. Why she had taken up with Mieko was a mystery. Mieko at twenty-six, was as serious, quiet, and inscrutable as Annie was energetic, emotional, and open. Maybe it was a natural consequence of being thrown together in the course of her friendship with Kate, or maybe, Mieko served as a kind of big sister.

Whatever the attraction, Lindy was glad that the girls had welcomed her. It made her feel like Annie was more a part of her life.

"I think they're at the theater," said Biddy. "Why don't I take you over, and your mom and dad can have a visit."

Annie blew Lindy a kiss and she and Biddy hurried away.

"Well, this is certainly a surprise," said Lindy. "Why didn't you call?"

Glen guffawed. "And miss seeing your expression? Anyway, Annie wouldn't let me. She wanted to surprise you."

"She did."

They walked back to the car, and Glen drove it to the front of the annex. A bellhop took the luggage. It was the same freckled-face boy she had seen cleaning glasses in the bar. He grinned a row of crooked teeth at her and led them inside.

She and Glen walked arm in arm across the lobby. Glen slipped his arm around her waist. Lindy stiffened as the image of Rebo and Juan flashed in her mind.

"What?" asked Glen.

"Nothing." She put her arm around him. It wasn't the same. She and Glen were married and . . . well, they were married. "Nothing," she repeated and gave him a squeeze.

Glen and Annie's suitcases were already in their room.

"The kid must have run all the way up the back stairs to beat us here," said Lindy.

"Be sure to give him a big tip," said Glen.

Lindy frowned.

"I can't stay. I just came to drop Annie off. Are you sure she'll be all right?"

"Positive. You can't stay a little while?"

"No. There's registration and a party. Then dinner." Glen paused. "It's a benefit. Lots of money for the Wurtheiser Foundation."

"I understand."

"And if I'm going to miss tomorrow's dinner to be here, I have to be very visible today."

"I said I understood."

"But I can stay an extra day. Until Wednesday morning."

"Great."

"I have to leave for Paris on Wednesday night, but I told Haddie to pack for me while I was here." Haddie was their Jamaican housekeeper. She had started with them as Cliff's nanny and had never left, and though she had never lived in, she was a part of the family as well as the brain behind the running of the Haggerty household.

"Paris? Again? This is the fifth time this year."

"The main operations have moved there. In fact, I'll probably be spending a lot more time there in the future."

"Oh." She scrutinized her husband. He had begun playing more golf, had taken up jogging. When Lindy had gone back to work, the signs of middle age had begun to appear in his gut and love handles. He was much sleeker now. Her working had been good for him, too. She always felt guilty about working when she had a family to take care of. But Glen was out of town more and more; and with the kids off at school, there was no reason for her to sit quietly at home. "Well, I'm glad you'll be able to stay longer."

"Me, too." He drew her to him and kissed her. Lindy put her arms around him, feeling herself respond.

"But I'd better hit the road if I'm going to do my share of fundraising." He gave her another kiss. This time a quick peck on the cheek.

"Sure," she said, trying not to let her disappointment sound in her voice. "I'll walk you down."

Lindy watched until the BMW had disappeared down the drive. Then she just stared into the space it had vacated. She should be grateful that he had to leave before he found out any of the details of what was going on in the camp, but she just felt lonely. In thirty-six hours he would be back, and then he would insist that she and Annie go home. Glen liked an ordered world.

He was well suited to his job in telecommunications. He wired the world and if something went wrong, he fixed it.

Well, he wasn't the only person in the communications business. What was performing arts if not communication? And when something in that world went wrong, you fixed it. Hell, that was her job. When something in a dance was not quite right, a wrong foot, a wrong count, or a traffic jam on stage, you fixed it.

But how the hell was she going to fix the disaster that had been brought on by Larry Cleveland's death? And with Annie here to worry about. If she had known that Annie would be coming home, she could have taken a few weeks off from work, and wouldn't be in this mess. It wasn't even like Jeremy needed her. Maybe she should side with Glen and insist that Annie go home. Maybe she should go with them.

She began walking slowly toward the theater. Annie had probably gotten the full details of the last few days—down to the nittus-grittus of Larry's sexual activity. She'd never be dragged away, now. She might have Glen's coloring, but she was her mother's daughter.

Company class had ended. Peter was out front killing the stage lights. "She's backstage," he said. "She's grown into a beautiful girl."

"She has, hasn't she?" said Lindy.

Peter shrugged. "Like her mom." He turned back to what he was doing.

Hmm, thought Lindy. A foray into gallantry, Peter. Not bad. She smiled all the way backstage.

All eight girls of the company were crowded into Andrea, Mieko, and Kate's dressing room. In the center of the crush, sat Annie, eyes wide, leaning forward in her folding chair absorbing every morsel of gossip.

With a sense of dismay, Lindy added herself to the melange. Somehow, the company had heard everything about the investigation. There was a very sophisticated grapevine in the theater world. Almost nothing went unknown.

After a few minutes, the group broke up for lunch. Lindy and Annie were walking down the hall to the stage door when Rebo came out of his dressing room. He froze for a second, flicked her an angry look, and strode down the hall in front of them.

"What's wrong with him?" whispered Annie.

Lindy hesitated, wondering if she should tell Annie about their fight. Better to tell her now before she heard Rebo's side of the story, and Lindy had no doubt that she would. Like her mother, Annie had an innate curiosity about the world around her. It was an onerous burden more times than not, a quality that propelled them headlong into life without considering the consequences. She couldn't change Annie any more than she could change herself, but at least she could try to guide her through the first rough passages.

"We had a fight," she said.

"That much is obvious," said Annie. "About what's been going on?"

"Indirectly. He and Juan were, uh, together at the annex last night." She faltered. She had never been forced to use stupid euphemisms before. What was happening to her? She sounded just like a Victorian spinster. "They were just enjoying each other's company." She paused. "Anyway, I told them I thought they should be more discreet."

"Because of Robert and Larry Cleveland?"

It hadn't taken her long to figure that one out. She should have known Annie would understand. She nodded.

"No wonder he's mad. You're supposed to stand by your friends, Mom, not try to change them."

Taken aback, Lindy pushed down the lump that was swelling in her throat. Even her daughter thought she was wrong.

"Annie, life can be pretty nasty. I just thought they should cool it. He'll get over it."

Annie's lips tightened. She had picked that up from Glen.

"They need to be thinking of our image until this is cleared up," said Lindy.

Annie's eyebrows quirked together. "When were you ever concerned about what other people thought?"

"Since I've become acquainted with murder."

"Daddy's going to be really pissed."

"Watch your language," said Lindy.

"Cool Jeep," said Annie as they came out of the student dining hall an hour later. The archaeologists' rusty heap was parked just outside the front door of the house. Donald Parker stood leaning against the dented fender, reading an almost-as-battered paperback. He threw it into the back seat as the two women approached.

"Hi, Donald," said Lindy. Annie stood with an expectant smile on her face. "This is my daughter Annie. Annie, Donald Parker. He's one of the archaeologists working on the premises."

"An archaeologist? Really?"

Donald shrugged slightly. "Just a student archaeologist so far."

"That's so exciting. Is your site near here?"

Leave it to Annie to use the appropriate archaeological term, thought Lindy. She interrupted before Donald could start on his favorite subject.

"What are you doing here?"

Donald pulled his gaze from Annie. "Oh, the old man's inside. We saw the Jeep again." He paused a moment to explain to Annie about the black Jeep.

"Anyway, this time we decided to watch it more closely. Got close enough to see the glint off the surveying equipment. The old man went ballistic. Practically had to hold him down."

Donald turned again to Annie. Lindy jumped in. "Did you see who it was?"

"Uh, no. He . . ." Donald nodded his head toward the house. "We convinced him to come tell Ms. Easton, instead of attacking them with our spades and sifting racks. I drove him over."

Just then the door opened and Dr. Van Zandt came out onto the porch followed by Marguerite.

"Really Emil," she said. "If there is someone trespassing—"

"No 'if,' Marguerite."

"Quite so. I'll inform the—the authorities. No, on second thought, I'll have the groundskeeper organize the staff to patrol the land. Would you be able to talk to Rogers before you leave? You can explain to him where you saw the surveyors."

"Excellent idea." Emil Van Zandt took Marguerite's hand in his and brought it to his lips. Donald looked amused. Annie was staring in star-struck wonder.

Van Zandt pulled his canvas hat out of his back pocket and crammed it on his head.

"Paaarker," he bellowed as he took the stairs two at a time.

"Yes, sir." Donald pull himself to full attention.

"Stay here."

Donald relaxed. "Yes, sir."

Van Zandt trotted off toward the lake and the groundskeeper's office.

Lindy and Annie said their goodbyes and made their way to the theater for the student rehearsal.

Before they had crossed the drive, Chi-Chi came running out of the annex service door. Lindy slowed down.

"Are you going to rehearsal?" asked Chi-Chi breathlessly.

"We're on our way now," said Lindy.

"If you have time, could you drop by the bungalow to check on Robert? He didn't sleep well last night." She lowered her voice, even though there was no one around. "His antihistamines aren't doing the job, but he didn't want to bother Dr. Addison. I strictly forbade him to go to the rehearsal today. He needs his rest."

"You want me to make sure he doesn't try to sneak in?" said Lindy.

Chi-Chi nodded. "I'd go myself. But the butcher just sent over a hundred pounds of chicken. They were supposed to send fifty of chicken and thirty of beef. And they forgot the veal completely. The chef is in an uproar."

Lindy patted her shoulder. "Get back to your chicken; I'll see about Robert."

"Tell him I'll be over as soon as I get this mess straightened out." Chi-Chi ran back toward the kitchen, waved at them over the back of her head, and disappeared inside.

"Go on over to the theater if you want," said Lindy to Annie. "Or you can hang out by the lake if you'd rather. Just follow the path around that rock formation. It's quite lovely."

"Don't worry about me, Mom. Go on with what you have to do. I can entertain myself."

Lindy nodded and went to make a quick visit to Robert. She

turned to give her daughter a wave, but Annie was deep in conversation with Donald Parker.

Lindy tiptoed across the porch of the bungalow and peered through the screen door. There was no light in the living room except the glow of the computer screen and the gooseneck lamp that sat on Robert's desk. Should she knock or just go in?

Then she saw Robert asleep at his desk. He was slumped forward, head resting on a jumble of papers. He must be tired, thought Lindy. He hadn't even folded his arms to pillow his head. They were hanging down by the sides of his chair.

She stood at the door deliberating on whether to wake him and move him to the couch, or to let him stay where he was.

Better to let sleeping dogs lie, she thought. She turned to go, then thought of Chi-Chi finding him slouched over the desk. She'd better wake him. If he was tired enough to conk out in his chair, he would probably go right back to sleep.

He must hate having to miss the preparations for the students' performance. It was obvious that rehearsal was where he was most vital. He seemed so inconsequential in the rest of his life. How awful to have your career cut short by an accident. Achilles tendons were as debilitating for dancers as they were for their namesake. Knees and ankles could be repaired, but the Achilles was never quite the same, even after surgery. It was heartbreaking. No wonder he needed Chi-Chi's tender love.

Lindy stepped inside, careful not to let the door slam behind her. She moved quietly toward the desk and touched Robert's shoulder. "Robert," she whispered.

No response. The man was dead to the world. "Robert." She gave him a little shake. Nothing.

"Robert, wake up," she said more loudly. A frisson of panic seized her, the same irrational fear that gripped a mother gazing at her sleeping baby, holding her breath until the child began to stir.

Robert didn't stir. She grabbed both his shoulders. His head lolled on the desk.

"Robert." This time she shouted his name.

She pulled him up and pushed him against the back of the chair, knocking over the nearly empty glass of Chi-Chi's power drink. The chair rolled away and his head fell back.

Then she saw the bottle of pills on the desk. He had been lying on it.

This time she let the screen door slam. She raced up the path. Two policeman were going in to the Loie Fuller studio. She slowed to a walk until they were out of sight. She wouldn't inform them now; they couldn't even search for a lost boy properly. She had to find Dr. Addison. She raced ahead, turned right down Two Rocks Way, and burst into the infirmary without knocking.

No one was there.

She spun around as if she could conjure up the doctor. Knocked on the door to the examining room, then opened it without waiting for a response. Dark except for the emergency light on the wall.

Dining hall. Or should she get the police? No. Grappel would interpret things in the worst light. She took the graveled path at a full run almost tripping as her feet lagged behind her body.

Two people were sitting on the bench across from the statue of Mercury. Stu and Dr. Addison. Their laughter registered in her brain; then the change of their expressions as she hurtled toward them.

"Robert." The name exploded out of her searing lungs. She grabbed Dr. Addison by the arm. "Pills. Bungalow."

A split second of comprehension and Adele was headed toward the infirmary. Stu pushed himself off the bench. "We'll wait for her at the bungalow."

Taking her by the elbow, he hurried her back down the path, moving at a speed that didn't seem possible for a man dependent on a cane.

She rushed ahead of him and into the room. And stopped.

Robert still sat in the chair. But the chair was facing the computer, not the desk. Lindy walked slowly toward him. Could she have hit the chair in her panic to get the doctor? Could it have turned around and stopped exactly in front of the computer screen? Maybe Robert had roused long enough to move it himself?

"Robert." She commanded him to get up.

But Robert didn't move.

The screen door slammed and Dr. Addison was kneeling by the sleeping man. She checked his pulse, lifted his eyelids, put her ear to his nose with a rapidity that left Lindy dazed.

"Where are the pills?"

Lindy pointed to the desk. She was afraid she might cry.

Dr. Addison snatched the bottle up and rolled it in her hands. "Benadryl. Empty. It must have been the last of an old bottle. I just refilled his prescription last week."

She pulled a stethoscope from her bag and ripped open the front of Robert's shirt. Buttons went flying.

"He's alive?" Stu had drained of color down to his lips.

"Yes."

"Thank God." He lifted a trembling hand to his eyes and rubbed.

"Should I get the police?" asked Lindy.

"No," said Adele. It was an answer that brooked no argument. Lindy swallowed.

"I need to get him back to the infirmary—quickly. I don't understand what could be causing this reaction." She looked at Lindy with an intensity that was frightening. "Without informing the police until I know what has happened. Imagine what Grappel will make of this."

"I'll get someone to carry him." Lindy ran out the door. She slowed to a walk as she passed the Fuller studio, then raced on again.

Ahead of her someone was walking toward the theater. Rebo. Damn. But he would be able to carry Robert to the infirmary without help.

"Rebo," she yelled.

He looked up and started to walk away.

"I need your help!"

He kept walking.

"Now!" It was a high-pitched scream. He turned around and reached her with the speed of a lean animal.

"It's Robert," she said already running back to the bungalow. She heard Rebo's steps behind her.

Robert was lying on the floor between the computer console and the desk. Dr. Addison bent over him. The chair had been pushed out of the way. Dr. Addison lifted her chin at the newcomer. Effortlessly, Rebo scooped Robert up and carried him out, already running. The others followed. Rebo turned immediately to the right.

"The infirmary is that way," yelled Lindy pointing down Two Rocks Way.

"Shortcut," he said. The others followed behind him, through trees and brush. Once Stu tripped on a rock that jutted up from the ground. Lindy grabbed his arm as he staggered and propelled him onward.

By the time she and Stu arrived at the infirmary, Dr. Addison was in the examination room with Robert. Rebo sat on the edge of her desk.

Lindy looked at him expectantly, momentarily forgetting their fight.

"She said not to disturb her." He was staring at his sandals.

"Thanks."

A slight shrug of his shoulders. He didn't look up. He wasn't going to let her off easy. But he had come through when she needed him.

"We should inform Chi-Chi," said Stu. He was still catching his breath, and the sentence came out in a rush of air.

"I'll go," said Rebo and pushed himself away from the desk.

"Don't alarm her."

Rebo shot Stu a caustic look and let the door slam behind him.

Neither Stu nor Lindy spoke when he had gone. Stu eased himself into the chair by the desk. Lindy paced back and forth across the floor, stopping to peer out the door on each turn.

In a few minutes, she saw Rebo and Chi-Chi hurrying toward them. Chi-Chi wore a white chef's apron over her jeans and blouse. It hung almost to her ankles.

She burst into the room and headed for the examination room door.

Stu stopped her. "Adele is examining him. She'll let us know how he is as soon as she can."

"What happened?" She looked at Stu, then turned to Lindy. "What happened?" she repeated.

"Chi-Chi, my dear," said Stu . His voice was quiet and controlled. "It seems that Robert . . ."

Chi-Chi just shook her head, continuously, mechanically, as Stu told her about Lindy finding Robert passed out at his desk, apparently of a drug overdose.

Lindy frowned. They didn't know that he had overdosed. It might just be a reaction to his medication; she had seen that happen before. She started to say so, but a look from Stu stopped her before she could utter a word.

Had Dr. Addison said something to him while she had been looking for help? The back of her neck began to tingle. Good God. The implications would be—what? That Robert couldn't cope with the strain of being questioned by the police, or by the events at camp, or Grappel's insinuations? The tingling moved to her stomach. Her throat felt dry. Or could those insinuations be closer to the truth than anyone wanted to admit? Surely, not.

Lindy glanced at Chi-Chi who sat perfectly still in the straight-back chair that Stu had pulled close to his. She admired her self-control. Instead of crying, wringing her hands, or pacing as Lindy had been doing minutes before, Chi-Chi sat calmly waiting. Marshaling her strength? wondered Lindy. It reminded her of Biddy. Two strong women. In control. Self-reliant. Or were they? Maybe, their sense of self-preservation maintained the facade of strength, a kind of emotional camouflage.

Footsteps sounded on the wood of the porch outside. Lindy sprang toward the door to turn the person away. Byron Grapple's simian outline loomed at her from behind the screen.

Unconsciously, Lindy looked at Stu.

Byron opened the screen door. "Chi-Chi."

It was all he said. He moved across the office and stopped at the examination room door. "He in there?"

"Yes, he is, Sheriff," Stu said firmly. "Dr. Addison is with him, and I'm certain that she would appreciate it if you would wait here with the rest of us."

Grappel's lips twitched as if suppressing a smile. Lindy fought the urge to slap him. Instead, she stepped toward Chi-Chi and put a protective arm around her.

Chapter
Eleven

"Sick, huh?" Byron Grappel pierced each of them with a skeptical eye. "So sick that he had to be carried to the infirmary like a baby." He ended this statement with a disgusted look at Chi-Chi. Lindy felt Chi-Chi's shoulder tense beneath her hand, and she tightened her grasp, warning her not to take the bait.

She was thinking furiously. Could they avoid talking to him until Adele emerged from the examination room? Maybe Adele would be able to explain what had happened. Say that he had reacted to the Benadryl. That it had been a mistake, and not what it appeared on the surface—that Robert had taken an overdose of some unknown drug.

They had left everything in the bungalow, except the bottle of pills. Lindy had seen Adele slip it into her pocket. It was a natural thing to do—she would want to refer to the dosage written on the label.

The silence in the room vibrated with tension. "I've had the bungalow secured," said Grappel. "Maybe I'd just better have a look around while we're waiting for the doc to do her thing." No one moved until the door had closed behind him.

"I'll be right back," Lindy said quietly.

Stu glanced at Lindy. "We'll be outside, Chi-Chi. Let us know the minute Adele comes out."

Chi-Chi only nodded. She had no energy for them. She was willing her husband to live. Lindy felt the power of her will. It pulsated from her. Lindy gave her shoulder another squeeze, and Stu followed her to the porch.

"What should we do?" asked Lindy quietly enough so the sound wouldn't carry back into the infirmary.

"Wait and see, I suppose."

Lindy sucked on the inside of her cheeks. Her mouth was dry. "I'm taking a walk," she said at last.

"I'll come with you."

Lindy nodded and began to walk down the path to the bungalow. She passed the spot of torn branches and trampled plants that marked their emergence from the shortcut. "This way."

Stu shook his head. "Once was enough for me. I'll take the path and meet you there."

Of course he knew where she was going, but she was glad that he was taking the long way. It would give her a chance to do some snooping. She set off through the trees.

A uniformed man was standing outside the bungalow when she came out of the woods. She wondered if the sheriff was already inside. As soon as the thought came to her, she saw Grappel walking up the path. She ducked back into the trees.

Grappel stepped onto the porch, then turned around and looked straight in her direction.

"You can come out now," he called in a low drawl.

Great sleuth, Graham, she thought with disgust. She stepped out into the clearing.

"Guess you wanna to take a look around." God, the man was ugly. Or maybe it was just the permanent sneer that made him seem so. "Might as well come on in."

Grappel tipped his head and motioned toward the door, a yokel mimicking the gallantry of the elite.

Lindy's eyes widened. She knew from experience that civilians weren't allowed in a secured area. She hurried forward before Grappel changed his mind. The other policeman followed her inside.

Her stomach rumbled as she took in the living room, still dark but for the light from the lamp and computer screen.

Grappel stopped in front of the computer. A green glow outlined the bulky muscles of his shoulders and arms.

"Well, what do we have here?" He sounded pleased.

Lindy felt her whole body go hot. Little prickling pin points rushed across her skin. She took a step forward.

He motioned the policeman over. "Take a look at this, White, and then go get the Polaroid."

Grappel moved aside to let the policeman look at the screen.

"Jeez," he said. "I'll get the camera." He passed Lindy on his way to the door.

"I'm really sorry," he whispered.

"What?" asked Grappel.

"Nothing. I'll get the camera." And he was gone.

"Might as well take a look," Grappel said again.

Lindy looked around and then realized he was talking to her. This had to be highly unorthodox. Instinctually, she summoned all of her rehearsal instincts. If you're going to look, look for the details, she told herself. A misplaced hand, a right foot instead of a left, one dancer too far downstage. Memorize the room. Look for the little mistakes.

"Well, come on. You wanted to see. Here's your chance." Grappel paused, then a satisfied smile spread across his face. "Might as well have an outside witness."

Her knees felt shaky. Witness? Witness to what? What the hell was going on?

She forced herself to move toward Grappel, afraid of what she might see. What hadn't she seen before that made him so satisfied now? The possibilities made her nauseous.

"I guess you could say that this wraps up the whole thing. Couldn't prove it before, but I can now." He moved aside.

Lindy stared at the screen.

I can't live with what I did to Larry Cleveland. You should never have married me.

Grappel scratched his head. Lindy was dimly aware of his arm movement in her peripheral vision as she tried to make sense of the words on the screen. "Never had evidence left on a computer before. Can't really put it in an evidence bag. Maybe I should make a backup disk."

For a wild moment Lindy wondered if she could lunge for the delete key before Grappel stopped her. But he'd be able to retrieve the text. And the other cop had seen it as well. No, it was out of her hands now. Robert had been responsible for Larry Cleveland's death. If he lived, he would be brought to trial. She might even have to testify against him. Jeremy would never forgive her. Chi-Chi would never forgive her. None of them—*Stop rambling,* she pleaded with her brain.

Grappel reached for the case of floppies.

"Stop." Lindy's voice was so strident that Grappel halted, hand outstretched, and looked around.

"Shouldn't you dust for prints before you touch anything?"

"What for?"

What for? Was the man a raving lunatic or just stupid beyond belief? "Because if nobody saw Robert type that on the computer, there's no evidence to say that he did." Lindy couldn't believe that she might be sealing Robert's fate, but a fragment of something she couldn't put her finger on told her things were not as they appeared.

Grappel hesitated.

Maybe she should let him muck up the scene. That way if they accused Robert of anything, he could get off on a technicality. Horror at her thoughts stopped her. If Robert had seduced or killed Larry Cleveland, he should be punished. It was a hideous crime. She shouldn't try to protect a monster that could do that to a seventeen-year-old boy. *If,* he had done it. It was a big *if* in Lindy's mind. Evidence or not, she had seen Robert in rehearsal. He was committed to his work and to his students. She didn't believe that he was capable of such a heinous crime.

Stop thinking, she pleaded again. Just look.

"Yeah, I guess you're right," said Grappel. "Don't want to contaminate the evidence."

The young policeman returned with the Polaroid and started taking shots of the room and closeups of the computer.

"You find the body?" asked Grappel moving out of the camera's way.

"Robert isn't dead," she retorted.

"Maybe, maybe not."

Repulsion welled up inside her.

"Hey, White, what the hell do you think you're doing?" Grappel barked out the question.

White turned around and held up a metal box. "I brought the fingerprint kit."

"You know how to use it?"

The young man blushed. "As well as anybody, I guess."

"Get on with it, then. Don't screw it up. So did you?"

Lindy realized his question had been directed to her.

She took a deep breath. "I found Robert asleep at his desk."

"That's what you call it, sleepin'?"

"Yes."

"Well, I guess you just better accompany me to my little office over there and answer some questions."

"I'd like to talk to my lawyer first." She thought for a terrifying moment that she was going to laugh. It was such an inane thing to say. Did witnesses even have the right to counsel? She bit the inside of her cheek until the tears came to her eyes. At least it kept her from breaking into hysterical laughter at the absurdity of the situation.

"Ain't no reason to start crying, now. I won't be swayed by a woman's tears."

She bit down harder. She blinked furiously and managed to get one tear to trickle down her face. She took a step closer to Grappel, to make sure he wouldn't miss her performance.

"Oh damn," he said. "White, forget the prints. I'll do 'em. Take her out of here."

"Yes, sir."

"And don't let her talk to anybody."

White took her elbow and led her outside. "I'm real sorry about this, ma'am."

"Are you?" she said defensively. "It seems to me that you people are trying a little too hard to find something wrong here."

"Oh no, ma'am." He shook his head. "You don't mind the sheriff. He does have a bug—well, he doesn't much care for the Eastons."

"No."

"But Ms. Marguerite. She's been good to the town. She's got a lot of friends there."

This was the first time Lindy had heard anything except how much the town wanted her land.

"She does?"

"Yes, ma'am. Most of us worked up here when we were kids. She treated us real nice and the pay was good. And the annex buys everything it can locally. And she donates a bunch of money to town projects and she takes an interest in the people."

"What about the people who want to build ski resorts?"

"There's always folks who aren't satisfied . . . in any town, I expect. But they're not most of us. Life isn't so easy all the time, but it could be a lot worse."

Lindy nodded.

"Would you just tell Ms. Marguerite that Abel White asked after her?"

"Of course. I'm sure she'll be grateful for your concern."

"You wanna go back to pumpin' gas, White?" yelled Grappel from the porch. "Or are you gonna finish up on those prints?"

Abel frowned and started to move away. "I never had to pump gas," he said quickly. "I made enough working here summers to go to school all winter. Comin', Sheriff." He trotted off toward the bungalow.

Grappel waited until he was inside, then strolled toward Lindy. "Now, Ms. Graham. Let's see about contacting your lawyer."

Situational ethics. Rose had used the term on their nightmare cruise to the Caribbean. Lindy had had to look up the definition. But how could you know what was ethical if you had to redefine it every time you got into a new situation?

This was only the first thought she had as she followed Grappel to the police sedan. He had changed his mind about questioning her at the studio. Once she had made that crack about the lawyer, he had decided to take her into the police station. She shuddered. What the hell was she going to do? She didn't even have a lawyer, except the firm that had closed their mortgage and made their wills. She wasn't even sure if she remembered the name, Hiller, Campbell, and . . . or was it Hillyer, Coville, and . . . Oh shit, she was in trouble. That's just what Grappel knew would happen. He wanted to rattle her. Then he would manipulate her answers. She could see it coming as surely as she could anticipate a turn going off balance, just by the preparation. She was an idiot. And where was Stu? Had he given up and gone to the house? Surely he wasn't still lurking in the woods.

Panic seized her as she saw the police car being driven across the drive toward them. What was she going to tell them? *Think now, so you'll get it right before they start asking questions.* But how little could she say? "Withholding evidence is not only a crime, Lindy, it can be very dangerous." Bill's words came back to her so clearly that she turned around to see if he had spoken. No such luck. But she did see Stu hurrying toward them. Thank God.

"What's going on here, Sheriff?"

"There was a note on the computer," Lindy blurted out.

Stu's mouth opened, and a look of disbelief spread across his features. "What?"

"A confession," said the sheriff complacently.

"No," murmured Stu. "No."

"I have some questions to ask this witness. And she wants to talk to her lawyer. Figure we might as well wait for him at the station, where I can put my feet up."

With a jolt of brilliant clarity, Lindy understood why people might be driven to murder. Because, at this moment, she felt like killing Byron Grappel.

"I'll come," said Stu.

"Suit yourself."

Grappel opened the back door, pushed Lindy's head down, and helped her into the backseat, just like any common criminal. And then a larger concern hit her. Annie was here, and her mother was being dragged ignominiously to the police station. Glen would be back tomorrow—in time to get her out of jail. What on earth had she done, just because of her antipathy for Grappel and her desire to protect her friends?

Stu got in beside her and propped his cane against the seat.

"Well, here we are," he said.

"You're a lawyer?"

"Among other things." He patted her knee. "All will be well." But his words didn't console her. Stu looked worried.

Stu guided her through the questioning. Lindy was glad to see that her words were being recorded by a tape recorder, and she insisted on waiting until they were transcribed before returning to the retreat.

The typist hadn't been happy about staying late, but Stu insisted that to cause Lindy any more distress would be harassment. Grappel consented with a brusque grunt. She made Stu read every word along with her. It seemed okay. She hadn't elaborated, just tried to remember exactly what had happened. The few times she attempted to speculate—for instance, why the chair was in a different position than when she had left—both Grappel and Stu had cut her off. She didn't attempt any more speculation after that. If they were going to pursue this, she would wait for her day in court. The idea sent a chill down her spine. Her heart raced and sputtered as she mulled over her answers as the police car drove them back across the mountain.

Sandiman opened the door, looking pale and drawn.

"Is Robert okay?"

"Alive. They are waiting for you in the drawing room."

Lindy's feet dragged as she followed Sandiman across the hall. Only Stu's presence behind her prevented her from bolting up the stairs and ducking under the covers of her bed.

Every head in the room looked at her expectantly—Marguerite, Chi-Chi, Ellis, Biddy, Adele, and Annie.

Lindy could hear her breath rushing out in shallow jerks. If she had said anything that pointed to Robert as the possible seducer of Larry Cleveland, they would turn on her. They had no idea that a more horrible accusation had been made by the sheriff. The corners of her mouth trembled.

Her eyes searched out Biddy's. Biddy gave her a reassuring smile and patted the cushion next to her on the couch. Ellis was already pouring her a glass of wine. Lindy sat down. She wanted to throw herself into Biddy's arms and cry. *Pull yourself together,* she begged.

Annie came and sat on the arm of the couch next to her.

Don't you know better than to sit on furniture arms, Lindy thought automatically. It was a ridiculous thing to be thinking. No one was concerned about good manners now. Annie slid off the arm until she was wedged into the space next to Lindy. Lindy put her arm around her and attempted a smile. "Never a dull moment around the Haggertys."

Annie smiled weakly. She looked young and vulnerable. She had learned pretty quickly that murder was not so much fun.

Waves of shock coursed through her like molten lava. Murder. It was what she had been trying to deny all day. Someone had murdered Larry Cleveland. She knew it and she knew that it wasn't Robert. Because suddenly all the "ifs" fell jarringly into place. Someone had tried to murder Robert, too.

Ellis handed her a glass. She almost dropped it.

"Mom, are you okay?"

"Sure, just kind of wiped out." She needed to be okay, and then maybe Annie would be, too.

Patting Annie's shoulder, she looked toward Chi-Chi. Her face was swollen from crying. She had broken down at last. Adele stood behind her chair. Without her glasses, her eyes were sharply focused—and angry.

"They've taken Robert to County," she said anticipating Lindy's question. "Under suicide watch." Her dark eyes flashed.

"They wouldn't let me go with him." Chi-Chi began crying again. "I'm sorry." She covered her eyes with one hand.

"You have every right to be upset." Marguerite's statement trembled with emotion. Ellis moved toward his sister, but she brushed him aside. She sat rigidly in her chair. The fine features of her face were set with determination. Gone was the gracious lady that had met them on their arrival, gone the weakened woman that had swooned the day they took Robert to the police station.

Her demeanor sent a chill through Lindy. Marguerite would protect her family, friends, and her mother's dream at all costs. Lindy could see it in her eyes. In the way she held her graceful hands deadly still in her lap. She would crush whoever tried to hurt them. Lindy just hoped she wouldn't be caught in the cross fire.

"He's going to be okay!" Chi-Chi's words cut into her thoughts. "He didn't do it. He didn't try to kill himself. He didn't have anything to do with Larry Cleveland falling down the cliff. He didn't."

"Of course he didn't," said Ellis. Everyone else added their assurances. Except for Stu who glanced at Lindy and looked down at his glass.

Lindy froze. Had she said something to the sheriff that would prove otherwise? Her mind went blank as fear burned through her. She had been so careful to be precise. And she was sure it wasn't attempted suicide. She could feel it. She could also feel someone watching her. She forced herself to look up. Adele and Marguerite were both staring at her. Were they daring her to disagree, or were they inviting her to make her stand with them?

The three of them stayed locked in each other's eyes, until the door opened and Jeremy came in with Rose and Peter close behind him. Sandiman closed the door and moved over to the drinks table. Jeremy followed him and poured himself a hefty amount of deep amber cognac.

He looked pretty close to death himself. Eyes dull, his complexion the color of cold ashes. He had been left to carry on the rehearsals by himself, while he should have been free to console Marguerite and Chi-Chi. He was worried about Robert, and probably about what Lindy had said to the police. Why hadn't Biddy helped him, instead of staying with Marguerite? Then she saw Biddy's face and understood. He had pushed her away again.

Rose and Peter stood uncomfortably on the fringe of the group and declined the drinks Sandiman offered them.

"We just dropped in to make sure that everything is on for tomor-row night," said Rose.

"The kids are ready. Is it a go?" asked Peter.

Lindy looked to Marguerite.

"Yes," she said. "Chi-Chi?"

"Of course, Robert would want us to."

"Really, Marguerite," said Ellis. "In light of all that's happened, we would be wise to . . ."

"God damn it, Ellis." Jeremy banged his brandy snifter on the table. It caught the edge of a marble trivet and shattered. Blood seeped from his hand.

Biddy was on her feet.

"Biddy, don't," said Lindy, but Biddy was already moving toward Jeremy.

You're just setting yourself up for another rebuff, she thought.

Biddy didn't stop until she was right in front of him. Ignoring his bleeding hand, she tilted her head up until she was looking straight into his face.

"Jeremy," she said. "Get a grip." She turned and marched out of the room.

The door shut behind her. Jeremy's face grew paler if that was possible. Rose, Peter and Lindy stared in open-mouthed astonish-ment. The others held an embarrassed silence until Adele crossed to Jeremy and began cleaning his hand with a towel that Sandiman had produced from a drawer in the table.

"Sorry," he said. "It was an accident."

"We're all very tired. Let's get some rest. Tomorrow will take all our strength," said Marguerite. She rose. Everyone else did, too. "You'll stay with us tonight, Chi-Chi. I've had the room next to mine readied for you."

Chi-Chi set her lips.

"Don't protest. You are not going to stay in the bungalow by your-self tonight. Come along, dear."

Chi-Chi followed her silently out of the room. The rest of them followed, except Stu and Ellis who were standing before the win-dow in quiet conversation.

In the hallway, Adele pulled Lindy aside. "Come to my office in the morning. We need to talk."

Lindy nodded and went upstairs to deal with Biddy.

Biddy sat on the windowsill. A cool breeze lifted the lace curtains. Lindy came to stand behind her, and they both stared out into the night air. The sky was an inky backdrop, studded with a million stars.

"The Queen of the Night's aria in *The Magic Flute*," said Biddy.

Lindy nodded.

"I've really done it now."

"Well, you certainly got everyone's attention."

"What did he do?"

"Stood there while Adele cleaned his hand."

"I hurt him. I shouldn't have done that."

"I think you had your reasons."

Biddy took a deep breath. "It was for his own good."

"I know."

Chapter
Twelve

Another day. Lindy blinked her eyes open without moving the rest of her. She concentrated on the raised pattern of the coverlet until her eyes came into focus. She had hardly moved during the night; the coverlet was unwrinkled.

Her body felt drugged, but she recognized the feeling for what it was. It was "tour tired." Waking up on tour was always worse than waking up at home. Each day on the road was crammed with back-to-back events, heavily scheduled so that there was hardly any downtime to regroup. You had to grab rest in small unplanned doses. A person had to be really flexible in order to make the most of what little relaxation time there was. It was an exhausting regimen. And when you were so tired that you thought you would die if you had to go on another second, you went on anyway. Then it was over, and for days or weeks nothing much happened; a few days off while you pulled yourself back to a functioning level, then daily rehearsals with an outside world waiting to distract and rejuvenate you.

Feast or famine. It was a way of life. An insular world that magnified every insult, every over-reaction, every insecurity. But it was also a glorious life culminating in pride, praise, and glimpses into the state that athletes called "the zone." Dancers had known about "the zone" for years. They just hadn't named it. When your body goes into overdrive, and you become the dance, the music, the sheer muscularity of the movement. And you soar.

Lindy's thoughts dropped painfully back to earth. And when you added accidents and possible suicide and murder to the schedule . . . the coverlet felt like a lead blanket. She shoved it aside and sat up. Biddy was still sleeping. Lindy had spent the night in Biddy's room, because she didn't want Biddy to be alone. She had heard her up wandering the room during the night, but after asking once if she were okay, Lindy had left her alone.

She forced herself into the bathroom and composed herself to face the day.

When she came downstairs for coffee, Peter was in the restaurant, sitting at a table by himself. She sat down across from him.

He handed her a piece of folded paper. "Jeremy's gone for the day. Says he'll try to be back in time for the afternoon rehearsal."

Lindy listened to his words as she read the same message written on the paper.

"That's all? He's gone? Didn't he say where?"

Peter stretched back in the chair. "I didn't see him. This was left in my box at Reception." He studied Lindy for a minute then put his hands behind his head.

"To the hospital?"

"Maybe, but Chi-Chi's here, looking about as substantial as that." He nodded toward the paper Lindy was holding. "If they wouldn't let Chi-Chi see Robert, I doubt if Jeremy will have any better luck."

Lindy let out a low growl.

"I know. We need him here. But he's feeling penned in and ineffectual. He can't help Marguerite and he's letting the company down."

"He told you this?" Peter and Jeremy were two men who kept their own counsel. Did they actually talk about things to each other?

"Didn't have to. I understand what it feels like." He leaned forward and finished off his coffee. "You want to take company class or shall I tell Mieko to do it?"

"Ask Mieko. I have something to do this morning."

"You want to tell me what?"

"Later."

Peter threw his napkin on the table and reached for his briefcase. "We're a team, remember? Nobody can make it on his own without the others; you taught me that."

Lindy watched him walk across the restaurant, stop briefly at Chi-Chi's post and give her a quick kiss on the cheek. A brooding, swarthy chrysalis emerging from his shell.

Too much symbolism, she thought. It must be the effects of the retreat's artistic ambiance. What she needed was some facts. She headed for the infirmary.

Adele's husky voice invited her inside. "Close the door, will you?" She motioned to the wooden door that was held in place against the wall with a wooden wedge.

Lindy kicked the wedge away and the door swung shut. She pushed until the latch clicked into place, then turned to Adele, her curiosity piqued.

Adele motioned for her to sit. She sat.

Adele stood up. "I'd like you to tell me exactly what you saw in the bungalow yesterday."

Lindy suddenly felt ill at ease. Was she being tested? "I thought you said *we* needed to talk, not just *me*."

Adele's eyes never left hers. "You talk, I talk, we talk."

Amo, amas, amat. She sounded like she was reciting declensions. Lindy took a deep breath. There was no reason not to tell her what the police already knew, she could probably find out anyway. But it was so hard to trust anyone when you were involved with death under unusual circumstances. A euphemism again. Murder. There, she had said it. To herself anyway. The police hadn't publicly declared that Cleveland's death was murder, but the sheriff suspected it, and against her will, Lindy had to agree. What she had learned of the boy didn't point to suicide, nor could she believe he was just wandering around at night and plummeted down the cliff. There had to be more to it than that. Was he on his way to some place specific? There was nothing out there except the archaeologists' camp. He could have been meeting someone. For a lovers' tryst? Or to break up with someone. Connie? They still hadn't found the boy. God, what if he was dead, too? And if he was, something was really rotten at the Easton Arts Retreat.

"Please." Adele sat down.

"I was just trying to get organized," said Lindy. She told Adele about Chi-Chi asking her to check on Robert, going to the cabin, and thinking he was asleep. She tried to include every detail, what she had seen, anything she might have heard. It was easier talking to Adele than to Grappel, but she still had the distinct feeling that she was being interrogated. Had Marguerite put Adele up to this?

"Did you notice anything in the room? On the desk?"

Lindy conjured the scene in her mind; let her mind's eye travel over the desktop. "There was the bottle of pills. His head hid them until I moved him away. A stack of paper. Several sheets of blue paper, and white ones spread in front of him."

Adele nodded

"A glass of Chi-Chi's power drink. Nearly empty. A jar of pens and pencils. A pen on the desk—" Lindy paused as a spur of realization grew within her. "Like he had been writing."

She stared at Adele. "Like he had been writing," she repeated. She wasn't being interrogated. Adele was leading her. Like a teacher encouraging a slow-witted student. No, like a psychologist guiding a client in denial.

"He had been writing. He never used the computer; Chi-Chi told us that the night we were in the bungalow. Robert wrote everything on paper, and she transferred it to the computer. The artist and the artisan. She laughed about it."

Adele nodded, her lips pressed together.

"The chair rolled back when I pulled him up. But only a few inches."

"And the computer screen?"

"It was on, but, no, I didn't notice if anything was written on it. Just the green aura. Then I came to look for you."

"Did anyone see you?"

Lindy thought back. "Possibly the police. Two of them were going into the Fuller studio, but I slowed down so they wouldn't get

suspicious." Lindy looked away, suddenly embarrassed. "I didn't
want to waste time explaining."

Adele smiled. Was it what Adele had expected of her, because it
proved to her Lindy was one of them, or was it relief for some other
darker reason? Oh hell, in for a penny in for a pound.

"Then we came back."

"And the computer screen?"

Lindy shrugged and shook her head. "I don't know. I was
shocked because Robert's chair was facing the computer, and when
I left it was facing the desk. I don't think I moved the chair by mistake, and even if I did, what are the odds of it stopping right in front
of the computer keyboard? It doesn't make sense."

Adele sat perfectly still as Lindy replayed the scene in her mind.
At last, she sighed. "I just don't know. I remember the glow, but I
don't recall anything written on the screen. Did you or Stu notice
anything?"

"No," said Adele. "I was completely involved with Robert, and
Stuart doesn't recall seeing anything. Men don't notice things the
way women do."

"Kitchen things," said Lindy.

A question formed on Adele's features.

"Kitchen things, the way women see things and interpret them,
have caught killers before and not just in fiction. You think someone
tried to kill Robert?"

"Don't you?" Adele put on her glasses and reached for a pen. She
rolled it between her thumb and fingers. "Now I'll talk." She contemplated the action of her fingers. "You know about Robert's allergies."

Lindy nodded.

"They're annoying, but not debilitating. A continuous dose of antihistamines keeps them at a livable level, but . . ." Adele pointed
the pen at Lindy. "Robert and Chi-Chi asked me not to mention it
to Marguerite. They didn't want to worry her." An expulsion of air
from her nostrils. "Everyone is so busy trying to protect Marguerite.
If there is one person on this earth who doesn't need protecting, it is
Marguerite Easton. Look at this place." Adele drew a circle in the

air with her pen. "She has us all jumping through the hoop." She plunged the pen toward the desk and the tip hit the blotter with a crack.

Lindy blinked.

"Because we want to, not because we're being coerced. She inspires that kind of loyalty." Adele cleared her throat and brought herself back to the point.

"Robert occasionally has trouble sleeping. Antihistamines affect some people that way. Some get drowsy, some get hyper."

Lindy nodded. That was why Robert's hands always had a slight tremor; he wasn't nervous, just reacting to medication.

"It isn't a perfect solution, but he doesn't need them in the city. He has nine whole months in which to clear his system. The downside is that he does need to be functioning while he's here, so I prescribe a light sedative to help him sleep on those nights when he's too wired."

Lindy's eyes narrowed.

"Exactly. One shouldn't mix antihistamines with a depressant."

"And I've seen him drinking."

"In moderation. With the lifestyle up at the house, not to drink would cause concern."

"It must put an awful strain on his system."

Adele nodded. "Between Chi-Chi and me and his own sense of duty, we kept things in a livable stasis. It's only for three months."

It was the second time she had mentioned the time element. Lindy thought she understood. Adele felt responsible for what had happened. She needed to go over all the details, so that she could learn if she had really been culpable in Robert's nearly fatal overdose.

"I knew you'd understand," said Adele.

Lindy's eyes widened. Was Adele a mind reader as well as a cardiologist?

"I could tell the first day I met you. There was a rapport."

There was? Adele had been friendly, but Lindy hadn't felt anything beyond general civility.

"You can imagine my—" Adele returned her pen to the holder

and placed her elbows on the desk. "Robert's system was coursing with Benadryl and tranquilizers. If you hadn't found him when you did, I doubt if anyone could have saved him."

"Thanks to Chi-Chi. She asked me to check on him."

"His recovery still isn't assured."

"Oh. I thought . . ."

"I did what I could, the usual standard procedures, but this kind of reaction induces a comalike state that can last hours or days. We'll just have to wait and see."

For a while neither of them spoke. Finally, Lindy ventured a question. "Could Robert have accidentally taken too much of the sedative?"

"No. He was extremely careful."

"Not even with all the extra stress he was under, Grappel and the night in jail?"

"No, I won't accept that."

"On purpose?"

"He would never do that to Chi-Chi, I don't care what the computer screen said."

"He wouldn't have seduced Larry Cleveland?"

"Never. He's been here thirty years and there has never been a hint of a complaint against him. Not even gossip."

Lindy was dimly aware that their roles had changed. Adele was letting herself be questioned. Maybe she didn't trust herself to try to figure this out alone. "Then he would have no reason to push Larry Cleveland down the cliff."

"No," said Adele. "But I'm following you. I don't think Larry Cleveland accidentally plunged to his death. In the most outrageous scenario, he might have slipped, but something would have stopped him before he hit the bottom. A boulder, a tree; he would have grabbed at a limb to break his fall."

Lindy nodded. It was just what she had done, climbing down the embankment to the stream.

"But he was found at the bottom of the ravine. I think someone pushed him or possibly even knocked him out and threw him over."

"That's what the sheriff thinks, but—" Lindy stopped while

ideas flew into place. It would have to have been more than a mere "poof" as Eric had suggested. She pulled out the image of the cliff where Larry had fallen. Not a sheer drop, but broken up with ledges, trees, and outcroppings of rock. She would have to take a closer look at that cliff. But not with Adele. She was beginning to like her, but she wasn't ready to trust her.

"In which case," said Lindy, "the real murderer might have caused it to look like Robert had committed suicide in order to throw suspicion from himself." The image of a hulking Byron Grappel came immediately to her mind. "But how? Could someone have tampered with his pills? Switched the dosage to a higher level? Would it have that effect?"

"Yes, but the person would have to be knowledgeable about drugs and have access to sophisticated equipment or another drug supply."

Lindy glanced unconsciously at the door of the examination room.

"It wasn't I."

No. Adele was too small to hoist the lanky Larry Cleveland over the cliff, even if she had reason. And what possible reason could she have? Lindy pushed any lurid speculations to the back of her mind. She would consider them later at her leisure. What she concentrated on now was the reason for Adele's confidence. Was she only trying to assuage her own fear that she had been negligent in caring for Robert? Or had she called in Lindy for a consultation in order to look at the problem from a different perspective. A second opinion. The scientific method.

Adele had taken off her glasses and was tapping them on the desk blotter. Finally, she shook her head. "If this is related to Larry's death, four days wouldn't be enough time for Robert's pills to inter-act with the Benadryl, even if he was taking twice as many as he should have."

"And he was gone one whole night, when he was at the police station. Chi-Chi said they wouldn't even let her give him his allergy medicine," said Lindy. "What about someone at the jail?"

Adele looked nonplused. "I have no idea. You'd think a person would at least be safe in jail."

"From that, anyway." Lindy leaned forward, an ugly idea forming in her mind as she spoke. "What about Chi-Chi's power drink? There was a glass of it on the desk. He had drunk most of it. Could someone have tampered with it?" Grappel hadn't mentioned the glass when he had questioned her at the station. Surely, they had held it as evidence.

"He drank it twice a day," she continued. "Chi-Chi made it fresh every morning." She stopped short. "Oh dear."

Adele shook her head.

"Then who—and why?"

"That's the mystery. And I don't have credentials in that area."

Unfortunately, Lindy did.

Murder and attempted murder. Lindy's mind recoiled from her own conclusions. She almost turned back to the infirmary to convince Adele that they had been too wild in their surmises. That they were jeopardizing Marguerite and the Easton Academy. But it was too late to go back. They weren't alone in their conjectures. Sheriff Grappel had already begun the awful process, and the only way they could help Marguerite was to find the real killer before Grappel arrested Robert. Unless it was Robert, and then she would be held responsible for destroying the Easton name.

She sat down on the base of a statue of St. Francis, wedging herself between the concrete birds at his feet. *O Lord, take this cup*, she thought.

She watched Abel White cross the clearing in front of the dining hall. She hailed him over. "Have they found Connie yet?"

Abel frowned. "The sheriff thinks he's probably out of the area. Maybe hitchhiked back home."

"I assume the parents have been notified, but I haven't seen them here."

"Well—they did get in touch with their secretary. Seems they're out of the country."

"They're on their way back?"

"Can't reach 'em. Gone hiking in some place in South America." Abel scratched his head. "Not my idea of a vacation, but I guess it takes all kinds."

And not Lindy's idea of concerned parents to send their kid to camp and not leave an emergency number where they could be reached.

"The secretary says they call in every Sunday. That's tomorrow. I sure hope he turns up okay."

"Me, too," said Lindy.

"Good day to you." Abel started to leave.

"Abel?"

"Yes, ma'am?"

"Did you look for the source of the drugs that Robert is supposed to have taken?"

"I think that's classified information. But I don't know, anyway. The sheriff handled it."

I just bet he did, thought Lindy. "Thanks, Abel."

"Sure thing." She watched him make his way down the path toward the Loie Fuller studio and Sheriff Grappel, then made her own way to the theater.

Rehearsal that afternoon was taken by Victor Slaton and Madame Flick. There had been no word from Jeremy. Lindy sat in the back of the house, once again doing nothing. Several more students had departed, and the rest seemed nervous. They had been through a revolving door of directors in the last few days. Robert was in the hospital, Jeremy had gone off to God-knew-where. Not to mention opening-night jitters. She was gratified to see several company members in the audience, showing their support. Kate and Mieko were in the aisle going over steps with two of the students. Annie was nowhere to be seen.

"We've been spurned for that cute archaeologist with the pony-tail," said Kate. "Leave it to your daughter to drop in unannounced and captivate one of the few straight men in the area. I wonder if he has a friend?"

The image of Annie's artistic cellist's hands digging for oyster shells brought a smile to Lindy's lips. Or maybe Donald had the day off. It was Saturday. A frown replaced the smile. She didn't know anything about Donald except that he was charming and worked for Dr. Van Zandt. Was that enough recommendation for a suitor for her daughter? Suitor? Yeesh, she needed to get back to the city. Next thing she knew, she'd be donning a bustle and a hobbled skirt.

Glen returned at seven o'clock, face pink from a day on the links, and feeling satisfied with the four hundred thousand dollars his company had raised. "They wanted me to stay for the farewell dinner, but I figured I'd better get over here and check on Annie and you. Where is she?"

Lindy wished she knew. "Out having fun. She's on vacation. And so are you."

They changed for the theater and went down to the bar for a quick drink before curtain. Glen enthused about every hole on the golf course; recounted sand traps, and bogies and birdies, and other terms that left Lindy befuddled. It didn't matter. She let him talk while she contemplated the shape of his nose, the white line where his hair met the back of his sunburned neck; anticipating the few days that they were actually going to spend together.

She took his arm as they left the bar. Glen stopped suddenly, his muscles tensing beneath her hand.

Lindy looked up. Surprise, relief, then guilt followed in quick succession. At first only the man's silhouette registered in her mind, all six feet of it. The lighting was muted in the hallway. It was just like the first time they had met. There had never been enough light to read his features in the Connecticut theater where a murder had just taken place. But she knew those features now without having to see them. Light blue eyes, as clear as the lake just outside. Straight nose. Mouth whose lips were thin but expressive, especially when he was mad at her, or when he had kissed her that one time when they'd first met. But it had never happened again. She had nothing to be guilty about.

"Bill," she said. Not an enthusiastic greeting, and she *was* glad to see him. They needed his expertise in crime.

Bill said absolutely nothing.

"What are you doing here?" she asked.

She felt Glen look at her. Then he stuck out his hand.

"Bill."

Bill extended his hand. They greeted each other like gentlemen. And why shouldn't they? They had met before. Glen knew he and Lindy were friends.

Another quick glance from Glen. She would have missed it if all her perceptions hadn't been working at full throttle.

"What *are* you doing here, Bill?" asked her husband.

Bill cleared his throat. Barely noticeably. It happened whenever he was about to bend the truth.

"Came to see the performance." His voice always took Lindy by surprise. It was resonant and full. She was sure that everyone in the bar behind them had heard his words.

"Really," said Glen.

Lindy managed a quick look at his face. Eyebrows and lips. Not a good sign.

"Actually, I invited him." Jeremy stepped up behind Bill so unexpectedly that Lindy jumped. "Good to see you, Glen. Glad you could make it."

More hand shaking. Lindy stared dumbly at the three men while she waited for her brain to engage. Bill here with Jeremy. So that's where he had gone. She had been thinking the same thing herself. Bill could, and would, help them. And now he was here. She allowed relief to override the other emotions his appearance had set off.

Jeremy and Bill pulled ahead of them on the way to the theater.

"I would have never guessed it," said Glen leaning down toward her ear. "Why didn't you tell me Bill was gay?"

The question took her by surprise. She had no reason to think he was. And a big reason to think he wasn't. But she didn't say so.

"And there I was thinking that . . ." His sentence trailed off.

"Don't tell me you thought he came to see me?"

"Of course not."

"You were jealous?"

"No."

"Not even a little?"

"Don't be ridiculous."

They took their seats and the house lights dimmed. Lindy just managed to pick out Jeremy and Bill a few rows in front of them as the lights faded to black.

She sat back to enjoy a rare night with her husband. She had left notebook and pen in her room in the annex. She forced herself not to take mental notes of the dancing, just watch and enjoy. This performance was a one-shot deal and not her responsibility.

But halfway through the opening ballet, her mind began to wander in another direction. Bill was here. Jeremy had called on him for his help; she was sure of that. But how on earth was she going to help Bill if Glen was around? And where was Annie? She had better be at the performance or she was going to be in big trouble. First with her mother—and then they would both get it from Glen.

She dragged her attention back to the action on stage. Several dancers were missing. It had been too late to rearrange the spacing to fill the holes left in the *corps*. A professional company would have had no problem with the adjustments. But students, some of them without stage experience, would have been thrown off with any last-minute changes. No. It was better to leave well enough alone. It didn't look too bad. Especially considering that most of the audience were family and friends.

There were probably a couple of critics in the house. Hopefully, they would take the upheaval at the retreat into consideration when writing their reviews. And by the next weekend, when the Ash company would be performing, surely, everything would be cleared up. Especially with Bill here. But she wouldn't think about him.

The curtain opened to *There Is a Time*, and Lindy indulged in the music and the movement, thoughts of the past, and the great dancers who had first performed the piece in 1953. Lindy had never seen those original dancers, except on film. José Limon, now dead, had captured the hearts and souls of the dancers he had worked with, and the generation of young students that would take their place. But dance was an ephemeral art; you couldn't hang it in a museum, or play it on your stereo system at home. There were dance films, but so much was lost when it was transferred to the two dimensions of the screen. Its life depended on reconstruction by dancers who had never seen the original. It was not always successful, but Robert had conveyed the spirit of the piece to these young dancers. And though the performance didn't have the maturity and understanding of a good professional cast, the enthusiasm and freshness of the students made up for the subtlety that their young minds lacked.

Lindy and Glen stayed in their seats at intermission. She perused the audience until she saw Annie wave at her from across the house. Lindy waved back, then squinted, as she tried to get a better view of the person seated next to her. Donald Parker in a denim shirt. Hair neatly combed behind his ears. A broad smile on his lean face.

There was only one major glitch in the second half of the program. And that was a lighting cue during a *pas de deux*, where three cues followed each other in rapid succession. But the dancers didn't seem bothered by it and neither did the audience.

The evening ended with everyone on stage. They even brought out the costume and stage crews. It was a lovely idea, thought Lindy. Usually the workers backstage were never given any outward show of thanks. Applause was a great way of building their self-esteem and showing them that it took more than dancers to make a successful performance.

She and Glen followed the crowd out to the lobby for the reception. The audience spilled out onto the lawn in front of the theater where additional refreshment tables had been set up.

Lindy watched Jeremy leave Bill and go to stand by Marguerite. She was exquisitely dressed in a creme floor-length gown, a shimmering oasis among the more casually dressed parents.

While Glen left her in search of champagne, Lindy scanned the crowd. She saw Bill perusing the room from the sidelines, taking in every detail. She continued to stare at him hoping to catch his attention before Glen returned. Maybe they could meet and discuss things in the morning before the town fair and fireworks.

Bill stared intently across the room. Lindy followed his line of sight directly to Annie whose position in the room made an equidistant triangle between them. Annie was looking back at Bill. Then her head turned slowly and her eyes met Lindy's. She looked away.

"Oh, there you are," she said as Glen handed her a glass of champagne.

"The boys snagged me." He drawled out the word "boys." Glen had never been able to accept the "theatrical affectation" as he called it, of calling dancers "boys" and "girls" even though they were really adults.

A few minutes later, they left the reception and walked up the stairs to their room in the annex.

Glen closed the door with a thud. "He isn't gay."

"Who?"

"Bill."

"I didn't say he was."

"You let me think he was. The boys had to set me straight."

"For crying out loud, Glen. What does it matter? Gay or not gay. Not all friendships are based on sexual preferences."

"But some are."

"You *are* jealous," said Lindy with a sparkle of satisfaction.

"No, I'm not." He pulled her close and kissed her. She kissed him back.

Chapter Thirteen

When Lindy awoke, the sun was shining through the window. It was going to be a perfect day for the town fair and fireworks. She lay in bed with a complacent smile on her lips. Competition, she thought, might not be good for the soul, but it certainly did wonders for your sex life. She looked over to Glen, lying on his side. He wasn't even snoring. She considered waking him. But no, she had things to take care of that wouldn't wait. She slid out of bed, tiptoed across the room and turned on the shower. Maybe she could catch Bill at breakfast.

Bill wasn't in the restaurant when she came downstairs. But Biddy was. Sitting by herself at a table by the window. Elbows on the table, chin cupped in her hands, she was staring out at the view. A plate of untouched food had been pushed out of her way.

Lindy felt an immediate stab of guilt. Biddy was upset, and Lindy hadn't given her a thought. Instead she had been having a grand old time with Glen as if she didn't have a care in the world. Well hell, it wasn't her fault. She had to make the most of what little time she and Glen spent together. Was that asking too much?

"Are you okay?"

Biddy looked up and then quickly away. She had been crying. Biddy only cried once a tour, when she needed to let off steam. At this rate she would be in debt to a whole year of tours before they returned to the city.

"Biddy." Lindy had meant it to sound sympathetic, but her own sense of inadequacy gave a harshness to her words.

Biddy pushed her chair away, and without looking at Lindy, hurried across the room.

Lindy stared after her, then sat down at the next table. *Great*, she thought. *I've insulted Rebo, neglected my daughter, hurt Biddy, and have two unexplained accidents hanging over my head.* She let that endangered head drop down on her folded arms on the table.

"Interesting place to sleep. Up late last night?"

Lindy turned her face to the voice. "Hi, Bill." She straightened up. "I've upset Biddy—and Rebo and—you name it."

Bill sat in the chair next to her. "You people don't need an investigator. You need a therapist."

Lindy smiled. "We'll settle for a college professor. I'm glad you're here."

"Right."

"Are you mad at me already? I haven't even talked to you yet."

Bill smiled and she immediately felt better. He had the most open smile she had ever seen on a man. Not that the rest of him was as congenial, not by a long shot. But he did have his moments.

"Jeremy asked you to come?"

Bill nodded, the smile disappearing as suddenly as it had come.

"It's a mess, one kid dead, another missing; then there's this sheriff." Lindy gesticulated in the air in explanation of what she thought of the sheriff.

"I've heard about Byron Grappel. I spent yesterday with Jeremy." His face relaxed, transforming his expression into a complete blank. Another trick he had. He was hiding something from her.

"What is it?" She tried to stop the rush of unease that had started in her gut and was working its way to her throat. But she already knew he wasn't going to tell her just by the nonlook on his face. Why had she bothered?

"There are a lot of things that Jeremy doesn't know about," she insisted. "Some things I learned yesterday while he was gone." No response. He was going to start yelling at her soon. She hurried on. "Dr. Addison thinks—"

He didn't yell. He laid his hand on her wrist and said very softly. "I want you to stay out of this." She wished he had yelled; she knew how to deal with that. Bill being quiet set her adrift. She could only stare back at him. His face was absolutely unreadable. Not a clue from his eyes, which looked back at her devoid of feeling. He had shut her out, completely, and irrevocably.

"Ah, there you are." Bill's smile reappeared as he greeted Glen and removed his hand from Lindy's wrist. It was completely natural, as if he were genuinely glad to see Glen. And, no doubt, he was. "Here, take this chair. I was just leaving."

Lindy watched his back as he strode away. He may not think he needed her, but he would before this was over. She turned back to Glen.

"Hi, hon." She smiled. It was a pretty sad attempt. How did Bill do it, she wondered.

The fair was in full swing when Glen and Lindy arrived at the town hall. The small paved parking lot was full, as was the used car lot across the road. Cars lined each side of the road, parked bumper to bumper on the grassy shoulders. Glen maneuvered the BMW into a meadow roped off for additional parking, and they walked back up the road to the entrance behind the clapboard hall.

To one side of the building, a multicolored striped tarp had been raised over groups of picnic tables. A country singer crooned from a small stage constructed at the front. Vendor trailers selling hot dogs, gyros, cotton candy, and ice cream were crowded together on a patch of flat ground nearby. Clouds of smoke, grease, and cooking smells battled each other in the air, attacking the nostrils and settling on the clothes of the people waiting in line.

They had to walk uphill to the fairway. Only it wasn't a fairway, but a meandering passage of hard earth, gutted and pocked by years of erosion. Every relatively flat piece of ground was covered with rides, games, and more food vendors. A ticket kiosk straddled a crack in the ground like a festive outhouse. Tinny music blared from every direction. Barkers chanted their come-ons: Three balls for a dollar. Win a goldfish. Are you a weakling or a he-man? It was hokey, dilapidated, and wonderful.

Sipping homemade lemonade, Lindy and Glen picked their way through the throng of children and parents. They dodged cones of blue and pink cotton candy held in sticky hands; jostled parents hurrying to keep up with their children, who ran ahead, jumping across crevices and scooting up the slopes of trampled grass in order to get to the next ride.

Their laughter brought back a whirl of memories. Cliff and Annie, eyes wide with excitement, mouths ringed in chocolate, clothes smeared with dust and mustard. Where was Annie? She hadn't even asked them for spending money. Lindy pushed her reminiscences aside and perused the swarms of revelers in search of her daughter.

A pink, four-foot inflatable bunny was jolting its way down the path from the upper level. Lindy recognized Rebo's legs beneath it. Juan and Eric, necks draped in plastic leis and bottles of bubbles on a string, followed behind.

"Have you seen Annie?" asked Lindy as they passed.

"A little while ago by the Tilt-a-Whirl," said Eric.

"She's with Paul and Andrea and the girls," said Juan. He was looking back toward the rides. So he wouldn't have to look at her?

Nothing from the bunny.

"Thanks," said Lindy.

She and Glen trudged past the carousel, sideskirting a line of waiting children. The faded shorts and mismatched tops of the locals outnumbered the designer clothes of the tourist children. But they were all having an equally good time. Organ music and snow cones were the great levelers of class distinction.

A waft of deep-fried food passed by them. A teenage boy held a paper plate out to a laughing young girl. He stopped for her to pull at a piece of batter-dipped onion. The onion slid across the plate as she pulled. Laughing harder, she popped the morsel into her mouth, oblivious to the traffic jam she was causing.

They climbed up a natural stairway of roots and rocks and stopped to watch boys firing air rifles at the Sitting Ducks trailer, then up to the Tilt-a-Whirl, whose precarious position on the ground gave additional meaning to its name. The ride itself looked ancient, small and in need of paint. It stopped with a squeal of gears. One group got off and the next hurried to find spaces. When they were settled and the operator had checked each bar, he shoved the gear arm forward, and the Tilt-a-Whirl lunged into motion.

Glen stood mesmerized as he watched the contraption go round and round. The ride's operator, a scrawny young man whose clothes seemed too big for him, leaned against the gear box. Stringy blond hair hung in his eyes as he pulled a cigarette from a crumpled package and returned the package to his pocket. He stuck the cigarette in his mouth and lit a match. Smoke curled up in front of his face. Lindy wondered if he had forgotten about the people going round and round on the ride behind him. He blew out the match and flicked it behind him. It landed on a pile of hay. Lindy's eyes widened until she realized that the hay had been spread to cover puddles left from the recent rain. Wet hay. She tried not to think about where the Tilt-a-Whirl would be during the dry season.

He pushed himself up, cigarette still dangling from the side of his mouth, and pulled the gear arm back. The Tilt-a-Whirl ground to a stop. Lindy took Glen's arm and guided him back to the 4-H Exhibit in the main building.

On their way back through the labyrinth of the fair, Lindy spotted Paul and Andrea in line for the Ferris wheel. It was on the level above them and they were too far away for Lindy to get their attention. She saw Kate and some of the company girls in line behind them. Annie was there. And so was Donald Parker. Maybe she should just have a little talk with Annie when they got back.

They passed Ellis and Stu beneath the tent canopy. Ellis was eating a sausage on a roll, stacked high with sauerkraut and relish. He looked as happy as the kids at the table next to them, where pizza slices, sodas, and French fries covered the table and their faces. Lindy's stomach growled.

Marguerite and Jeremy were coming down the stairs from the ex-

hibition room as Glen and Lindy came inside. They paused while
Lindy introduced Glen to Marguerite. She wondered if she should
stall them long enough for Ellis to finish eating; sausage and sauerkraut had to be right up there with home fries and gravy. But Jeremy
had already begun leading Marguerite out of the building. *You're on
your own, Ellis,* Lindy thought, and made her way toward the pro-
duce table.

Rows and rows of tables covered in blue-checked oilcloth were
crowded into the room. The floor boards were unpolished and dusty
from the parade of viewers. Lindy stopped in front of a gigantic
tomato. It was sitting alone on a white Styrofoam plate; a red ribbon
lay next to it. To its right, another tomato, smaller but perfectly
shaped, had taken the blue ribbon.

"Why do you think the smaller tomato won?" asked Glen. "What
is the criteria for a prize-winning vegetable?"

"Fruit," said Lindy. "Tomatoes are fruits."

Glen shrugged. "They may be fruits, but they're vegetables to
me."

Next came the pies, wedges cut out, filling oozing onto the
plates. Then cakes, breads, and plates of cookies. Almost all had rib-
bons by them: blue, red, white, yellow. A contest where everyone
won, even if it was only an honorable mention.

Down the next aisle were crocheted baby booties, hand-knitted
afghans, and colorful patchwork quilts.

"Are you done yet?" asked Glen. "I want to see the tractor pull at
four."

"What do they pull?"

"I'm not sure, but I want to see it."

She followed him out of the building and through the parking lot,
dodging exiting cars and others waiting to take their places. Glen
helped her jump across a brackish ditch. In front of them, a meadow
had been leveled by a bulldozer. To one side was a stand of bleachers. In the clearing, a yellow-and-green tractor chugged toward the
trees. A rope was attached to the back and a team of men strained to
keep it in place.

"Tug of war," said Lindy.

The cheers of the crowd mixed with the groans of the men as their muscles bulged with exertion. Glen was already climbing onto the bleachers, groping his way over spectators until he found an empty spot. A cheer erupted from the crowd and another team of men replaced the first.

"Who won?" asked Lindy.

Glen shrugged without taking his eyes off the arena.

"The tractor," said a man in front of them.

"Oh." She sighed, shifted her weight on the aluminum bench, and thought wistfully of the delicately stitched quilts they had just left.

It was a long day. Lindy had seen the dancers from the retreat spending their money freely on the rides and games. Rose's head occasionally appeared above the crowd. Biddy had joined the company girls, having brushed aside Lindy's invitation to join Glen and her, saying they should spend the time together. The few times Lindy had seen her in the crowd, she appeared to be having fun.

She caught a glimpse of Peter more than once. But she hadn't seen Bill. She should have invited him to come along. Did he feel left out? Not Bill. He never had trouble fitting in.

By eight o'clock, they were tired, dusty, and stuffed with junk food. They followed the line of people, strollers, and the occasional dog to the high school where the fireworks were being held. Flares were positioned down one side of the road to light the way and to warn approaching traffic. Police stood on the asphalt, their flashlights dancing crazily in the darkness as they moved people to the side. Behind them, the carnival noises and lights receded and the chirrup of crickets and the throaty croaks of frogs took their place.

In the dark, the playing field looked just like any other patch of meadow, except for the outlines of the goal posts at each end. Telephone poles topped by floodlights prevented total darkness, and a halo of yellow emanated from the band shell at the back of the field.

The high school band, in gold and burgundy uniforms, tooted patriotic songs and marches. The clarity of the tunes ebbed and flowed as the sound shifted on the breeze. Glen and Lindy stopped at the edge of the field. The one stand of bleachers was packed with spectators. Others had brought blankets or folding chairs, and were claiming their territory. Children whirled glow-in-the-dark necklaces. The smell of bug spray permeated the air.

The band oompahed into a new song. On cue, the people on the bleachers rose and faced the bandstand. Those on the grass around Lindy and Glen stood up. It must be a ritual they all knew, because only when their hands were placed on their hearts and they began to sing, did Lindy recognize the distorted notes of *The Star-Spangled Banner*. She was not alone; other confused outsiders got to their feet and stood in respectful silence.

" . . . and the home of the braaave." Cheers and a smattering of applause, and Lindy saw Marguerite step to the front of the stage. She was accompanied by the band director and another man who introduced himself as the mayor over the squeal of feedback from the microphone. This was met with several catcalls and whistles. He thanked the band director whose name was lost in another squeal of feedback. The mayor looked over to the side of the band shell. When he began again, the amplification had been sorted out.

Then he introduced Marguerite, though he said she needed no introduction. Marguerite stepped to the microphone. She was wearing a red suit dress; its cut buttons caught the light and flashed iridescent beams into the darkness. She began by welcoming everyone, but instead of listening to her speech as she had planned, Lindy found herself studying the surrounding faces as she often did the audience in search of their reactions. A woman stood next to her, a brood of children hanging on her flowered shirtwaist and a baby asleep at her feet. Catching Lindy's eye, she leaned over. "That's Marguerite Easton, one of our finest citizens."

"Is she?" Lindy moved closer to the woman. She felt a sticky hand grab her knee. "What does she do?"

"Just about everything. She owns most of the property around here. Has a camp for artists and such. She's also responsible for most of the jobs for our young folks. It ain't easy for young people to find jobs around here these days." She looked down at her hovering brood. "I expect all these young'uns will be working for Ms. Marguerite before they go off to school. Couldn't ask anything better, could we, Toby?" The boy released Lindy's leg and nuzzled into the woman's skirt. "All my children have worked for her, and my Billy does most of his hardware business with her groundskeeper."

The lights on the band shell began to dim until the night was lit only by the stars and a sliver of moon.

"Don't know what this town would do without her." It was now too dark to see the woman's face, but Lindy could imagine her expression just from the heartfelt gratitude in which the words were spoken.

The first loud boom brought her attention back to the fireworks. The air was lit with a circle of blue stars. Then a whistling sound and a spray of orange erupted from each star. Lindy leaned into Glen. He put his arm around her.

"Isn't it romantic?" she sang quietly as the air was split with another thundering explosion.

The sky continued its display of pyrotechnics, followed by smoke and the fallout of ripped cardboard wafting down on the heads of the observers. A boom and a spray of white fountain that filled the sky; a chorus of oohs and ahs from the crowd, then an answering boom, but in the distance.

"Somebody from Thorton Township gettin' in on the act," said a voice nearby. Appreciative laughter.

A multiple set of booms and the sky was filled with green, white, and orange.

"Isn't that Annie?" Glen pointed in front of them. Lindy followed the direction of his hand as the outline of Annie and Donald, arm in arm, faded into the night.

"Who's she with?" asked Glen not waiting for Lindy's answer. Before she could reply to his second question, the air lit up again. They had a perfect view of Annie and Donald wrapped in a lengthy kiss.

"Damn it," said Glen as he moved toward the unsuspecting couple.

Lindy grabbed his arm. "Don't embarrass her. She's eighteen. He's a nice boy."

Glen pulled away. The sky lit up. Annie and Donald were gone. "Wait till I get my hands on her."

It was a ridiculous thing to say. Glen and Lindy had never even spanked their children. They were both adherents of the then current philosophy of "time outs."

"I'm sure we can trust her to be intelligent," said Lindy.

"I'm not worried about her intelligence; I'm worried about her hormones."

"Don't worry." *But,* thought Lindy, *I'm definitely having a little mother-daughter talk with her tomorrow.*

"I'm her father. I'm supposed to worry."

Lindy smiled in the darkness and gave him a kiss.

It took forever to get out of the parking lot, dodging tree stumps, holes, and other vehicles anxious to get home. They followed the line of cars along the winding road, while the police force waved their flashlights to keep them moving. The search for Connie Phillips had been halted because of the extra staff needed for the fair. Only one dispatcher had been left at the station to answer emergency calls. Lindy had learned this from Stu that morning. The man was a storehouse of information. She wondered briefly if he had any ideas about Larry Cleveland's death.

It was almost midnight when the BMW drove through the gates of the Easton retreat. Sandiman came rushing down the steps before they could drive around the back to the annex parking. He must have been watching for them. Glen slammed on the brakes. The passenger-side window lowered and Sandiman stuck his head in, his face a ghoulish mask. "They're all at the archaeologist camp. There was a landslide. Your daughter is there, too. I thought you would want to know."

"Was anyone hurt?" Lindy tried to ask. The image of Dr. Van Zandt buried in rubble took her voice away. Not Annie. They had just seen her at the fireworks. "Was anyone—" She began again, but

Glen overrode her. "How do we get there?" The panic in his voice only increased the panic Lindy couldn't express.

"Back down the main road, a quarter of a mile, big boulder on your left, follow the dirt road." Glen put the car in drive, Sandiman hung to the window and ran along as Glen turned the car around. "It isn't paved—bumps—be careful."

Glen accelerated the BMW back onto the driveway, leaving Sandiman staring after them, a solitary, black silhouette against the lights of the porch.

The car screeched as Glen sped past the boulder that marked the turnoff. He had to back up to make the turn onto the dirt road. They careened through the darkness, the headlights producing bizarre forms as Glen raced toward the archeologist camp. Even the BMW's shocks couldn't contend with the twists and bumps that rushed toward them. Lindy grabbed the armrest to steady herself; her seat belt prevented her from knocking her head on the ceiling.

"Slow down," she said in as even a voice as she could muster. "I'm sure she's all right. She probably got back just before we did."

Glen ignored her. His hands gripped the steering wheel as he hunched forward in concentration.

"Slow down, you won't help anybody if you wreck the car."

"I'll never forgive you if you've let anything happen to Annie," he said. It was said softly, almost to himself. Lindy felt all the panic, all the worry, all the warmth drain out of her. Was he blaming himself or was he blaming her?

"What?"

"I knew I shouldn't have left her here. Couldn't you just have taken care of her?"

Lindy waited for her heart to start up again and her brain to clear. He was blaming her. Which was absurd—he was here, too—how could he think she was responsible for a landslide? It was just his fear talking. She felt the side of her mouth quiver, ordered it to stop. She wouldn't cry. Annie was fine. He'd see.

At last, the dim shadows of cars and Jeeps parked haphazardly on the side of the road warned them they were near the site. Glen pulled off the road, threw open the door and began to run toward the eerie fingers of light that shone through the trees. Lindy followed right behind. Stumbling on rocks and branches, she finally skidded down the last few feet of the path and into a scene from a disaster movie.

Where the tents and worktables had been, a hill of boulders, mud, and brush now covered shafts of wood and torn canvas. The Jeep had been pushed off its ledge and lay on its back in the stream, right where the young archaeologists had been digging two days before.

Lindy shook her head to clear the whirring in her ears, only to realize the sound had come from the emergency generators that were running three makeshift floodlights, attached to tree trunks around the camp.

And then she saw Annie running toward them. "Oh, Mom, they've lost everything!" Her face was streaked with mud.

Glen grabbed her as she passed. "Are you okay? Are you hurt?"

"I'm fine, Daddy. Let go." She wriggled free. "Sandiman told us when we got back, so Donald and I caught a ride down. It's awful. All their work—" The rumble of shifting rocks cut off her words.

There was a scrambling on the pile of sludge that covered the tents. Someone was pulling a gesticulating figure away. Another person joined them and escorted a protesting Dr. Van Zandt to the clearing where Lindy stood with Glen and Annie.

Van Zandt was limping. His trouser leg was torn from the knee down. Bill supported him under one arm, Dr. Addison held the other. Only a smear of mud across the shoulder of her blouse marred her otherwise immaculate appearance.

Bill stepped away from the two doctors and moved toward Lindy. "No one was at the camp when it happened." His voice was grim. He was wearing jeans and a tee shirt that had once been white, but was now torn and covered in dirt and grime. "Dr. Van Zandt returned to . . ." He paused, then gestured behind him. "This." He wiped his forearm with his hand, then wiped his hand on his shirt. "He was pretty upset; one of the students came looking for help. We found him digging in the rubble. That's how he hurt his leg."

Dr. Van Zandt pulled away from Adele. Suddenly mute, he stood looking at the destruction, shaking his head slowly from side to side. "Everything, everything, everything," he whispered. Adele motioned to one of his assistants and turned to Bill.

"We'll take him up to the house."

"Come on, Doc," said the girl who had taken his arm. "We'll come back tomorrow and salvage what we can." She pulled him away.

"You okay?" asked Lindy.

"Just dirty." The expression on Bill's face frightened her.

Donald trudged up at that moment looking even dirtier than Bill. "Nothing much we can do here tonight," he said. He took a shaky breath. Annie slipped her arm around him. Lindy felt Glen start to move.

"Why don't you guys get in the car," she said. "We'll give you a ride back."

Annie and Donald turned to go.

"Thanks, Bill," said Donald.

Bill only nodded.

Annie gave Bill a long look before she turned and started back up the hill.

"Come on, Lindy," said Glen. "Give you a ride, Bill?"

"No thanks. I'll just stay here for a while."

"Be careful," said Lindy over her shoulder as Glen led her away. But Bill was staring out over the shattered remains of the camp.

"Where do you think you're going?" asked Glen.

"With Donald." Annie's hand rested on the car door. They had stopped in front of the main house to let Donald out. A group of archeology students sat on the front steps.

"It's late."

"Daddy, it's barely past midnight. I'll be back soon, I promise." She slammed the door.

"Want me to chaperone?" asked Lindy.

"We'll both chaperone. I'll park the car and meet you back here."

Lindy followed Annie across the drive. Five dirty, unhappy faces watched them approach.

"Ms. Easton's arranging for us to stay up here tonight," said

Donald. "She doesn't want us back at the site until she's sure it's safe. The old man is not happy about it."

"No, I am not." The words rumbled through the doorway, preceding the speaker who limped across the porch and sat down heavily on the top step.

Marguerite, still dressed in red, followed close behind.

"Emil, you cannot go back there tonight. Chi-Chi is preparing the guest rooms for your staff, and I have a room ready for you in the main house."

Emil shook his head stubbornly.

Marguerite sat down on the step beside him. She accomplished it with the ease of a young woman.

"I won't have you placing yourself at risk until we know what caused the landslide and if there is danger from more. I'll have the park service come and take a look first thing tomorrow."

"Don't bother. I know what caused it. And it wasn't the rain."

So that was why Bill had stayed behind, thought Lindy. He was going to look for clues of vandalism. In the dark? What if there was another slide? Should she send someone back to look for him?

Her questions were answered before she could voice them. Bill, accompanied by Stu and Ellis, emerged from the trees near the dining hall. Bill looked dirtier than when she had left him a few minutes ago. There were blotches of mud on Stu's trousers.

Emil helped Marguerite to her feet.

"Stuart Hollowell, you are incorrigible," she said.

"I just slipped. Could have happened to anyone."

"No more roaming around at night, do you hear me?"

Stu and Ellis hung their heads like two chastised boys.

"Thank you for rescuing them, Bill."

Bill flashed his wide smile at her.

She smiled up at him.

Lindy cast her eyes heavenward. Bill had been there all of one day and had already made a conquest. She moved closer to him as the others began to file inside.

"How did you get back so fast?"

"As the crow flies, more or less. I saw something move on the path above the site, and when I went to investigate, I found the two of them. Stu on his butt on the ground, and Ellis trying to get him up."

"Did you find anything?"

Bill's eyes widened. "Wasn't that enough?"

Damn, he could be so infuriating. He knew exactly what she had meant. And he had purposely deflected her question back to her.

She felt an arm link through hers. "We'd better go," said Annie. "Daddy will be wondering where we are."

She practically dragged Lindy toward the entrance of the annex.

"Did you and Donald have a fight already?"

"No." But Annie's scowl said otherwise.

"Are you sure? You don't look very happy," said Lindy.

"I'm just tired." Annie slowed down as they reached the top of the stairs to their rooms.

"Mom?"

"Yes?"

Annie was studying the texture of the carpet at her feet.

Lindy waited. Annie was not usually at a loss for words.

"Bill—" she stopped.

"What about him?" asked Lindy trying to figure out where this was going. Was Annie worried about what had happened at the camp? Was she frightened? Maybe she should have Glen take her home in the morning.

"Nothing." Annie ran down the hall to her room without even saying good night.

Chapter Fourteen

"Tomorrow?" asked Lindy.

Glen looked up from the breakfast menu. "They've moved the Paris meeting to Wednesday afternoon, so I'll have to catch the Tuesday evening flight out of JFK." Glen closed his menu. "I'll take Annie home with me. I'm sure Haddie will stay over until you get back."

"Annie could stay here." Lindy sipped her coffee. "If you think I can take care of her." She looked over the rim of her cup.

"What are you talking about?"

"Last night you seemed to think I wasn't doing a good job of overseeing her."

Glen looked confused.

Lindy hurried on before she lost her nerve. "You said you'd never forgive me if anything happened to her."

"I didn't say that."

"Yes, you did—when we were in the car."

"No, I didn't. Why would I say something so stupid?"

Lindy shrugged. "I don't know, but you did."

"You must have been hearing things."

Annie joined them at the table. She looked unhappy; her eyes were puffy from lack of sleep. She opened her menu, hiding her face from her parents.

"Lover's quarrel," Lindy mouthed to Glen.

Glen's mouth opened. He looked relieved.

"Annie," said Glen. "I have to leave tomorrow morning instead of Wednesday. So you'd better pack tonight. We have to get an early start."

The menu came down. Annie eyed both parents then returned to reading. "I think I'll stay here," she mumbled from behind the menu.

Glen put down the coffee cup he had just picked up. It hit the saucer with a rattle. Annie's menu landed on the table with a thud. Two sets of brown eyes locked on each other. The Haggerty stand-off. Lindy had lived with it for years. She leaned back in her chair to wait it out.

It was cut short by a waiter returning to take their breakfast order.

"So who is this Donald Parker?" asked Glen.

Annie's eyes rolled back in her head. "So that's it. Really, Daddy. I'm not a child. I'm eighteen."

"For two months."

"Sooo?"

"We don't know anything about this boy."

"Daddy, I've been living away from home for two years. I think I can judge if someone's nice or not." Her tone held just enough exasperation to trigger Glen's fight instinct.

"I'll be the judge of that," said Glen.

"Really? Well, I'm not the one you should be worried about." Annie flicked Lindy a look that could have meant anything.

"Be ready to leave by eight o'clock." Glen picked up the morning newspaper.

They ate breakfast in silence. Annie played with her food. Glen read as he ate; Lindy just waited for it to be over, while she tried to figure out what Annie's last statement had meant. At last, Annie pushed her chair back and got up.

"No," she said and walked away.

"Time for a little mother-daughter talk," said Lindy and followed Annie out of the restaurant.

Lindy caught up with her in the driveway. "Let's take a walk around the lake."

"I can't," said Annie. "I'm helping Donald and the others clean up the mess."

"It will just take a few minutes. Did you two have a fight?"

"No, why should we have?"

Lindy shrugged. "I don't know. You just seem unhappy."

"Jeez Louise, Mom. Dr. Van Zandt just lost years of work and you think I'd be worried about some man?"

They walked in silence. It must be teenage hormones, thought Lindy, as she guided Annie toward the lake. She had always been a good-natured child. Even the usual angst of adolescence had seemed minor when compared to her brother, Cliff. But she had spent the last two years away at school, and it struck Lindy that she had missed out on a lot of Annie's growing up.

They passed the man-made beach. Students were already in the water; Monday was their day off. Jeremy had even given the company the day off. Lindy hadn't questioned him why.

"It's just that Daddy and I want you to be happy." The second she opened her mouth, Lindy knew she sounded just like a parent from a fifties sitcom. She was out of practice.

Annie threw her a look that her statement deserved.

A man was opening the boat rental shed. Shiny aluminum canoes sat upside down on wooden racks.

"Want to go for a row on the lake?"

"No."

"Come on," said Lindy. "You always want to do everything. Where's my enthusiastic little girl?"

"I'm not a little girl, and I'm not going home with Daddy."

"He's just worried about you."

"I'm not the one he should be worried about."

"So you've said." Lindy turned to face her. "Who should he be worried about?"

Annie crossed her arms and refused to look at her. Lindy pulled her chin up. Annie's eyes flashed with anger.

"I'm not stupid, Mom. I know what's going on and why you want to get rid of me." She dropped her gaze back to the beach.

Which is more than I can say for myself, thought Lindy.

"Care to elaborate?"

"You know what I'm talking about."

"Annie, I don't have a clue." Lindy was beginning to lose her patience. She felt tired and harassed, and she didn't feel like dealing with a belligerent daughter. "Could you try working with me here? Give me a hint."

"Bill." Annie's face crumpled and tears began to fall from the corners of her eyes.

"Bill?" Did Annie, like Glen, resent her "indulging in disaster?" "What about Bill?" she asked slowly. An uglier idea was taking hold in her mind.

Annie dug the toe of her sneaker into the sand, then smoothed it out again. Lindy watched her repeat the action, while she tried to calm herself enough to talk.

"Annie . . ." Lindy reached for Annie's shoulders, but she pulled away.

"You have a lot of nerve." Annie's voice broke. "You come down on Rebo and Juan, you try to keep me away from Donald, and all the time you have Daddy and your lover here at the same time—in front of everybody."

Lindy reeled back.

Annie's tears were dropping onto the sand. She wiped her arm across her nose. "How could you?" she cried and began running along the shore, leaving the beach and scrambling over the path that skirted the lake.

At last reaction kicked in and Lindy ran after her. It only took a minute to catch up to her. Angry and hurt, she spun Annie around.

"How dare you!" It was all she could do not to slap the girl for her wrong-headedness and lack of trust.

Annie tried to pull away. Lindy gripped her more tightly. "Listen to me, Miss Know-it-all. And listen good. Bill and I are not lovers, we are friends."

Annie gave her a sullen look. Lindy shook her hard. "Whatever gave you such an idiotic idea? We have never been lovers. And even though it is none of your business, I will let you know that I have *never* been unfaithful to your father. Not in twenty years of marriage— and yes— there have been plenty of times when I could have been. So before you go throwing around any other accusations, be sure you've got the facts right." She gave Annie a shove and stalked away, furious, mortified, and a little self-righteous. She and Bill were not lovers. Their relationship had absolutely no physical overtones. They made sure of that. Because although it was unspoken, they both knew if they once overstepped the bounds of propriety . . . but it was better not to think about that.

As soon as Glen found out that Annie was going to the archaeologists' camp, he took off after her. Lindy went to look for Bill, but he wasn't to be found. He was probably at the camp, too. Great, she thought, he and Glen together, after what Annie had said. She shuddered at the thought. She just hoped that Annie had come to her senses and would not cause any trouble between the two of them.

She would deal with that later if necessary. Right now she had another matter to clear up. It couldn't be put off any longer.

The sight of the pink rabbit bobbing along toward the beach sealed her fate. She fell in step with the rabbit.

"Going to the beach?"

No answer.

"I didn't know bunnies could swim."

The bunny stopped. Rebo's head peered out from behind it. "You got something to say?"

"How about 'I'm sorry for being such a jerk'?"

"That's a start." He stuffed the bunny under his arm.

"I'm not a hypocrite; I don't know why I reacted like that. You know I love you and Juan." She swallowed. "And I'm glad you love each other."

"You are?"

"Sure." She took a deep breath. "Looove—" she sang.

"—And sex—" he added.

"Make the wooorld go round," they sang together.

Lindy punctuated the sentiment with a kiss in the air.

Rebo smiled back, his teeth flashing white against his ebony skin. Almost his old smile. They were making progress.

"You were just trying to protect us. Juan says we can't expect you to stop acting like a mother, just because you're our boss."

"Juan said that?"

"Yeah, sometimes the boy gets right to the heart of the matter."

"Pax?"

"You bet." Rebo opened his arms. "Three-way hug." They stood there for a second in a silent embrace, Rebo, Lindy, and the pink bunny. Rebo dropped his arms. "Now that we're back to normal, have I got dirt for you."

He walked over to the nearest tree and sat the bunny down at the base. "You stay here, Jasper."

Taking Lindy's hand, he led her down the path that would eventually lead to the archeologist camp, or what was left of it.

"His name is Jasper?"

"Jasper the Friendly Bunny. You like it?"

Lindy could only shake her head. They had walked about ten minutes when Rebo stopped, looked around, and stepped into the bushes, dragging Lindy after him. Before she could ask where they were going, Rebo put his finger to his lips.

"Afraid I'll scare the wildlife?" she whispered.

Wordlessly, they descended the slope through swarms of insects, climbed over decomposing logs, pushed away overhanging branches, and tripped over rocks that jutted out of the ground. It wasn't a path, but it had been used as one. She followed Rebo along a line of trampled grasses and underneath a dying oak, its wood charred by lightning.

Rebo stopped abruptly as they came out onto a ledge. He looked around as if he thought they might be followed. Below them were the ruins of the archeologist camp and the tiny figures of Van Zandt's staff moving across the rubble.

He led her along the edge of a granite wall. Giant boulders had fallen onto the end of the ledge. A few saplings struggled for life in the dirt that had settled in the crevices between them.

Without warning, he disappeared. "In here." His voice was an echo. She looked more closely and saw the overlap of rock and the fissure just large enough for a body to squeeze through. Pushing aside thoughts of snakes and bats, Lindy forced herself inside.

It was pitch-black. Not even a slit of sunlight showed through the crack.

"Rebo?" she asked tentatively. Her voice echoed back to her. Gooseflesh broke out on her arms and the back of her neck.

"Ta da," came a triumphant voice from the darkness. Then an eerie yellow lit the dark. Hulking shadows loomed out at her, moving, growing, surrounding her. She fought the urge to run screaming for her life.

Rebo placed the Coleman lantern on a makeshift table in the center of the cave. Lantern? Table? Cave? Holy shit. She looked around the chamber. A store of soda and junk food was stacked against one rocky wall. A pile of magazines and another lantern sat on a wooden crate next to a sleeping bag. A plastic baggie of what had to be marijuana (there was a roach clip sitting next to it) and a plastic cup filled with pencils, pens, and unused condoms were placed beside the sleeping bag. Holy shit, she thought again.

"You should see your face." Rebo laughed. The sound bounced off the walls and rebounded in her ears from every direction.

"Shhh."

"No one can hear us," he said. "Juan and I tested it."

"You didn't."

"Not that, Lindelooloo. One of us stood outside while the other one yelled and whistled. Couldn't hear a thing."

"It's unbelievable."

"Welcome to Larry Cleveland's cave of iniquity. *We've* been doing a little sleuthing since *you've* been tied up with all your family matters." Rebo shot her a condescending look, his face ghoulish in the exaggerated shadows.

"He had a real thing going. Gave 'em sex. Made 'em pay. And nobody's talking. They're sure that dumbass sheriff is looking for a murderer, and every one of them thinks he's going to pin it on them."

"Have you looked around?"

"You mean, searched the joint? Yep. Nothing's here." He paused, a look of satisfaction growing on his face. "Nothing, but somebody's been here, and recently."

"Connie Phillips?"

"Got it in one, Lindecleverly." His look of satisfaction increased. He moved to an unlit corner and pulled out a crumpled shirt. He spread the shirt open with the inside of the collar facing Lindy.

She leaned forward to see. A neatly printed label was ironed onto the fabric. CONNOVER PHILLIPS. "Jeez."

"The sheriff can think he's left the area; I'm not going to tell him otherwise. But I think Connie's still here. Hiding out somewhere during the day and sleeping here at night. And . . ." Rebo put up his hand to stop her question. "I think if we hang out here tonight, we'll catch him at it."

"Do you think he killed Larry Cleveland?"

Rebo shrugged. "Or knows who did. If I was that kid, I'd be scared shitless."

"I guess it would be stupid to inform the sheriff."

"Are you nuts? He'll arrest the kid on some trumped-up charges or scare him into saying that Robert is a pederast. From what I hear, there's no way Robert's involved in this. His record is spotless, as they say in the movies."

Lindy massaged her temples. "Connie could be in danger."

"No shit. I say we find out what he knows and then decide what to do with him."

"We could be jeopardizing his safety."

"We'd certainly be doing that if we turn him over to that homo-phobic—"

Lindy cut him off. "You're right. God, this is hideous."

"So try to sneak away from your hubby-do after dinner, and we'll stake out the joint."

Rebo doused the light and they were plunged into darkness. Lindy felt a hand enclose her arm and pull her forward; her shoulder scraped the wall, and she was pushed out into the sunlight.

They scrambled back up the slope. Lindy waited below the path until Rebo checked to make sure no one was coming. He pulled her up the final few feet, then covered the entrance with a log and broken pieces of brush.

"Do you think the police know about the cave?" she asked as they made their way back to the camp compound.

"No way. Their imagination died in the back seat of their daddy's Chevy."

"How on earth did you find it?"

"Just needed to know where to look."

She raised an eyebrow at him.

"Had one just like it at the Baptist Youth Retreat back in Springfield."

"You didn't."

Rebo looked shocked. "Well, we didn't have any weed; it was a church camp, but cheap wine pretty much did the trick."

Lindy could only shake her head and try to figure out how the hell she was going to get away that evening.

Rebo retrieved Jasper from the base of the tree and headed off toward the lake. Lindy returned to the house. As she reached the top of the steps, she saw two figures sitting on a wicker settee at the far end of the porch. A shaft of sunlight illuminated the shape of Bill's head, bringing out the gray and blond strands that intermingled with the soft brown of this rest of his hair. Bill always kept his hair short around the hairline and longer on top, as if he couldn't decide whether to be a policeman or an intellectual. She took a step toward them. At least they were outside. Bill in the out-of-doors was more approachable than when he was inside. There, he seemed to tower over you, making his tall, slender frame appear overpowering and his voice thunderous. His head was bent toward Jeremy's.

They jumped when Lindy approached. She half expected them to shove a copy of *Playboy* magazine beneath the cushions.

She stopped and stood over them, trying to give herself a psychological edge. It wasn't much of an edge. With Jeremy at nearly six feet and Bill slightly over, even sitting they were almost as tall as she was.

"Would you fellas like to tell me what's going on?"

They stared at her as though she were a Bedouin camel asking directions in a New York deli.

"Okay, let me rephrase that," she said when it was clear neither man was going to speak. "Tell me what the hell you two are up to."

Bill's face went completely blank. Jeremy stared beyond her shoulder. She had to fight the urge to turn around and see if anyone was there.

She brought both hands to her hips. As an intimidation technique it was singularly lacking in success. They remained mute.

She tried again. "I know Jeremy brought you here because he's worried." No reaction.

She turned on Jeremy. "Don't you want to know what I learned while you were gone?"

He shot Bill a look that could only be described as desperate.

Bill caught Lindy's eye. "What did you learn?"

"You first."

"No deal."

Anger spewed up inside her, overriding her good sense. Didn't he realize they had to work together on this? It was the only way. Connie might be in danger. One boy was dead. Robert close to death with God-knew-what hanging over his head. This was no time for a battle of egos. But that was her rational self talking; her angry self refused to listen.

"Just like the old days, huh, Brandecker?" She paused long enough to glower at him, then turned on her heel and stalked into the house.

She had reached the stairs before she realized that she should be going to her room in the annex. Part of her insisted that she turn around and tell Bill everything. After all, he was the ex-cop; he'd know what to do. But she had to cool off first. It never did any good to talk to Bill when you were angry, he just turned it back on you . . . or out-yelled you. She climbed up the stairs hoping Biddy was in her room.

* * *

"Sorry about breakfast yesterday," said Biddy. She was looking better than she had in days and Lindy immediately felt better.

"I wasn't at my best, either. I've missed you."

"Me, too." Biddy moved to the table and put on her glasses. "I've been making some notes."

At last, thought Lindy. Notes were a big part of their life together. Not only were there theater notes and rehearsal notes, but they had taken to writing down their ideas about the other "misadventures" they had been involved in. Note-taking hadn't really been pivotal in catching the murderers, but at least it gave them a clearer picture of the situation and had led them closer to the truth each time.

Lindy pulled another chair to the table and sat down.

Biddy opened her notebook and began to read. "Larry falls down the cliff. The sheriff says it was suicide or murder." She made a face. It never got any easier accepting murder as a fact of life. "He takes Robert in for questioning, then Robert is found unconscious with a suicide note on the computer. In the meantime . . ." Biddy flipped a page. "This boy Connie has gone missing. And Bill Brandecker shows up." She lifted both eyebrows in question.

"Don't look at me. It was Jeremy's doing."

"I thought it must have been. Even at your maddest, most impetuous moment you would never have him here with Glen."

Lindy went rigid. "Why?"

"Why?" Biddy's eyebrows disappeared beneath her curls. "Are you kidding? With the way Glen feels about your being involved with murder? Not even you would be nuts enough to rub it in his face. No matter what the stakes."

Lindy let out her breath.

"What?"

"Annie just accused me of having an affair with Bill."

Biddy laughed. "Ridiculous. Bill's too much of a gentleman and you're too faithful. You're both hopeless. What gave her such an absurd idea?"

"Appearances."

"Oh those," Biddy said dismissively. "You're in the arts. You should be used to it by now. Can we get back to my notes?"

"Please. I guess I was a little distracted."

"So get over it. Then there's the landslide at the archaeologist site, which Dr. Van Zandt insists was no accident. Anything else?"

"Rebo found a cave that Larry was using for his wild nights with the other students."

"Wow." Biddy scribbled it into her notebook.

"He thinks that Connie is hiding there at night. He wants me to go with him tonight to see if we can catch him and find out what he knows."

Biddy pushed her glasses to her forehead. "Great."

"But how the hell am I going to sneak out with Rebo when Glen is here?"

Biddy brushed the air with her hand. "I'll take care of Glen. I'll get him talking about golf or something."

Lindy pulled her chair closer. "Okay, pal, what else do you have?"

"The police study of the cliff where Larry fell shows that he didn't fall down it but arced over it. Found that out from Marguerite, who found it out from Sheriff Grappel. The most loquacious cop I've ever been around."

"He's bound to have made so many procedural errors that if someone does get tried for murder, he'll probably get off."

Biddy sighed. "But that isn't really the point is it?"

"Appearances," they said together.

The retreat's reputation would be destroyed," said Lindy.

"Taking the Easton name with it."

Lindy nodded. "So where's the motive?"

"Well, the town wants the land for development . . ."

"But I've talked to several locals who don't feel that way at all. In fact, I got the impression that it's only the mayor and some local real estate people who are pushing that. Most of the town seems satisfied with the Eastons' patronage."

"Hmmm." Biddy wrote this information into a column in her notebook.

"If Larry's death was suicide, it would be bad for a while, but it would eventually blow over," said Lindy.

"Yeah, I can't see how they could tie suicide into a scheme to ruin the Eastons."

"Unless Robert had seduced him as the sheriff and the note implies." Lindy rubbed her temples. "That would certainly ruin the reputation of the camp."

Biddy slapped her palm on the table. "But everybody, I mean everybody, says that it isn't true."

"People have been fooled before."

"I won't believe it."

"Me neither, not yet. But just to take the absurdity one step further: If Robert seduced him and then Larry threatened to expose him, Robert might have been desperate enough to push him over the cliff."

"And we can kiss the retreat's reputation goodbye," said Biddy.

"Or it might be as simple as a lover's quarrel between Connie and Larry. And Larry goes over the cliff."

"Not Connie, too."

"I'm afraid so. It seems Larry had his hands in everybody's pants. God, how sordid."

"So it all comes down to two options, so far," said Biddy.

"Two?"

"Sex or real estate."

Lindy opened her hands in a question. "Whooo could aaask for anything more?"

"So why is Bill here?"

"Not a clue. He's worse than usual this time. About as communicative as one of those faces on Mount Rushmore."

"It must be bad."

"I think you're right."

Glen was stretched out on the bed, freshly showered. His hair had left a damp spot on the pillow.

Lindy crept over and gave him a kiss.

"Uumm," he said.

"How was the morning?"

He opened one eye. "Grueling and dirty. Come here." He reached out one hand.

"I'm dusty and icky."

"I don't mind."

They missed lunch and most of the afternoon. Glen headed back to the shower.

When Lindy stepped out of the shower, Glen was already dressed. "I think I'll wait for you in the bar. Maybe they have something to snack on." He gave her a lascivious look.

"Just remember we're dining with the Eastons tonight."

"Will do." He grabbed his jacket and shut the door behind him.

When she came downstairs, Rebo was coming out of the bar.

"Don't forget our date."

"I won't."

"Bring some better shoes." He looked down at her four-inch stilettos.

"I stashed my Nike's in the downstairs closet."

"Good. See you then."

"Have you seen Glen?"

"He's in the bar with the boyfriend wannabe."

"With Bill?"

"Yup.

"Doing what?" She couldn't imagine them actually trying to carry on a conversation.

"Last time I looked they were pissing on the chair legs."

"What?"

He stretched his mouth into a broad grin and champed his teeth down. "Claiming their territory."

She left him at a run. They were sitting at a table with Stu, Glen looking self-assured and Bill decidedly unhappy. Was it because of her or was something else bothering him?

Bill looked relieved when he saw her, then his face cleared of expression. He was beginning to really piss her off.

"Good evening, Stu." She ignored Bill.

"You look lovely, my dear. Shall I get you a drink? Marguerite says to come over whenever you're ready."

"I'm ready."

Glen and Stu got up.

"Coming, Bill?" asked Stu.

"I'll be over later," said Bill.

They left him idly turning his wineglass on the table.

Chapter
Fifteen

The good news at dinner was that Robert was awake, lucid, and would recover. Chi-Chi had finally been allowed to see him, accompanied by a policeman, while another stood on duty outside the door. The rest of the news was bad.

Robert denied having tried to kill himself, didn't remember taking anything besides his normal dose of Benadryl, and insisted that he never used the computer. He became agitated at the suggestion he had killed Larry Cleveland and had to be sedated.

The sheriff, of course, had not believed him and was holding him on suspicion of murder. If he had any real evidence, he was not saying, a departure from his normal habit of verbosity.

Chi-Chi had returned to her duties at the annex with a ferocity that struck fear in her employees.

Lindy sat between Jeremy and Glen at the table. Across from her Biddy was flanked by Bill and Stu. Ellis and Marguerite sat in their usual places. Biddy concentrated on Stu, Glen talked with Ellis. Lindy had nothing to say to Jeremy or Bill, and she didn't want to risk catching their attention if she talked with Marguerite; she held a quiet communion with her plate. Conversation, what little there was of it, was polarized at each end of the table: Jeremy, Bill and Marguerite and Stu, Glen and Ellis, with Biddy and Lindy the no-man's land between them.

It was with relief and anticipation that Lindy finally pushed her chair back and followed the others to the library for coffee. Bill and Marguerite took their coffees off to the side and spoke in low tones, leaning toward each other in an attitude that said they were not to be interrupted.

Lindy went to stand by Ellis who was alone by the unlit fireplace. He looked like he needed cheering up. She smiled at him; it was the best she could do. There was nothing to say that could make any of them feel better. The worst had happened. Whether Robert was really guilty or not, the reputation of the camp would be seriously jeopardized.

Ellis finally looked at her with that look of slight confusion she had seen several times before. She found herself wondering if, perhaps, he was becoming just a bit senile.

"Why is he avoiding me, what have I done?" He was looking not at Lindy, but across the room. "We used to be such good friends." Ellis murmured the words. Lindy followed his gaze across the room to where Stu and Jeremy stood by the book shelves.

She stifled her irritation. Another lover's quarrel, and at a time like this.

She was thinking of some platitude to cover her consternation, when Glen joined them. He was beginning to get on her nerves, too. At first it was nice to be the center of her husband's attention for a change, but after two days, his hovering was becoming annoying and his presence was interfering with her ability to find out what had happened to Larry Cleveland and why.

Now, on top of everything else, she had to figure out a way to ditch him for the next few hours in order to set an ambush for Connie. She felt ridiculous and guilty, but most of all impatient.

She gave Biddy a nod. Biddy rose from the sofa and carried her coffee toward them. As soon as she arrived, Lindy said, "I think I'll go check on Annie."

"I'll go, too," said Glen and made ready to follow her. She widened her eyes at Biddy, who immediately asked him what a par was.

"Good night, Marguerite," said Lindy.

"Good night, my dear."

Bill looked at Lindy curiously.

"On second thought, I'll just stay here for a while," said Glen, beetling his eyes at Bill. Lindy made her escape.

If Bill wasn't any use to her as a partner, at least he made a good diversionary tactic. Glen could follow him around all night for all Lindy cared, it would keep both of them out of her way. She stashed her heels in the shrubbery and laced up her running shoes. She wouldn't take time to change. Her black cocktail dress would be prefect nighttime camouflage.

Rebo was waiting at the path. With an amused look at her outfit, he disappeared into the woods. Lindy followed.

Creeping as stealthily as two lumbering bears, they made their way toward the cave until Rebo stopped her with a sharp movement of his hand.

"He's here."

Lindy could only take his word for it. The night was pitch-black. Rebo slipped into the crevice dragging her with him. The yellow light of the lantern assaulted her eyes making it impossible for her to see.

Her vision came into focus just in time to see a raised stick crash down on Rebo's head and Rebo fall to the ground.

"Stop!" she cried. "We're friends." About as original as "Halt, who goes there," but it seemed to work. Connie Phillips, arm raised for another blow, backed up. Rebo moaned and the boy threw himself past Lindy toward the opening.

He landed on the rock floor, spread eagle, letting out a sharp cry. Rebo held on to one ankle.

"You little shit. We're trying to help you," he said.

But Connie had curled into a ball, his arms covering his head. Rebo transferred his grip to the boy's armpits and hauled him up. He carried the fetal Connie over to the sleeping bag and dropped him unceremoniously onto it.

Lindy winced. The thin layer of Qualofil wasn't much protection from the hard ground. Connie yelped when his butt made contact.

"Look, kid, we don't want to hurt you." Sergeant Friday from

Dragnet. Lindy would have laughed if Connie hadn't looked so petrified.

She knelt down beside him. He was shivering. She placed a motherly hand on his shoulder. He flinched away. She suppressed her impatience. Good cop, bad cop, she coached herself. "It's all right," she said in her most soothing voice. "We want to help." She felt him relax a little, then look cautiously at Rebo.

"I'm in deep shit, aren't I?" Connie whispered.

"Got it in one, amigo." Rebo squatted down on his haunches. "You want to tell us what this is all about?"

Connie shook his head vigorously.

Rebo stood up.

"Okay, okay." Connie cowered against Lindy's knees.

"Just start at the beginning," she said.

"I don't know where the beginning is." Tears welled up in Connie's eyes. "Shit." He wiped them away.

"Why did you run away?" prompted Rebo.

" 'Cause Larry got killed and nobody cared. They just put in his understudy, like he had sprained his ankle or something." Connie wiped his eyes again. His hands left a raccoon mask of mud across his face.

"It may seem like that to you, Connie, but people do care," said Lindy. "They're trying to find out what happened. And you can help them."

Connie shook his head again.

"Just get to the point, my man." Rebo flexed his shoulders. It was a ludicrous gesture, but it unleashed Connie's tongue.

"They're trying to make it out that Larry killed himself. He would never." He took a breath. "He loved himself too much."

Rebo caught Lindy's eye. "What do you think happened to Larry?"

"They killed him. And they're going to kill me, too."

"Who?" Rebo and Lindy both spoke at once. He had caught them completely off guard.

Connie lunged across the sleeping bag. Rebo's large hand brought him up sharp.

"Tell us—we want to help you. Don't tell us—you can tell it to the sheriff."

Connie shook his head again.

"Stop doing that or you're gonna knock yourself out," Rebo said shrilly, dropping out of character.

Connie stopped, then stared up at Rebo, rhythmically blinking his eyes. Rebo threw up his hands and started to walk away.

"Nobody much liked him." Lindy had to lean forward to hear his words. "I did, though. He used to bring kids here. Sometimes he brought me."

"Did you ever come here with anyone else?" asked Lindy.

Connie's eyes widened. "No. Only Larry could bring people here. And nobody could tell. Robert would have sent us home."

"Robert didn't know about this place?"

Connie started to shake his head, then looked up at Rebo and stopped. "No." He switched his troubled eyes to Lindy. "Did they call my mom and dad?"

"They're still trying to reach them."

"They'll kill me if they find out I'm . . . you know . . . gay."

If I were your parents, thought Lindy, *I'd kill you if I found out you were having sex of any persuasion.* She pushed the thought aside as another thought took its place. His parents would "kill" him. Isn't that what he meant when he said "they" would kill him? Was it just a teenage expression? She asked him.

"No." His eyes never left Lindy's, seeking comfort there, comfort that should have been given by his own mother. "I mean really kill. Me and Larry were sneaking down here one night and we heard these voices up above us on the path. I was really scared, but Larry told me to come inside and wait for him." Connie paused and Lindy carefully moved to the floor to sit beside him.

"I thought for sure we were going to get caught, but when Larry finally came back, he just laughed and said it was no problem. He had that smile on his face. You know, the one he got when he had just found out something that he could use."

"Did he tell you what it was about?" Rebo's voice sent Connie scuttling close to Lindy. She put her arm around him.

"No."

Larry must have overheard something that he shouldn't have, and he must have recognized the voices or seen who it was. He was planning to use it against them. Blackmail. But it had backfired. Someone who wasn't afraid of Larry. Some one who was willing to kill a boy in order to cover up—a relationship? A plan? Someone who was stronger than he was. Could Robert have pushed him over the cliff? He was much smaller than the teenager, but adrenaline had been known to give people enormous strength.

"Connie," she said softly. "The police are saying that Robert seduced Larry and then killed him in order to keep it secret."

Connie tried to push her away. "No way. Robert never did any of those kind of things. None of the teachers here did." He started to cry in earnest now, not bothering to wipe away the tears that coursed down his cheeks. "Not Robert. It was whoever was on the path that night. And now they want to kill me, too. But I don't know anything."

"Robert is in the hospital," said Lindy, strengthening her grip on the boy. "The police think he tried to commit suicide because of what he had done."

A pained cry erupted from the boy. He threw his head backward into Lindy's shoulder. She held on.

"He couldn't have been here that night. We waited until he checked the dorm. He always did that after the counselors went to bed. We hid in the bushes until we saw him go into the bungalow and turn out the lights. He couldn't have made it to the path before us."

Lindy felt her own breath release and realized that she hadn't breathed for several seconds.

Connie's arms were suddenly around her, shoulders shaking with his sobs. An inconsolable boy, alone. She rocked him gently until his breathing steadied and the trembling had subsided.

She looked up to Rebo. He stood over them, feet spread, arms akimbo, a quizzical expression on his face.

"What should we do?"

"Keep him away from the sheriff. I'm beginning to get some nasty ideas about him."

"Me, too," she agreed.

"We can keep him here tonight and put him on a bus home to-morrow."

"If the sheriff has done an even half-assed job, his picture will be posted everywhere." She felt Connie nod his head. So that was out.

Connie was becoming heavy in her arms, fatigue replacing fear as Lindy rocked him slowly toward sleep.

"Damn. Talk about your rock and hard places," said Rebo. He pulled his bandanna from his head and mopped his face. "If we tell Brandecker, he'll have to tell the authorities. Too bad the man's so damn scrupulous. If he weren't, we could dump the kid on him." He paused, then grinned. "And you could be having one hell of a lit-tle fling on the side."

They finally decided to leave Connie there for the night. He was already asleep when Lindy lowered his head gently to the sleeping bag. Rebo volunteered to stay with him. It was getting late or Lindy would have argued. If Grappel discovered them, God knows what he would make of it. But they had no choice.

Rebo followed her to the ledge.

"Don't worry mama, I'm strictly monogamous, and . . ." He placed his finger on her nose. "I don't do children."

She brushed his finger away and hugged him. "I have total confidence in you."

"You do?"

She nodded and began her climb back to the path.

"Oh, I forgot to tell you," Rebo whispered. "You do that good."

"What?"

"That mother thing." Then he vanished, leaving her staring at the rock wall. Smiling, she climbed upward.

She retrieved her heels from under the bush and crept upstairs. The room was empty. She had a brief image of Glen following Bill around to prevent him from keeping a midnight rendezvous. Lord, if he only knew.

She had barely jumped into bed and pulled the covers up, when she heard the door open. She yawned theatrically and asked in a sleepy voice, "Where have you been?"

"Talking to Bill." Glen threw his jacket on a chair and kicked his shoes underneath.

"That's nice."

"He's not so bad once you get to know him."

No, he wasn't, agreed Lindy and closed her eyes, this time for real.

Chapter
Sixteen

Annie and Lindy stood in the driveway until Glen's car was no longer in sight.

"Well," said Lindy. "Just us girls."

"Mom."

Lindy knew from Annie's tone where she was going. "The least said, the better."

"I'm sorry."

"You're forgiven. But the next time you get any wild ideas, ask first." Lindy moved away.

"Where are you going?"

"To see a man about a horse." And, she added to herself, to try to think of something besides platitudes before she got there. She started back across the pavement. Two black sedans sped up the drive and stopped in front of the house. Car doors slammed and a cadre of Easton lawyers hurried up the steps.

She hadn't gone far before she saw Rebo coming up the path. He was walking funny. As he got closer, she could see a patchwork of scratches across his face and arms. His complexion was a chalky brown.

"Little shit bolted," he said. "I was graciously offering him a Pop-Tart for breakfast when he kneed me in the balls and took off. By the time I was a baritone again, he was nowhere to be found.

Though I tried." He held out his scratched arms as evidence. "The forest fought back."

"What do we do now?"

"Let the sheriff find him," Rebo grunted. "I don't care what you do, but I'm going to go straddle an ice pack." He limped away.

Lindy felt her options disappearing. She couldn't tell Bill about finding Connie. Especially now that he was out there somewhere unprotected. Bill would be bound by his sense of jurisprudence to tell the sheriff, regardless of how he felt about him. And Lindy knew exactly how he felt. If he wouldn't put up with sloppy thinking from an amateur, he certainly wouldn't condone it in a professional. But he would still feel compelled to act within the law. Damn the man for his honesty.

She headed for the theater. She'd look in on company class while she tried to figure out what to do. The company started each day with a ballet class. As Rebo had told his students, ballet was the foundation of their art, and its classical structure might inspire a little order to her thoughts.

She went through the front door and into the lobby; it was faster than walking around to the stage door in the back.

Rose was looking at the student pictures when Lindy walked inside.

"Morning," she said then turned back to peruse the picture in front of her.

Lindy came to stand beside her.

"You know," said Rose. "He's not at all what you'd expect from hearing about him."

Lindy looked at the picture. Larry Cleveland smiled back at her. "I thought the same thing when I first saw it," said Lindy.

"Kind of reminds me of that riddle."

"What riddle?"

"You know, that one about what enters on four legs, does something on two, and then exits on three." Rose shrugged. "I don't remember how it goes exactly."

" A baby, a youth, and an old man," Lindy answered. "But I don't follow you."

"Well, here is the 'baby', blond, blue-eyed, handsome . . ."

"Yeah?"

"Then there's the boss." Rose pointed to the closed door of the theater where Jeremy was teaching company class. "Blond, blue-eyed and handsome, only older. And then . . ." She turned toward the glass front of the theater. "There's him." Ellis and Stu passed in front of them, looking comfortable and unhurried, their quarrel apparently resolved, out for a morning stroll. "No longer blond, but I bet he was, blue-eyed, still kind of handsome, and walking with a cane."

"Hmmm," said Lindy. "It is a weird coincidence, isn't it?"

"Is it?" Rose pondered for a moment. "I wonder. The Eastons seem to have a penchant for the—"

"Blond, blue-eyed, and handsome," finished Lindy.

"Hmmm," said Rose.

Lindy felt calmer after watching class. Ballet was so well ordered. One exercise built on another until all the body parts were warmed up and working; smaller movements grew into larger ones, requiring more and more strength as the class progressed. And when the final exercise was finished, the body was primed and ready to work. Sounded like good technique for an investigation, too, thought Lindy. Start with the small and build to the larger picture. Pay attention to each separate part until the whole situation made sense. But how to do it?

She began organizing each incident sequentially, then took them apart and looked for common threads. A dead boy, a staged suicide, a landslide. Sex and real estate. A powerful family, loyal friends and employees, and the disgruntled few. Where was the pattern? Marguerite, powerful, beloved, unyielding; Ellis, well bred, but slightly befuddled and anachronistic; Stu, the family friend. Was that just Marguerite's euphemism for Ellis's lover? But they were over sixty. As if sexagenarians didn't have sex, thought Lindy, disgusted with her own prejudice. Prejudice? Byron Grappel, hating the camp and Robert, because of Chi-Chi, or because of something else? And what about Adele? She had slipped the bottle of pills into her pocket. It seemed perfectly reasonable at the time, but was she hiding something? Was she involved or was she in danger? And who had typed the suicide note on the computer?

It had to have been someone after they had taken Robert to the infirmary. Why else would the chair have been moved? Someone typed the note and turned Robert's chair to face the computer. Someone who didn't know that Robert didn't type. Good Lord, had she interrupted the killer after he had placed a potentially lethal dose of drugs in Robert's drink? Had he been there watching her? Then typed the note after they had taken Robert away?

She sprang out of her seat; the cushion flipped up and she hurried up the aisle. She had to talk to Bill. He knew something that she didn't. Something that Jeremy had told him. He'd have to tell her. She'd trade him information if he wanted to play it that way. Between the two of them, they would be able to figure it out.

She stopped as soon as her hand reached the bar of the lobby door. Or could it be that Jeremy knew who the killer was? A cold sweat broke out on her face. Her stomach churned. Maybe Robert really did know how to type; she only had Chi-Chi's word for it that he didn't. Shit, her imagination was running wild. This was doing no good. It was time to humble herself before Bill.

She didn't have far to look. Bill was coming around the back of the theater. A knapsack was slung over one shoulder. He braced himself when he saw her.

She walked slowly forward. She was no more prepared to encounter him than he was ready for her. Inexplicably, she felt that their friendship was about to be tested. She waffled a minute wondering if finding the killer would be worth the price. And why it had come to this. Was it because of everyone's assumption of their sexual involvement, or was it that they really didn't have each other's trust?

He was waiting for her, standing his ground, not making the first move. She took a steadying breath and walked up to him.

"Hi." *Great, Graham*, she thought. *Brilliant opening.*

No smile. Just an intent look. "I feel a trap here," he said finally. And there they stood, being stubborn. Just like many times be-

fore. Only this was different. She could feel it as sure as she felt the
sweat gathering in her armpits.

She groped for something to say. Every possibility fled her brain,
leaving it blank and stupid. The silence continued.

"You want to see what I have in this bag?"

Had he just made the first step? Or was he deflecting her again?

"Etchings?" As a joke it fell flat. Stop being glib, she warned herself. "Yes."

He turned away. She followed him across the graveled clearing
until he stopped at a table and plunked the bag onto it. They sat
down. Lindy watched him press open the plastic clasp and pull out
a brown lunch bag.

Lunch? She watched warily as his hand reached inside again.
This time he pulled out a flashlight, which dragged a surgical latex
glove along with it. He tossed the glove aside. "A makeshift evidence kit. Adele gave me the gloves."

Her interest increased.

He turned on the flashlight and opened the bag. He didn't have
to tell her not to touch it. He knew she wouldn't. Somehow that fact
made her feel better.

He shined the flashlight into the bag. Lindy peered past it to
three tiny pieces of metal. "What are they?"

"Remnants of dynamite caps."

"You found these at the site?"

"Above it."

So that's where he had been. She smiled her approval.

"Just dumb luck. And not usable in court."

"But—"

"Found and removed from the crime scene by an amateur. Like I
said, not much use."

Crime scene, she thought, but she said, "You're not an amateur."

"These days I am. But at least we know."

Lindy wondered if it was disappointment she heard in his voice,
or just resignation. Over their months of friendship, she had learned
that he had given up his job as detective in the NYPD because his

wife, an actress, had thought it wasn't classy enough. He had quit and she had left him. That was fourteen years ago and that was all he had ever said on the subject.

"Are you going to tell the sheriff?" She knew the answer.

"As a matter of formality."

She nodded. But his next statement shocked her.

"I suggested he look. Yesterday." She watched his jaw tighten then relax. "This morning the area had been contaminated, big time."

"You think he destroyed evidence."

Bill quirked his head to the side. "He missed these."

"I wish you'd yell at me," she blurted out. "You're being much too accepting. It's not like you."

He smiled. A shadow of his usual one. "I haven't spent much time with the company before this, Lindy. I don't like it."

"We're that bad?" She tried for a casual tone, but she felt hurt.

"Just the opposite." He folded the ends of the bag and returned it and the flashlight and glove to the knapsack. "Will you tell me what you've found out?" He held up his hand. "No reciprocation."

But she understood now. Jeremy had told him something in confidence and he wouldn't betray it. He was caught between his loyalties and he was unhappy.

She told him about the day she found Robert slumped over his desk. About the chair being turned the wrong way and her surmises as to why.

Bill only nodded as she spoke as if he had expected as much. But the story about finding the cave and Connie clearly surprised him.

"You should have told me. I wondered where you were off to last night. I would have followed you, but I couldn't detach your husband."

"I'm sorry."

"You planned it that way."

She nodded.

"Figures!" Now, he yelled. "Of all the stupid—did you stop to think of the repercussions? The kid could be in danger—you could be in danger." Then he stopped as abruptly as he began. He grabbed the knapsack off the table. "Never mind," he said in a quieter voice. She watched him walk away.

She added Bill to the list of people she had pissed off that week. The others had forgiven her. Hopefully, he would, too.

Lindy sat for a while alternating between watching Bill's back as he walked toward the house and staring at her shoes. If he had been honest with her from the beginning, she would have told him what she and Rebo were planning. And if she had told him, he would have handled it much better than they had done. They had let Connie get away, and now he was wandering around frightened and possibly in danger.

Then it occurred to her that Bill had not asked to see the cave. She started to run after him, then stopped, dropping abruptly back onto the bench. He didn't want to know. He didn't want to be in the position of having to tell the sheriff. He was tying his own hands. They had wanted his help, had even brought him here, and they were making it impossible for him to act efficiently. Making it impossible for him to act at all.

At least he was still here. Watching, putting the pieces together. And she would help him, in her own way. She would make the cave her business. Discover everything she could, and then take it to Bill.

She followed the path past the back of the theater, made certain that no one was nearby, and ducked into the brush. She followed the trampled grass through the trees, downward, fighting back at branches, climbing over rocks and decaying wood. Always looking behind her. It seemed to take forever. Once she was sure she had gotten lost. She backtracked until she found a landmark that she recognized. She kicked herself mentally for not paying more attention on her first trip down with Rebo, rather than depending on him to lead the way. She wouldn't be so careless in the future.

At last she stepped out onto the ledge and looked around. To her left was the wall of granite and the cave. She turned to her right. Open space stretched out before her, though the view was dissected by the spires of trees. She scanned the distant walls of growth, looked down and found blue patches of the stream where it showed through the trees. And right below her, separated by a sharp drop and a mangle of greenery, the archaeologist camp.

Lindy recognized Annie's dark hair among the students that loaded rocks and debris into wheelbarrows, then carted them away. The barrows disappeared behind an outcropping of rock and reappeared empty. The Jeep had been salvaged; she could see a dented fender behind a copse of trees. An orange backhoe pushed rocks out of the stream. Water oozed from its shovel as the operator deposited the load onto the shore where it would eventually be carted away.

But the figure that stopped her eye was Dr. Van Zandt. His back toward her. Arms by his side. Looking over the ruin of his camp. The destruction of years of backbreaking, eye-damaging labor, and thousands of years of archaeological evidence. She knew he was feeling every scrape of the backhoe as if it were scoring his own back.

He must have decided to continue with his research—why else clear the area?—though the integrity of the beds was now compromised. Just like the dynamite site, she thought with a shudder. She turned her focus back to her investigation.

She visually drew a line from the backhoe up the side of the cliff, past the ledge where the Jeep had been parked. She had to duck her head to see beyond the tree that marred her view. She took a few steps along the ledge, keeping the line "as the crow flies," in her mind. Traced its projected route to the promontory where the dynamite charge might have been detonated. She didn't have a clear view. It was surrounded by green shrubs entwined with the flowers of climbing honeysuckle. She turned back to the face of rock behind her. Followed it back to the right to the slope she had just climbed down.

Then she let her eyes roam upward, looking for a place that someone might have stood talking, making plans—her head shot back to the promontory above the camp site. Making plans to blow up the camp. Good Lord. And if Larry Cleveland had overheard them—

He probably thought he was in fat city. Did he recognize the voices? Or did he sneak back up the bluff and actually see them? She could kick herself for not asking Connie how long Larry had been gone. She searched her mind for what he had said, his exact words, "when he finally came back." Did that mean he had been gone long enough to climb up and actually see who was talking? Or just that to a frightened boy the time seemed interminable? It could make the difference. If it was someone whose voice he recognized that would probably leave Grappel and the townspeople out, unless Larry had been in trouble with the police since he had been here. That was unlikely. Marguerite would only call in Grappel as a last resort, knowing the way he felt about Chi-Chi and Robert. So maybe Larry had seen who it was. And now he was dead.

Lindy scanned the area above her, looking for a spot for a rendezvous. There were too many damned trees. She climbed back the way she had come until she regained the path. To her right, the path sloped upward to the theater. To her left, it took a downward swing until climbing again into the woods. The same path she had taken for her morning jog. She walked slowly, looking through the trees, waiting for a glimpse of the water. She followed the curve of the path until she saw the guardrail and remembered stopping to talk to Ellis. Ellis pointing to the lookout where Larry had "lost his footing."

She swallowed her agitation. Ellis? He had said that he didn't mind a little tasteful development as long as they didn't get too close, and with thousands of acres, that wouldn't be much of a difficulty to overcome. The idea stretched the limits of her imagination. Then why not just sell? Because he couldn't stand up to Marguerite. That was pretty evident in the way she treated him, as if he were a child that needed overseeing. Chi-Chi had told her that Marguerite didn't think any of them had quite grown up. It could make a man resentful.

She was standing at the rail, hands gripped tightly on the green bar. Had Ellis been standing there that night, plotting with someone? No, it didn't make sense; you couldn't even see the campsite from where she was standing. If you were planning to blow something up wouldn't you stand where you could see it? Point and discuss and trace trajectories?

She slipped under the rail before her good sense could stop her. Hugging the inside edge, holding onto branches, rocks, or anything that might be stationary, Lindy shuffled around the spur of land. She could feel the breeze on her face as it whipped past the promontory. She kept her eyes glued to the ground, checking the earth beneath her for any signs of cracking or instability. When she reached the ridge, she pulled a sapling down in her hand, gave it a yank. It seemed firm. She scooted out to the edge and looked down. The orange backhoe dumped another load of rocks on the shore. It was a perfect view. She could even see the ledge where the Jeep had been parked. And above it, on the same eye level from where she stood clinging to a tree, she saw the remnants of what had been an outcropping of granite, now just the jagged edges of rock where the rest had been blown away and hurtled down the side.

She dragged her gaze from the scene and willed herself to look downward. Tangled growth marred her view. She tried to orient her eyes to where she thought the cave might be. There were several patches of gray among the greenery, but she wasn't sure which one was the cave. But what she did realize was that the police were correct. Larry Cleveland hadn't slipped off the edge. Bushes and scrub oak grew out from the face. He could have grabbed one and broken his fall, and if that had failed, there was a flat area not more than ten feet below. After that, the land plunged straight down. Hitting the first ledge might have killed him, but that wasn't the point. Larry Cleveland had ended up at the bottom. And though Lindy leaned out as far as she dared, she couldn't tell where the bottom was. What she could tell was that Larry would have to have flown to get to the bottom, and if he could fly, he wouldn't be dead.

Lindy inched away from the precipice, scrambled back up the side as fast as her shaking legs and racing heart allowed. She ducked back underneath the rail and held onto it until her heart slowed and her breathing was almost back to normal.

"Lindy."

She spun around and swallowed the scream that erupted from her throat.

"Sorry, I didn't mean to startle you."

She laughed, a nervous sound that rang harsh in her ears. "Just contemplating the beauty. You took me by surprise." She turned what she hoped was a warm smile on Stu.

"It is magnificent, isn't it?"

She nodded and turned to look at the view while she got herself back in control.

He joined her at the rail, feet apart, hands resting on his cane in front of him, the breeze ruffling his shirt as he looked out on the land. He reminded her of a dashing sea captain, standing on board his vessel, looking out over his crew and at the vast sea, the wind whipping at his face as he sailed into adventure.

She found herself smiling.

Stu sighed. "It's good to see someone enjoying themselves. I was afraid that recent events would sour your regard for us."

"Not at all. It's wonderful to know a family that has accomplished their dream. I have a deep respect for the Eastons."

"As do we all. But the retreat is Marguerite's dream." His sentence trailed off as he took in the view. He tapped his cane on the ground and winked at her. "Ellis and I just like to have fun. Which reminds me, I'd better get back before he comes looking for me. I'm afraid this stupid hip operation has made him a little overprotective."

They walked back toward the camp in companionable silence. Sure enough, they met Ellis on his way down the path.

"I was beginning to get worried," he began.

Stu shot Lindy an amused "what did I tell you?" look. "Well, my dear friend, not only am I safe and sound, but I picked up a lovely lady as well."

She left them at the dining hall, watched for a few minutes as they strolled back toward the house, then ducked inside to see if she could scrounge up some leftovers before going to the afternoon rehearsal. One day she would start scheduling lunch into her life.

Chapter
Seventeen

"Places." Peter looked around the stage to make sure everyone was in position. He jumped down from the apron and walked up the aisle toward the tech table.

Lindy crammed the uneaten portion of her bagel into her dance bag and hurried down to the stage.

"Where's Jeremy?" Peter asked as they passed.

"I've got Rose talking to him about something that couldn't wait."

"Smart thinking. Get started before he can extricate himself. We could all use a normal rehearsal for a change."

Lindy nodded. The music started. Mendelssohn's *Italian Symphony*. Jeremy had choreographed it for their last European tour. He had made a few changes after seeing it performed for four weeks, and this was the first time the new version would be put before an audience. That was one of the many things that she admired about Jeremy. He was never content to just choreograph a piece, then let it run like a movie, never to feel the choreographer's hand again. He was always reshaping, refining, and honing each step until it was exactly as he imagined it. It made it a little more difficult for the dancers to remember which version he had done last, but it kept the dancing alive and the dancers on their toes, at least metaphorically. They were never allowed to become complacent about their work.

It was one of the qualities that had been responsible for their rapid rise in the dance world.

Mieko jumped onto the stage, feet tucked beneath her. She continued across the Marley floor, swirling and stretching in a curved arc, picking up Kate and Laura from the opposite wing.

Jeremy, like other contemporary choreographers, used ballet as the basis of his movement, but freed and transformed by the modern techniques pioneered by Doris Humphrey, Martha Graham, and the next generation of choreographers, José Limon, Merce Cunningham, and Paul Taylor. He eschewed the use of point shoes, finding their boxed toes clunky, and considered the dependence of classical ballet on upright balance a hindrance to the vitality in the movement that he sought. The Mendelssohn was danced in soft ballet slippers dyed to match the skin color of the dancers. During the performance the girls would be costumed in silk gym shorts and tees, the boys in silk pajama bottoms and bare-chested. The reds, oranges, and golds of the fabric mixing freely among the cast members.

Today they were wearing practice clothes. No one wore tights and leotards like they had during the first years of the Easton retreat. These days, dancers clothed themselves in shorts or sweatpants and tee shirts and sweaters. Whatever was comfortable and didn't hinder the movement of the body.

The girls exited and Paul and Andrea entered from upstage. Paul slid across the stage until he was sitting at Andrea's feet. From there, he partnered her in an arabesque, then a pirouette, holding her by the ankle instead of the waist. The pirouette ended at a tilt. Unlike its balletic counterpart, the off-balanced position was intentional. Paul stood and brought her back to balance, then moved away as she stayed poised on one foot. He slid again just as she dove forward, parallel to the floor. He caught her in both hands and she hovered above the stage, then curved into his arms. Her feet touched the ground and she pulled him to his feet.

It was playful and fun, a side of Jeremy he rarely showed to the nondance world. Actually, it was a side of himself that he rarely showed to anyone. But that joy was inside him. It came out in his choreography without a struggle. If he could only learn to spread it around in his own life.

Her thoughts must have conjured him up. He was suddenly beside her. She steeled herself. Rose was supposed to have kept him until the rehearsal was well underway. Should she offer to let him take over?

She decided against it. Instead of acknowledging him, she kept her attention concentrated on the stage. If he wanted to take over, he would have to tell her so. He watched the dancing, and slowly the worried lines of his face began to smooth, the tiredness disappeared until a slight smile hovered on his lips.

"Do you mind if I just watch today?" he asked finally.

"Of course not," whispered Lindy. He walked back to sit with Peter. She returned her eyes to the stage. Paul went into another slide, but he had been distracted by Jeremy's sudden appearance and he slid too far to the right.

"Paul," Lindy yelled.

"Right." He scooched over in time to catch Andrea and cradle her in his arms. Lindy smiled. They were young and energetic and both had impeccable technique. When Lindy had first returned to work, Paul had partnered an old harridan of a dancer who had wormed herself into a job with the company. That partnership had been hideous to watch.

Murder does have a certain convenience, thought Lindy.

One dancer entered from each wing, until eight of them were curved around the stage in a semicircle behind the couple.

"Over," said Lindy. She waved her hand toward stage right. Three dancers adjusted their spacing without missing a step. A well-oiled machine. She gave them a thumbs-up and settled in to do her job.

At the end of the Mendelssohn, they changed over to the second piece they would be performing, a suite of Gershwin preludes that they had toured for the last six months. No major glitches there.

The third and final piece of the evening was set to music by Mozart. It would have its first performance on Saturday night.

The adagio began. Rebo moved onto stage from the upstage left wing. He seemed to gobble up the space around him. From the other side of the stage, Eric repeated his movement to the opposite side on the next phrase of the music. Then they moved toward each other diagonally downstage until they met in the center. They circled each other slowly, legs stretching and bending in the air, torsos curving, like two awakening tigers. Then Rebo rolled Eric across his back. Eric's pointed feet made an arc in the air, then he landed with a ripple of muscle. Mieko entered from downstage, walking backward in a curve until she came between the two men. After a brief trio, Eric left the stage, and a courtly duet for Mieko and Rebo began.

"Eric," called Lindy. His head popped out from the wing he had just exited. "Let's push that passage to the wing. Wider arc, bigger steps, and get there sooner."

He saluted her and disappeared back into the wings. She brought her attention back to Rebo and Mieko. He lifted her as if she were weightless. Lowered her to the ground without her seeming to ever land. Lindy allowed herself a few moments of sheer pleasure.

"Foot," she barked automatically.

Mieko stretched her foot and the energy seemed to continue past her body and show visibly in the air.

"Good." She glanced back to Jeremy, but he was frowning at the stage. She returned her focus to the dancing.

He had choreographed this piece specially for the anniversary celebration. His tribute to Marguerite. He had struggled with it, never quite satisfied, and he had still been making changes in the parking lot when they boarded the bus for the Easton retreat.

Lindy and Biddy had finally put their collective feet down, and told him he was not allowed to make any more changes until after the performance on Saturday. Of course, he hadn't listened. He was nothing if not driven.

And there was the problem of his personal life as well as the genius of his art. He was driven, but none of them understood exactly what was driving him. They had learned a few things about him, things that had left them reeling with the discovery. Lindy often found herself wondering just how many skeletons were living in the closet of Jeremy's life.

Once again, the thought of him seemed to conjure his presence. He was walking down the aisle. No doubt he was about to make "just one more change."

"Sit," she said.

"But—"

"Sit." He sat, next to where she was standing, two rows from the stage. She knew he would waylay the dancers as they left the theater and make suggestions, or have them try out a new step in the driveway.

She turned to him, put her hands on her hips and screwed her face into an exaggerated scowl.

He flipped his hands out, an "I wasn't doing anything, really, I wasn't" look of feigned innocence on his face.

But just as she was about to respond with a smile. His look disintegrated into one of deep sadness. She wanted to put her arms around him, comfort him as you would a child. But she didn't. Jeremy was very affectionate, as long as he was giving out the affection. He didn't seem to have the knack of accepting any in return.

Sure enough, Jeremy had cornered Rebo and Mieko on the pavement in front of the lobby just after rehearsal.

Lindy hoisted her dance bag to her other shoulder. "Bad boy, bad boy," she sang as she passed them.

"Last time, I promise," Jeremy called after her.

Sure, boss, she thought. Well, at least it would keep his mind off the entangled events of the last few days. Only four more days left. They needed to wrap this up and get on with their work. They were leaving for Europe again in two weeks. There was a lot to do, and they needed Jeremy to be focused on his work.

She had been so lost in thought that she didn't see the police car until she was almost upon it. Abel White was loading a cardboard box into the backseat. A disconnected telephone sat on top of the box.

"What's going on?" she asked.

"The sheriff has decided to call off the search for the Phillips kid. He figures he's taken off by now." Abel tossed the box onto the seat and slammed the door. "I'm not so sure, though. The family secretary still hasn't heard from him. You'd think the boy would call home to say he was okay." Abel scratched his head. "If he was planning to go home."

Lindy nodded and continued on her way. Too bad Abel White wasn't the sheriff, she thought. She would be inclined to tell him that Connie was still around, or at least had been until last night. Where was he now?

Byron Grappel was climbing the front steps. She followed him inside. Realizing he was about to enter the drawing room, she hurried to catch up.

Bill and Marguerite cut off their conversation as the sheriff and Lindy entered.

Bill flashed Lindy a wry smile.

She shrugged her shoulders back at him and stood her ground.

Grappel stepped to the side leaving her a clear view of the sofa and Chi-Chi sitting there looking like she hadn't slept in a week.

Bill stepped in front of him, blocking the intimidating look he had shot at Chi-Chi.

Lindy readied herself for the confrontation.

"I've called off the search for Phillips," said Grappel trying to direct his statement past Bill to Marguerite and Chi-Chi. Bill slowly crossed his arms.

Lindy stood perfectly still. What would he tell the sheriff? Situational ethics, Bill, she pleaded silently. She sent the subliminal message with all her concentration. She didn't think for a minute that it would work, but it was all she had.

"Unless any of you know where he is."

Lindy held her breath. Then she heard the barely perceptible rattle in Bill's throat. He was going to bend the truth. She was afraid to move, as if any change in the room might throw off the tenuous balance of Bill's decision. She watched his face clear of expression, then he turned from the sheriff.

"Found these." Bill scooped up the paper bag from where it had been sitting on the coffee table.

She couldn't see Grappel's reaction; she was still standing behind him. She took the chance and eased to his side.

"What?" Byron's dislike for Bill was palpable in his tone of voice and the brevity of his question.

"Fragments of dynamite caps, found at the scene of the landslide."

"Got any witnesses?"

Bill shook his head.

"Then it don't mean shit to me." He reached for the bag. Bill moved it away.

"Then I'll just keep them."

"That might be evidence," protested Grappel.

"Make up your mind, Sheriff, usable or not usable. Then let me know." Bill folded over the top of the bag and walked out the door. As far as effective exits went, it was right up there with the best of them.

Grappel glared at the door. Lindy was surprised that it didn't burst into flames. Then he redirected his frown to Marguerite. "You'd better call off Dick Tracy, there. He screws around with any more evidence, I'll arrest him as accessory after the fact."

Lindy felt a cold stab of fear deep in her gut. Get a grip, she demanded. Grappel was no match for Bill.

As soon as the sheriff had swaggered out the door, Marguerite sank onto the couch next to Chi-Chi.

"Oh dear," she sighed.

"He can't do that, can he?" asked Chi-Chi.

It was obvious they had both placed their hopes in Bill. It made Lindy feel proud in a vicarious way. Just to be his friend. If they were still friends . . .

"Don't worry about Bill," said Lindy, but she hurried out to look for him.

He was sitting on a boulder that jutted out into the lake. It was surrounded by tall grasses that grew in the shallows and it took her several minutes to find him. She walked up behind him. He didn't look back at her, though she knew he must have heard her. He had probably watched her as she made her way around the lake in search of him. He was holding a stalk of grass between his long fingers.

"Situational ethics," she said.

"Rationalization." He folded the grass stalk over and over until it was a small rectangle, then tossed it into the water.

"Whatever. Mind if I sit down?"

"If you think Annie won't mind."

She sat down.

"She's been sending me some pretty conflicting signals," he continued, still staring out at the lake.

"She'll get over it."

"I envy you."

She tilted her face trying to get a better look at his.

He twisted another stalk of grass from the clump and began folding it as he had done with the other one. "I have a son."

"You do?" It came out before she could think. He had never mentioned that he was a father. Never even hinted at it during their lunches or the occasional walk in Central Park.

"He was seven." Lindy waited for him to go on. The past tense. Was the boy dead? Was that why he had never spoken about him. But he said "have." I have a son.

"Is he . . ." She let the question die. She couldn't bring herself to ask him.

"He's in his third year of veterinary school." He tossed the now-mangled grass into the water and watched it float away. "In Idaho. About as far away from actresses and New York cops as he could get."

Lindy stretched out her hand, meaning to give him a reassuring pat. Thought the better of it. Grasped her knees instead.

She saw him smile. Not the smile that always made her feel better, but one that took him into himself, away from her. "Seeing you with Annie makes me realize what I've missed."

"Don't you ever see him?" she asked, trying to keep her voice free from any inflection that might be taken as judgment.

"Not much. Claire was determined to have her own way. I decided not to pursue it. Thought it might hurt him more to be caught between two warring parents. She got what she wanted, which was to get rid of me."

He yanked at another piece of grass. Lindy wanted to put her hands over his and stop him, but she didn't.

"I gave up too easily. Before the year was out, she had lost interest in acting and married a dentist in Westchester. He became Steven's father." He tossed the grass, now crumpled like the others into the water.

This time she did allow her hand to come to rest on his shoulder, just like she would with any hurting friend. Appearances be damned.

But he moved away. "I won't make that mistake again." He stood up.

She jumped to her feet, rattled by the intensity of his statement. Was he talking about her or about the murder?

"Sheriff Grappel is threatening to make you an accessory after the fact," she said.

"Hot air. The man's a troglodyte."

"We've only got four more days."

"*You* only have four more days. I have all the time in the world. I won't give up on this, either." He gave her only a millisecond to see his meaning before he erased all expression from his features.

She felt relieved and sad at the same time. Warmed that he had given her another brief glimpse into his life and yet disturbed by what she had seen. And then from the back of her mind she heard the echo of Marguerite's words to her brother: "You give up too easily."

Bill raised a questioning eyebrow.

She shook her head. She was beginning to see patterns in everything. It was just as confusing as seeing no pattern at all.

Chapter
Eighteen

As they made their way back around the lake, Lindy told Bill what she had discovered that afternoon. Bill's only response was, "So the cave is within hearing distance of the ledge."

Obviously, he had figured out everything else without her.

"But if he was killed because he heard a plot to dynamite the archaeological site, why is Robert being held for molesting and possibly murdering him? I don't see what one has to do with the other."

"I doubt if they are related at all."

"So why is Robert being held?" she persisted.

"I'm working on it," was all he would say.

They parted on the upstairs landing and she realized for the first time that Bill was staying in the main house instead of the annex.

Already a part of the family, she thought ungenerously and stomped off to see Biddy.

Biddy looked up from the windowsill when Lindy came in; her head went right back to her book. "They brought your clothes back."

"Are you still reading that regency romance?" asked Lindy.

"I finished it. Loaned it to Marguerite." Biddy turned the page.

"You didn't."

"Thought she could use some distraction." Biddy glanced up briefly, then returned to the book. "Caught her reading it twice today." She stopped reading long enough to give Lindy an arch look.

"So what's that?"

"Another one."

"You're kidding."

Biddy reluctantly closed the book. "They're kind of fun if you speed-read through the sex scenes."

"Most people read them for the sex scenes."

"I know, but somehow sex is just more interesting in the flesh than on the page." She held up a hand, like the Pope's blessing. "Usually, but don't ask. My last foray into *that* was singularly uninteresting. You'd be amazed at how many boring men there are out there."

"There's always . . ."

"Don't even get started."

"Is that why you're spending so much time with Marguerite? Are you avoiding Jeremy?"

"I'm not avoiding him. Just staying away until he pulls himself together. This time if he wants my support, he's going to have to ask for it."

They dressed for dinner and met Annie in the restaurant. It was obvious that she was trying to work her way back into her mother's good graces. She was animated and enthusiastic about the camp. Did odes to Dr. Van Zandt. Questioned them about the investigation, and showed concern for Robert and the missing Connie. But she left them as soon as the last forkful of dessert passed her lips.

"Hot date?" asked Biddy.

"Certainly looks like it."

The two of them lingered over coffee, catching up on the things they had missed in their three days apart. After dinner they wandered into the bar where the company members had settled down to cards and board games. Biddy left to finish her book. Lindy hunkered down to a serious game of Scrabble with Rose, Peter, and Mieko.

It was almost midnight when Mieko went out on the word *quicker*. Lindy said good night and went back to the main house.

She was just going upstairs when Marguerite came out of the drawing room. She was wearing a rose sateen dressing gown that shimmered in the light cast by the chandelier. But the color only accentuated the pallor of her face, and the clinging fabric hung about her frame, making her seem frail and old.

"Oh, Lindy, good evening. I couldn't sleep. I came to look for my book."

Nothing like a good romance to chase away the cares of the day, thought Lindy.

Marguerite's hands were empty.

"Didn't find it?"

"No, maybe I left it in the library." Marguerite began to go down the hallway.

"I'll help you look," said Lindy. With a pang of regret, she realized that she didn't trust Marguerite to climb the stairs safely by herself.

They had just come to the door of the library when they heard voices. The door was ajar. They stepped inside. Stu, Ellis, and Jeremy stood at the opposite end of the room, their backs to the door. Ellis attempted to put his hand on Jeremy's shoulder, but Jeremy jerked away.

Instinctively, Lindy tried to pull Marguerite back into the hallway. This was not a scene they should be eavesdropping on. Marguerite held her ground.

"What is the matter?" asked Ellis. "You used to always tell me everything."

"Get away from me." Jeremy's voice was so strident that Marguerite jumped. Lindy put an arm around her, more intent than ever to get her away. Whatever was going on, she didn't need to hear it. Lindy was sure of that.

Stu's voice broke into the tension between the two men. "Jeremy, Ellis has always been good to you. Why on earth are you treating him this way?"

"I think Ellis knows."

Ellis only looked confused. Lindy could see his profile: his cheek, flushed pink in the light, his mouth turned down in an expression of befuddlement.

"I don't," he said quietly. "What have I done?"

Jeremy took a step backward; ran his hand over his eyes. "I think you killed Larry Cleveland."

Ellis dropped into the chair. Marguerite swayed in Lindy's arm. Horror overtook her and she tried once more to pull Marguerite away. But Marguerite was rooted to the spot.

"That's preposterous," said Stu.

"Is it? Tell him, Ellis."

Ellis only looked up at Jeremy with sad eyes.

"Tell him," Jeremy repeated, his voice growing quieter and colder.

"Tell him what? I don't know what I'm supposed to say."

Stu took a step forward as if to protect Ellis. "Tell me what?" He directed the question to Jeremy.

Jeremy ignored him. Lindy watched his shoulders tighten, and prepared herself for the worst. "Did Larry threaten to tell, Ellis? Is that what happened?"

Ellis glanced up at Stu. Stu touched Ellis's hair. Then his head snapped toward Jeremy. "I think you've lost your mind, Jeremy. If anyone killed Larry Cleveland it must have been Robert. How could you accuse Ellis of something so utterly despicable?"

"Because he buggers little boys."

Ellis buried his face in his hands and a sob burst through his fingers. A shudder rolled through Marguerite. Her hand gripped Lindy's where it was holding her around the waist. Lindy tried to drag her away and then gave up. It was too late to spare her now; they might as well hear the rest of it.

She was wrong.

"I don't, I don't." Ellis's denial came out muffled from behind his hands.

"What about me?"

Marguerite gasped. Lindy was afraid she would collapse but somehow she remained on her feet. The men in the room were too intent on each other to hear her.

Ellis slowly raised his head. The glow from the library lamp caught the tears that ran down his cheek and held them crystallized in its light.

He shook his head slowly. "I don't. You were the only one." He breathed in sharply. "Because I loved you."

"You disgust me." Jeremy spun around and came face to face with Marguerite. Lindy could only guess at Marguerite's reaction, but she knew she would live with the memory of Jeremy's shocked eyes for a long time to come. And she knew in that moment, that he would never forgive her for what she had heard.

Jeremy's mouth opened as if to speak, then he crashed past them and out of the library. A few seconds later, Lindy heard the front door bang shut.

Marguerite was dead weight in her arms. Stu looked at Lindy, pursed his lips and turned to comfort Ellis.

Lindy dragged Marguerite upstairs and rang for Sandiman.

By the time Adele arrived, hastily dressed, Lindy was furious. Furious with Jeremy, with Ellis, with Bill, with the world.

She banged on the door to the room which Sandiman had told her was Bill's. At first there was no answer, then it opened a crack, and Lindy pushed her way inside.

"You knew!" she screamed. "You knew and you didn't tell me. How the hell do you think *this* is going to affect the family, the camp? Talk about your damned repercussions—how the hell are you going to get them out of this?"

Bill looked slightly dazed. The bed behind him was rumpled. His hair was disheveled. He was wearing a navy-blue bathrobe. He had been asleep. She didn't know whether to laugh or cry or run.

Bill tightened the sash of his robe.

Terry cloth, she noted. She took a step backward. If she crept away now, would he remember this in the morning?

"Oh no you don't." His hand closed around her arm and he pulled her into the room. "Now, that you've got my attention, I would like to know what you think you know."

"Jeremy—Ellis—They—"

Bill dropped his hand. Lindy's anger died and was replaced by sadness. At what Ellis had done. For the trust he had betrayed. For what he had done to a young boy. But most of all because Jeremy had not trusted his friends enough to tell one of them. "Why didn't he—" She had to stop to swallow the quaver in her voice.

"Why didn't Jeremy tell you? Or Biddy? Lindy, sometimes there are things in a man's life better left unsaid."

Like your son, she thought. But he had told her. Jeremy hadn't. "But he told you."

"Trust isn't a contest, Lindy." He stopped to let his statement sink in.

"He accused Ellis of killing Larry Cleveland. Marguerite and I overheard them; I couldn't get her to leave." To her dismay, she felt a tear slip out from the corner of her left eye. She stared past Bill, willing it to stop, while she felt it trickle down her cheek and roll beneath her chin.

Bill wiped it away with a brush of his finger.

"Is it true?"

He stepped past her and sat down at a table by the window. Not Queen Anne like the one in her room, but a Sheridan tea table with fluted legs. She followed him and sat down in the chair opposite. The surface of the table separated them, and Lindy wondered if Bill had chosen to sit here to create a distance between them. Surely, after what she had learned, he wouldn't try to keep her uninvolved. She waited.

"I don't know if it's true," said Bill. "But when Robert apparently attempted to commit suicide—"

She started to protest. Bill stopped her with a glance.

"Apparently, not necessarily *did*—Jeremy realized something was terribly wrong."

"So he called you."

Bill nodded.

"And you dropped everything and came to the rescue."

Irritation flickered in Bill's eyes. At least, Lindy thought it was irritation. She was glad to see any emotion. It meant that he hadn't shut her out yet.

"I wasn't that busy."

"Poor Marguerite. Just imagine what she must be feeling."

"I'd rather not." Bill leaned back in the chair and Lindy realized how tense he had been only a second before. "She and Jeremy both suffer from rampant over-responsibility. Jeremy already thinks he's responsible for what has happened."

"That's ridiculous."

"For those of us with a little rational thought left." He flashed her a quick amused smile. "But you understand how it goes. 'If only—if only—' "

Lindy nodded. She did understand. If Jeremy hadn't let Ellis seduce him all those years ago. If he had told. If he had arrived at the retreat a day earlier. It was absurd, of course. It was just like Jeremy.

"So what are"—she paused, then took the plunge—"we going to do about it?"

"We are going to try to figure out what really happened."

"We are?"

"Yep." Bill leaned forward again. "I'm afraid this will take all of us. I came here to help Jeremy find out if Ellis was a viable suspect before his sexual history came out. If there were more boys than just Jeremy . . . Well, you can imagine. A history of sexual abuse in one of the most prestigious art camps in America? It would be devastating."

It would be more than devastating. How many boys could have been seduced? The thought horrified her. And pity for the children and disgust at Ellis consumed her for a second. She pushed it aside.

"He said Jeremy was the only one."

"He did?"

"Because he loved him." The sound of that mournful plea still burned in Lindy's ears.

Bill stood up and walked to the closet. "A thirty-year-old man has no right to love a fourteen-year-old boy—that way." Bill had spoken into the closet, but his voice filled the room.

Lindy shuddered.

He returned with his little black book, but Bill used this black book for taking notes. He wrapped the flaps of his robe more closely around him and sat down.

He pulled a pen from inside the notebook and clicked the point out. "Okay," he said barely above a whisper. "Take me through everything that has happened. Point by point with every"—he smiled,—"roving thought you've had about them."

For an hour, Lindy talked. Bill wrote. He only interrupted her for clarification of something she said, though he did stop writing when she told him about the fight with Rebo and what it was about. She didn't want to; she felt bad enough about it without telling Bill. She wondered if that was why Jeremy had gone to Bill and not her. Had he been in doubt of her loyalty? Bill had to bring her back to the point, but she saw in his eyes that he understood where she had gone in her few moments of silence.

She didn't tell him about Annie's accusations. That had nothing to do with anything.

Finally, she leaned back in her chair, exhausted. "I just can't believe that Ellis would kill anybody."

"Not very objective, but it does you credit." Bill closed the notebook. "For what it's worth, I'm not convinced that he did, either."

"You're not?"

"Why now? If this has been going on for years, why lose control now?"

"Ellis seems, I don't know, confused sometimes. I thought maybe he was getting senile."

"Senility doesn't create murderers."

"If he were being blackmailed?"

"With his money? Try again."

"What if he loved Larry Cleveland?" She had forgotten to tell him about Rose's riddle. Larry, Jeremy, and Stu. She told him now.

Bill pressed two fingers to his temple. "I just feel that there's a larger issue here." He laughed softly. "I know. Feelings are pretty lame investigatory tools. I must have picked it up from you."

It was an insulting thing to say. So why did it make her feel warm inside? "Yeesh," she said, as much at her thoughts as for the situation.

"Aptly put." He glanced at his watch. Glen never slept with his watch on, she noted. She felt herself blush. Shit.

"But it's going on two o'clock. Unless you're planning to stay, I suggest you go back to your room and get some sleep. We both have a busy day ahead of us."

She fled to the door. Bill was still sitting in the chair when it closed behind her.

Chapter
Nineteen

L indy taught company class the next morning. She had walked through the Easton house earlier, accompanied only by her own footsteps. There was no other sign of life, not even Sandiman. She let herself outside. The day was overcast with a chill in the air. *To match my feelings*, thought Lindy.

She grabbed a cup of coffee in the student dining hall. Everyone was preparing for class and she had the room to herself.

And now she stood on the stage, leading the company through their exercises at the *barre*, correcting placement with a touch rather than voiced encouragement. She felt turned in on herself, impatient to be away and looking for a murderer, instead of watching *rond de jambes* and *grand battements*.

She cut them loose for lunch. In the afternoon, Victor Slaton and the other teachers would begin rehearsing for the next student showcase. It would be performed in a few weeks when another professional company would be in residence. Would the camp still be operating in a few weeks? She could only pray that it would be. On Sunday, the Ash company would return to the city. That gave them only four days—three and a half—to find out the truth.

At two o'clock, she began rehearsal. Jeremy was not in the theater. No one from the main house had made an appearance that day. She hadn't seen Bill. Biddy had left after lunch to spend the afternoon with Chi-Chi going over last-minute details for the program for Saturday night. Lindy wondered how Chi-Chi could even be functioning with the worry that must be consuming her.

Lindy mechanically made corrections, while she tried to keep one part of her brain focused on discovering anything she had missed concerning Larry's death. Her thoughts were interrupted by explosions of panic every time she thought about Jeremy and what their first confrontation would be. And whether it would be their last. Would he ever forgive her for stumbling into that hideous scene the night before?

Lindy was surprised when the last piece finished and the rehearsal came to an end. She sat in the house and watched the company file past her.

Kate and Mieko stopped briefly by her seat. "That spacing is much better in the last section. Thanks," said Kate. Lindy had no idea what she was talking about. She had rehearsed them on automatic pilot.

The stage lights went out, then the house lights. Still she sat. *Hell, get out there and do something even if it's wrong,* she thought. And there was a good chance that whatever she might do would be wrong. Should she try to talk to Ellis? No, better leave that to Bill. So what could she do? She had begun walking up the aisle without realizing it. The house was completely black, but it didn't matter. She knew her way around a theater whether she could see it or not.

"Lindy." An urgent whisper that made her jump. She peered into the darkness looking for the source. She knew it was Jeremy's voice. He hadn't wasted any time. At least he had not sent her a note firing her without confronting her. His dark shadow gradually came into view.

"Are you busy?"

She shook her head, then realizing he might not be able to see the movement, said, "No."

The shadow rose from the row of seats. "Let's go for a drink—away from here."

They drove in silence, the white Land Rover that belonged to the family taking the curves of the road with ease. Its occupants felt anything but ease.

They passed through the gates onto the county road, passed the turnoff that would lead them into town, and took the entrance to the state highway. Several exits later, Jeremy turned onto an offramp. A cluster of the usual freeway hotels sat by the access road. Jeremy pulled into the parking lot of one of the larger ones and shut off the engine. Without looking at her, he got out of the car and slammed the door. She was opening her own door when it was pulled out of her hand, and Jeremy was helping her out. She was afraid to look at him.

With her eyes on the ground, she followed him into the bar, sat across from him at a corner booth, and listened while he ordered her a white wine and himself a gin and tonic. A summer drink, she noted distractedly. She didn't think her stomach could handle the wine, but when it was placed before her, she took a swallow, and felt herself begin to relax.

Then she looked up at him and immediately wished she hadn't. She looked away.

"Lindy."

"Jeremy."

Their words came out at the same time. They both stopped. Then Jeremy said in a voice husky with barely controlled emotion. "It's my fault."

Without a thought, Lindy was out of her side of the booth and sitting next to him, her arm around him. She didn't care if he liked it or not. "It was Ellis's fault. He was the adult. You were a child."

Jeremy shook his head. "It wasn't like that."

She had been here before. Pressing Jeremy to talk about his past. Watching impotently while he wrestled with the ghosts that peopled his life. She wished he would just clean house once and for all. How many bizarre things had happened to this man in his forty-something years?

"Ellis was warm, and loving, and . . . gentle."

"I can imagine," she said, but she tried not to.

"And it made me feel special, a delicious secret that only the two of us shared. I think he did love me."

"And do you think he loved Larry Cleveland, too?"

A quick jerk of a shrug. "I guess. Ellis was different when he was younger. Maybe not the brightest person in the world, but he was so imaginative; we'd—he'd tell me stories about his travels, find wonder in every little thing he saw. He came here in the summers just to make Marguerite happy. But he was happiest, he said, just out discovering the world. He said he would take me with him. Then before I knew it, the summer was over. When I came back the following year, I had a girlfriend, and he never touched me or made any kind of advances again." He stopped long enough to take a slow controlled breath. "But he was always there for me. We'd still talk about our dreams like two old friends."

He lifted his glass and held it to his lips without drinking. Then he drained half of it, returned it to the table, and pushed the glass away out of reach. "Not the answer," he said.

"No," she agreed.

"You should have known him before. Back then, he humored Marguerite because she was his only living sister. He loved her, of course; everyone loved Marguerite. It was impossible not to. But he's turned into a kind of lap dog, hasn't he?"

Lindy had to admit that lap dog was an appropriate description. Attentive, loving, but distinctly ineffectual. Even Stu had to prep him on what to say to the reporters. Would a man like that be capable of killing? And if he were, could he carry on with his life as though nothing had happened?

"Do you really think a man like Ellis could lure a strong, streetwise kid like Larry Cleveland out onto a precipice and throw him over the side?" It sounded absurd even before she had finished the statement.

His head lowered. He reached one hand to hers that still lay across his shoulder and clung to it. For all the times she had wished Jeremy would accept someone's support, she now wanted to free herself of the responsibility it demanded. She tightened her fingers around his. She held her breath, wondering what the next step would be. Then he laid his cheek briefly on their hands.

It only lasted a second, but she felt that she had just witnessed an unprecedented act of acceptance.

"I was just so angry. I let my emotions get the better of me and instead of protecting Marguerite, I—" He broke off. Lindy watched him relive that moment of discovery as she relived her own part in it.

"Marguerite doesn't need protecting," said Lindy. "If I'm sure of anything, I'm sure of that. I think she's the strongest person I've ever met."

She said it more forcefully than she had intended. Jeremy looked startled. "I'm hardly ever sure of myself," he said.

"Most of us aren't. It's the human condition." She gently cuffed the side of his jaw and removed her arm from his shoulders. "And that's something we can both be sure of."

"So what are we going to do?"

It was still "we." First with Bill and now with Jeremy. Two for two. She felt a glimmer of hope.

"I was supposed to let Bill handle it," he said. "But I lost my temper. Now, I've messed up his game plan."

"Don't worry about Bill. He's a man who can think on his feet."

"I wish we had never come."

"I don't believe that. Would you want Marguerite to face this alone?" She didn't add that Marguerite had been there for him when he was facing his own demons.

He shook his head. "She must hate me."

"If I've learned anything about Marguerite in the last few days, it's that she is probably castigating herself for letting you be seduced by Ellis. I think you should talk to her."

"I can't face her."

"Yes, you can."

A flash of lightning cracked above them as they left the bar. It was quickly followed by huge pelting drops of rain. They hurried past parked cars and jumped into the Land Rover.

"God, I'm dense," said Lindy. "Look."

She pointed to the car in the space next to them. A new, black four-wheel-drive.

"There must be a hundred of those around here. They seem to be the transportation of choice these days."

"I know," said Lindy, catching a glimpse of a Donald duck inner tube in the back seat. "Let's just take a look through the parking lot, anyway."

Jeremy drove along the parking lot while Lindy jotted down the license numbers of two black Jeeps. They tried the next motel. None at all, but it was near dinnertime; not too many people had returned for the day.

The rain stopped as suddenly as it had started. They entered the third lot just in time to see three men get into a black Explorer. New and shiny except for the splashes of mud on the fender. Lindy wrote down the tag number.

They drove past. The Explorer backed up and drove out of the parking lot. Jeremy swerved the car around. Lindy grabbed the armrest.

"I've seen that guy. The one getting into the back seat," said Jeremy.

"He probably lives around here."

"Did you get a look at him? He's definitely a city boy. I saw him talking to Byron the day I took Chi-Chi in to see Robert."

"In that case, Poncho, follow that car."

Jeremy followed at a discreet distance, if there was such a thing. The Explorer exited the highway, headed in the direction of town and subsequently the Easton property. They were the only two vehicles on the road. White car following black. Like Hopalong Cassidy, thought Lindy and wondered if they were on a fool's errand.

They had passed the turnoff to town when the Explorer turned abruptly into the woods. Jeremy slowed down, then followed it. A PRIVATE PROPERTY sign was posted to a tree by the side of the road.

"Guess who owns this," said Jeremy without taking his eyes off the rutted road.

"The Eastons?"

Jeremy nodded. He sped up. The Land Rover hit a bump. Lindy bit her tongue.

There was a glimpse of black in front of them.

"This is a surveillance, not a chase, Jeremy. We don't want them to know we're following them."

Jeremy braked, then continued on at a slower pace. Suddenly they were out of the woods driving along grass-covered meadows. In front of them, pulled onto a lookout was the black Explorer. All three men stood by the hood of the car.

"Car trouble?" asked Lindy.

Jeremy began to reverse the car back into the woods. He pulled it alongside the road and shut off the engine. He motioned for her to follow. They crept along the edge of the woods until they had a clear view of the men and car. The men were now looking out over the valley below them. One turned back to the car. Lindy watched him unroll the white tube that rested on the hood and spread a huge sheet of paper across it.

"A map?" whispered Lindy.

"Yes, damn it."

At that moment the rain reappeared, drenching Lindy and Jeremy and pelting the men and the paper. One of them hastily rolled it up. Then the three of them jumped back into the car. Without a word, Jeremy and Lindy ran back to the Land Rover. There was no sound of another engine.

"Do you think they'll wait it out?" asked Lindy. A crack of lightning answered her, followed by a rumbling that seemed to fill the air. "What should we do?"

"Get the hell out of here, and figure out what's going on." Jeremy was already backing the Land Rover into the road. He turned sharply to the right. The left side of the car dipped as the wheels sank into the soft leaves and mud on the side. Jeremy shifted into second. The wheels gained purchase and the Land Rover shot back onto the hard dirt of the road.

They were almost to the paved road when Jeremy slammed on the brakes. Rocks and dirt sputtered outward as the Land Rover lurched to a stop. Ahead of them, a log stretched across the width of the road.

"Shit." Jeremy pulled on the emergency brake and got out of the car. Lindy followed him, keeping one eye on the way they had come in case they were overtaken by the black Explorer.

Jeremy began dragging the log out of the way. Lindy leaned down to help him just as a metallic ping rent the air. Then another. And another. She looked up in time to see Jeremy throw himself toward her. She hit the ground with a thud, smothered by the weight of his body across hers.

Her first thought was that he was dead. Then he lifted his head. His eyes were round and glazed. "Shit," he said.

"No shit," she replied. He rolled off her and dragged her back to the Land Rover, crouching along the passenger side and opening the door without standing up. He pushed her into the front seat, then climbed past her. The driver's window was gone. Pellets of glass lay in a pile along the frame and spread across the seat. Jeremy swept them away with his forearm and hunched down behind the wheel. The engine roared up; they sped out of the woods and onto the county road.

The rain was coming down in thick sheets. Even with the windshield wipers on high the windshield was coated in water. Rain sliced diagonally across Lindy's window. She could see nothing.

She looked out the back window, resting her chin on the top of the front seat. It was impossible to tell if someone was following them. There was no sight but a curtain of rain, no sound but the barrage of drops on the roof, and the feel of the stinging spray that assaulted them through the shattered window.

Lindy didn't know how Jeremy got them back to the Easton retreat. She barely could make out the wrought-iron letters as they passed underneath the entrance to the camp. Jeremy pulled into the garage at the back of the house and told the mechanic on duty to find Bill.

"And some towels," yelled Lindy after the man who rushed wild-eyed away.

She and Jeremy stood quietly dripping at each other for a few minutes. Then she became aware of a towel being draped around her neck. Jeremy's face disappearing behind a cloud of white terry cloth. She started to laugh, teeth chattering.

"It isn't goddamn funny." Bill's voice was as menacing as the thunder that resonated behind his words.

He stood glaring at both of them for a second, water dripping from his hair, his rain-drenched shirt clinging to his shoulders and chest. She looked away.

Bill began circling the Land Rover, opened the door, rummaged around, and pulled a pen knife from his pocket. A few minutes later, he reemerged, holding his hand in a fist. He opened his fingers. A pellet of metal rested on his palm.

Jeremy and Lindy peered into his hand as if it held the secret of the philosopher's stone.

"BB," he said. He walked away from them, then turned back. "Do you want to tell me what happened?"

"He's annoyed," whispered Lindy.

"You're damn right I'm annoyed," Bill bellowed. Even Jeremy flinched. "You could have been killed."

"With a BB?" asked Jeremy.

"Yes, with a BB. A hit to the eye could have gone straight to your brain. A shattered windshield could have sent you both over a cliff."

"It wasn't our fault," said Lindy. "We were ambushed."

Bill's growl echoed in the rafters as they followed him out of the garage.

Showered and changed, Jeremy and Lindy sat drinking tea in the drawing room while Bill paced up and down in front of the window. When they came to the end of their adventure with the black Explorer, Bill stopped pacing.

"I'm going into town," he said. "I don't know when I'll be back."

Lindy waited until the door slammed behind him. "And you're going to face Marguerite," she said softly.

Jeremy shot her a quick look as if asking for a reprieve.

"Go," she said.

He went.

*   *   *

Lindy sat for a while longer, sipping tea and listening to the sound of the storm outside, then she climbed up the stairs. On the landing, she overtook Stu, drenched to the skin, filthy with mud and leaves, and limping slowly down the corridor.

She rushed up behind him. "My God, Stu, are you all right? Shall I get Adele?"

"No, I'm fine." He didn't turn around but waved her away with his hand. His voice sounded gruff and impatient. Well, no wonder. He had had a shocking week like everyone else, even more so considering what he had learned about Ellis the night before. And now he had been caught bedraggled and dirty and was probably embarrassed.

But when he finally turned to her, his usual smile was in place, and Lindy wondered if she had imagined that undercurrent of pain and frustration.

"Are you sure?"

"Yes, I just got caught by the storm. In my hurry to get to shelter, I tripped. No harm done except to my clothes." He smiled a sheepish smile. Then the humor faded from his face, leaving only a crescent of a mouth and two tired eyes.

"Try not to be harsh in your judgment of Ellis and Jeremy, Lindy. These things happen." With a nod, which looked chivalrous in spite of his waterlogged appearance, he went into his room.

Yeah, Stu, she thought. *Shit happens.* Then she kicked herself mentally for her sarcasm. He was probably exhausted from shoring up the Easton family while dealing with his own convalescence and emotional upheaval. She wondered if Ellis and Marguerite realized how lucky they were.

Chapter
Twenty

Several diners were leaving the restaurant as Lindy and Biddy arrived. "Where did all these people come from?" Lindy asked Chi-Chi as she led them to a table for two.

"The annex is open from July until the middle of September. We cater to nature lovers and sportsmen as well as art patrons." She placed her fingertips on the table and leaned forward. "We close before hunting season opens."

It didn't surprise Lindy that Marguerite was against hunting for sport. And it was just as well. Chi-Chi didn't look as though she would make it through the evening, much less until the middle of September.

"When everyone clears out, why don't you join us for coffee?" asked Lindy.

"Sounds wonderful."

Lindy watched Biddy watch Chi-Chi as she walked back to her station.

"What?" Biddy stared back at her from across the table.

"Just thinking."

"Oh, that. For a minute I was afraid you were conjuring up my future. And I left my Tarot cards in another lifetime." Biddy flipped her palms upward in a gesture somewhere between "C'est la vie" and "Little Suzy Sunshine."

"So what did you do today?" she asked.

"I was going to ask you the same thing." It was a deflection that would make Bill proud, Lindy thought unhappily. There had not been too many times in their life together that Lindy had kept anything from Biddy, and most of those times had involved Jeremy. Here she was again, stuck between her two friends. Irritated with both of them that they were so busy protecting themselves that they couldn't talk to each other.

Biddy shot her a quizzical look. "For starters, bail has been denied." She waited for Lindy's reaction. "The judge felt that in view of the possible suicide attempt it would be irresponsible of him to allow Robert to return home. So they're transferring him . . ." She paused while a waiter bade them good evening and handed them menus. "To the county jail. Evidently a step above the local pokey. As if that's any consolation."

"Criminy." Lindy glanced toward Chi-Chi's post, but her view was blocked by a statue of Diana draped in a tunic of concrete folds.

"Yeah, she's taking it pretty hard; driving herself like a maniac," said Biddy. "I figure it won't be long until she collapses. And where will that leave everybody else?"

"She virtually runs the whole operation, doesn't she?"

"No virtually about it. Chi-Chi *is* the retreat."

Lindy closed her menu and rested her elbows on the table, clasping her hands together and staring at her knuckles. She heard Biddy sigh. When she looked up Biddy was searching her face.

"Lindy . . ."

"Huh?"

"There has been no sign of Marguerite, Ellis, or Stu today." Biddy's eyes held hers. She had to fight the urge to look away. "What's going on?" It was more challenge than curiosity.

Lindy could only shrug and hoped her face wouldn't give her away. She held no illusions about that, though. Biddy had always known how to read her. It was their understanding of each other that had made them inseparable friends during their career as dancers, and had sustained them since being reunited through their work for Jeremy. Now that she thought about it, Jeremy was the one thing that threatened their trust in each other. Resentment bubbled up from somewhere deep inside her.

The waiter returned, took their orders, and left. But his interruption hadn't made it possible to change the subject. Biddy was waiting.

"There've been developments." Lindy couldn't even look her friend in the face.

"You don't want me to know." Bitterness was antithetical to every part of Biddy's being. Hearing it now made Lindy want to throw herself at Biddy's feet, beg for forgiveness, and tell all. But she couldn't. Only Jeremy could tell her something like that, and she doubted if Jeremy ever would.

"I'm caught between loyalties," she mumbled.

"Oh well," said Biddy. "I wouldn't want you to be dis-loyal." She dragged out the last word.

"Biddy, you know that you're my best friend in the whole world."

Biddy lifted an eyebrow.

Lindy closed her eyes.

"It's about Jeremy, isn't it?"

Lindy looked up. Biddy was pulling at her hair with both hands. She was upset, and who wouldn't be? "What hideous thing has he dumped on you this time?" Biddy's voice was hard. Biddy's voice was never hard. Lindy felt like confessing to anything if she would just sound like her normal self.

A movement caught in her peripheral vision.

"Biddy."

"I'm sick of him and his self-involvement. He's not the only person in the world who has suffered. The rest of us get on with it."

"Biddy—"

"I'm fed up with him. He can just go worry himself to death."

"Biddy—" This time she said it more urgently. Jeremy was standing next to the statue of Diana. Greek god and goddess. They were both the same shade of gray.

"I'm quitting."

Lindy's jaw dropped.

"Don't—" But it wasn't Lindy who had spoken.

Biddy's jaw dropped, and the two of them sat staring open-mouthed at each other across the table.

"I need you."

Biddy blinked and slowly turned her head in the direction of the voice.

Lindy wondered if it was possible to vanish into thin air. Her thoughts spread out in all directions. Any thought was preferable to thinking about what was happening right here.

What was Jeremy doing in the restaurant, anyway? Christ, if people thought Dickens relied too heavily on coincidence for his plots, they should try spending a week on tour with a dance company. *The stage is all the world*, she thought. Keeping any semblance of a private life was definitely a problem in such a confined existence. Everything was magnified, exaggerated. Between gossip, overheard conversations, fallout from arguments that hit those who just happened to be nearby, privacy was impossible.

Lindy reined in her thoughts. Jeremy and Biddy hadn't moved. She considered sliding under the table. Ludicrous. Willed herself to disappear. Impossible.

"Excuse me." She deserted the table still holding onto her napkin. Halfway across the room, she literally ran into Chi-Chi.

"I was just on my way over. Everyone is gone now."

"Good, let's take another table."

Chi-Chi frowned.

"Biddy and Jeremy need to talk business." Serious business, she added to herself.

"They don't need us?"

"No. Let's just get a strategic table so we can make sure they aren't disturbed."

They sat down at a table across the room but with a view of the entrance and a less obvious view of Biddy and Jeremy, who were still in the same positions as when Lindy had left them.

She narrowed her eyes at them. Places, please. Curtain go.

Jeremy sat down. Lindy consigned him to his fate and turned her attention to Chi-Chi.

"Biddy and I spent the morning getting everything set for the performance on Saturday."

"You're incredible," said Lindy. "How do you manage it?"

"Staying busy is the only thing that is keeping me from falling apart." Chi-Chi looked as though she might fall apart anyway.

Lindy reached across the table to put her hand on Chi-Chi's. "We all have absolute faith in Robert's innocence."

"Innocent men have gone to prison before." Chi-Chi tried for a smile, but her lips twisted, and she hastily covered her mouth with her napkin.

"Marguerite's lawyers are the best there are," Lindy said with conviction. At least she assumed they were. "And Bill is working on finding out what really happened. He won't give up."

"You trust him, don't you?"

"Absolutely." She was saved from wandering into that mine field by the waiter placing her plate in front of her. He poured Chi-Chi a cup of coffee.

"Should you be drinking that this late?" asked Lindy.

"Decaf. I'm having enough trouble sleeping as it is. Marguerite still insists that I stay at the house, but I miss the bungalow. There's something about sleeping in your own bed . . . even if it's empty." Chi-Chi struggled with her face again.

"It won't be for long. I'm sure of it."

After dinner, Lindy walked Chi-Chi back to the house. Sandiman informed her that Bill had not returned. She wandered back to the annex where Kate informed her that Annie had gone out with Donald. That was another situation that Lindy needed to deal with. Glen's accusation of her incompetence in handling her daughter still rankled. She returned to the house, too restless to go to her room. She sat on the porch to wait for Bill to return. She would also be able to see when, and she had to admit , *if* Annie came back to her room at the annex.

She was sitting on the stone steps, hands between her knees, rocking slowly back and forth like an inmate of Bedlam, when Bill's gray Honda pulled up to the steps. Donald jumped out of the driver's side and ran around to open the passenger door. Lindy jumped up. Donald? Driving Bill's car? Something had happened to Annie. Where was Bill?

Before her thoughts worked themselves into words, Annie bounded out of the back seat. She and Donald hoisted Bill out of the passenger's side of the car.

In the porch light, Lindy could see a large scrape across his left cheek, and a smear of mud—no blood—under his nose.

She hurried down the steps. "What happened?"

"Lucky punch," said Bill.

"You should have seen him, Mom." Annie tried to take Bill's arm, but he gently eluded her. "He was great."

Ah, another conquest, thought Lindy. But she was grateful for this one. She followed them up to Bill's room, Bill clutching his ribs while trying to fend off Donald and Annie's attentions.

Lindy went immediately into the bathroom and came back with a wet washcloth.

"He saved my butt," Donald explained.

"There were four of them," said Annie. "Four of them." She held up four fingers in case her mother had missed the point.

Lindy pushed Bill onto the bed. He grunted as he sat down.

"Four of whom?"

Annie and Donald began talking at once.

"These local guys—the same ones as before—"

"They came to the table and started harassing us—"

"And then—"

"They started pushing Donald—"

"I thought my goose was cooked for sure—"

"Bill was at the bar—"

"But we hadn't seen him. We didn't even know he was there."

"And suddenly there he was—out of the blue." Annie shot Bill an idolizing look.

Lindy rolled her eyes. Bill had the decency to look embarrassed.

"I was there getting a take on the locals," he said.

Lindy wiped the blood off his lip. He winced as the cloth touched his cheek.

"Really, Bill, brawling in a public bar . . ." she said.

"It was kind of fun."

"For crying out loud."

Bill tried to take the cloth from her, then grabbed his side instead.

Without thinking, Lindy dropped to her knees and began to feel his ribs. "Is anything broken?"

Bill was holding his breath. "They mainly got the fleshy parts," he said through clenched teeth.

"Right, tough guy."

She continued to press his sides until she had reached the bottom of his rib cage. He seemed okay.

"You can stop that now," he said.

She looked at her hands resting on his abdomen. "Oh." She moved her hands away.

Bill finished exhaling.

"You should have seen him, Mom, he took on all four of them."

"And finished them off—like that." Donald snapped his fingers.

"Then the other guys in the bar threw them out and bought us all beers."

"That was the worst part," said Bill. "Beer." Bill hated beer. "But it was safer than the wine. I doubt if the bartender would know the difference between a Chateau Neuf de Pape '83 and a Gallo 2000." He started to laugh, then stopped and ran his hand over his stomach.

"So did you learn anything from the locals?" asked Lindy.

"That these guys were the town troublemakers. They've been stirring up feeling against Van Zandt and company. All that crap about the Native Americans building casinos. And—that Grappel has looked the other way while they do it."

"Criminy." Lindy sat down on the bed. Bill winced.

She slid over a respectable distance from him and looked at Annie, but Annie was too steeped in admiration to notice.

"Who started that idea, anyway?" she asked Donald.

"There was some article in the local newspaper."

"Stu said the editor was in favor of development."

"I talked to the man," said Bill. "An ex-hippie. It seems that the article was an editorial written by him, urging people not to let anyone, including the Native Americans, develop the land."

"He's antidevelopment?" asked Lindy.

"He's an ex-hippie," Bill repeated.

"But what about those lurid headlines when Larry was killed?"

"Even ex-hippies have to make a buck." Bill gingerly shifted position. "And the real estate people turn out to be two retired schoolteachers from New York. They rent summer cottages."

"And the mayor?"

"For the last thirty years. He might be in favor of some development, but he didn't strike me as the type to condone murder in order to pave the way for it."

"Then—"

"I think the Eastons have a skewed view of the local mindset."

Lindy shook her head slowly. "Not all of the Eastons. Marguerite told us that she had friends in the town. She never doubted them."

"Well, that leaves Ellis." Bill paused. "Stu is not an Easton."

Not even by marriage, thought Lindy. "So that puts us right back to—"

"Where I came in." He gave her a look that could have been interpreted in several ways, then pushed himself off the bed. "But I would like to get some sleep before the night is over."

"Sure," said Donald. He backed toward the door. "Thanks. Thanks a lot."

Annie stood on tip toe and kissed his good cheek. "You were wonderful."

This from a girl who only yesterday had accused him of being her mother's lover. Wonders never cease, thought Lindy.

By the time Lindy reached the door, Donald and Annie were already chattering away down the hall. Bill had followed her over.

"You're sure you're not hurt."

Bill laughed. "What a question."

"Bill . . ."

"Good night, Lindy."

She swallowed. "Good night." She backed out the door. It closed in her face.

Chapter
Twenty-one

"Wake up."

A groan came from under the pile of covers on the bed across from hers.

"Wake up," Lindy repeated.

A mass of cinnamon curls appeared, followed by two blinking eyes.

"How can you sleep when I'm dying of curiosity? Do you still have a job? Did you quit? What happened?" Lindy fired her questions toward the lump in the other bed.

"What time is it?"

"Eight o'clock."

Biddy nestled back into the covers.

Lindy climbed out of her own bed and stood over Biddy. "Biddy."

"Huh?" came the lazy reply.

Lindy yanked the covers away. Biddy sat up. "Ugh." She scrubbed her hair, then looked up, blinked a couple of times, bringing her eyes into focus, then said, "Let's get breakfast. I'm starved."

"Thank God." Lindy sank back onto her bed.

"Well, don't sit down. Let's get going."

Thank you, thank you, thank you, she chanted inwardly as she went to take the first shower.

* * *

"So, then he said, would I consider staying on. I said of course, and then we went to bed."

"You did?"

"Not together, dingbat." Biddy popped a piece of English muffin into her mouth. "When I got back to the room, you were dead to the world." She swallowed, and reached for her coffee. "So I ate the sandwich you left me. Thanks."

"I didn't hear you."

"You were too busy yelling at whomever you were dreaming about."

Lindy's eyes widened. "I don't remember dreaming."

"Just as well. You were giving somebody hell."

"Myself, probably. We've got three days, counting today. *If* we go on with the performance."

"Jeremy is afraid Ellis killed Larry," said Biddy.

"I know. And if it's true, Marguerite can kiss the retreat good-bye."

"The sooner it's over, the sooner she can get on with whatever she has to do," said Biddy, momentarily losing interest in her food. Then she stuffed the rest of the English muffin into her mouth.

"So many people depend on her."

"She should have thought of that before she let that chicken hawk brother of hers hang around the camp."

"She didn't know," said Lindy. "I'm sure of that. You should have seen her reaction."

"She didn't know about Jeremy, maybe. But that doesn't mean she didn't know about Larry."

"I'm not sure I like where you're going with this."

"Look. Lindy. I think the world of Marguerite, too. Everybody does. But I have no doubt that she would do anything she needed to do in order to keep her mother's dream alive. And I also think there are more than a few people who would help her."

"Criminy. Sometimes your thought processes are scary. But why kill Larry? That would bring certain scandal. She would have been smarter to kill Ellis."

"Her own brother?"

about Ellis and Larry? Adele? She had access to drugs and—Lindy grasped for an image just out of her consciousness. Surgical gloves. She could have typed the message with the gloves on. No prints. Hmmm. Had they found prints on the computer? But Adele was only a little over five feet tall. If anyone had gone over that precipice in a fight, it would have been Adele.

She was surprised to see Byron Grappel and two state troopers coming up the path from behind the theater. One look at his face sent a shiver of fear through her. He had found the cave. Had he also found Connie? She turned down Two Rocks Way hoping to avoid the sheriff.

"Ms. Graham."

She stopped. The way Grappel pronounced her name filled her with disgust.

"Sheriff. I didn't know you were here."

"Got a tip. Don't suppose you know what I found down there." He jerked his head over his shoulder.

She tried to look stupid. It wasn't that difficult. She felt pretty stupid. "You want to tell me?" she asked blandly. She had to admit she was getting better at this deflection business.

"Larry's love nest." He smiled, his teeth small and pointy. Too small for his mouth. It was the first time she had noticed his teeth. Details, she thought. It's in the details, just like rehearsal, something not quite right. Something you might ordinarily overlook, but once you discovered it, and fixed it, and the dance flowed smoothly, it would seem so obvious.

"Well, good for you, Sheriff." She pulled her mouth into a rictus smile. "Gotta run." And she ran.

She didn't stop running until she was back at the house. Surrounded by thousands of acres of forest and mountains, it seemed like she was just running in the tiny circles of house, annex, theater, and studios. Just like a rat in a cage. It was ridiculous. How could you feel penned in when you were in the middle of wilderness?

What details was she missing? Did Chi-Chi feel penned in? Maybe she hadn't wanted to learn the hotel business. And now she

"Why are we even talking like this?" The idea that someone would kill a seventeen-year-old boy was horrifying enough. That it was most likely someone they knew made her sick. "I'm feeling overwhelmed here. None of this makes sense."

"Unless it was just an accident." Biddy glanced over Lindy's shoulder. "Wow, what happened to him?"

Lindy turned around to see Bill coming toward them. He had a glaring bruise on his cheek.

"Fistfight in the local bar," Lindy whispered as Bill approached the table.

"I'm going to be gone for a few hours," he said. "Don't do anything stupid until I get back."

Biddy laughed. "You can only be stupid when he's here to enjoy it."

Bill took the beginning of an exasperated breath, thought the better of it, and exhaled. "Let me rephrase that. Don't do anything stupid. I'll be back this afternoon."

"But where are you going?" It was a hell of a time for him to take off. They needed to catch a killer.

"To check out TriCon Enterprises."

"The license plate?"

Bill nodded.

"They were able to trace it already?"

"The city never sleeps," said Bill. And with that, he left them.

Biddy and Lindy separated outside the restaurant. Biddy went to make sure that Jeremy was teaching company class. Lindy wandered from master class to master class, while she desperately tried to figure out a reason for Larry's death. And do so before that afternoon, when she would have to push aside her snooping and teach a rehearsal techniques class and then talk the class through Jeremy's company rehearsal that afternoon.

Had she missed any clues, any motivations? She went over the list of people involved, dismissing each of them in turn. Chi-Chi, if she found out Robert was cheating on her with a young boy? There was a real motive for murder. Stu, jealous for the same reasons, was stuck. Marguerite controlled the lives of a lot of people here. Did one of them resent her manipulation? She gives them a chance, and then like indentured workers who had to buy from the company store, they could never pay off their debt? Or was it really about sex? Did she dare call Connie Phillipses' home to see if he had returned? Or would that muddy the water? Bill picked a hell of a time to leave them.

She paced up and down the hallway, then went into the library. She retrieved the Phillipses' number from the Rolodex on the desk. Punched in the numbers. The secretary informed her that Connie had not yet returned home. She sounded irritated as if his absence were adding to her normal workload.

"Really, Ms. Graham. We stopped worrying about Connover's tendency to run away years ago. A headstrong child. He can take care of himself." A curt goodbye and Lindy was listening to a dial tone.

Why did people bother having children if they weren't willing to care for them? God, it made her angry. If Annie or Cliff had run away from camp, she would have dropped everything and gone to look for them. She ached for the lonely, frightened boy who could be anywhere and for whom no one seemed to care.

Please, just let him be far away from here.

It was a long day, made longer by the increasing agitation that enforced inactivity always brought on. She taught her rehearsal techniques class; explained what Jeremy was doing as she and fifteen students sat in the audience watching rehearsal. She had them pick out techniques that she had told them about; pulled out her notebook and showed them how to take notes in the dark.

They were enthusiastic and a bit awestruck that their teachers actually knew what they were talking about; had studied long and hard to be good at what they did; that their ability to fix a step or a movement hadn't sprung full-blown from the air.

Like other young professionals she had encountered, they seemed unaware of the dedication it took to be proficient at what you did. They expected to be good. An entitled generation, they were taught

to believe they deserved the best. The consequences of their actions were clouded by lenient teachers, indulgent parents, and peers
whose only care was to have a good time.

Did they understand that Larry Cleveland had courted disaster
because of his behavior? After their initial shock, it seemed to Lindy
that they had dismissed him from their lives. What had Rose said?
Some of them would have been glad he was dead if they were old
enough to realize it.

Had they been on the wrong track all the time? The older generation taking too much responsibility for what had happened, the
younger generation not taking enough? In their concern for the
Easton family, had they been wasting their energy, when they
should have been looking for a murderer among Larry's peers?

She decided to put Rebo back on the case. Find out what the students were thinking now. If they had any more ideas about why
Larry Cleveland had died.

She left Peter, Jeremy, and Biddy discussing that night's tech rehearsal. She wandered aimlessly through the camp. Time was running out. If they didn't find the real culprit, Robert would be held
and then tried for the death of Larry Cleveland.

She walked into the student dining hall. Like any camp dinner,
sounds of dishes, laughter, and benches scraping on the concrete
floor filled the air. She grabbed a bottle of water. Drank it down. She
walked back out into the growing dusk.

"Hey, Babbalindy." Rebo stopped. "You look a little poor, pitiful,
and pearlish. What gives?"

"What's that Poe story about the guy in prison where the walls
and ceiling keep moving closer and closer until they're about to
crush him?"

"I think that was a Flash Gordon movie."

"Figures."

"So what's the prob? You closing in on the killer or is life closing
in on you?"

"The latter."

"Well, here's something that should cheer you up." Rebo thrust out his hip and crooned, "Your boyfriend's back." He thrust out the other hip and grinned.

Lindy didn't try to correct his misconception about her "boyfriend." She went to find Bill.

Bill was back, but he was not to be found. She still hadn't found him when she made her way toward the theater and the tech rehearsal.

It had begun to rain again. She changed into jeans, threw a sweatshirt over her tee shirt, and grabbed a poncho from the hall closet. She felt waterlogged and cold. As she sploshed across the driveway, Annie was getting out of the old red Jeep. She looked tired and dirty, but amazingly energetic after a Sisyphean day of hauling rocks.

She had thrown herself into the rehabilitation of the archaeologist camp with the same vigor with which she approached all of life. It didn't hurt that a cute, attentive archaeologist was driving the Jeep. Annie jumped out and waved goodbye as the Jeep gurgled and belched down the driveway and through the trees.

Lindy waited for her and gave her a hug.

"Mom, you'll get all dirty."

"Nothing wrong with a little dirt," said Lindy. "I see they got the Jeep running."

"Donald says it has nine lives."

"He's pretty nice, huh?"

"Yeah." Annie smiled up at her mother.

Lindy watched the rain drip off her daughter's hair and run down her face, feeling like the luckiest person in the world.

"I'm going to miss him."

"Oh?" said Lindy, a little surprised. "Is he going somewhere?"

"There's only another day or two of clearing to do. Then they go back to the university to try and scrounge up some more equipment, and we'll be leaving to go back home."

"Ah," said Lindy. At least they hadn't made plans to spend the rest of Annie's vacation together. That would have put Glen through the ceiling. "Well, maybe he can visit before you have to go back to Geneva."

"He has his work and I have mine." Annie heaved the sigh of the young and in love.

"It's the Haggerty way of life."

Annie frowned, then smiled. "But I have a date in an hour. Donald's parking the Jeep and trying to find something with a top." She gave Lindy a quick kiss and took off toward the annex. "Drive carefully," Lindy called after her. *And,* she added to herself, *don't stay out late, don't have sex, don't drink and drive. Don't*—The list went on until she was in the theater, her notebook open, pen poised for the first correction, and the music began.

She didn't need to take many notes. The tech was practically a formality. The company had been rehearsing in the theater for nearly two weeks. Their spacing was flawless. Peter had been playing with the lights for days. They were out of the theater by 10:30.

Lindy had just come out of the lobby and was heading to the annex for a drink when Rebo fell into step beside her.

"Oh, Lindetection," he whispered. "I have a little present for you."

He turned and walked backed toward the theater. She followed him.

"What is it?" she asked as Rebo led her to the back of the theater and into the stage door.

"Our runaway is back."

"Oh shit."

"That was my first reaction. I kept myself and the crown jewels at a safe distance and came to get you."

Lindy started to run.

"Don't worry. Rose is guarding him."

Lindy burst through the door of the boys' dressing room. Rose was standing next to the makeup table, arms akimbo—Valkyrie with Heidi braids.

Connie was sitting in a chair next to her, looking about as forlorn as a sixteen-year-old runaway could look.

He jumped up when Lindy entered. A look from Rose, and he dropped back into his chair.

"It's okay," said Lindy. It wasn't okay, and Connie probably knew it, but being a mother, her first concern was to reassure him. "Why did you come back?"

Connie shifted in his seat. "I'm really hungry," he mumbled.

"No prob, my little ball buster," said Rebo. "You give us a little light confession and I'll get you a little light repast." He grinned his best Jack Nicholson grin at Connie.

Connie cast an anxious glance at Lindy.

"Nobody's going to hurt you. Just tell us why you came back, then you can eat."

Slightly heartened by the prospect of food, Connie began his tale.

"I got to thinking about what you said about me not being safe, so I was hitching back to the city."

Lindy nodded.

"Well, I was about halfway there when it hit me."

Hit him. "What hit you?" He didn't look injured.

"The book."

"You were hit by a book on your way to New York?" asked Rebo incredulously.

Connie smiled tentatively. "Hey, you're kind of funny."

Rebo circled his hand in the air. "That's what the kids in my high school always said. Get on with it."

"The book. Larry had this book. It was probably all in the book."

"What book?" three voices asked in chorus.

"Larry's notebook. It was, you know, like a diary."

Of course. A notebook, thought Lindy. Talk about a detail staring you in the face. She and Biddy made notes of suspects in a notebook. Bill kept his notes in his black notebook. Hell, she spent most of her days in the theater with a notebook in her hand.

It made perfect sense that Larry would keep a written record of who owed him what, the indiscretions he had seen or heard that he might be able to use later. Someone that active in the summer camp blackmail business would need to keep his accounts straight.

And she had been so caught up in thinking about real estate, sex, fingerprints, and surgical gloves, not to mention all the other dead ends, she had missed the most obvious. She wanted to kick herself.

"Do you know where he kept this notebook?"

Connie nodded. "I saw him writing in it one night when he thought I was asleep."

"In the cave?" asked the three voices.

Connie nodded. "But when I came back to get it, the cops were there. I waited until they left and then sneaked in to look for it."

Rose, Lindy, and Rebo leaned forward. Connie broke into a real smile.

"Did you find it?"

Connie's face fell.

"And don't nod or shake your head," said Rebo. "Just say 'yes' or 'no.' Got it?"

Connie stopped his head on the first nod. "Yes. But no. It was gone."

"Did it look like the cops were carrying it when they left?" asked Rebo.

Connie looked at him warily. "No."

"So if the cops don't have it, who does?" Rebo looked at Lindy.

"They could have found it, and put it in an evidence bag. Or somebody's pocket. God forbid Grappel should carry on an intelligent search for anything."

"Or body," added Rebo. "For which we can be grateful, at least in one case." He raised an eyebrow toward Connie.

"He's really mucked up this whole investigation," said Rose, her contempt rolling out with her words.

"On purpose, if you ask me," said Lindy.

"He could have found the notebook and be keeping it to himself," Rebo suggested. "If it fails to implicate Robert, or if it implicates the dimwitted sheriff or any of his dimwitted friends, he just has to toss it, and no one will be the wiser."

"But there were two other cops there, too," said Connie.

"Maybe they're all in cahoots."

"I don't think so," said Lindy. "This seems to be the sheriff's private vendetta. But how to prove it?"

"Well, while you figure it out, I'll go raid the mess hall. Back in a tick." Rebo slipped out the door.

"Rose, you better see if you can find Bill. He'll know what to do." Rose looked over at Connie, who immediately slumped back in his chair. "You're sure you'll be okay with that one?" A flip of her chin indicated what she thought of Connie.

"Yes, he's just a boy."

"Well, don't get too close to him." And Rose was out the door.

"If I hadn't left, I would have gotten the notebook, and Robert would be out of jail."

Lindy had to fight the urge to go over and hug him, but she wasn't about to let him get away again. " 'What ifs never helped anybody, Connie. At least you were brave enough to come back."

"I was?"

"And Robert is really lucky to have a friend like you."

"He is?"

Lindy nodded. She wondered if Connie had ever been given a compliment before.

"If Robert ever comes back," he said.

They heard the stage door open and close. "That was fast," said Lindy moving toward the door.

Another door opened and closed. An expletive followed. It was not Rebo. Another door. Lindy shot a frantic look at Connie then motioned toward the window.

He bolted across the floor and threw himself at the window. Connie and the screen disappeared into the night; at least the window had been open. Lindy jumped into the closest chair and began to straighten the makeup in front of her.

She heard the door squeak behind her.

She looked around. Byron Grappel's surprised expression stared back at her. Then it turned into a malicious grin.

"Well, lookee here," said the sheriff.

Lindy wondered briefly if he'd gotten his sheriff's persona from *The Dukes of Hazzard.*

"Where're you hiding him?"

"What are you doing here, Sheriff?"

This time Grappel wasn't distracted. "Where is he?" He began scouring the room with his eyes, taking in the costume rack, sweeping underneath the makeup table. Then his eyes came to rest on the jagged edges of screen left in the window.

"Ms. Graham, Ms. Graham," he scolded. "You and Dick Tracy are causing me no end of grief." He shook his head slowly. Lindy wished Rebo were here to give him a good shake. "Tampering with evidence, hiding a material witness. You two are gonna get in real trouble."

"I have no idea what you're talking about, Sheriff. Who is Dick Tracy?"

Grappel took a step toward her. "Don't try to change the subject, Ms. Graham. You know who I'm talking about. I figure Connover Phillips, you know, Connie—pretty name don't you think?—knows that Robert Stokes killed that other little pervert. Way I figure it, Connie's just plain scared shitless that it's gonna happen to him, too."

"You forget, Sheriff. Robert's in jail. How could he possibly hurt Connie?"

"Well, the kid didn't know that when he ran away did he? Maybe he still doesn't know."

Grappel took one more step toward her, then pulled out another chair and sat down. Lindy instinctually scooted hers away from him.

Grappel leaned forward. "Why do you want to protect somebody that does that to little boys? What's wrong with women like you?"

Gee, Sheriff, is this a trick question? she thought. At least, he seemed to have dismissed the broken window as Connie's means of escape. Maybe she could keep him talking until Rebo got back.

"What kind of woman is that, Sheriff?"

"Hell, you're attractive, you got a husband. He don't look too bad."

"What does my husband have to do with it?" It was hard trying to stall a man who made your skin crawl.

"What I can't figure out is why he'd let you hang out with crud like this. I'd never let a wife of mine work here."

It was too much. "Well, it's a good thing for me I'm not married to you."

"No reason to get prissy, Ms. Graham." He stood up. "Well, I hate to leave such charming company, but I figure Connover has had time to get to the cave by now. That's where he's been hiding, right?" He waved his hand dismissively. "I'm not gonna hurt him. I don't guess you believe me, 'cause of the kind of people you're used to. He just needs to come down to the station and answer a few questions, is all."

He nodded to her and closed the door behind him. She heard his footsteps hurrying down the corridor and the stage door slam.

She took a second to think, then dismissed the idea of trying to find Rebo or Bill. It would take too long, and by then no telling what Grappel would have done to Connie. She grabbed a box of Kleenex off the makeup table. At the stage door, she dropped the first tissue. If it worked for Hansel and Gretel, why not her? She just hoped Rebo was up on his fairy tales.

At the stone steps, she dropped another one and followed Grappel down the dark path toward the cave. She ran out of Kleenex two forks before the overgrown path to the cave. She dropped the empty box and pulled off her sweatshirt.

"Psst." Lindy jumped. "Psst."

A white hand motioned to her from the dark. With a quick glance left and right, Lindy plunged into the thick underbrush.

Connie's colorless face peered up at her from the darkness.

"Thank God," said Lindy.

"That guy must think I'm really stupid."

"We've got to get back to the house."

"I know the shortcut." Without another word, Connie took her hand and pulled her into the woods. Darkness enveloped them. The trees closed like a blanket above them.

Dense brush and vines wrapped around her as Connie pulled her headlong into increasing blackness. They crashed into branches that slapped at Connie and then rebounded into Lindy. Connie gripped her hand, not letting go even when she tripped and fell headlong into a wet pile of composting forest debris. He yanked her up and dragged her forward until her feet finally caught up with the rest of her.

Her lungs were screaming, her mouth was gritty with dirt and tasted of decay. She could hear Connie panting as they struggled on. She had no idea in what direction they were traveling. She wondered if Connie did.

And in a heart-stopping instant, she wondered if Connie had killed Larry Cleveland.

Chapter
Twenty-two

The thought turned her muscles to stone. Connie whiplashed into her, then yanked her violently forward, grunting against her weight.

Then suddenly they were standing on gravel. The light from a security lamp bathed them in its yellow glow. Still holding hands, they gulped in air. In front of them was the back of the student dorm.

"Home free," gasped Connie.

They began to run up the path toward the main house. Connie stopped abruptly and Lindy plowed into him.

Stu was walking down the path toward them, whistling in the night air. He stopped when he saw them. His cane chucked up a piece of gravel and sent it into the shrubs by the side of the path.

"What on earth?" he said, taken aback.

"Thank God, Stu." It was all that Lindy could get out. She took a deep breath. It hurt her lungs, and her relief made her weak in the knees.

Connie spun around. She held onto his hand. "It's all right now, Connie. We're safe."

She pulled him toward Stu. "We've got to find Bill. The sheriff—"

"Connover Phillips," said Stu in a voice sharp with surprise.

"Everyone has been worried sick about you. Where have you been, you young rascal?"

"No time," gasped Lindy. "Got to find Bill."

"By all means," said Stu. He took Connie's elbow. Connie tried to pull himself free, but Stu had a firm grip. "And you, too, Sheriff. Now this is a surprise." Stu was looking past Lindy's head. She whirled around. Byron Grappel, hand on his black holster, stepped from the shadows.

Connie began to struggle. Stu dropped his cane and put his other arm around Connie's chest, trapping the boy in front of him.

"You shouldn't run from the police, Connie," said Stu. "The police are your friends."

"He's not my friend," yelled Connie. He twisted and squirmed but couldn't free himself from Stu. "He took the book." He glared at the sheriff.

"What book?" asked Grappel.

"He took it so nobody would know who killed Larry. Let me go." Connie wrenched to the side. Stu was thrown off balance, but managed to grab the back of Connie's shirt. Connie yo-yoed backward and fell onto his butt. Stu hauled him back up.

"Would you please stop struggling? The sheriff just wants to ask you some questions."

"Like what damned book is he talking about."

"You didn't find Larry's notebook in the cave?" asked Lindy. If he hadn't, then who had it?

Byron wrinkled his nose. Probably to activate his brain. "I don't know anything about a damned notebook." And then he looked at Stu.

Holy shit, thought Lindy. Grappel really didn't know about the notebook, but it was clear from his face that he expected Stu to. Had Stu been a spy in their midst?

Connie lunged to the side; this time Stu lost his balance. His arms flew out reflexively. Connie scrambled away on all fours, then pushed himself to his feet and took off down the path.

"Stop him!" yelled Stu.

"He won't get away," said Grappel. "I'll just call for some backup. He can't get far. It's pitch-black out there."

"You fool, they heard us."

"Huh?"

"The night on the ridge; now go get the little bugger."

Grappel turned and lumbered a few steps, then stopped. He turned back to Stu. "Robert killed Larry, right?"

But Stu had grabbed his cane and was running after Connie, faster than Lindy thought was possible for a man with recent hip surgery.

Grappel just stared down the path. Lindy took off after Stu. She heard Grappel behind her, but didn't stop to look around.

They ran until the path joined the one that led to the archaeologist camp. Rounding a curve, she saw Stu's uneven gait and beyond him, a shadow, running wildly. There was a cry, and the shadow dropped to the ground. As she got closer, she could see Connie rolling back and forth on the gravel, holding his knee.

Then Stu was upon him. He pulled Connie up and dragged him to the side of the path. Lindy made out the silhouette of the green guardrail against the murky sky. She slowed down; Grappel barreled past her, then came to a halt.

"What the hell are you doing, Hollowell? I just want to ask the kid some questions."

Enclosed in Stu's arms, Connie had gone deadly still. Hunched over, one hand holding his knee, he stared at Lindy with fearful eyes.

Stu sighed. A long deep resigned sigh. "Sorry, Byron. It's too late for questions. These two little shits were too greedy for their own good."

Connie shook his head, and kept shaking it long after he realized it would do no good.

Grappel just stood peering through the darkness at the man who held the boy poised on the edge of the cliff, a quizzical expression on his face. "You mean . . ."

"I mean, you idiot, that Larry Cleveland tried to blackmail me."

"But Robert Stokes killed Cleveland."

Stu turned to Lindy for the first time. "The good sheriff, my dear, is a man with little brains. No imagination." He chuckled. "And then when you least need it, the fool has an inspired idea."

Byron Grappel looked as confused as she felt.

"Things took a turn for the unexpected, and I had to do a little improvising. It would have all been fine, Byron, in spite of the fact that Lindy, here, stumbled onto Robert's body before it was quite a body. But I forgive you, my dear. How were you to know?"

"But, Byron . . ." Stu shook his head. "Fabricating evidence. It shows a gross lack of intelligence. Robert never used the computer. If he had left a note it would have been written on a piece of paper."

He turned again to Lindy. "I assure you, my shock was genuine that day you told me about the suicide message."

"You killed Cleveland and then tried to kill Robert?" Grappel's hand reached toward his holster.

Stu glanced at his hand. "Byron, it's too late for heroics. You're an accessory to murder, a principal in the destruction of Easton property; you'll be held for tampering with evidence, corruption, and sheer incompetence. There's nothing for it but to get rid of these two and get on with life."

"Why, Stu?" asked Lindy.

"Ah, Lindy dear, remember how this land looks in the light of day? I could have made Ellis a fortune. Freed him from Marguerite's constant demands."

He let go of Connie long enough to sweep his hand across the vista. Lindy saw Grappel slowly unsnap his holster. "Why? Because like Everest, my dear Lindy, it is there."

A guttural cry escaped from Connie, and he flung himself backward against Stu. Stu staggered, and they both fell to the ground and slid underneath the guardrail. Connie tried to roll away, but Stu, unhampered by a weak hip, now that they were both on the ground, held fast. Connie struggled blindly, dragging Stu toward the edge.

Grappel had his gun out of his holster. It swung back and forth in the air as his hand moved with the two struggling figures.

"Don't shoot!" screamed Lindy. "He's just a boy." Grappel ignored her and crashed through the brush where the guardrail came to an end. Lindy followed, driven on by adrenaline, her good sense held in abeyance by her need to save the boy who had trusted her.

Grappel's beefy arm suddenly swung to the side, stopping her dead. She peered beyond him. Stu had managed to get Connie to his feet. The boy had begun to shake with blind terror, uncontrollably, like a seizure.

"Hold still, you little shit," growled Stu. "Think, Byron. It's your only chance. This one is history. You can't stop me. Just take hold of Lindy for a minute. I'll do the rest. Then life will be yours. Chi-Chi will be yours."

Grappel's arm moved so quickly, Lindy had no time to react. It closed around her and dragged her up against his body. She gagged on the musky scent of his sweat. He growled, low and guttural into her hair. "Run, damn you."

He loosened his hold. She breathed in a spastic breath and yelled at the top of her lungs. "Cooonnie!" The sound echoed around her. Stu and Grappel stood as if stunned. Connie blasted his heel into Stu's shin, and he dove headlong toward Lindy.

Grappel fired his gun in Stu's direction. It must have been a reflex action, for the shot went wide. The bullet lodged into the earthen wall above the ledge, sending a spray of dirt, mud, and pebbles into the air.

Lindy's hands flew to her ears, the ringing reverberating in her bones, shutting out everything around her.

Stu staggered backward and slipped in the loose dirt.

And then everything began to slow down, happening in fractured pictures and sounds. Stu flailing his arms. The ground beneath him giving way. At first just a piece no larger than a piece of garden flagstone. Then, the entire point was gone. All at once. The top half of Stu's body seemed to bend away from them. His arms flew out to his sides. And the rest of the ledge dropped like an elevator, in one huge piece, Stu dropping with it.

His screams echoed back through the crunching and whooshing of earth, mud, rocks, and brush as they thundered down the face of the cliff and piled onto the ledge ten feet below; then swept it, too, toward the depths of the chasm.

Connie crawled away from the encroaching devastation, heading for the guardrail as the earth gave way behind him. Grappel pushed past Lindy, knocking her off her feet. He made a grab for Stu, but Lindy knew that Stu was beyond his reach.

And then the rest of the world upheaved. Grappel was thrown backward, and Lindy slid downward with the rocks and dirt until her back was caught against a tree—one of the saplings that had gotten a toehold of life between the boulders.

She watched in horror as Grappel followed Stu over the side, only now there was no side, just a deluge of melting earth. She made a feeble attempt to grab the sheriff as he slid past her. Felt her own feet being washed away and grabbed the tree with both hands. She held onto it as if it were a thousand-year-old sequoia instead of a tenuous little runt easily torn from the earth.

She heard another scream. Connie's. Then she squeezed her eyes shut and prayed, as the thunder of shifting earth drowned out everything else.

After an eternity, the rumble seemed to recede. She could distinguish individual cracks and thumps as the earth resettled below her. She was still alive. Her eyes refused to open, as if that slight movement would cause another shift in the ground. Her hands grew numb as she fought to retain her tenuous hold of the tree.

Bands of pain tightened around her forearms, cramping her muscles. Her grasp weakened as her arms went into spasm. Oh, God, Annie would be left here alone.

"Lindy."

She opened her eyes. Bill was lying on his stomach on the rock above her. It was his grip on her forearms that had cut off the circulation to her hands.

"Let go of the tree and grab my wrists."

But she couldn't move. Her hands were frozen to the tree. More ground gave way beside her, covering her legs with mud.

"Now." Bill's voice was loud enough to start another landslide.

She let go. Felt two arms beneath her grip. Wondered why she had never noticed how muscular he was. Felt herself being lifted up as the debris fell away below her.

Then she was being carried back to the path, Bill's body trembling with exertion and adrenaline.

"Connie," she said.

"He's okay."

She felt her heart pound in relief. Connie was alive.

Her feet hit the gravel with a crunch.

"Goddamn it!" Bill bellowed.

She lifted her eyes to his and cringed at the look on his face. "That was close."

He started laughing. It grew until the woods rang with the sound.

"Bill," she said. "You're hysterical."

He stopped as abruptly as he had started, a strange expression on his face. "Yes, I am." He wrapped his arms around her and they clung to each other until the sound of running replaced the echo of Bill's laugh.

Lindy turned her head, afraid to lose her fragile grasp of another human being. As if the world might yet swallow her up if she let go. Connie was leading the pack, favoring one leg and shored up by Rebo and Rose. Peter, Jeremy, Biddy, and Annie followed close behind them. Every face, etched with fear, leapt out at her like masks from a Greek tragedy.

Bill's chin was resting on the top of her head.

"I think you had better stand on your own now." But he didn't let go. "It wouldn't do to have your friends, family, and coworkers find you in the arms of the other man." He tapped the top of her head with his chin. "Even though I'm not the other man."

That made her look up. "Well, there isn't any other other man."

"A comforting thought." He pushed her gently into one arm and helped her toward the approaching crowd.

Chapter
Twenty-three

The entire camp had been aroused by the sounds of sirens and megaphones as the emergency teams began the arduous job of nighttime rescue. They stood along the path, watching quietly as a stretcher was hauled up the side of the cliff and rolled away to the waiting ambulance. Byron Grappel was still alive, barely. The disjointed scream of the ambulance echoed back at them as it made its way across the mountain.

They watched the crew carefully pull themselves back up the face of the cliff. One carried a broken staff of wood, a piece of Stu's cane they had found sticking out of the earth like a symbol of surrender.

Stu was dead, his body crushed beneath tons of rock and earth. The rescue squad had dug only far enough to establish that he had no pulse. Then they cordoned off the area and left two patrolmen to guard the site until the morning, when it would be safe to extricate the body without endangering the lives of the rescuers.

The others trudged back up the path, ushering the campers along in front of them. Rebo had scooped up Connie and carried him in his arms. Lindy focused on the boy's fingers where they clasped the back of Rebo's neck.

She thought that she should feel sad, but she felt nothing—only

Annie's arm linked through hers and Bill's presence close behind her, but not touching her. She could make out the individual shapes of the leaves of trees that encroached on the path—could hear the crunch of the gravel as it shifted under their feet. Funny how aware she was of everything but feeling; it didn't seem right.

They passed the blinking lights of the rescue vehicles parked in the circular drive. Lindy narrowed her eyes against their painful brightness, blurring them until only an aura of red surrounded her.

She felt the hardness of the stone steps of the house. Sandiman opened the door. He turned without a word and led her to the drawing room. He had forgotten his diamond stickpin, and his tie was askew. She followed behind him, taking courage in this unprecedented display of human frailty.

She sat on the sofa, Annie molded to her side. Watched Bill cross to the window, leaving clumps of mud and leaves on the carpet. Then the smell of coffee and Sandiman's bony fingers placing a cup on the coffee table before her. The coffee was black and too sweet, but she drank it.

She felt Bill and Annie look toward the door and saw Abel White step silently into the room.

"It seems . . ." he said. The first word came out in a squeak, like an adolescent boy's changing voice. He cleared his throat. "It seems," he began again, "that I'm the acting sheriff." He raised his eyebrows making the statement a question.

"Hell of a first case." Bill came to stand beside him. His voice seemed to reassure Abel.

"I guess this could wait until the morning, but—"

"No," said Lindy. At least she thought she had spoken. She must have. Abel had stopped talking and was looking at her with an expression that could have been embarrassment, but might have been pity. "The sooner we do this, the sooner Robert will be home."

The sun wouldn't rise over the mountain peaks until later, but the early-morning birds had begun to call to each other outside the window by the time Lindy had finished telling her disjointed story.

Abel assured her that he would hear it again when she was "feeling better." As if she would ever feel better after what she had witnessed. She shivered.

Adele's haggard face appeared before her. "I think that's enough, Abel."

"Yes, ma'am."

"How are Ellis and Marguerite?" Lindy asked her.

"Sedated," Adele said matter-of-factly. "And I suggest the same for you."

Lindy shook her head.

"Trust me, you do not want to dream tonight." Adele glanced toward the window. "What's left of it."

"Connie?"

"A twisted knee—scraped and bruised . . ."

Lindy read the unspoken words in her pause.

"Body and soul," Adele agreed. "But your friends are with him. He won't be alone when he wakes up." In an instant, Lindy understood Adele's loyalty to Marguerite. He wouldn't wake up alone, like the small, lonely girl who had not awakened alone, because an older school girl had become her friend.

Lindy felt the first stab of emotion she had felt since the horror of the night before. Maybe Marguerite would be there for Connie, too. Tears sprang into her eyes. "Tired, I guess," she managed to say and tried to smile, then burst into embarrassing, uncontrollable crying.

"I'll just get back to the station," said Abel White, backing away. Lindy could only nod as she tried to stop the unstoppable tears that streamed down her face. She tried not to think about Bill's reaction to this spectacle. She risked a look in his direction, but he was staring out the window, one hand braced against the frame.

Biddy opened the door when Adele and Annie led Lindy back to her bedroom. Then she was gone, and Lindy heard the sound of the bath being filled. That brought a fleeting smile to her lips. Leave it to Biddy to know that what she needed most in the world was to wash away the grime and the memory of that night.

She soaked for a long time, listening to the murmurs of the three women who waited for her in the bedroom. She finished off the bath with a hot shower, letting the water sting her skin and turn her flesh pink with its heat. Then she put on the tee shirt that Biddy had hung on the towel rack and stepped into the room.

Adele held a glass of water in one hand and a pill in the other. "No arguments," she said. "I don't make a habit of handing out sedatives. These are unusual times."

Lindy understood. She took the pill and drank it down with the water, climbed into bed, and kissed Annie good night. Then she watched Adele and Biddy accompany her daughter out the door.

She immediately felt drowsy—almost missed the tap at the door.

"Come in." Her voice already sounded far away.

Bill stood in the doorway.

"I don't bite." Her words were slurred, but she couldn't seem to help it.

"I don't believe that for a minute." But he came to her side and smiled.

"What? You better hurry, I'm fading fast." A yawn drove the point home.

"Get some sleep." He pulled the covers up to her chin, and with a look that Lindy didn't attempt to comprehend, he kissed her on the forehead and tiptoed out the door.

It was afternoon when she awoke with a start.

"Not to worry," said Biddy. "The company is at the beach until the dress rehearsal tonight. Robert is back and the body is gone."

"Life goes on," Lindy croaked.

"You got a better alternative?"

Lindy shook her head. "Strangely enough, I'm hungry."

"That's my girl," said Biddy and hauled her off the bed.

Later that day Lindy repeated her statement to Abel White. Annie had finally been pried from Lindy's side to spend the day with Donald at Dr. Van Zandt's cleanup effort.

They hadn't seen Ellis or Marguerite, or Bill or Adele. Jeremy had shown up briefly, just to make sure she was okay, and then left them to closet himself with the Eastons. Robert and Chi-Chi had moved Chi-Chi's things back to the bungalow and hadn't been seen since. That had brought a ribald comment to Biddy's lips, and they had laughed, tentatively at first, then with real enjoyment.

Now, she and Biddy sat in the shade of the boulders by the lake, listening to the sounds of dancers determined to have fun. Connie had been carried out and was sitting in a beach chair under an umbrella, his thin shoulders covered by a striped towel. He was surrounded by his peers, who chatted and laughed and handed him sodas and pieces of fruit.

In the evening, Lindy would oversee the dress rehearsal just like any other day on tour. Even though none of them was sure they would be performing the following evening. Like inertia, they continued their activities until forced to stop. It was the only way to approach life.

And that thought brought her painfully back to Stuart Hollowell. What had driven him to commit murder and betray his dearest friend? Just for the momentary excitement of building a ski resort or luxury hotel? Because it was there, he had said, right before he had plummeted to his death.

Self-assured and unrepentant, until that final cry of surprise and fear that still haunted Lindy's memory. For an intelligent, energetic, life-loving man to come to that. It was such a waste. And though he had paid the ultimate price for his actions, it was those left behind, Marguerite and Ellis, especially Ellis, who would suffer most.

And Connie, a timorous boy, now showered with attention for a few minutes of one day. What would happen to him? How would he survive with the memories of what had happened to him that summer?

Lindy stood up, pulled her shirt over her head and walked across the beach to the water. She waded in until her legs were numb below the knee. Then she dove in, the freezing water taking her breath away, and she swam until she could swim no more. She came back to where Biddy sat, and stood over her, shivering, teeth chattering, and dripping onto the romance novel that Biddy held unread in her hands.

Then they gathered up their things and went to the house to get ready for rehearsal.

Lindy stood backstage watching as the company began the Mendelssohn symphony. She would eventually take her place in the audience, notebook at the ready, but not yet.

Connie Phillips sat on a stool near the wings. Rebo exited and gave the boy a thumbs-up sign.

"You seem to have made a conquest," said Lindy.

Rebo was counting under his breath, readying himself for his next entrance.

"Children are such a big responsibility." He sighed dramatically, batted his eyelashes, and leapt back onto the stage.

She watched from the wings as the dancers moved deftly through the steps. Connie came to stand next to her.

"Pretty cool, huh?" she said without taking her eyes from the stage.

Rebo finished a turn at that moment and flashed them a grin.

"Do you think I can stay at camp?" asked Connie.

"If it's okay with your parents," she said. "I'm sure Robert and Marguerite would love for you to stay."

"My parents won't care," he said.

No, Connie, I don't think they will, she thought. Maybe Connie could find the family he needed and deserved here. Jeremy had, and he had turned out all right. Robert and Chi-Chi would be at the New York school to guide him through the winter months. In spite of a horrendous beginning, Connie just might have a bright future ahead of him.

"You want to sit out front with me?" she asked.

"No, I think I'll just stay here."

She left him gazing raptly at the stage, and felt a flicker of warmth as she made her way to her seat in the house. Just tiny at first, but growing larger and warmer, pushing away the horror. By the time she opened her notebook, she had lost her dread of touching it. She began to write, and Stu Hollowell and his schemes of empire slipped away like the slow fade of stage lights at the end of a dance.

Chapter
Twenty-four

Saturday after lunch they gathered in the drawing room—the tech members of the Jeremy Ash Dance Company, the teachers, Adele, and Robert and Chi-Chi—to hear Marguerite's pronouncement of whether the show would go on or not.

"It will be our new beginning," she said. And so they filed out the door: Peter and Rose to ready the theater, the teachers to inform their students, Adele to her infirmary, and Robert and Chi-Chi to prepare the programs.

And the reporters. They had arrived early that morning. Abel White had given them a statement, blushing against their rapid-fire questions and clicking cameras. Then he sent them off to view the accident site, accompanied by two hulking state troopers with the order to clear the area by afternoon.

Lindy, Biddy and Jeremy sat around Marguerite's chair trying to make sense of the events of the last two weeks.

Marguerite sat frail as paper as she listened once more to Lindy's story of Stu's final minutes, the chase through the woods, Grappel's realization that it had been Stu who killed Larry Cleveland and not Robert.

"He'll stay here of course," said Marguerite, when Lindy brought up the subject of Connie's future. "I'm not turning him over to that secretary, and God knows when the parents will deign to return. Can you imagine parents not bothering to cut their vacation short when their child was almost murdered?" Then her indignation dried up. "But I don't suppose we know the whole story. One seldom does, does one?"

It was a question fraught with meaning, and the interruption brought about by Sandiman entering with a tray of lemonade was welcomed with relief.

Bill entered on Sandiman's heels, having finished questioning Abel White about Byron's condition and White's plans for pursuing the inquiry. Lindy just hoped that Bill had not overwhelmed him.

"Byron is awake, more or less." His voice filled the room. "He was able to make a statement. He admitted to setting off the dynamite and typing the computer message. He swears he thought that Robert had killed Larry and was just trying to make things easier for the prosecution."

He took a glass that Sandiman handed him, eyed it, and then put it down on the coffee table. He started to pace. "With what Lindy and Connie verified about the events of Thursday night, and the fact that they found a bottle of tranquilizers among Stu's possessions, I'd say he's probably telling the truth."

"But why do such a horrible thing?" asked Marguerite. "Making up that terrible note, it's unpardonable."

"Well, we don't need to worry about him being pardoned. Byron Grappel will be living off the taxpayers' money for a long time to come."

"They would have realized it was a fake, wouldn't they?" asked Biddy. "I mean, what if they had believed it?"

"It was a stupid thing to do, Biddy," said Bill. "But I don't think Grappel really cared whether it was used as evidence or not."

"Then why go to all that trouble?" asked Lindy.

Bill shrugged. "A wild guess? He wanted to destroy Chi-Chi's love for Robert. It was a good thing you discovered Robert when you did. Grappel might not have tried to kill him, but I bet anything he wouldn't have attempted to save him." Bill sighed. "The agonies of unrequieted love."

"Do sit down, Bill," said Marguerite; the hint of a smile hovered at the edges of her mouth.

Lindy fought for control and then burst out laughing. "Unrequited love?"

Bill looked embarrassed. "I don't know where that came from."

Marguerite patted his knee. "Shakespeare, I believe. It's quite okay, Bill. The retreat has that effect on people."

Sandiman opened the door and held it open in his most imperious fashion. Behind him, Annie and Donald stood side by side, mud-splattered and grinning. Abel White ushered them into the room. Annie was holding a package that dripped murky water onto the carpet.

"Look!" she exclaimed and rushed forward to Bill, presenting the disgusting object like a frolicsome puppy. Lindy rolled her eyes and leaned forward to see.

"The bulldozer dredged it up. It was sitting there in the pile of rocks. Can you believe it?"

Bill took it from her. Water seeped from the mangled, swollen pages of what had once been a blue spiral notebook. Sandiman appeared with a silver tea tray and Bill dropped the book onto it.

Then he carried it over to a table with everyone following behind. He took out his penknife and began to turn the pages as the rest of them crowded around him. Some of the pages were unreadable, torn or covered with ground-in mud. On others, pencil entries had faded from view.

After a few minutes, Bill began turning the pages even more carefully than he had done before.

"Hmm," he said, placing the tip of the knife gently on the page. "Here it is, and as luck would have it, the entry was made in ink. Thank you, Larry, for your foresight."

Bill began to read aloud, his sonorous voice filling the room as he became engrossed in the story that unfolded. Larry had left Connie in the cave and gone to see who was meeting on the path so late at night. He overheard Stu and Byron making plans for dynamiting the archaeology site, the first of several disasters they had planned in order to nudge, the word was surrounded by quotation marks, Marguerite into letting Stu take over the development of the land.

"That's why he was so against the town's attempts to develop the land," exclaimed Annie. "He didn't want them to have it, because he wanted it for himself."

That piece of deduction won her one of Bill's wide smiles.

Yeesh, thought Lindy.

A few entries later, Larry mentioned his appointment with Stu at the ledge. His expectation of sudden wealth. *Big time!* were the last two words he ever wrote.

Annie, Donald, and the notebook went off with Acting Sheriff White to make their statements.

Wordlessly, the others moved back to the sofa and surrounding chairs, while Sandiman replaced the lemonade with something stronger.

"But how did the notebook get in the stream?" asked Biddy.

"It flows right beneath the path," said Bill. "Stu probably just tossed it over thinking that with all the rain, the swollen waters would carry it away." He took a glass of white wine from the tray Sandiman held. He studied the liquid, then with a look of appreciation, he took a sip. "And it would have if they hadn't dynamited the site and covered it under rubble." Bill laughed. "If I ever complain about life not being fair, I'll remember that notebook. Brought down by their own iniquity. It's downright . . ." He lifted his glass toward Marguerite. "Shakespearean."

The fiftieth-year anniversary performance was a gala affair. The parking lot and driveway were festooned with colorful lanterns; tables of hors d'oeuvres were placed in the clearing in front of the theater, and white-coated bartenders served drinks from portable bars placed strategically among the group of theatergoers.

They were dressed for opening night, even though this opening was in the middle of the New York wilderness, surrounded by trees and rocks and wild animals whose calls could be heard in the distance. Slinky floor-length gowns stood next to above-the-knee cocktail dresses. Tuxedos mingled with outlandish bohemian outfits that identified their wearers as the cutting edge of the artistic avant guarde. The air hummed with conversation—about art, about sports, about murder.

Into this crowd walked Marguerite Easton in a magnificent golden gown, its silk charmeuse train spreading out behind her. And to either side, her escorts, dressed in black tuxedos, looking tall, athletic, and handsome as befitted a royal retinue. Jeremy and . . . Bill?

Lindy did a double take, then poked Biddy in the ribs.

"Wow," said Biddy.

After almost two years of friendship, this was the first week Lindy had seen Bill wearing anything but flannel shirts, sweaters, or the occasional tweed jacket for teaching. But Bill, first in a tee shirt, biceps firmly developed, and now in a well-fitting tuxedo, took on a whole new dimension in Lindy's mind.

He shot Lindy a quick glance as he and Jeremy escorted Marguerite into the theater. Not quite comfortable in the role, thought Lindy. It made him even more endearing.

"Jeremy doesn't look so bad, considering," Biddy said.

"I'm sure he's been flagellating himself for accusing Ellis of murdering Larry. Did he say anything to you?"

Biddy shook her head. "You know, it's that old two steps forward, one step back thing."

"That's our Jeremy all right," Lindy agreed.

They followed the others inside.

Before the curtain rose, Marguerite came onto the stage and gave a welcoming speech. She was perfectly poised, and her voice was strong and warm. What it must have cost her to face all those questioning eyes was staggering to the imagination.

"The woman's got guts," said Biddy under her breath.

Lindy could only agree.

The evening ended with Jeremy's tribute to Marguerite Easton, his mentor and friend. With music by Mozart, it began with the trio for Eric, Rebo, and Mieko. The *pas de deux* for Mieko and Rebo that followed was filled with seamless partnering, languorous extensions, and sensitive musicality. Not a rustle in the audience disturbed the beauty of the movement. They were joined by the full company, costumed in white chiffon and silk, in a joyful hymn of praise. And throughout the piece, Jeremy sat in his seat, head bowed, not once looking at the stage.

"Jeez. He'd better get over it," said Biddy. "We leave for Spain in ten days."

"He'll get over it," Lindy assured her, but she was not so sure herself.

On Sunday morning, the bus was loaded and goodbyes were said. The dancers filed up the steps and took their places inside.

After an ardent goodbye to Donald and a promise to meet on the following weekend, Annie was marshaled onto the bus by Kate and Mieko.

Only Lindy and Biddy stood outside, waiting for final instructions from Jeremy, who had decided to remain a few days with the Eastons. He and Bill were standing on the porch with Marguerite, who waved to the company members as they climbed into the bus.

They watched Jeremy walk down the steps and across the drive.

"I'll be back in a few days."

"We'll be fine," said Lindy and let him give her the customary theater kiss on the cheek.

He turned to Biddy. "Marguerite needs me. Ellis needs me."

Biddy nodded and let herself be kissed in turn.

"I'll be back next week," he said.

"Take all the time you need. We'll manage."

"I'll be there." He started to walk away, then turned back and kissed Biddy—on the mouth, quickly, awkwardly, but definitely a real kiss.

Then Lindy and Biddy were staring at his back as he took the steps of the porch two at a time. Lindy swore she could see Bill smiling.

"Wow," said Biddy. "Take all the time you need."

Lindy saw the cluster of faces at the front window of the bus disappear as she led a befuddled Biddy up the steps. She smiled as she saw the conspicuous disinterest of those who had hastily taken their seats.

She pushed Biddy into her seat and turned to the driver.

"Home, James."

And the bus rumbled away.